Praise for Manda Collins

READY SET ROGUE

"Displaying a deft hand at ch[...] an engaging plot spiced wit[...] able flair for graceful writin[...] crisp wit, Collins launches the [...] on a high note." —[...]ist (Starred review)

"*Ready Set Rogue* has an assortment of bold, brilliant female characters and showcases the strength and resourcefulness of women." —*Fresh Fiction*

DUKE WITH BENEFITS

"A delight to see a classic Regency hero so smitten with a truly unusual heroine. Driven by multiple passionate scenes and the hunt for a murderer, it's a swift and intense read. A bluestocking Regency romance of unusual intensity." —*Kirkus Reviews*

"Intense romance." —*Publishers Weekly*

"The romance is lovely, with both hero and heroine falling into love the way people do in life outside of books—in a slow tumble and a sharp drop, all at once." —*New York Times* bestselling author Sarah MacLean

"This is a terrific historical romance . . . I definitely have to recommend." —*Night Owl Reviews (Top Pick!)*

"A delightful book full of romance, intrigue, and mystery, *Duke with Benefits* should be on your to-buy list for July!" —*Romance Reviews Today*

"A delicious romance with a curious mystery thrown in to spice things up!" —*Fresh Fiction*

Also by Manda Collins

One for the Rogue
Wallflower Most Wanted
Good Dukes Wear Black
Good Earl Gone Bad
A Good Rake is Hard to Find
Why Lords Lose Their Hearts
Why Earls Fall in Love
Why Dukes Say I Do
How to Entice an Earl
How to Romance a Rake
How to Dance with a Duke

Rogue, Set, Match

TWO NOVELS IN ONE

Ready Set Rogue

&

Duke with Benefits

MANDA COLLINS

St. Martin's Paperbacks

Published in the United States by St. Martin's Paperbacks, an imprint of St. Martin's Publishing Group

For information, address St. Martin's Publishing Group, 120 Broadway, New York, NY 10271.

www.stmartins.com

ISBN: 978-1-250-84811-6

Printed in the United States of America

St. Martin's Paperbacks edition / March 2022

10 9 8 7 6 5 4 3 2 1

Ready
Set
Rogue

Chapter 1

The Marquess of Kerr was having a very bad day.

As if breaking an axle on his ancient family traveling carriage on the most deserted portion of the drive from London to the south coast hadn't been inconvenience enough, there was also the fact that his favorite horse was miles back, tied behind the coach carrying his baggage and valet. To compound his situation, after instructing the coachman and outriders to wait for help, he'd set out on foot for the coaching inn some three miles up the road only for the skies to open up and release a deluge not felt on Earth since the Great Flood, he was convinced.

If it hadn't been for a chance meeting with his cousin the day before, he'd not have been traveling to the downs at all. But the news that his late aunt Celeste had done what she'd always threatened—left her estate to a bevy of blue stockings—had meant beating a hasty path to her manor house near the village of Little Seaford before any of her hangers-on arrived. At least that had been the plan when he set out. At this rate all four harpies would have descended upon Beauchamp House before he had a chance to so much as hide the silver.

Thus it was that when he reached the Fox and Pheasant

he was not only wet, muddy, and exhausted, he was hungry. Which, as his old nanny could attest, made for a very grouchy Torquil, indeed.

Despite the rain, the inn yard was bustling with activity, as the bright yellow mail coach, which had just arrived, released its passengers into the already crowded doorway of the hostelry.

Cursing beneath his breath, Quill elbowed his way through the crowd until the quality of his garments seemed to register with them and, despite their own fatigue, the passengers began to defer to him. All save one.

Had he been in a better mood, he might have noticed the auburn-haired lady's curvy figure or her warm brown eyes behind her spectacles. But he was too annoyed by her blatant disregard for him as she shoved in front of him carrying a small, but obviously heavy, trunk. And as if that weren't enough, she had the bad manners to drop the aforementioned trunk directly onto his booted foot as he attempted to slip around her.

"Hell and the devil!" he cursed as the weighty box landed. Despite the thickness of his boots, they were no match for whatever it was she traveled with.

"Oh dear," the woman said, crouching at once to clutch the handles of the offending thing. "I am so sorry. I should have waited for the coachman, but I was so afraid to leave them, you see. They're quite valuable."

But when she heaved on the trunk, it was obvious that she'd need a bit of help lifting it. Wordlessly, Quill pushed away her hand that gripped the handle and took both sides in his own grasp and lifted it.

"What are you carrying in this, madam?" he asked as he jostled it up close to his chest. "It feels as if you've weighted it with gold bars."

It was only then that he took a moment to really look at her. And was intrigued despite his annoyance. She really was quite pretty despite the spectacles and the obviously dated gown.

Before she could respond to his question, however, the innkeeper rushed over. "My lord, I am so sorry you were accosted by this"—he waved his hand in the direction of the lady, as if unable to come up with a suitable description for her, finally settling upon—"person. I'll have our finest room made up for you at once. Be gone with you, madam. His lordship has no wish to be bothered by the likes of you."

Wordlessly he gestured to a footman, who stepped forward to take the trunk from Quill, wincing as he did so.

"There's no need for rudeness, Stepney," Quill chastised the innkeeper. "It was an accident, nothing more. Please have your man carry the lady's trunk wherever she has need to take it."

"Oh that is too kind of you, my lord," the young woman said with a bright smile. "I would have left them in the coach, but one hears such tales about the mail coach and the thievery that takes place even amongst the passengers. I simply could not risk them. My books are so necessary to my work, you understand."

As she spoke, Quill noticed that her eyes were a clear green. And at her confession, something clicked into place. Of course. She was a governess. That would explain the spectacles and the books. She was likely on her way to a new position.

Before he could respond, however, Stepney bowed deeply and ignored the governess. "Very good, my lord. I'll see to it at once. Now, if you'll follow me I'll see you to your room."

And since the young woman was already directing the footman into the taproom where she was doubtless going to have a meal before she joined the rest of the passengers on the mail coach again, he gave her one last look, then followed Stepney up the stairs.

Grateful he'd thought to bring a small bag with him when he left the traveling chaise, Quill was soon bathed and wearing a fresh change of clothes. If his cravat wasn't as skillfully tied as his valet might have managed, then the clientele of the Fox and Pheasant would simply have to make do. Deciding to dine downstairs in the taproom rather than alone in his room, he was nearly at the bottom of the stairs when he heard a feminine shout. A premonition had him racing the rest of the way down and hurrying into the dining room, which took up the entire width of the building. Though it was still daylight, the lack of windows made for a dimly lit room, the only light source coming from the lamps on the tables and in sconces on the walls.

But it wasn't too dark for him to see the little governess standing defiantly before a great lummox of a man who clutched a hand against his cheek. "I'll no' take tha' from the likes o'ye," the man growled, launching himself forward and gripping the lady by her upper arms. "Who d'ye think y'are?"

In the tradition of all bystanders everywhere, the rest of the taproom seemed to settle in for a spectacle. At least that's how it seemed to Quill, who pushed his way forward, and snapped, "Unhand the lady at once, sir."

If there was one thing Quill could not abide, it was a man who laid hands on a woman. And there was something about seeing this particular lady in the other man's grip that made him particularly angry.

Not pausing to consider the wisdom of his actions, and not waiting for the fellow to obey his orders, Quill pulled her away from the ruffian and stepped between them, watching as her attacker lost his balance in his surprise and fell backward into the table behind him.

Standing over the man, lying in angry shock on the floor, Quill scowled. "Let that be a lesson to you that there are consequences for the mistreatment of ladies traveling alone. I don't know how things are done in the dark hole from whence you hail, but in the civilized world, men treat women with decency and respect. Especially when they are not noticeably under someone's protection."

Turning away from where the man sat stunned, he turned his attention to the governess, who was gaping at him with suspiciously bright eyes.

"I . . . I don't know how to thank you, my lord," she said, her voice shaking. "If you hadn't arrived when you did, I fear things would have gone very badly indeed."

Handing her his handkerchief, Quill led her to a booth on the far side of the room, where he gestured for her to take a seat.

"Why are you still here?" he demanded tersely, his residual anger making him short. "The mail coach should have departed by now." And as he quickly scanned the room, he saw that the others who had crowded into the inn with her were missing.

Wincing, she looked down. "The driver took on more passengers here, and he claimed there was no room for my trunks. When I refused to leave them behind, he left without me." As she finished this disclosure, she lifted her chin and glared defiantly at him, her eyes bright with anger. "They are necessary for my studies and I saw no reason why I should be the one to give up my trunks when there were plenty of others with far larger ones. It was grossly unfair."

"Surely you could have had them sent after you," Quill pointed out with a raised brow. From his time at university he knew that books were essential for study, but it was hardly practical for her to give up her seat for them. Any employer of merit would see the necessity of paying to have them delivered once he was informed of her situation. Which brought up another question. "Why didn't your employer make arrangements for your travel? Surely governesses are not required to travel on the common stage. I know my father always sent the traveling carriage for my sister's teachers. Or at the very least a hired carriage."

At this, she raised a brow in annoyance. "I know my gown is not of the first stare of fashion, but I hardly think I'm so drab as to be mistaken for a governess." She pursed her lips. "Not that there is anything wrong with governessing, you understand. It is a respectable profession—and one of the only ones available for a single lady of gentle birth."

Quill surveyed her appearance, taking care not to be seen doing so—a skill every young gentleman perfected in his teens lest he be forever receiving raps on the knuckles from his mama. On closer inspection, her gown, while dark gray in color, was well made. And her modest bonnet was constructed of if not the finest silk, then at the very least not the meanest. Even the trunk of books that she had lowered to the taproom floor beside her was not cheaply made. In short, he'd judged her wrongly from the start. What he'd concluded to be a lady in reduced circumstances was actually just a lady of modest tastes.

He felt his brow furrow. "If you are not a governess then, who are you?"

It was a highly inappropriate question considering they'd never been properly introduced, he knew. And it would be highly unusual for him to do the honors himself. Was she an actual governess, she'd likely read him a scold that would blister his ears. But, she didn't seem to take offense at the inquiry. "I am independent scholar," she informed him, her pride in it evident in her squared shoulders and elevated chin.

And to his surprise, she offered him her gloved hand. "Miss Aphrodite Wareham, Ivy to my friends."

His hand was already clasping hers when the name registered, and it was all Quill could do to stop himself from dropping the offending extremity and turning his back on her. But good manners had been instilled in him almost from birth, and he had been taught not to be rude to a lady. No matter how grasping or conniving that lady proved to be.

He gave a quick, mirthless laugh. "I might have known we'd meet on the road to Beauchamp House. Since it is, after all, the family estate you and your cohorts wish to steal out from under my family's nose. Well, I beg leave to inform you, madam, that while my late aunt was eccentric, she was not without family protection. And we will not stand for this scheme you've concocted. No matter how you might protest your friendship with my aunt."

Her nose wrinkled in confusion. "I don't know what you mean, sir," she said with a little shake of her head. "I never met Lady Celeste while she was living. Indeed, I wish I had for I'd have offered up my sincere thanks for her generous bequest."

She frowned, tilting her head as she scanned his face. *She was quite skilled at playing the puzzled innocent,* he thought bitterly.

"I assume from your accusation that you are Lady Celeste's relation?"

As if she didn't know it already. Hell, he'd not be surprised if she'd arranged for her little contretemps with the man earlier to gain his sympathy.

He sketched a mocking bow. "Torquil Beauchamp, Marquess of Kerr, at your service." Rising to see her still maintaining her air of bewilderment, he continued with a disgusted shake of his head. "But you doubtless knew that already. Tell me, how long did it take you and your friends to choose my aunt as your target? For I have little doubt she proved a ripe pigeon for plucking given her generous nature and genuine interest in scholarship. I know there must not be much opportunity for fortune in the arts for ladies. You must have been beside yourselves with glee when you found her."

But rather than let his derision break her, she seemed to gain strength from it. "I'm not sure where you get your information, my lord, but I have never met your aunt before in my life. Nor am I acquainted with the ladies you refer to as my cohorts. As far as our scheming to somehow steal your family estate out from under you, I was given to understand that Lady Celeste owned Beauchamp House outright and that it was not included with the rest of the Beauchamp estates, which is what made it possible for her to bequeath it to us in the first place."

Her color was up and she was bristling with anger now, which Quill had no doubt was genuine. Well it might be, given that her plans were being challenged instead of what she'd likely thought would be smooth sailing on her trip to take possession of her new home.

Let her be angry, he thought with a pang of self-mockery at how quickly he'd fallen prey to her wounded-innocent act. She was probably as mean as a snake and twice as venomous.

The Beauchamps were not known for their pacifism. And as the head of the family, Quill didn't mean to let a passel of scheming harpies lure him onto a rocky shore in hopes they could take an estate that had been in the Beauchamp family for hundreds of years.

"Then, my dear Miss Wareham," he said coldly, not believing her protests for a moment, "you were sadly misinformed. And I will do my utmost to ensure that you and the other ladies who tricked my aunt are not only prevented from taking ownership, but are prosecuted for your fraud."

Chapter 2

"I might have known it was too much to ask that you were simply a kind stranger," Ivy fumed, angry with herself as much as at Lord Kerr. No man with that much polish could fail to be a scoundrel beneath his burnished exterior. She'd been a fool to let his championship against the taproom bully sway her to let down her guard. Even a little.

She'd been around enough of her father's noble pupils to recognize aristocratic good manners when she saw them. She'd seen any number of lordlings and gentlemen bow politely to her one moment, then pinch the maid on the bottom as soon as they thought they were out of sight. Lord Kerr was no different, only his grasping had been of a less crude variety.

If she was less certain of the validity of her claim upon Lady Celeste's estate, Ivy might have been more frightened by the marquess's threat to stop her and the other heirs from claiming their inheritance. But as soon as the letter from Lady Celeste had arrived, along with another from her solicitor, Ivy had asked for her father's assistance in determining whether it was legal.

Though Lord Alton Wareham, a former Oxford don who'd left the university upon his marriage, hadn't spoken to his family in some years thanks to their less-than-welcoming attitude toward his wife—Ivy's mother—he'd kept in touch with his cousin, a solicitor with clientele in the aristocracy. And upon consultation, the cousin had assured both Lord Alton and Ivy that the bequest was not only valid, but that if Ivy did not wish to risk losing her inheritance, she should travel at once to Beauchamp House and stake her claim.

As the eldest in a family of seven daughters, Ivy had been more than eager to embark on the journey. Not only because she looked forward to making use of the impressive library mentioned in Lady Celeste's letter, which was said to contain any number of Greek transcriptions that had never been made available to the academic community, but also because she was desperate to escape the mayhem of her family home.

She'd spent most of her life caring for her siblings and when that lady was subjected to yet another confinement, to her mother. Though her father had been born the younger son of the Duke of Ware, his unsupported marriage had cut off any financial assistance he might have expected from his family. And so, it had been in a modest house on the outskirts of Oxford where Ivy and her siblings had grown up. It wasn't an unhappy family. But Ivy was more than ready to strike out on her own scholarly path—to get out from under the influence of her father's tutelage and to establish herself in her own right. And if it let her also escape the responsibility of caring for her younger siblings, so much the better.

In short, she was looking forward to taking up her shared tenancy of Beauchamp House, and no amount of bullying from the Marquess of Kerr would persuade her otherwise.

"But, nephew of Lady Celeste or not," she continued, her spine ramrod straight, "you will soon find yourself disabused of these notions. You do not think I would pack my trunks and leave my home on merely the hint of an inheritance, do you?" She would indeed have done such a thing, given her desire to escape her parents' unruly abode, but Lord Kerr didn't need to know that.

He looked down his aristocratic nose at her, his blue eyes narrow with dislike. "I have no notion what a woman like you would attempt, madam," he said coldly. "You have proven yourself to be brazen enough to hoodwink an elderly lady into bequeathing a valuable family estate to you. Why should I be surprised at anything you do?"

She gasped at his words. By referring to her as "woman," he'd essentially called her respectability into question. If she were a man, and if she believed in dueling—a truly barbaric practice that was long overdue for dying out—she'd have called him out. As it was, she was a lady and would pay no attention to the slurs of a man who had proved himself to have very little claim upon the title of gentleman.

Turning her back on him, she hoisted her trunk of books with some difficulty, letting the exhale of exertion hiss through her teeth lest he realize just how much effort it took, and carried it and her valise to a table not so very far from his. (She'd have gone farther, but she greatly feared that she would drop the trunk, embarrassing herself before her nemesis.)

No sooner had she collapsed as genteelly as she could into her chair, than the innkeeper appeared at her side, his narrowed busuy brows, his smile less than polite. "This taproom is for paying customers only, miss," Mr. Stepney said with a pointed look at her trunk, as if it was taking up a seat that was also meant for paying customers. "If you would like to hire a room for the night, I'll just take your payment now."

Well aware that Lord Kerr and the rest of the dining room were watching with interest, she mentally calculated the amount of money in her purse, which, she feared was not enough for even the smallest room here. Her passage on the mail coach had used the bulk of her funds, and her father had insisted that traveling with a full purse would invite cutpurses and pickpockets to prey upon her. Or so he'd said—she rather suspected it was another attempt on his part to keep her from leaving, but she'd called his bluff and gone anyway.

Smiling up hopefully at the proprietor, she said, "You seem like far too kind a man to eject a lady from your establishment, Mr. Stepney, is it? I assure you I will only be here for a little while. I am expecting a carriage from Beauchamp House near Little Seaford this afternoon." A bald-faced lie, but she was desperate. It was bad enough for a lady traveling alone to fend off the rough customers of a taproom, but if he forced her into the inn yard she didn't like her chances of surviving unscathed.

The innkeeper frowned, but before he could respond, she felt a presence at her back. "She will be traveling with me, Stepney," said Lord Kerr smoothly. "We are both bound for Beauchamp House so I thought it best to spare her the indignities of the mail coach."

Stepney's look of suspicion turned into a leer as he glanced between the marquess and Ivy. "Very well, my lord. Will you be needing another room then?" It was clear from his tone that he thought the question unnecessary.

"I don't think so," Kerr said to Ivy's shock. If the ill-tempered marquess thought she would let him get away with ruining her reputation then he was sorely mistaken.

She opened her mouth to set the innkeeper straight, but the Lord Kerr continued, "I've hired a carriage for the drive so that we can leave in a short while. My own is in need of further repair so I will leave my coachman to see to it from here. Miss Wareham may have a place in the hired coach. For propriety's sake I'll join my valet in the second carriage."

Ivy could not have been more shocked if he'd casually announced that he drank the blood of virgins and howled at the moon. She'd judged him wrongly, she supposed. At least when it came to his desire to ruin her reputation. But as soon as Mr. Stepney had stepped away, the marquess said in a low voice only she could hear, "I'll not risk any damage to your reputation lest I find myself at the other end of your father's pistol being forced into a marriage with you. That is just what this farce needs to make it an actual circus."

She clenched her teeth, anger making her hands shake. "I wouldn't marry you if you were wrapped in gold and carrying every last missing fragment of Greek poetry," she spat.

"Then we are in agreement on something, it would seem," he sneered. "And if you are wondering why I am in such a generous mood, it's because I won't have you ruining my good name in these parts. My family has owned property here for hundreds of years and we are well known in the district. And the sooner we get to Beauchamp House and speak to my aunt's fraud of a solicitor, the sooner I can get back to London and get on with my life."

"I might have known you'd be playing dog in the manger with Beauchamp House," Ivy said shaking her head in disgust. "You don't want me or the other ladies to have it, but you don't actually want it for yourself either. Just another family property to languish empty while you and the other Beauchamps 'live your lives' in your actual homes. What a charming portrait of aristocratic generosity you paint."

"I'd mind my tongue if I were you, Miss Wareham," he said with a smile that didn't reach his eyes. "Else I shall change my mind and leave you to the charming Mr. Stepney's care."

Recognizing the truth of his threat, she bit her tongue on the sharp retort she longed to let fly. "My apologies," she said falsely. "If the hired carriage is ready, perhaps I'd best go ahead and climb in, to spare us both further argument."

With as much dignity as she could muster, she attempted to hoist her book-laden trunk once more, only to be forestalled by Lord Kerr who wordlessly lifted it without so much as a grunt of exertion—really it was too unfair that men were endowed with such strength. Especially men like the marquess, who it was unlikely was ever called upon to lift more than a fork at his lavish dinner table. Though a quick glance at his close-cut jacket and skin-tight breeches showed that he must be doing some sort of exercise on a regular basis.

The villain. Why could he not be as fat as the Prince Regent and as weak as a kitten?

"Come along, Miss Wareham," he said without waiting to see if she followed. "The sooner we get to Beauchamp House, the sooner we can have you on your way back to Oxfordshire."

Rather than argue, she trudged along after him, looking forward to the moment when he'd be forced to accept just how wrong he was. About her, and about the matter of Lady Celeste Beauchamp's bequests.

There would be time enough for gloating then.

Despite her earlier upset and sparring with Lord Kerr, Ivy fell asleep almost as soon as the hired carriage departed from the inn. Her day had begun before dawn and she'd gotten little rest the night before because she was eager for her journey.

By the time the conveyance pulled to a stop some hours later, she was awake and ready to see her new home. But night had fallen as they traveled, so all she could see was the glow of lamplight through the windows. A real look at the manor house would have to wait until tomorrow.

She was surprised to see that it was Lord Kerr who opened the door of the carriage rather than a footman.

"Don't just sit there gaping, Miss Wareham," he said extending his hand in to her after he let down the step. "You'll catch flies."

Her desire to stretch her legs after hours in the carriage

was at war with her determination to be as uncivil as possible to the man who had insulted her motives so thoroughly earlier. But, she thought as she grudgingly took his proffered assistance, he had offered her safe passage to Beauchamp House—no matter how ugly the motive—so she relented.

No sooner was she standing on her own two feet than she was pulled close in a strange lady's embrace. "You must be Ivy," said the woman with a slight northern burr. "We thought you'd never arrive. We've been waiting this age. You're the last to arrive and though Lady Serena did assure us that you'd be here soon enough, I did have my doubts let me tell you, Ivy. May I call you Ivy? It's such a lovely name, though Lady Celeste's letter did say that your given name is Aphrodite, which I must say is a mouthful so I'll just use Ivy if you don't mind. Though if you insist of course, I shall call you Aphrodite, it's your name after all."

She could have continued on forever, Ivy was certain, had the young lady not glanced over into the bemused countenance of Lord Kerr. Her gray eyes grew wide and her mouth formed an O of surprise.

Taking a moment to catch her breath, Ivy glanced behind the talkative lady and saw three more ladies, a very dignified man she assumed was the butler, and a footman arrayed upon the front portico.

"Give her a moment to get her bearings, Miss Hastings" said the curvy brunette, who seemed a bit older than the other three. Smiling to soften any chastisement in her words, she continued. "That chatterbox, Miss Wareham, is Miss Sophia Hastings who along with her sister Miss Gemma Hastings, here"—she gestured to the plainer girl next to her, with beautiful dark chestnut hair in contrast to her sister's light brown locks—"is another of Lady Celeste's heirs."

"I'm Lady Daphne Forsythe," said the tall blonde, who was perhaps the most beautiful creature Ivy had ever seen.

But her awkward manner kept her from the remoteness that her looks might have imbued her with. "I am a mathematician, Sophia is a painter, and Gemma studies fossils. You study ancient languages." This last was said as if an accusation, but Ivy got the feeling that there was no harm meant by the girl's brusque manner.

"Indeed I do, Lady Daphne," she said with a smile at the other girl. "But I'm sorry ma'am," she continued to the woman who'd spoken up first. "I didn't hear your own name in that list of introductions. Might you be Lady Serena Fanning?"

"She is indeed, Miss Wareham," said Lord Kerr before Lady Serena could speak up. "And I suggest we all go inside so that we can discuss this business somewhere other than the front stoop where all and sundry might listen in."

Rather than protest at the marquess's bad manners, the other ladies nodded in agreement and allowed the butler to usher them all back into the front entry, where Ivy handed the man, whom she learned was called Mr. Greaves, her cloak and asked that her trunk and valise be taken up to her room. She would have liked to wash off her travel dirt before getting into yet another argument with the marquess over the late Lady Celeste's disposition of Beauchamp House, but she'd seen the glint of annoyance in Lord Kerr's eyes at seeing her fellow heirs waiting for her, so she knew it was coming.

"Let's retire to the parlor, shall we?" Lady Serena suggested as she led them upstairs into a well-lit chamber furnished with comfortable chairs, a couple of sofas, and a merrily burning fire.

Ivy could tell that Sophia wanted very badly to ask her a dozen more questions, but something—perhaps Lord Kerr—kept her silent until they were seated. "I had not expected you to be traveling with a gentleman, Miss Wareham," she said as if unable to keep her peace any longer. "Is he your betrothed?"

Both Ivy and Lord Kerr spoke at once.

"Good god, no!"

"Perish the thought!"

Lady Serena laughed. "Well, that was certainly heartfelt. Sophia, I can assure you that this fellow—though he does seem to have arrived with Miss Wareham, is my cousin the Marquess of Kerr, and he was likely on his way here when he met Miss Wareham on the road. Is it something like that, Quill?"

The marquess, who was looking as comfortable as a hen in a foxes' den, inclined his head to Lady Serena. "Something like that, Serena, though I must confess myself surprised at finding you here. I should have expected you to have more family feeling than to be welcoming these interlopers into Aunt Celeste's home."

"Interlopers?" Sophia asked, her nose wrinkling in puzzlement. "What can you mean?"

"The bequest is quite clearly spelled out in your aunt's will, my lord," said Lady Daphne firmly. "My solicitor made sure of it."

"As did ours," said Miss Gemma Hastings, with a firm nod. "Else we'd not have traveled such a great distance to come here."

Enjoying the sight of Lord Kerr confronted by others who were on her own side, Ivy pushed up her spectacles on her nose so that she might better see his chagrin. Of course, being Lord Kerr, he showed no such thing.

"My own solicitors are looking for loopholes as we speak, ladies," he said with a shrug. "And I fear you are all doomed to disappointment. I will, of course, do what I can to ensure you safe passage back to your respective homes."

"Quill," Lady Serena said sharply, "I think you are

mistaken—both with regard to Aunt Celeste's will but also her wishes. Why do you think I am here?"

For the first time, Ivy saw a crack in his lordship's veneer of certainty. He frowned. "I don't know. I suppose I thought you brought Jeremy here to visit the seaside. And mistakenly thought these ladies were guests."

"Jeremy is her six-year-old son," Lady Daphne helpfully informed Ivy. "A bright child though not as good with maths as I was at that age."

Ivy's eyes widened, and even Lord Kerr looked shocked.

"Daphne," Sophia hissed, "that's not something you should say aloud in front of the boy's mother."

"I was only stating a fact," Lady Daphne said puzzled. "If I were Jeremy's mother I would wish to know that he is lagging behind."

Clearly Lady Daphne was lacking the ability to censor her thoughts, Ivy thought. That would make for an interesting tenure in Beauchamp House for them all.

Perhaps wishing to change the subject, Lady Serena said, "I did not bring Jeremy here to enjoy the seaside. Aunt Celeste asked me to act as chaperone for her heirs for the next year as they compete to see who will eventually become the owner of Beauchamp House."

A silence fell over the room, and Ivy could feel the shock of the other girls because it mirrored her own.

"Compete?" Lord Kerr asked, looking as flummoxed as the rest of them.

"Perhaps you'd better come have a private chat with me," Lady Serena said to the marquess. Turning to the four heiresses, she said pointedly, "And you ladies can go get Ivy settled in to her room. I daresay she'd like to rest after the journey she's had. I'll see you all in the morning."

Knowing a dismissal when she heard one, Ivy gave one last look at Lord Kerr whose frown was thoughtful as he stared at his cousin. He might have been unpleasant, but he was the last connection to her life before Beauchamp House, and Ivy found herself reluctant to leave him.

But Sophia slipped an arm through hers and smiled with understanding. "Come on," she said leading her to the doorway. "I'll ring for hot water. I know the first thing I did as soon as I got here was freshen up."

Diverted by the promise of fresh clothes and rest, Ivy went along.

Chapter 3

"You should leave, Quill," said Serena baldly as soon as the door to the parlor closed behind them. "I don't know what maggot you've got in your head about Beauchamp House, but you need to get back into your carriage and return to London."

He waited until they were safely inside Celeste's library before speaking up. Quill had never known either his aunt or Serena to fall prey to the sort of feminine whims that led other ladies to be taken in by frauds, but in this instance he was convinced that it had happened to them both. Why else would his aunt have concocted a contest that determined who would inherit a manor house that had been in the family for centuries?

"You shouldn't speak cant, Serena," he said, scowling as he opened the cupboard doors behind his aunt's desk in search of something alcoholic. "It doesn't suit you. And I'm surprised that you of all people would go along with such a ridiculous plan."

At last in the back of the cabinet, behind a stack of Minerva Press novels, he found a decanter. Pulling it out, along with the glass beside it, he held up the crystal to the light.

Opening it, he sniffed. Port! He gave a sigh of relief and poured himself a glass.

Serena watched all of this in annoyance, her arms crossed over her chest. "What do you mean, me 'of all people,' cousin?" she asked sweetly. "I hope you're not referring to my late husband, else I shall be forced to toss you out on your ear myself."

Quill had the grace to feel sheepish. He also well remembered that until he'd grown strong enough to hold her off, she'd been quite good at pinching the tender skin beneath his bicep when he kidnapped her dolls or used her fans as sails for his self-constructed sailboats on the pond. Surreptitiously he slipped a hand beneath his arm at the remembered pain.

Still, even Serena had to admit that her late husband had been a charlatan of the first order. Though he could hardly say as much now. Instead, he took a sip of the excellent port—thanking the gods that his aunt hadn't been too much of a stickler not to buy her liquor from the smugglers that populated the coast.

When he saw that Serena was waiting for a response, he shrugged. "I simply thought you'd had enough of being lied to," he said simply.

"And what makes you think that I'm being lied to now?" she asked, not deigning to acknowledge his veiled mention of her late husband's perfidy.

By the time Quill had learned that his dear cousin's husband, who had spent every last farthing of her dowry, had died on his way to the continent with his mistress, it had been too late to do what he wanted—which was call out the bastard. So instead he'd seen to it that she was well taken care of and that her young son, Jeremy, was not in want of male relatives to substitute in the role of father figure. He knew all too well what it was like to grow up as the only male in a house full of women.

Grateful that they weren't going to go into the details of Fanning's bad behavior again, Quill latched on to her mention of their present problem. "Can you truly believe that Aunt Celeste would have invited four strangers into her home—where she surrounded herself with everything she loved: books, art, artifacts, academic papers—and not only given them free reign but involved them in some sort of competition for it? Our Aunt Celeste? Who disliked people almost as much as she loved books? It's laughable. She is very likely shouting at us from beyond the grave, telling us to get them out of her house and away from her things!"

Though he'd been very fond of his aunt, he knew better than anyone just how much of a misanthrope she could be when it came to interacting with people she didn't know. He'd never heard the full story, but his mother had hinted once that a failed romance had left Celeste with a sour attitude toward the *ton* and a dislike of town. It was impossible to reconcile the Celeste he knew with the sort of woman who would invite strangers into her home—no matter how lonely she might have become.

"When was the last time you actually visited her, Quill?" Serena asked pointedly. "For someone who claims to have known her so well, you weren't exactly the most doting of nephews, were you?"

"I visited," Quill protested, feeling heat creep up his neck. "I was here last summer, I think." Or was it the summer before? He'd been busy in London for the past few years with the lords and dealing with repairs and updates to the farms at Kerr Castle, the seat of the Kerr marquisate in Dorset. But he'd managed to write to her once a month like always, hadn't he? And it wasn't as if he was her only nephew. He had male cousins. Not to mention Celeste's own living sisters and brothers. There was no need for him alone to have come visit so often.

But you were her favorite, an insidious little voice whispered in his head. *You and Serena. She was here. Where were you?*

"Not enough," his cousin said flatly. "I don't blame you. You have responsibilities as the head of your family that the rest of us don't. But you cannot simply waltz in after she's made preparations and set into motion what she wished to happen after she was gone and cut up rough because you weren't consulted. You weren't here. And this competition—however crass you might think it is—is how she wanted to dispose of Beauchamp House."

It *was* crass.

That, he admitted to himself, was the part that pained him most. That his aunt—who for all her dislike of going out into company in London was as elegant as anyone he'd ever known, his own mother included—would have put up her home as the prize in a crude competition amongst a group of strange women. It wasn't anything he could ever have imagined the Lady Celeste Beauchamp he'd known doing.

"But why did she do it?" he asked Serena, who clearly had been privy to more of his aunt's thoughts on the matter than he had. If he'd ever got an inkling of such a thing from her witty letters to him over the last year he'd have dropped everything and rushed to the south coast at once. "Why these women in particular? And why give up Beauchamp House? I know grandfather gave it to her outright, but surely she was aware of its history as part of the Beauchamp properties."

Serena suddenly looked exhausted and gestured for him to give her the rest of his port. And since there didn't seem to be another glass, he poured a bit more and handed it over. Closing her eyes as she savored the wine, Serene gave a sigh of appreciation and set the glass down. Taking a seat in the well-cushioned chair across from Celeste's desk, she rubbed the spot between her brows.

"You know that Aunt Celeste was a bit of a bluestocking in her youth," she said finally, looking up at him with eyes so much like Celeste's.

"Of course," Quill responded, taking a seat behind the desk. He'd always thought it was a masculine desk for his aunt, but there was something commanding about it. And taking a seat behind it for the first time showed him why perhaps she'd kept it on moving into the house. It would be difficult to manage a household from a delicate ladies' desk like the one his mother had in her sitting room. "It was from her that I first learned about Greek and Roman myths. Not to mention Latin."

Serena laughed. "Me too. She was determined that her nieces as well as her nephews would have a working knowledge of the classics."

"Always banging on about what passed for female education in England." Quill nodded in agreement. "She was nothing if not a determined follower of Wollstonecraft. If she told me once, she told me a thousand times not to marry an empty-headed society chit."

"Which you've managed to avoid," Serena said. "Along with matrimony of any kind."

"Not for want to effort on Mama's part," he retorted with a grimace.

"Well, if you remember our aunt's views on education," Serena continued, "then you will also recall how much she prized feminine success in languages, the arts and sciences."

"So, what, these four are here to be educated according to some guidelines set forth by Aunt Celeste?" Quill asked, frowning. It made sense, he supposed. But there was the matter of Miss Wareham—she had no need for an education considering her profession.

Suddenly, it came to him. "No, Miss Wareham is the one who will teach the others. It's why she was carrying all those blasted books." He grinned. "I'm right, aren't I?"

"You really do think you know everything, don't you?" Serena asked exasperated. "Miss Wareham is the daughter of Lord Alton Wareham, former classics professor at Oxford. She's a gifted translator and scholar of ancient Greek in her own right. She is here because Aunt Celeste read one of her translations of Sappho and thought it was far more nuanced than any she'd read by the dozens of men who attempted it."

Quill frowned.

He'd known she was some sort of scholar. No woman clasps a trunk of books to her bosom with that sort of ferocity without knowing their value. And some sense had told him they weren't novels. But Sappho? He thought back to the few Greek poetess's verses he'd read and felt a spark of interest flare. Perhaps there was more to the prim Miss Wareham than he'd originally thought.

"Shall I ring for some smelling salts?" Serena asked with a knowing look. "Or better yet a block of ice to cool your heated thoughts?"

"Certainly not," he responded resisting the urge to run a finger beneath his collar. "So, Miss Wareham is a classics scholar. And she's to teach the others?"

"Hardly," his cousin retorted. "They are all experts in their own right, and that is why Aunt Celeste chose to leave the house to them. Or so I've surmised. She only asked that I come live here with them for the year while they get acclimated, and didn't tell me about her purposes in leaving it to them. Though she did praise them all as accomplished ladies whose expertise is to be commended."

"That sounds like Aunt, at least," Quill said begrudgingly. "And this . . . competition?"

He had difficulty even saying the word, the concept was so vulgar. If word of this got out, the entire Beauchamp family would be the laughingstock of the *ton*, not that he was generally given to caring what the gossips said. But as the head of the family, he did have a responsibility to prevent the sort of talk a scandal like this could cause.

"They're all to spend a year in residence here, working on some project in their chosen field," Serena said. "If any of them should move away before the year is up, she'll forfeit her inheritance. There are of course exceptions for the death of a close family member or medical catastrophe. But any or none of them could inherit according to the terms of Aunt's will, depending upon their ability to remain here. At the end of the year they should each have some new project completed that will contribute to the body of work by female scholars and artists. I suppose that, ultimately, is Aunt's purpose in choosing them."

"It's absurd," Quill said with a shake of his head. "But not, I suppose, entirely outside the realm of things I would expect from Aunt Celeste. She was nothing if not a champion of her bluestocking causes."

"So you'll agree that you've behaved like an ass and will apologize to Miss Wareham, then?" Serena's look was one he well remembered from childhood. He hated it when she was right.

"Let's not be hasty," he said raising his hands. "I didn't know the full story when we met on the road. And though I am persuaded that she is here as the result of a legitimate invitation from Aunt Celeste, I still don't necessarily condone having four strangers inherit Beauchamp House."

"Oh, give over, Quill," Serena said rising. "You're worse than Jeremy when he's trying to wiggle out of a bath. Just admit you were wrong and go back to London. There's nothing for you to do now but wait and see."

But he wasn't convinced that she was right. "Perhaps I will just remain for a while and get to know them. It would hardly be polite if the head of the family were to avoid them all. I am nothing if not cordial, after all."

"What rot." But Serena didn't try to talk him out of it. "I suppose if you're going to stay, I'd better have Mrs. Bacon prepare a room for you. Though I daresay Greaves has already done so. You always did have the servants wrapped around your little finger."

"Because I'm irresistible," Quill said with a wink.

He hoped that was still the case. Because he was going to need every wile at his disposal to convince the four potential heiresses to give up their claims on Beauchamp House.

Chapter 4

"How did you manage to meet Lord Kerr on your journey?" Sophia asked as she thumbed through the books that Ivy had just unpacked from her trunk.

Across the room, the lady's maid who'd been assigned to Ivy on her arrival was brushing out the mud-streaked traveling cloak she'd worn earlier, having already unpacked the few gowns, underthings, and shoes she'd packed. Well aware of the quality of the other girls' gowns, Ivy suspected that compared to their bags, hers had been quite sparsely packed. Even so, she wasn't one to dwell on such things. And she wasn't here to discuss fashion, she reminded herself.

At Sophia's question, however, she glanced nervously at the servant. The last thing she wanted was to be the subject of gossip below stairs. But when Sophia noticed her glance, she shrugged it off. "She's going to learn the full story from his valet anyway, aren't you Polly?"

The maid blushed. "I'm sure I don't know, miss." Turning to Ivy, she curtsied and said, "You let me know, miss, if you need help after your bath. I don't mind helping. I've never been a lady's maid before so I want to do things right and proper for ye."

"Thank you, Polly," said Ivy with genuine gratitude. It

would appear that she and Polly would both be learning how to deal with new situations. "You may go now, if you like. If I have any questions, I'll ring." It was a polite lie, but she was comfortable with it. If she was going to have a maid, she wasn't going to give the girl a hatred of her on the first evening by ringing in the dead of night.

As soon as she was gone, Ivy glanced up to see all three of the other ladies looking expectantly at her.

"Fine," she said with a huff and gestured to the small sitting area in the corner of her enormous bedchamber. "But if you don't mind, I'd like to have a cup of tea while we have this uncomfortable conversation." Upon learning Ivy had missed supper, the maid had insisted on ordering a plate of cold food and a pot of tea sent up.

Despite her missishness around her new acquaintances, Ivy was starving and bit into one of the delicious watercress and cucumber sandwiches. Likely realizing that they'd not get any information until the newcomer was comfortable, Gemma played mother and poured for them all.

"The food has been excellent so far," Lady Daphne said as she picked up a lemon tart. "Lady Celeste must have employed a very skilled chef. Our own chef at home demanded five hundred pounds per annum but my father said he was worth every penny. Perhaps Lady Celeste paid more. Though this house does not seem to be as nice as ours, the food is better than even Pierre's."

Ivy exchanged looks with Sophia and Gemma who both widened their eyes at the beautiful blonde's pronouncement.

"Daphne, dearest," said Gemma casually stirring sugar into her tea, "it isn't generally the thing to discuss how much one pays one's cook. Or to speculate upon the salary of the cook in a home where one is a guest."

Quite sure the family cook at home would have retired immediately if such a sum were offered to her, Ivy tried to imagine what five hundred pounds would look like spread out on a table, and failed.

"You keep saying things like that," Daphne said with a puzzled frown, "but if one doesn't discuss such things openly, how do they know how much they should pay? It makes no logical sense. If I were setting up a household, I would very much wish to know how much I should pay my cook. Otherwise I'd risk paying too much. And though I enjoy good food, I wouldn't want to fall prey to a schemer."

"It's not polite," Sophia said patiently. "Like telling the footman that his legs look quite strong."

Ivy choked on her tea, prompting Gemma to pound her on the back.

"But my father says that about horses all the time," Daphne protested. "I don't see what's so bad about it. Doesn't a footman need strong legs to help him carry things?"

"People are not horses," Gemma said on a laugh. "Really, perhaps it should be a good thing not to speak about anyone's . . . ah . . . parts from the waist down."

"That sounds like a sensible idea," Ivy said, wondering how on earth Lady Daphne managed to mix in polite society without saying something that would ruin her.

But Daphne waved off the warning. "I already know not to talk about buttocks and penises," she said. "I'm not a complete simpleton."

After the other three had recovered from their coughing fits, she continued. "I suppose I shall add legs to the list of things I shouldn't speak about. Really the list is quite long. It's a wonder I find anything to speak about at all. At least there is nothing about maths that can get me into trouble."

"I daresay none of us would know them if there were," Ivy said with a smile. It must be very hard to live life in Lady Daphne's skin, she reflected. For she could tell it wasn't a lack of intelligence that kept the other lady from knowing what not to say, but a genuine lack of understanding what made it so objectionable. She herself found societal strictures to be quite ridiculous at times.

"Perhaps we should return to my earlier question," Sophia said looking slyly at Ivy. "How did you manage to arrive here in an entourage that included the Marquess of Kerr, Miss Wareham?"

Sighing, Ivy knew she'd have to tell them or they'd speculate. "I missed my place on the mail coach at the Fox and Pheasant, and his lordship kindly offered to convey me to Beauchamp House. There's really nothing more to it than that."

"He seemed quite angry when you arrived," Daphne said. "And serious about keeping us from inheriting Beauchamp House."

"Though from what Lady Serena said about a competition, it doesn't appear that any of us is assured of inheriting," Sophia said, her light brown brows drawn. "That was the first I'd heard of anything like that."

"Me too," Ivy said. "I thought we each were to inherit a share of Beauchamp House. But it sounds as if we only inherit if we can remain here for the entire year."

"I certainly have no plans to leave before the year is out," Lady Daphne said fiercely. "Have you seen the library? It will take that long at least for me to catalog the mathematics collection."

"Nor do we," said Sophia, clasping her sister's hand in hers. "I plan to paint to my heart's desire while I'm here. You've not seen it by day, Miss Wareham, but the light is incredible reflecting off the sea."

"The cliffs here are well known for the number of fossils they've produced," Gemma added with a grin. "So his lordship can quite discount any notion of running the Hastings sisters off."

"And I've only just arrived," Ivy said firmly. "He might be unhappy with his aunt's decision on how to bequeath her property, but clearly Lady Celeste wanted us here, and no amount of complaints on the Marquess of Kerr's part will convince me to leave."

"Then we're agreed," Sophia said with a decisive nod. "Now, we should leave you to finish settling in."

"We'll see you at breakfast, Miss Wareham," Gemma said, giving Ivy an impulsive hug. "I'm glad you're here. Now we can begin living our year in scholarly retreat properly."

"I wish you would all call me Ivy," she said as she followed the trio to the door. "My given name is Aphrodite, of course, but my baby sister could only manage 'Ivy' out of it, so Ivy it is. And I think it suits me better, to be honest. I am far too prosaic to be an Aphrodite."

"The goddess of love, was she not?" asked Sophia with a speculative look. "I can see you that way. Do promise me you'll pose for it? I'd love to capture all that lovely auburn hair."

"Do not start that, or we'll be here all night," Gemma said tugging her sister to the door. "Good night, Ivy."

The rest of the ladies exchanged their good nights, and Ivy shut the door behind them.

Turning, she gazed around at what was to be her inner sanctum for the next year. With fine carpets and expensive wall hangings, it was far more finely furnished than her own bedchamber at home in Oxford. And for a moment, she felt a pang of homesickness that no amount of silken finery or expensive trinkets could soothe. She'd longed to escape her mundane existence for so many years that she'd never imagined that once achieving her dream she'd feel frightened by it.

She let the tears flow for a few minutes and then pulled

out her handkerchief, blew her nose, and shook away her doldrums.

If she had to face Lord Kerr over the breakfast table, she'd do it after a good night's sleep so she could rebut his arguments properly.

Gathering her nightgown and underclothes, she headed for the dressing room and the hot water Polly had left for her.

Once she'd washed and prepared for bed, Ivy took one more look out at the moonlit view from her window then moved toward the large bedstead.

The bed had already been turned down—Polly again, she supposed. And as she climbed up onto the soft mattress, Ivy noticed a tidily folded missive on her pillow. Had it been there before, when the other ladies were here? Or had one of them left it?

Propping the pillow against the headboard, she settled back against it and stared at her name written in a fine copperplate on the message. Breaking the seal, she began to read.

My dear Miss Wareham,

If you are reading this, I have died under mysterious circumstances. And I must beg you to do your utmost to discover who has robbed me of the chance to meet you and the other three young ladies whom I have chosen to invite into my home, to compete for the chance to call it your own. It was my greatest wish to meet the four of you. To welcome you as fellow scholars, and to share with you my own love of language, mathematics, art, and investigation of the natural world. But for some weeks now, I have become aware that someone near to me has wished me dead before that meeting could happen. At first I thought the accidents were merely accidents. An imagined shove as I stood on the cliffside. My own clumsiness when the heel broke off my shoe as I descended the stairs. A weak shelf that allowed books to crash down upon me in the library. But now it has become clear to me that there is someone who wishes me dead. I am quite certain I am being poisoned, and I fear each day will my last.

You will perhaps wonder why I entrust this information to you, my dear Ivy, whom I have never even met. And the answer is quite simple. I have made a study of you—of all of you young ladies whom I have chosen for study at Beauchamp House—and you have struck me as the most, how shall I put this? The most capable of managing more than one task at a time. Do not mistake me. I believe all of the others—and indeed my own niece Serena, to whom I have entrusted you in my absence—to be clever and devoted to finding truth, but you, dear Ivy, are the only one who has been forced to pursue your own studies while also assisting someone else with theirs. And that, I believe, with a father like yours, must have taken some degree of guile. I do not blame you, of course. Indeed, it only makes me admire your abilities more. For not everyone is able to maintain two tracks of thought at once.

It is for this reason that I tell you all of this. It is most unfair, I know, to saddle you with this task just as you are ready to finally embark upon your own solitary, scholarly journey, but I'm afraid it's not to be helped. There is too much at stake for me to rest easy knowing that there is a murderer so near Beauchamp House. I know at this point only that they wish to end my life. But I do not know the why of it. Perhaps there is something in the house itself that they seek, in which case now your own life and the lives of the other young ladies are also in danger.

In thanks for your assistance in this matter, I've left a token of my appreciation for you in the library. You will find it inside the glass-front case on the east wall. I've already informed Serena that it belongs to you, so do not worry about removing it. It is yours now and I hope it will do you some good in your studies. In return, I hope that you will confide what I have told you in my nephew, the Marquess of Kerr. He will be quite angry that I have left Beauchamp House to you and your fellow bluestockings. But he is a good man, and will do his utmost to help you in this matter. I trust him, Ivy, and so too should you.

I do so wish we could have met in person, my dear, for I've long suspected you of possessing the same inner fire for knowledge that I myself had at your age. But it was not to be. I shall simply have to content myself with the knowledge that we will meet in the afterlife, where we will talk to our hearts' content about everything and nothing.

Yours in scholarship,
Lady Celeste Beauchamp

Ivy stared down at the letter. Then, more slowly, she read it again. But no amount of rereading would dispel the meaning of the words that Lady Celeste herself had penned for the express purpose of informing Ivy that she'd been murdered.

When she'd first learned that none other than the renowned Lady Celeste Beauchamp had left a portion of her South Downs estate to her, Ivy had thrilled at the prospect of using the bluestocking's famous collection of scholarship on ancient Greek and Latin poets and philosophers for her own studies. She lived in Oxford, of course, but the Bodleian Library and its world-class collection was off limits to ladies and even if that weren't the case, she suspected her father would have forbidden her from going there. He had taught her to write and read any number of languages, but he still considered some of the works discovered in the remains of the Hellenistic world to be improper for a lady—his daughter in particular—to be exposed to. So, the hope that Lady Celeste had collected some of those forbidden works was far too tempting a prospect for Ivy to overlook.

What she had not considered was that she would find herself called to solve a murder on her first night in Beauchamp House. Or that Lady Celeste herself would beckon to her from beyond the grave.

Unbidden, the Marquess of Kerr's handsome face rose in her mind. And despite her earlier annoyance with the man, she knew that she had to tell him about this. Not only because he had clearly spent a great deal of time here at Beauchamp House and could therefore assess better than she could who was likely to have wished his aunt dead. But also because Lady Celeste was his aunt. He clearly held her in great affection and would do his utmost to find out who had killed her.

And her benefactress had asked her to tell him. That was ultimately the fact that made Ivy don her dressing gown. Hoping that the marquess was still awake and in the library, she squared her shoulders and made her way downstairs.

Chapter 5

Too wound up for sleep, Quill remained in the library after
Serena had gone up to bed, wishing it wasn't too chilly for
him to go for a swim. As a youth he'd spent many a summer
night burning up restless energy that way. He'd been forbidden from doing so alone, of course, but when had that ever
stopped him from doing something? On more than one occasion he'd been joined by his cousin, Dalton, Serena's brother,
who had also been a favorite of Aunt Celeste. All three had
viewed Beauchamp House as a refuge from the responsibility and strictures of their parents' houses—somewhere they
could behave like typical young people rather than the children of peers, and in both Quill's and Dalton's cases, rather
than the heirs to two of the oldest titles in England.

He was staring out the window into the darkness when a
noise at the door to the chamber made him turn around.

"My lord," said Miss Wareham as she stepped diffidently
into the room. "I hope I'm not disturbing you."

Quill was silent for a moment as he let himself drink her
in. Gone was the dull traveling gown. She'd exchanged that
for a perfectly respectable white night rail and robe that covered far more of her than an evening gown would have. At
least that's what he told himself even as his heart skipped a

beat at the idea of seeing her in such attire. And her shiny russet locks, freed now from their pins, cascaded over her shoulders in a riot of red curls that glinted in the firelight.

He'd known she was attractive—had categorized her as such almost as soon as he saw her in the Fox and Pheasant earlier that day—but even that observation hadn't led him to imagine what she'd look like in such dishabille. Well, that wasn't quite true, he amended. His mind had conjured her in much fewer clothes than this before he'd realized just who she was. But any such imaginings had been snuffed out as soon as he'd known her destination. The reality of facing her here, now, in her virginal bedclothes, however, with her lovely red hair framing her face like a halo was far more tempting than his fantasy had been.

So, yes. She was disturbing him, but likely in a way she didn't even comprehend.

Suppressing the urge to tell her just that, he said instead, "I was too restless to sleep. It takes a bit for me to settle in to a new place. So there's no harm done."

Moving farther into the room, she set her candle down on one of the large library tables and wrapped her arms across her chest. "It's chilly in here," she said frowning. "I hadn't expected it this close to the sea. I thought it was supposed to be milder here."

Wordlessly, he looked away from her and moved over to kneel before the fireplace, stoking the embers back into a blaze. "It's still early spring," he said on standing, brushing his hands together more for something to do than to remove any soot. "The breeze off the channel keeps the air fairly cool until summer."

But she wasn't paying him any mind; instead she scanned the shelves that lined the walls behind him.

"Looking for something in particular?" he asked, noting

the impatience flash in her gaze before she replaced it with polite indifference. "Something to read before sleep, perhaps? Something to steal?"

Her brow furrowed at his question. He'd meant it to be playful, but her response told him that it had come off more sharply than he'd intended.

"I'd hoped you'd decided to stop treating me like an opportunist here to steal your inheritance from you," she said, pursing her lips. "I have it on very good authority that you've a great many houses as part of the Kerr estate—ones much grander and more impressive than this one. I do not understand why you cannot manage to accept the loss of this one. Unless, of course, like most boys you dislike sharing your toys."

She said this last part dismissively over her shoulder as she stepped past him and openly began to read through the shelves on the far wall.

Turning to watch her move from shelf to shelf, he sighed. "I suppose I deserve that after the way I behaved this afternoon. But let me assure you that it's no petty childhood jealousy that made me distrust you and your compatriots, Miss Wareham."

This must have surprised her, for she turned and looked at him through narrowed eyes. "No? Then what?"

He thrust a hand through his hair, fighting the urge to look away. "Have you never faced the removal of a childhood memory?" he asked, finally. "Never wished to hold onto the last bastion of somewhere that gave you comfort?"

Arrested, she tilted her head. "And that's what this place was for you?" she asked. "A bastion of comfort?"

He wasn't sure why, but Quill felt more exposed in that moment than he would have if he were stark naked. But he knew he owed her an explanation. Especially after the way he'd treated her earlier. "For me, for Serena, and for my cousin Dalton," he admitted. "Our own homes were not particularly . . ." He broke off as he tried to think of a word that wouldn't shock her. He could hardly tell her about the debauchery that had reigned in his own house before his father died. And the circumstances of Serena and Dalton's upbringing weren't his to reveal. "Let's just say that we found our visits to Beauchamp House to be a relief from our own homes."

Something flashed behind her eyes. Sympathy? Or something else? Quill wasn't sure, but he couldn't fail to note the way she squared her shoulders. As if she'd come to a decision.

Abandoning her scan of the bookshelves, she turned fully to face him, her hands clasped before her so tightly that her knuckles were white with it. "Lord Kerr," she began, her green eyes shadowed with trepidation. "There is something I must tell you."

Quill felt his stomach drop, and a pang of disappointment ran through him. Now she'd admit that she and the others actually *had* found some way to trick Aunt Celeste into leaving them Beauchamp House. The whole business of the competition had sounded like a farce, and though he'd known his aunt to possess a playful streak, he'd never guessed it would reveal itself in such a way. Certainly he'd not supposed she would play fast and loose with the disposition of Beauchamp House, where she'd spent so many happy years.

"Then by all means," he drawled, allowing every bit of the world-weary ennui that cloaked him in town to settle over him. "Tell me all, Miss Wareham. I confess I am curious to hear how you all managed it, never having set foot in Beauchamp House before. It must have taken a great deal of coordination amongst the four of you."

But if he'd expected her to surrender completely, he was

to be disappointed. "What?" she asked, her nose wrinkled in puzzlement. "I thought we'd just put that behind us. And yet, here you are with accusations again. You are like a dog with a bone, Lord Kerr. Honestly!"

"If not that, then what is it you wish to tell me?" he demanded, exasperated. He'd never thought himself to be a particularly emotional man, but since he'd met this chit on the road he'd gone through more feelings than a year in London had elicited from him. He must be sickening for something. "You can hardly blame me for jumping to conclusions when we've just been speaking about my earlier suspicions."

"I can blame you all too easily," she retorted with a scowl. "But I will not because I am tired of being at cross purposes with you. And I do not believe your aunt would like it."

Indicating with a wave of his hand that she should go on, Quill waited.

"I found a letter from your aunt waiting for me in my bedchamber," she said, her fine features marred by worry. "I greatly fear that Lady Celeste was murdered."

"What the devil do you mean 'murdered'?" Quill demanded, shocked despite his foreboding at the bespectacled beauty's pronouncement. "What did this letter say?"

From the pocket of her robe, Miss Wareham produced the letter. Opening it, Quill recognized his aunt's hand at once and began to read.

When she was finished, Quill found himself shaking his head in bemusement. "I must confess, when I suspected someone of doing away with Aunt Celeste, I assumed it was one of you four heiresses," he admitted with a frown. "It never occurred to me that someone would kill her for any other reason than an inheritance. She simply wasn't the sort of person who could inspire the sort of enmity that would provoke someone to murder."

"I greatly fear that your aunt suspected otherwise," Ivy said with sympathy in her eyes. "I know it is difficult for us to see our loved ones as others see them, but was there anyone in the village or in her circle of acquaintances who might have resented her for some reason? Or even someone in the household?"

"I've been away for long enough that I may not know all of the staff she's hired in my absence. So it is possibly one of them. Though I can't imagine it. Aunt Celeste was brusque at times," he said with a sad smile, "but only with those who attempted to suggest that because she was a female she couldn't be taken seriously as a scholar. When I was a boy I recall she had a particularly scathing correspondence with the president of one of the Royal Societies about his refusal to publish the findings of one of her bluestocking friends. It was quite a scandal—well, with my mother, at any rate. She was never very supportive of Aunt's intellectual pursuits. But that was decades ago. And I cannot imagine that fellow held a grudge for that long."

"No," Ivy agreed. "That doesn't sound like something that would prompt her murder now. I must confess that I cannot imagine why someone would kill her. Though my only understanding of her is as the generous benefactor who chose me amongst dozens of classics scholars as one of her heirs. And from what you and your cousin Lady Serena have told me, she was much admired. It seems mad to think of the lady you've both described as being the victim of something so vicious."

"That's a good point," Quill admitted. "At this juncture we don't even know if she was murdered or not. After all, from what the local physician said, she died of natural causes. She was rather young, I admit, but it does happen. I wasn't here at the time, of course, and neither was Serena, so we don't know what the days were like leading up to her death, but surely if there was something untoward, the servants would have reported it."

"Perhaps they didn't know what was going on," Ivy said thoughtfully. "I believe there are any number of poisons that can act quickly and without giving away their presence in the body."

For what felt like the hundredth time, Quill castigated himself for not rushing to Beauchamp House as soon as he'd learned of Celeste's death. It had felt unnecessary, since she was the only person he'd cared about there, and her body was to be brought to Beauchamp family cemetery at Maitland Hall, the seat of the Duke of Maitland. His own mother, Celeste's sister and another daughter of the fourth duke, had been devastated at the loss of her sister—despite their differences—and had insisted upon burying her beside their parents. Now Quill realized that the haste with which it had all been taken care of had made it virtually impossible to suspect anything untoward in his aunt's manner of death. Certainly neither he nor his mother had suspected murder.

"It's too late to know now," he said with a shake of his head. "Though I could question the local physician, and even Mrs. Bacon, who was here at the time."

"What of her maid?" Ivy asked. "I know many lady's maids know their mistresses' lives even better than *they* do sometimes."

"I have no idea," Quill admitted. "I'll ask Mrs. Bacon when I see her in the morning."

The room was silent for a moment as they considered what their first move should be in investigating Lady Celeste's death.

Finally, Ivy cleared her throat. "I do not like to remind

you, my lord," she said with a troubled glance. "But your aunt asked that we keep our investigation a secret from anyone else."

"Of course we must," Quill said nodding. "We don't wish to alert the killer to the fact that we've figured out it wasn't just natural causes. And besides, that it would put you in danger, which is why you must let me see to all of it. Really it's the most sensible way to handle things, you must agree."

But he was disappointed to see Miss Wareham roll her lovely green eyes. "I most certainly do not agree. I will keep things quiet, of course, but I must insist upon being part of the investigation. Your aunt entrusted this information to me, after all. Not you. If she wished for you to conduct this investigation alone, then she'd have left the letter for you."

He disliked admitting it, but she was right about that. Aunt Celeste and her silly bluestocking tendencies. Didn't she realize the danger she was placing Miss Wareham in by telling her about this? But he supposed his aunt had known what she wanted, and for all that he disliked the idea of Miss Wareham in danger, he had little doubt that she was every bit as courageous as a man would be in her place. Perhaps more.

"Fine," he said with a shake of his head. "We will work together. But you will let me question Mrs. Bacon and the physician initially. It will look more natural for me to be the one with lingering questions about her death. And I promise I'll share anything I learn with you."

She looked as if she weren't quite convinced of his sincerity, but finally Miss Wareham nodded. And with one last wistful glance at the bookshelves, she crossed the room to the door. "I'll just go back up then. I bid you good night, Lord Kerr."

Before she could open the door, however, he spoke up. "I think if we're to work together, Miss Wareham, that we'd better call ourselves by our given names. I don't think my aunt would have any objections, given her feelings about equality between the sexes."

Turning back, her hand on the doorknob, Miss Wareham gave a short nod. "All right then, my lord."

"Quill," he reminded her with a smile. "Call me, Quill."

"Very well, Quill," she said, a little breathlessly.

"Good night, Aphrodite," he said softly, liking the feel of the word on his lips, like some sort of incantation. Her green eyes widened behind her spectacles at hearing him speak her actual name. But she didn't correct him. And if he wasn't mistaken, there was a blush rising in her cheek. Perhaps there was more of the pretty scholar's namesake in her than she'd previously let on.

But then she seemed to come back to herself, straightening her spine and saying firmly, "Good night, Quill." With that, she stepped out, shutting the door behind herself with an audible click.

He stared at the door for a moment before what she'd told him returned to the forefront of his mind.

Someone had murdered Aunt Celeste.

He thought back to the last time he'd seen her, just a few months ago. How she'd teased him about his decision to put off marrying for a few years yet to, as she put it, gather his rosebuds. She'd cautioned him not to wait too long. Could that have been because she saw her own life was almost at an end?

She had confessed to feeling a bit under the weather but blamed it on the French cuisine his mother insisted upon in Castle Kerr. Had it been something more? Had someone been poisoning her beneath his roof? It was not to be borne.

If someone had deliberately put an end to Lady Celeste Beauchamp's life, then he was damned if he'd allow the miscreant to run tame as if nothing had happened.

And something else occurred to him, now. If the motive for Celeste's murder had been something related to Beauchamp House, then the ladies who stood to inherit the manor were in danger too.

He trusted Serena, his valet York, and those servants who'd been at Beauchamp House since his boyhood, but that was the extent of it. If he was going to learn more about his aunt's poisoning, he'd need to have someone here he could trust. Someone who had loved Celeste as much as he did.

Searching the desk for writing materials, he quickly scratched out a message. Finding some sealing wax in the drawer, he melted it and quickly pressed his signet ring into the crimson liquid.

When he reached his bedchamber, he found York waiting for him. "I'd like this to go to London first thing tomorrow," he told the man he trusted with his life. "If you cannot find someone to go, then I'd like you to go yourself."

The other man's surprise showed in his raised brows, but that was the only sign he gave of recognizing his master's agitation. "Very good, my lord." After pocketing the missive, he went back to brushing out Quill's greatcoat.

Feeling somewhat more sanguine about his task, Quill readied himself for sleep that did not come.

Chapter 6

Despite her difficulty sleeping, Ivy awoke at her usual early hour the next morning and was pleased to find that Lady Daphne and Miss Gemma Hastings were seated at the breakfast table when she arrived.

"How pleasant to find that I am not the only early riser amongst our little band," she said as she returned from the sideboard with a plate of eggs and toast and took a seat next to Lady Daphne. "I presume, Miss Gemma, that your sister does not share this proclivity?"

Biting into a piece of toast, Gemma shook her head. "No," she said with a frown. "Sophia tends to stay up quite late and as a result ends up sleeping late too. It made for many a schoolroom battle when we were younger, I can assure you. She could never understand why she should keep regular hours when she felt more alert in the evenings. She was always falling asleep during our lessons."

"It can hardly be considered an aberration," said Lady Daphne returning her teacup to its saucer, "when so much of society spends the season keeping those kind of hours. It is really only the lower classes who value regulated schedules such as you describe, Gemma, and that's mostly because they tend to work in factories which require it. Is not your father an industrialist? You are surely aware of this as his daughter. I'd think anyone who makes their fortune in such a manner would be."

Ivy had thought perhaps she'd imagined the mathematician's excessive good looks the night before, but the bright light of day only proved Lady Daphne Forsyth to be more beautiful than Ivy had first thought. Taller than the other ladies, her figure was not so buxom as to be vulgar but not so svelte to be thought unfeminine. And her golden hair, arranged in fashionable ringlets that perfectly framed her face, was like something an actual Greek goddess would possess—which made Ivy feel rather inadequate to her given name.

The girl's lack of tact, however, she had not imagined, and after posing her question to Miss Gemma Hastings, Lady Daphne simply sipped her tea, as if she hadn't just called the Hastings family common. Or at the very least, called attention to their position in a class lower than her own family hailed from.

Given that her own family was often made aware of its fall from the exalted heights of society by ladies of a similar rank to Lady Daphne, who sought to depress any pretensions Ivy and her sisters might have to raise themselves through marriage, Miss Hastings was maybe more sensitive to such pointed comments. And lord knew she'd been insulted in far subtler ways than Daphne had just done. Even so, Ivy was unable to stop herself from coming to Gemma's defense.

"If you are suggesting, Lady Daphne, that Gemma is vulgar for valuing the merits of maintaining a regulated sleep schedule," she said tightly, "then you must surely call me vulgar too, for I am also someone who values waking before the morning has passed."

At Ivy's annoyed tone, Lady Daphne frowned in puzzlement. "I didn't call Gemma vulgar," she said with real confusion. "I merely pointed out that people of her social standing tend to value such sleeping regularity. I fear I am an aberration to my own class, for I also would rather not sleep the day away. But then, I can get by on only a few hours of sleep without much trouble. Sophia, it would seem, is far more suited to the life of an aristocrat despite her being born the daughter of an industrialist."

Gemma placed a hand over Ivy's but said to Daphne, "I understand what you meant, my dear. I fear Ivy hasn't got used to your plain speaking yet. It will take her a bit, as you well know." Turning to Ivy, she continued, "She means no insult, I can assure you. And Sophia, the wretch will likely be quite pleased to know she is suited to the life of an aristocrat. God knows Papa has told her that often enough."

"I seem to lack the ability to make my words fit into the sort of polite chatter that is needed to converse without insulting my listeners, Ivy," said Daphne with an apologetic smile. "I hope you won't hold my clumsy speech against me. By all accounts you are considered to be a brilliant linguist and I should hate to think we will live together in Beauchamp House for the coming year and you will hold me in dislike all the while. I truly did not mean offense."

Despite herself, Ivy was touched by the apology, which seemed heartfelt at least. "Do you truly not recognize it when your own words could be construed as insulting?" she asked, curious about the other girl's deficiency.

Daphne's beautiful features twisted in unhappiness. She nodded. "I never mean it, but I am always saying the wrong thing to someone. I tend to avoid polite company because of it. Which is quite acceptable to me, since I would rather spend my time working on calculations and constructing proofs. It can be lonely at times, but so few people are able to understand my work that it is not all that interesting for me to converse with them anyway."

Ivy certainly wouldn't be able to say the first thing of sense about mathematics. What a lonely existence Daphne must have. And yet, she didn't seem particularly unhappy. Indeed, she was sanguine about her situation. Ivy was sure of it.

"I wonder," Daphne continued, "why Lady Celeste included me in this group at all, given how different my own talents are from yours. If any of us is the odd woman out, it is I. Though for that matter, why did she choose any of us?"

At the mention of their benefactor, Ivy recalled to mind her own task set forth by that lady. "Did any of you know much about Lady Celeste before you received word of your inheritance?" she asked. "I know that I had never met her before, but it seemed as if she knew quite a bit about me, and my studies."

Sophia's appearance in the doorway of the breakfast room delayed their discussion for a moment while they waited for her to fill a plate and join them at the table.

"We didn't move in the same circles," Gemma said with a wry smile given Daphne's earlier statement about the Hastings social placement. "But I was aware of the brief pieces she contributed to a small journal a few of her bluestocking friends published about her findings amongst the fossils of the South Downs. We shared a friend in common. But we never met. And I certainly didn't expect to be invited to remain in her home for a year so that I could excavate the cliffs myself."

"And she was quite well known amongst the fellows of the Royal Society," said Sophia with a shrug. "Though I never met her either. Not even when my painting was shown. She apparently didn't make the journey to town very often. Especially not this last year."

Ivy frowned. "What was different about this past year?"

she asked. Had word of Lady Celeste's poison-induced illness made its way to London? And if so, who had spread the word of it?

"The first night we were here, Mrs. Bacon told us that Lady Celeste was ill for much of this past year," Daphne said. "The local physician was never able to learn what the cause was, but it seemed to come and go. And the unpredictability of it made her reluctant to travel given that she never knew when an attack would overtake her. I should have thought such an illness would prompt her to seek out a Harley Street specialist, but she allowed sentiment to keep her loyal to her local physician. Which is quite maddening when one considers that her foolishness may have caused her untimely death."

Biting her tongue, Ivy reminded herself that Daphne was not being purposefully insulting about Lady Celeste. And her frustration mirrored Ivy's own. Especially since determining the cause of her demise was something she—a classics scholar for heaven's sake—had been entrusted with. What on earth did she know about investigating crime? She might as well have been asked to solve one of Daphne's mathematical equations.

"So, the servants were aware of Lady Celeste's condition?" Ivy asked, stifling her self-doubt for the time being.

"Certainly," Gemma said with a nod. "And when you consider it, they often know far more about our lives than we know about one another. I know our maids have been privy to more of our scrapes and misdeeds than our parents have been."

"Which is all for the best," Sophia said with a grin. "Else we'd neither of us been allowed to travel to the south coast at all. Mama and Papa are sadly rigid about their ideas regarding feminine behavior. Much more so than the upper ten thousand if Daphne is to be believed."

Having only one maid who served all five of the Wareham sisters, Ivy was perhaps not as familiar as the other ladies were about life with personal servants. But even in their small household, with just a handful of servants, there were certain things about the Warehams that their maids knew better than those with whom the family socialized.

"Why are you so curious about Lady Celeste's illness?" Daphne asked. "It is unlikely to have been something that would linger in the household, as by all accounts she was the only person in Beauchamp House to suffer from it."

Mindful of her agreement with Lord Kerr to keep their investigation of Lady Celeste's murder to themselves, Ivy shrugged. "I was merely curious. Never having met the lady, I was foolishly wondering if there may have been some way of preventing her death. Which is silly now that I consider it. Especially since there is nothing to be done about it now."

"But hardly unusual," said Sophia gently. "When someone you love dies unexpectedly I think there is always a tendency amongst the mourners to wish it hadn't happened. And we, all of us, owe so much to Lady Celeste. I know neither Gemma nor I would have been able to devote an entire year to our passions without our benefactor's generosity. And I dare say it's the same for both of you."

Ivy nodded in agreement, but Daphne shook her head. "My father allows me to do as I please so long as it doesn't bring ridicule on the family."

Sophia bit her lip, stifling laughter. "Most of us, then," she amended with a wink at Ivy. "And even Daphne would wish to be able to thank Lady Celeste."

Before Daphne could object—and her mouth opened as if she was going to—Ivy broke in. "Of course she would. No matter how pointless it is to wish something that happened in the past hadn't occurred. Isn't that right, Daphne?"

"I suppose so," said Daphne with a frown. "But really it is not realistic to dream of the fantastical. It will only lead to disappointment. It is far more sensible to acknowledge a bad thing has happened and then to move on."

Smiling ruefully, Ivy decided a change of subject was in order. "Have any of you seen Lord Kerr this morning?" Knowing that the inquiry would lead to speculation from the others, she added, "One of his bags was brought to my room by mistake so I wished to let him know."

"I feel sure you could have your maid take it to his valet," Sophia said raising her brows.

"If you wish to engage in an affair with Lord Kerr," said Daphne baldly, "then you would do far better to summon him to your bedchamber to retrieve the bag."

Sophia and Gemma covered their startled laughter with coughs. Ivy felt her face turn red with mortification. "I most certainly do not wish any such thing, Daphne. I truly only wished to return his bag, I can assure you." Though the notion of what an affair with Lord Kerr—Quill, as he'd asked her to call him—would entail gave her a moment's pause as she considered it. Even so, she would hardly admit to it here in the breakfast room.

"I believe I saw him headed toward the servants' quarters on my way here," Sophia said once she'd managed to stifle her laughter. "Perhaps he was in search of his bag."

But Ivy knew precisely what his lordship was in search of and it wasn't his fictitious missing bag. He was beginning the investigation into Lady Celeste's murder without her, curse him, which was not the plan that they'd agreed to. She might have known that all his promises to work together with her to find his aunt's killer had been mere pretense. He was distrustful of her from the start so it should come as no surprise that he didn't trust her enough to include her in the questioning of the servants. No matter that his aunt had asked *her*—not her high-handed nephew to find out who killed her.

Rising, she threw down her napkin. "I shall simply have to seek him out downstairs, then. Pray excuse me."

Chapter 7

"You still make the best scones in the county, Mrs. B," Quill said, fighting the urge to pat his stomach after consuming three of the housekeeper's famous pastries. It was unusual for a housekeeper to undertake such a task, of course, and many cooks would not condone an interloper in their kitchen. But since Mrs. Bacon only made one thing—scones—the cook at Beauchamp House, a no-nonsense woman named Mrs. Mason, overlooked the irregularity when the chatelaine came in search of flour and butter.

When he was a boy, Quill had spent many a happy hour at the broad kitchen table where the servants took their meals. There was something about the easy manners of the servants—a family, though none of them were related—that offered him a welcome reprieve from the stifling formality of his own home. Of course, Beauchamp House itself had been less formal too, but he'd never have managed a trip to the kitchens in Kerr Castle without receiving a swift reprimand. Here he knew that there would be no repercussions, no matter how his aunt might chide him when she found him wiping crumbs from his mouth.

"You're the only one who ever said so, my lord," said the

housekeeper with a fond smile. "You and his grace, the Duke of Maitland, that is. Though it wasn't a great mystery since the pair of you could eat a kitchen's worth of food in your day."

"In my day!" Quill raised a hand to his chest. "You're not saying I'm an old man, now, are you? I confess I'm pained to hear you say so."

"But you are old, cousin," piped up Jeremy from the chair beside Quill's where he was doing his best to consume his third scone. "Least, to me you are. Though Mama says I shouldn't call old people old."

"That's because when one is old, young Jem," said Quill wryly, "one doesn't like to be reminded of it. Certainly not by young rapscallions who declare they're going to break one's scone-eating record."

"Uncle Dalton says records are made to be broken," said the boy, chewing unrepentantly.

The marquess would have responded, but Mrs. Bacon's curtsy toward the doorway made him turn.

Her expressive green eyes narrow with suspicion behind her spectacles, Miss Wareham—or Ivy, he corrected himself, though it was a devilishly prosaic name for such a fiery creature—stepped into the kitchen warily. "I do apologize for intruding Mrs. Bacon," she began, "but I was told I could find his lordship down here."

Having stood as soon as he saw her, Quill nudged Jeremy, who had missed the lady's entrance so wrapped up in his scone was he. "Mind your manners, Jem."

The look of chagrin on the child's face would have been comical if Quill weren't sure the panic had been seeded in some sharp word from Jeremy's late father.

"It's all right," he told the boy in a low voice. "You stood as soon as you knew." He placed a comforting hand on Jeremy's shoulder, and they both bowed to Miss Wareham.

"I didn't realize you were not alone, my lord," she said

looking somewhat deflated. "I had heard you were in the servants' hall and . . ."

And she'd suspected him of questioning them without her, he guessed. But the opportunity that presented itself when he'd found Jem lingering in the kitchen waiting for Mrs. Bacon's scones to come out of the oven had been too much to resist. The presence of Ivy, a newcomer, would likely inhibit the older woman from speaking frankly.

Even so, he wasn't about to help her reprimand him. One had to take advantage of opportunity when it came to call.

"And, Miss Wareham?" he asked, brows raised.

"And," she said with a speaking look, "I thought perhaps you were searching for your missing bag. The one that inadvertently was left in my chamber. I suppose when the bags were brought in yesterday one of yours got mixed in with mine."

Her eyes told him not to correct her, and it was rather good as reasons for seeking him out went. Though a more correct lady might have had her lady's maid perform such a task by having her converse with his valet. But something about the simplicity of her gowns and the self-sufficiency she evinced made him suspect that Miss Wareham did not enjoy the services of an abigail. At the very least not one all to herself. "Ah, yes," he said with a nod. "I am glad you spoke up. I noticed its absence last evening, but didn't wish to disturb you by sending my valet for it."

Looking ill at ease, Ivy bit her lip, causing a host of less-than-polite thoughts to flood his imagination.

"Would you like a scone, Miss Wareham?" said Jeremy, very effectively puncturing Quill's wanton imagination. "There's some left ain't there, Mrs. B?"

"I'll just get you a plate, miss," said the housekeeper bustling around as she set a place at the table for the interloper—as if she entertained parties in the kitchens every day.

"Oh, I . . ." Ivy began, but when Jem stepped forward and took her hand in his, she gave one helpless look at Quill before giving in to the child's tug and following him. "I suppose I could have one. Though I've just had breakfast."

"You won't let a little thing like that keep you from the county's best scones, will you, Miss Wareham?" Quill asked with a grin. "I thought you were bolder than that."

"Do you have scones at your house, Miss Wareham?' Jeremy asked, watching avidly as Ivy spread butter followed by gooseberry jam on her scone. "They're my favorite."

Ivy smiled indulgently at the boy, revealing a dimple in her left cheek that Quill hadn't noticed the night before. "Indeed I do, Jeremy," she assured him. "Though I must confess that my absolute favorite confection from our cook is her lemon tart."

"You surprise me, Miss Wareham," said Quill, biting back a grin. "I shouldn't have thought you would have a taste for tarts." It was juvenile of him, but he found himself fighting a boyish impulse to tweak her pigtails, or in this case, to tease her with double entendres. "It is unusual, I think, for a lady to express such a desire."

Her lips twitched, and he had no doubt that she'd understood the jest. "There's a great deal you don't know about me, my lord," she said guilelessly. "Indeed, I must confess myself surprised that you prefer scones to tarts yourself. I was given to understand that men of your social station possessed an insatiable appetite for them. At least, that is what I hear from the gossip." It was clear from her expression that she didn't approve of it, either.

"Well, we don't *all* enjoy tarts," he said feeling as if he needed to defend himself against her censure. "I will grant that a great many titled men seek them out. But that doesn't mean that we all do. Some men, myself amongst them, are more selective about the . . . desserts we choose."

"I like all kinds of sweets," Jeremy offered helpfully. "Biscuits, cakes, tarts, Christmas pudding."

At the mention of pudding, Ivy covered her mouth with her hand, and her cheeks turned red with the suppression of laughter.

"I think perhaps we've bored Miss Wareham enough with talk about ways to quench her sweet tooth, Jem," Quill said, clapping the boy on the shoulder even as he exchanged a wry grin with Ivy. "If you're finished with your scone, why don't you go see if York will let you assist him with polishing my boots. I know you enjoy it."

"I like to see my face in them," Jeremy said with a grin, pushing his chair back from the table at once. Then, mindful of his manners, he gave Ivy a very correct bow. "Good day, Miss Wareham."

When the child was gone, Ivy gave Quill an exasperated look. "You should be ashamed of yourself speaking like that in front of a child." Though it was clear from the ghost of a smile that still lingered on her pink lips that her ire wasn't serious.

"You're the one who brought up tarts," he said defensively. "I was merely expressing my surprise. Surely there is nothing wrong with that."

"Certainly not," she conceded with a shake of her head. "If, that is, you do not then imply that I enjoy spending time with ladies of ill-repute. Which, I should inform you, is not far off from what that villain in the Fox and Pheasant said to me."

At the mention of the man he'd rescued her from at the inn, all humor fled from Quill. "What do you mean?" he asked, wishing he'd beaten the villain when he had the chance.

"Calm down," she said, tilting her head in puzzlement at his sudden change of mood. "I shouldn't have said anything. It's long gone anyway."

"What did he say, Ivy?" he pressed her, his eyes pinning her in place with their intensity.

"Just something about how I shouldn't be surprised at being treated roughly if I kept such low company," she said, looking down at where her hands lay clenched on the table. "He saw me speaking to one of the women lingering in the taproom. I suspected she might be . . . in need of help. Sometimes there are circumstances so desperate that a woman has only the choice between virtue and survival. And I thought perhaps I could assist . . ."

Quill cursed under his breath. "So he thought you were working together. That's why he put his hands on you."

Nodding, Ivy said angrily, "It infuriates me that the same men who use women like that will turn around and shame them as if the men themselves are innocent of any sin. I work sometimes at a home for unfortunates near my home in Oxford, and the stories I've heard there would make your hair curl."

"An inn in a town you've never been to is not the same as a home in Oxford, Ivy," Quill said with a shake of his head. "A home which I daresay your father has visited to ensure it's safety so that you can go there with no harm to your reputation."

But Ivy's pained expression told him it wasn't so easy as that. "He doesn't know you go there," he guessed.

"No," Ivy admitted with a shrug. "If I'd informed him he would forbid me from going at all. And those women need help. My help."

"Oh, they need to be able to translate ancient Greek?" he asked with a sarcasm he regretted almost immediately. His dislike of her putting herself in danger was just so consuming that he had trouble filtering his words.

"No," she said with a scowl. "I teach them how to read so that they might better themselves. Perhaps get a job as a clerk in a shop. Or maybe a copyist if they are able to learn to write their letters. I won't be ashamed of it, my lord, so you needn't try."

Sighing, Quill wiped a hand over his face. "I apologize. I was rude. I simply do not like to imagine you placing yourself in danger like that. Certainly if I'd known that was what precipitated the actions of that man at the inn I'd have dealt much more roughly with him."

"It wasn't perhaps a wish to keep me out of danger that led you to start questioning the servants without me this morning, was it?" Ivy asked, her eyes knowing. "Because I cannot help but think that's what made you come down here this morning. But thankfully for me, Jeremy interrupted. Else you'd have spoken to all of them before I even got a chance to come below stairs."

"I was only thinking of your safety," he said scowling. Lowering his voice, he leaned forward. "Someone *murdered* my aunt. If you think for one minute I'm going to allow you to place yourself in similar danger then you are sorely mistaken."

"I know she was murdered," Ivy hissed. "I was the one she chose to tell, and I hope you won't forget that. Your aunt obviously thought I was capable enough to handle the task, so kindly let me do it. Indeed, it was I who invited your assistance. Not the other way round. So I will thank you to remember that."

"My aunt was just as pigheaded as you are when it came to her thoughts on the role of ladies in society," Quill argued. "And I loved her. But that doesn't mean I always agreed with her."

"In this instance," she said haughtily, "you have no choice. I will investigate this matter. Whether you wish to assist me is entirely up to you."

And as if the matter was settled, she rose from the table, brushed off her hands, and turned to exit the kitchen.

Despite himself, Quill was impressed with her determination. But that didn't mean he would let her risk her own safety. He'd simply have to find a way to protect her. Against her will if necessary.

Wordlessly he stood and followed her.

Chapter 8

Ivy found Mrs. Bacon in the dining room, overseeing two of the housemaids as they polished the enormous cherry wood table. She felt Quill's presence behind her but chose not to remark upon it. If he were going to assist her in this matter, then he would have to follow her lead.

As soon as the trio became aware of their presence, they dropped into curtsies.

"Mrs. Bacon," Ivy began, "I wonder if I might have a word?"

But to her frustration, the older woman looked to Quill first, who nodded, before turning back to Ivy. "Of course, Miss Wareham," she said with a smile. "Would you like to step into my parlor?"

"If it's not too much trouble, Mrs. B," Quill responded, "that would be ideal. It's a matter for some discretion."

Biting back a sharp retort at having him intrude upon her task, Ivy nodded, and shook her head silently at Quill when he gestured for her to precede him.

Once inside the tiny room, which the housekeeper had made cozy with embroidery, a few bits of mismatched furniture, and a comfortable-looking chair, they declined to sit as Ivy thought it best if they got straight to the point.

"Can you tell us a bit about the servants employed by the house at the time of Lady Celeste's death?" she asked, trying to sound both authoritative and kind. No easy task, she realized.

At Mrs. Bacon's frown, Quill spoke up. "We only wish to know if there has been anyone who gave my aunt any trouble. Or who perhaps felt slighted upon her death. I know many of the servants here have been at Beauchamp House since I was a boy.

"What's this about, my lord?" Mrs. Bacon asked, her brow furrowed with worry. "Has someone been complaining because they didn't receive a bequest in her ladyship's will? For I won't stand for that sort of behavior from any of my staff. Just let me know who it is and I'll have him out on his ear at once."

Before Quill could jump in, Ivy hastened to reassure her. "No, no. It's nothing like that. I simply wondered, whether it might be worth finding out some of the history of the people who have kept Beauchamp so well these last years. And to find out who might have caused your mistress trouble. I should hate to think one of us might inadvertently invite them back, not knowing their history here."

"That might not be a bad idea, Miss Wareham," said Mrs. Bacon approvingly. "It would be a shame if someone tried to ingratiate himself with you young ladies in such a way. But aside from her ladyship's maid, who left because there was no lady for her to serve anymore, and the steward, who retired to live with his daughter, we haven't lost anyone in the past several years. We tend to keep the same staff on for years at a time. Which is why it's such a shock to lose someone. Or for that matter to hire someone new."

"I should imagine so," Ivy said with a nod. "Well, I can assure you that the other ladies and I have no plans on dismissing or hiring anyone anytime soon."

Rather than appearing reassured by this pronouncement, Mrs. Bacon only looked uncomfortable, as if she felt Ivy was trying a bit too hard to win her over. "I . . . that is to say . . . very good, Miss."

Clearing his throat, Quill spoke up. "Mrs. B, I know it's perhaps a difficult subject, but might we talk for a moment about the particulars of my aunt's illness? I wasn't here for her, you know, and it pains me to think that she was suffering."

Ivy was relieved that Quill had decided to ask the question himself, for the housekeeper's entire manner softened as she took in his genuine grief. "I wish I could tell you it was quick and painless, my lord, but I'm afraid it was anything but. She suffered for several months before it finally took her. And indeed it was hard for all of us. I think it preyed upon Dr. Vance's mind the most, though. He was so helpless, you see. Everything he tried failed. Until one day my lady just slipped away. And there was naught any of us could do."

Quill, Ivy noticed, had to struggle to keep his composure. "Why didn't she tell me, Mrs. B?" he asked with a sigh. "Any of us? If we'd known she was ill, I know I would have been here at a moment's notice."

With a soft look, Mrs. B shook her head. "That's just what she didn't want, my lord. Your aunt was a proud lady. And she didn't wish for you to remember her like that. Ill, and looking nothing like her vibrant self. I did ask more than once if she'd like me to contact her family—for I knew that you, and Lady Serena, and his grace would wish to come— but she would never agree. Said you all had your own lives and that besides, she wanted you to remember her as she was before the illness."

Wishing she could touch him, Ivy had to content herself

with standing at his side, hoping her presence would offer some kind of comfort.

"I suppose you're right, Mrs. B," he said with a shake of his head. "I just can't help but think of what might have been."

"You and I both, my lord," said the housekeeper. "And, as I said, Dr. Vance was most troubled of all."

"You never said what her illness was," Ivy said tentatively, not wishing to impose upon Quill's grief, but also wishing to know if Dr. Vance had any suspicions.

"That's because none of us knew, Miss Wareham," said Mrs. Bacon. "Dr. Vance could never discover exactly what it was that ailed her. He thought at first it might have been something she'd eaten. But by the end, he was convinced it must have been a wasting disease of some kind. But he never said what."

"Is his office still in town, Mrs. B?" Quill asked, exchanging a look with Ivy. "On the same street as the blacksmith's shop?

"Aye," the housekeeper nodded. "And I know he'd be happy to see you, my lord. If only to relay his sympathies in person. I've known him for many a year now and I don't mind telling you that he took your aunt's death quite hard."

"Thank you so much for your assistance, Mrs. Bacon," Ivy said, hoping the conversation might have thawed relations between them. But she had no such luck.

"I'm happy to help, Miss Wareham," Mrs. Bacon said stiffly. Then turning to Quill, she offered a broad smile. "If there's anything you need at all, my lord, I hope you won't hesitate to ask."

"Of course I won't, Mrs. B," said Quill, breaching their formality to buss the older woman on the cheek. Which made her blush like a giddy schoolgirl, Ivy noted. Were there no lengths to which this man would not stoop to sway people to his side?

Allowing him to guide her from the room and up the servants' stairs, she would have spoken as soon as they reached the main floor but he shook his head and indicated she should wait. Only once they were safely in the little study Lady Celeste had used for handling household business did he give her a nod that indicated she could speak.

"What on earth did I do to make that woman detest me so?" Ivy demanded with a huff as she stalked over to the fireplace. "You would think I'd burst in demanding she hand over her most prize possessions at gunpoint!"

Quill, easy as ever, strolled over and bent to stoke the fire, standing far too close for Ivy's comfort. When he did not respond immediately, she glared at him. "Well?"

Straightening, he shrugged. "I've known Mrs. Bacon and Greaves and many of the other servants since I was in short coats. You cannot expect to be in Beauchamp House for one day and have them treat you like a treasured friend."

"I did not expect that," Ivy insisted, though a small voice in her head reminded her that perhaps she had. "At least," she amended, "I didn't expect her to simply tell me everything. But why did she look on me with such suspicion? I wasn't rude. Or demanding."

"She lost her employer, whom she has served for almost thirty years just a few months ago," he reminded her quietly, not mentioning that he too had lost his aunt. "And now she has to accustom herself to not one, but five new mistresses including my cousin and the four of you bluestockings. Can you blame her for being a bit stiff with you?"

When he put it like that, Ivy was forced to agree that perhaps she'd not been altogether fair to Mrs. Bacon. "I suppose that is a great deal for one to take in," she conceded. Then, not wishing to dwell on the housekeeper's obvious dislike, she asked, "What did you think about the physician? Might it be worth a visit to the village to see what he has to say?"

His jaw tight, Quill nodded. "If he knew my aunt was being poisoned and did nothing to find the culprit, I warn you now that I will not be answerable for my actions."

Ivy fought the urge to lay a consoling hand on him. What was it about this man that brought out her protective instincts? It wasn't as if he was a weakling who needed it. And he certainly wouldn't thank her for it. His posture projected strength where any other man would seem vulnerable. Was it just a product of his position as a peer of the realm with the weight of generations bolstering him? Or was it something more personal? Like his upbringing? Cursing her own dangerous curiosity, she kept her hands to herself.

"Then perhaps you had better let me pay a call on the good doctor," she said. "That way you won't be tempted to do something rash."

"Like hell," Quill snapped, then recalling to whom he spoke perhaps, he sighed. "My apologies, Miss Wareham. I seem to have forgotten my manners."

But Ivy, who had grown up in a household where young men in need of tutoring ran tame, was hardly offended. "It's nothing I've not heard before," she assured him. "Or said myself from time to time. Though I hope you won't tell my mother. She has corrected me for my unruly tongue more than once."

If she'd expected him to be surprised by her confession, she was disappointed. Instead he gave a quick grin. "Why am I not surprised?" he asked with a laugh.

The diversion lightened the mood somewhat and it was with a bit less ferocity that Quill said, "Why don't we both go to the village to see the doctor. That way you can keep me from doing anything rash."

"And what purpose will *you* serve?" she asked with a raised brow, unable to keep from baiting him.

"I'll keep you from doing anything your mother would find improper," he said, extending his arm to her.

"I look forward to seeing you try," Ivy responded taking his arm. "I can swear in several languages."

"But that's no impediment to me, Miss Wareham," he said as he shut the library door behind them. "So can I."

Chapter 9

To Ivy's frustration and disappointment, however, Lady Serena had scheduled a tour of Beauchamp House and the surrounding grounds that morning.

"Now that you're all finally here," she explained to Ivy and Lord Kerr as they stood near the door to the servants' quarters, "I can show you just what it is that Lady Celeste built here. Beauchamp House is more than just its magnificent library and scholarly collection. It's also a working farm, and boasts a pottery staffed solely by women."

Despite her vexation at not being able to question the doctor, Ivy's interest was piqued by Serena's mention of the pottery. "I had hoped to go into the village today—" she began.

"But surely that can wait, Miss Wareham?" asked the marquess with a speaking look. "I know I said I'd accompany you, but perhaps it would be better if we go another day."

Recalling how he'd attempted to question Mrs. Bacon without her, Ivy was skeptical. "You would be willing to wait, my lord? And will promise not to travel into the village on your own without me?"

Lady Serena frowned, looking from Ivy to her cousin and back again. "Clearly I've missed something here."

Holding Lord Kerr's gaze, Ivy raised a brow in question.

After a moment, he let out a breath. "Fine, Miss Wareham. I will promise not to go into the village without you. Though I must warn you that our errand is a time-sensitive one."

"What errand?" Serena asked, her brows snapping together in suspicion.

"Nothing mysterious, cousin," Lord Kerr said holding up his hands to protest his innocence. "I merely offered to escort Miss Wareham into the village to purchase some ink."

"Ink?"

Before his lordship could elaborate, Ivy interjected. "I prefer to use a very particular brand of ink for my translation work. And I realized upon unpacking that I'd left my own behind. But it can wait."

The other woman looked skeptical, but didn't argue. "So you'll join the rest of us, then?"

After one last speaking look at Lord Kerr, Ivy nodded. "I would like to very much."

"Then take yourself off, Quill," said Lady Serena, slipping an arm through Ivy's. "This outing is for ladies only."

It was only after they were out of earshot of the marquess that Lady Serena continued. "I hope, Miss Wareham, that you will accept a word of advice."

Still unsettled by the hasty reversal of her plans for the day, it took Ivy a moment to realize she was expected to respond. "About what, Lady Serena?" Though she had some idea about whom it might pertain to.

They had just reached the double doors leading into the library, when the chaperone turned to face Ivy before she continued. "My cousin is a very handsome man, Miss Wareham, but he is a notorious flirt. He is an honorable man, but like all men, he doesn't always think before he acts. I should hate to see you come to harm because of it." She paused, and Ivy saw a shadow cross her face.

"Lady Serena?" Ivy asked, concerned. "What is it?"

But whatever it was had passed, and the chaperone shook her head a little. "Nothing, my dear. I am doubtlessly being overprotective. Just promise me you will not take Quill too much to heart."

Thinking back to the pull of attraction she'd felt between herself and the marquess, Ivy nevertheless waved away Lady Serena's warning. "I can assure you, my lady," she said firmly, "that I'm in no danger of succumbing to your cousin's charms. He may be handsome, but he's also stubborn and not just a little arrogant."

Serena narrowed her eyes, as if trying to discern the truth of Ivy's denial. Then, biting back whatever retort she'd been about to make, she opened the library door and pulled her charge into the chamber that would never stop setting Ivy's heart to beating faster.

If she was in danger of losing her head, it was over the first-class collection of manuscripts, books, and artifacts in this room, she thought as her eyes scanned the floor-to-ceiling shelves with something like wonder.

"Were you able to find Lord Kerr, Miss Wareham?" asked Sophia, looking up from where she stood perusing one of the cabinets where Ivy knew the art books were shelved.

Feeling Serena's gaze on her, Ivy tried to look nonchalant. "I did, thank you, Sophia." Stepping farther into the room, she crossed to glance out the window looking out over the gardens. "I wish you would call me Ivy. It will be a tiresome year if we all stand on ceremony with one another for the duration."

"I can see nothing objectionable in that," Serena said from where she'd moved to remove a thick, bound leather volume from one of the shelves. "And as I said before, you must call me Serena. I am serving as your chaperone of course, but we're of an age, I think. And I hope we can become friends."

Before any of them could reply, Lady Serena continued. "Now, are you all ready for a tour of the house and gardens? My aunt left strict instructions about what areas and features she most particularly wished for you all to see." She held up the volume in her hand to emphasize her words.

Daphne looked up from where she was seated at one of the large library tables with a stack of books before her. "Must I go too? I've only just started in on this fascinating account of the Goldbach conjecture . . ."

"And I'm immersed in this history of Dr. Harvey's dig at Stonehenge," Gemma added looking vexed. "Perhaps you should take only Sophia and Ivy for this first tour, Lady Serena. After all, we don't wish to disrupt the household with a large party traipsing here and there."

But Lady Serena would have none of it, much to Ivy's relief. Despite her wish to begin investigating the circumstances of Lady Celeste's death, she too wanted some time alone with the contents of the library and the idea of being off on a tour while the others had free reign in the magnificent room sent a pang of outright jealousy through her.

"Come along, Gemma and Daphne," Sophia said, reluctantly turning from the art books. "If Lady Celeste wished us to see these parts of Beauchamp House, then I daresay it was important to her. The least we can do for the poor woman's sake is to do as she wished. Without her we'd not be here at all."

"I hate it when you're sensible," Gemma groused, though she stood and tugged a still-reluctant Daphne from her chair.

"I suppose it will still be here when we return." Daphne gave one last longing look at her chosen tome.

Without any sort of preplanning, the four ladies stood in

a row before Lady Serena, who smiled approvingly. "Excellent. Now, you've seen the library, so let's go downstairs and start in the entrance hall."

As they made to follow her through the double doors, Sophia took Ivy's arm. "You don't suppose Lord Kerr will make an appearance do you? I should very much like to study those cheekbones a bit more. He'd make a very good Mars for my study of the war god and his lady."

"Why don't you just ask him to sit for you?" Ivy asked pettishly. Something about the other lady's interest in the marquess set her teeth on edge.

But Sophia shook her head, and slipped her arm through Ivy's companionably. "Men are the most wretched models I've found. They are impatient as can stare, and don't take orders very well at all. Much better to just get the details in the usual course of things and use my imagination for the rest."

The artist had a point, Ivy conceded. Lord Kerr was nothing if not headstrong.

"I have no idea what his plans were for the rest of the day," she said with diffidence.

Was it her imagination or was Sophia smirking at her?

Really, she thought, if she'd known her tenure at Beauchamp House would entail so much scrutiny from her fellow bluestockings, she would have remained home.

But as they reached the second-floor landing she saw the portrait of Lady Celeste and immediately felt a pang of guilt.

Not only had her benefactor chosen her to share Beauchamp House, she'd also, for some reason Ivy hadn't figured out yet, deemed her trustworthy enough to solve her murder.

If she had to endure some teasing from the other ladies, then so be it. She'd endured worse from her brothers at home.

And besides that, she was hardly some wilting violet who couldn't stand up for herself.

She was made of sterner stuff than that.

Aloud, she said, "Enough about the marquess. This is part of our inheritance, Sophia."

At Sophia's look of surprise, Ivy raised a speaking brow. "For bluestockings only."

Gemma and Daphne, who were just ahead of them, turned. "Bluestockings only," Daphne said with a nod. "I like it."

"As do I," said Gemma grinning.

"I believe we've got our motto, ladies," Sophia said with a laugh. "Beauchamp House, for Bluestockings Only."

And, however reluctantly we might accept them, Ivy added silently, *relations of Lady Celeste Beauchamp.*

Despite his instinct, which was to make his way to the village posthaste to meet with his aunt's physician, Quill curbed the impulse and decided to take Jem out to see his horses.

Starved for male attention, the boy was elated when his older cousin appeared at the nursery door and requested his company for a trip to the stables.

"Since you've not seen his lordship in a long while, Master Jeremy," his nanny, Mrs. Ellis said firmly, "I will allow it. But no more sneaking down to the kitchens without asking first."

Trying and failing to look contrite, the boy nodded vigorously but couldn't conceal the grin that overtook his face.

"She seems like a good sport," Quill said as they made their way down the back stairs to the door leading out to the stableyard. "Not at all like my old nanny, who'd have skinned me alive for a stunt like the one you pulled this morning."

Jeremy shrugged. "I suppose so. Mama thinks I don't know, but I heard her telling Mrs. Ellis not to be too hard on me. On account of Father."

The boy spat out the last word, as if it left a foul taste in his mouth.

Yet another sin to lay upon the grave of the late unlamented Lord Fanning, Quill thought grimly. "Is that so? Does it bother you?"

The boy pondered the question for a moment. "I don't know 'xactly. On the one hand I like not getting into much trouble."

"Who wouldn't?" Quill bit back a smile.

"But I don't like it that they treat me like a baby." He looked up at his cousin, a fierce look in his countenance. "I'm *not* a baby."

Knowing it would be exactly the wrong thing at this moment, Quill suppressed the urge to ruffle the boy's hair. Even after the difficulties he'd faced when Fanning had terrorized both the boy and his mother, Jeremy managed to maintain a sort of quiet dignity that the marquess couldn't help but be proud of.

"Certainly not."

They were crossing the side yard now, and the stables were just in sight.

"I know Mama thinks I need coddling because of what he did," Jeremy said, a note of frustration in his young voice. "But I don't. I can take care of myself. And her too."

He paused, and Quill waited for him to finish.

"I couldn't when he was alive, you know." His expression was that of someone many years older. "I was too little then. But I'm not now. I'll never let anyone hurt her again."

Placing a comforting hand on the child's shoulder, Quill said, "Of course you won't. You're a good man, Jem. I'm sure your Mama knows it."

"I let her down, Uncle Quill," the boy said with a sigh. "But I won't do it again."

Unable to let the boy continue in this vein, Quill knelt

before him. Looking into eyes that were so much like Serena's, he said firmly, "You have nothing to be sorry for. You were no match for a man like your father. And I know beyond a shadow of a doubt that your mother believes the same thing."

"But he hurt her, Uncle Quill," Jem pressed on. "And I couldn't stop—"

Hoping that Fanning was roasting in Hades, the marquess interrupted his small cousin. "Do you blame your Mama for not defending herself better? Do you believe that she should have been able to stop him?"

That gave the boy pause. His brow furrowed. "What? Of course not. She's just a lady and—"

"I'll stop you right there, boy," said Quill with a laugh. "Never let your Mama or any of Aunt Celeste's heiresses hear you call any of them 'just a lady' if you know what's good for you."

He stood, and they resumed their trek to the stables.

"But they *are* ladies," Jem said, puzzled.

"True enough," the marquess agreed, "but that doesn't mean that they're defenseless. You certainly wouldn't like it if they were to call you 'just a child' would you?"

"Of course not," Jem said heatedly, as if someone had called him that. Then, Quill could almost hear the realization come to him.

"Oh."

"Yes," Quill agreed. "Oh."

"So that's what Auntie Celeste meant about not treating ladies like children?"

"Something like that," Quill agreed. "So, let's have no more lamentations from you over your helplessness in the face of a man three times your size. You and your Mama did your best in a difficult situation. And there's an end on it."

Looking thoughtful, Jeremy nodded.

Then, as if the discussion had allowed him to cast off a heavy cloak of guilt, he brightened. "Do you think Graham in the stables will let me brush out your grays?"

Relieved that he'd managed the conversation with some degree of success, Quill clapped the boy on the shoulder. "I think that can certainly be arranged."

Chapter 10

"It's a shame we weren't able to visit the pottery today because of the rain," Ivy said that evening as the residents of Beauchamp House sat in the drawing room after dinner.

To her surprise, she meant the words. Though she'd been reluctant to pause her investigation into Lady Celeste's death with something as seemingly trivial as a tour of the house, the hours spent in the company of her fellow heiresses had proved to be both informative and entertaining. And Lady Serena had proved to be quite knowledgeable about all the considerations her aunt had put into the decoration and improvement of her estate.

"Unfortunately, Miss Wareham," said the marquess from where he stood with one shoulder against the sitting room mantle, "you'll find that this part of the country is prone to unexpected showers at this time of year."

"If we're reduced to discussing the weather," Sophia said with a shake of her auburn curls, "then I shall simply be forced to do something scandalous in order to alleviate my boredom. Pray, do not make me do it."

There was a hint of the absurd in her tone, but Ivy got the feeling that the artist would not be above making good on her threat.

"There is no need to resort to drastic measures, Miss Hastings," interjected the marquess with a staying hand. "I will change the subject immediately. I shouldn't like my cousin's first foray into the realm of chaperonage to be a failure, you know."

Serena gave him a speaking look. "I will thank you very much to mind your own business, Kerr. I am quite able to handle whatever attempts at scandal these ladies attempt to dish out." After a quelling look in Sophia's direction, she turned to Ivy. "Perhaps you can tell us a bit more about your translation work, Ivy."

Feeling all eyes turn on her, Ivy felt herself flush. "Oh, it's not very interesting to talk about," she demurred. "Just a process of reading the original, then trying to capture the essence of it using our own language."

But she wasn't to be let off so lightly.

"A great deal of Greek poetry is rather shocking, isn't it, Ivy?" Gemma asked, her blue eyes glinting with slyness. "At least, that's what one of the essays I read about the Elgin marbles said."

Before Ivy could confirm or deny the question, Daphne spoke up. "I was quite disappointed by the marbles when I was finally able to view them. I was expecting the male mem—"

"Daphne, dear," Serena interrupted, "it's not the done thing to discuss such things in mixed company, you know."

"Or any company," said Sophia in a low voice that only Ivy, seated beside her, could hear.

Unable to stop herself, Ivy looked up to see how the marquess had reacted to Daphne's slip up. To her surprise, he was looking right at her.

Their eyes met, and she felt a zing of awareness run through her before she quickly looked away.

But Serena's next words diverted her attention away from the marquess.

"Perhaps you can recite one of your translations for us, Ivy?" Seeing the entreaty in her chaperone's eyes, she gave an inward sigh.

She hated reciting poetry above all things.

Not because it was difficult. But because it had been a regular evening entertainment in her father's house for the children to recite. And her father had been nothing if not demanding when it came to the ability of his offspring to recall every cadence and emphasis of a verse.

When she was very young, Ivy had suffered from a slight stutter, and it would resurrect itself, it seemed, only at those times when she most needed to be able to speak with confidence and ease. Which, during her childhood, had been those evening recitations.

Still, she could see that Serena was desperate for some way to divert attention away from Daphne and her inappropriate chatter. And she'd long ago managed to rid herself of the impediment.

"I suppose I can recall a few of them," she said, inclining her head toward Lady Serena. "Perhaps a bit of Sappho's song to Aphrodite."

A hush fell over the room, and Ivy felt the attention of the others in the room like a tangible thing. The weight of it almost took her breath away, until she managed to shut everything out but the words, and began to speak.

"Splendour-throned Queen, immortal Aphrodite,
Daughter of Jove, Enchantress, I implore thee
Vex not my soul with agonies and anguish;
Slay me not, Goddess!"

And so she began to recite her own translation of the celebrated poet's only complete work—the rest had been discovered in mere fragments, their complete sentiments left to the ravages of time and the abyss of imagination—which she had laboriously worked on for nearly a year. She'd debated whether the first word was *poikilothron* or *poikilophron*—something that hadn't ever been settled amongst those who had transcribed the lyrics from the original Greek—finally deciding on the latter, which meant "many-colored throne" rather than "many-colored mind." After all, she'd reasoned, it was far more likely for a throne to be multicolored than a mind.

As she said the words, aware as she did so of her own role in bringing thoughts and ideas that had first been sparked in the ancient world, she felt a small shiver run through her. As if Sappho herself was bestowing some otherworldly approval from the ether.

When she'd finished, the room was once again silent, only this time it was a lull before the other occupants erupted in praise and applause.

"My dear, Ivy," said Sophia, hurrying over to give her a brief hug, "you must never try to speak of what you do as dull again. It's breathtaking to think that you were able to wrangle those beautiful sentiments out of the unintelligible squiggles that make up the Greek language."

"Sophia was never very fond of languages," said Gemma wryly as she kissed Ivy's cheek. "But she's right. I can actually read Greek but I sincerely doubt my own translation would be anything but workmanlike and prosaic at best. You've made the words spring to life."

"Shall I ring for some tea?" asked Daphne, standing awkwardly on the other side of the room. Clearly she had not been as moved as the Hastings sisters, Ivy thought wryly. At least she could always count on the mathematician to keep her from becoming too full of her own importance.

From where she stood beside Lord Kerr, Serena gave the blonde girl a look of exasperation. But rather than chide her, she simply said, "That would be lovely, Daphne. Thank you."

The spell broken, they drifted into different corners of the room, and Ivy soon found herself standing with the marquess near the fire.

"I hadn't thought about Greek poetry since I was at school," said Lord Kerr with a wry smile. "And then it was not for the beauty of the language."

Ivy felt her cheeks pinken. She knew quite well what this marquess and his schoolmates had found of interest in ancient poetry. There was quite a bit of it—much of which Ivy had read herself in the original—that could be called licentious.

"I understand that is how many young men become acquainted with the classics," she said primly.

He tilted his head. "But not young ladies?"

"Since the vast majority of young ladies are not taught either Greek or Latin," she said tartly, "then I would say, no. Not young ladies."

"But you were taught both, weren't you, Miss Wareham," he said with a grin. "So, perhaps you too spent some time with the *classics*." He said the last word with an emphasis that left her in no doubt of what he meant.

"My father was not very keen on it," she admitted, not meeting his gaze. "But I was able to convince him that it was impossible to gain a true understanding of the classics without having read everything Catullus has written. Even that which might be considered prurient."

She had, in point of fact, made her father's daily life miserable until he agreed to let her read Catullus. But they had agreed that neither of them would tell her mother about it—ever.

"How clever," the marquess said with an approving nod. "And unlike most schoolboys who claim to read Catullus merely to improve their fluency in Latin, you have bolstered your own case by actually becoming a Latin scholar."

"Yes." Ivy fought the urge to roll her eyes. "Years of study and hard work were simply a ruse to allow me to achieve my actual goal—reading the naughty verse of the most celebrated Roman poet of all time. Which, by the by, isn't even his greatest work."

"When you put it like that," Quill said with a shrug, "it sounds absurd. Which is likely why it isn't a scheme employed by more people. Far too much trouble."

Unable to stop herself, Ivy laughed. Then, thinking about what he'd said, she asked, "You weren't, by any chance, speaking of your own excuses for reading classics, were you? That explanation seemed far too well-rehearsed to have been invented on the spot."

For a fraction of a second—so quickly that Ivy wasn't even sure it had happened—the marquess's gaze rested on her mouth. Then he met her gaze with his own. "I was a schoolboy once, Miss Wareham," he said with a half smile. "Perhaps you can test my knowledge of Catullus some time."

It was said in an unexceptional tone. The same way that he might have suggested they go for a ride in the park, or take a turn about the room.

But his eyes told a different tale, and Ivy felt the blush that had rested in her cheeks for most of their conversation spread to her chest. And lower.

Before she could respond to his words, they were interrupted by the arrival of Lady Serena, who looked between them with suspicion. "Did I miss something?"

"Not at all," Lord Kerr said to his cousin with an easy smile. "We were just discussing various methods of teaching the classics to schoolboys."

Ivy could have kicked him.

At the mention of schoolboys, Lady Serena's eyes lit with interest. "Oh, indeed? I should very much like to hear your views on the matter, Ivy, since I am considering how best to settle Jeremy's education. Though he is a bit young yet."

"I've just remembered I need to speak to York about something," the marquess said before Ivy could respond. "I'm sure Miss Wareham will be able to steer you right, cousin. She is well versed in the matter."

Ivy stared at his retreating back for a moment. She wasn't quite sure what had just happened, but it had been unsettling.

"You don't mind, do you, Ivy?" Lady Serena asked, frowning a little. "I wouldn't wish to impose."

Seeing that the chaperone was, indeed, looking troubled, Ivy sought to reassure her. "Of course not, Lady Serena. Now, what do you wish to know?"

And the two ladies discussed how best to prepare Jeremy for the rigors of classical languages.

But a part of Ivy's mind was still thinking of that moment of heat in Lord Kerr's eyes.

Mindful of the danger in spending too much time in the company of a certain classics scholar, Quill spent the next several days immersing himself in estate matters. Aunt Celeste had left the day-to-day operations of the farm and the rest of the estate business in the hands of a very capable steward. But there was always hard work to be found if one was looking for it. And aware that any more suggestive conversations with Miss Wareham might lead him down a path he wasn't quite ready for, Quill took advantage of that fact.

Repairing fences and visiting tenants kept him busy. But not too busy to think about the circumstances that had brought him to Beauchamp House in the first place.

Now that he'd met and spent some time in the company of all four of the lady scholars his aunt had chosen to bestow her estate upon, he wasn't as angry about the situation as he'd been when he first set out for Beauchamp House.

All four ladies were, so far as he could tell, knowledge-able about their areas of study and, far from being the social outcasts or tight-lipped scolds he'd been afraid of, would not embarrass the Beauchamp name—excepting Lady Daphne, perhaps, but she was quite lovely, so she would probably not face too much censure in the *ton* for her plain speaking.

Lady Celeste's decision to leave her home to strangers still rankled, however. And he could not deny that the fact she'd asked Miss Wareham to find the person who killed her stung.

Then again, he'd known her his whole life yet failed to no-tice she was in trouble. It was no wonder she'd decided to ask a young woman she'd never even met for help instead of her self-absorbed family.

He might have kept on avoiding the ladies of the house un-der the guise of manual labor were it not for Miss Wareham, who found him one afternoon almost a week later, brushing out his grays in the stables.

"I would have thought a marquess might not wish to dirty his hands with work better suited to a stable lad," she said from the other side of the stall door. "Though your horses seem to think you do a good job."

"You might be surprised at the sort of work a marquess is required to do from time to time," Quill said without look-ing up. "I would not ask one of my servants to do something that I myself wouldn't be willing to do."

He felt her gaze on him, and wondered what she saw when she looked at him. A pampered aristocrat playing at being a servant for a day? Or perhaps she saw a man who had been too caught up in his own life to pay attention to his dying aunt? Either way, he had a feeling she wasn't impressed by him. Which was just as well, since there was no need for them to be friends. There might be some attraction there, but he had a feeling she'd value her independence too much to get entangled with any man. And of all the ladies he'd ever met, she was the least likely to be swayed by his title. It was intellect she valued, and though he wasn't a simpleton, nor was he the kind of man who spent his days with his nose buried in a book.

"Even emptying chamber pots?" she asked with gentle skepticism.

She had him there.

Unable to resist looking up, he did and saw that her rosy lips were curved in a smile.

"Perhaps not that," he amended, standing up straight and giving the horse one last pat before turning to exit the stall.

As he neared her, Miss Wareham watched his progress, stepping back as he reached the latched gate and allowing him to open it.

"You've been avoiding me," she said when he'd latched it back and turned to face her.

It wasn't a question, and he didn't condescend to her by pretending it was.

"Perhaps," he agreed, crossing his arms over his chest. "Though there has been plenty to keep me busy."

"Shall I take your behavior as a confirmation that you won't help me find out whether your aunt was actually murdered?" she asked, not sugarcoating the question.

Quill was grateful for her forthrightness. It would make his refusal to work with her that much easier to deliver.

"You may," he said with an air of finality he didn't feel. "My aunt may have chosen to confide her suspicions to you, but I have only known you for a week or so. That is hardly enough, in my book, to prove your trustworthiness. For all I know, you and the other three benefactors conspired to have my aunt killed as soon as you learned you stood to inherit her estate."

She looked as if he'd slapped her.

"You don't believe that, surely?" she asked, her eyes wide with shock.

Relenting a little, he shook his head. "I don't believe it, no. But it's possible. And until I know you well enough to judge with my head and not my . . ." He paused, realizing what he'd been about to say. "Until I know you better," he amended, "I can't trust you."

Miss Wareham looked nonplussed.

"Is there something about me that you don't understand?" he asked, growing impatient with her refusal to see reason.

"Yes," she said, standing up straighter and stepping closer. "I don't understand how a man who purports to have loved his aunt more than anyone in the world could possibly stand by and let her murderer go on about his merry way."

She took another step.

"I also don't understand how, if getting to know me enough to find me trustworthy is your goal," she continued, her eyes flashing, "you can spend almost an entire week avoiding me."

He opened his mouth to respond, but Miss Wareham poked him in the chest with her forefinger. "If you want to know what I think," she said with a toss of her head, "I think that you, Lord Kerr, are behaving like a spoiled little boy. Your aunt didn't leave her estate to you, and so you're punishing her by refusing to search for the person or persons who killed her."

"Now just a minute, Miss Wareham," he began, her words sticking like a barb in his chest, "I won't allow you to—"

"Oh, do not tell me what you will or will not allow," she said with disgust. "You've made it clear that you have no interest in finding your aunt's killer. So, I will simply have to do it myself. Which is hardly a surprise, since if you want anything done well, it's best to call a woman."

She turned and, before he'd judged the wisdom of such a move, he grasped her by the shoulder. "Stop."

Turning to face him, she glared. And to Quill's surprise, there were tears glistening in her eyes.

"What?" she demanded, holding herself back from him, their only contact, his hand which was now resting softly on her shoulder.

They were silent for a moment. He reached up, and with his thumb, stroked away the tear that had fallen onto her cheek.

"Why do you care so much?" he asked hoarsely. "You didn't even know her."

"Because she chose me," she said in a low voice. "She believed in me. In my abilities." She looked up and he realized she was utterly sincere.

"Perhaps you don't know what it's like to move in a world where your every decision is scrutinized, questioned, doubted," she continued. "Where even your father, who taught you himself, doesn't believe you're good enough to be a real scholar. Where the associations and societies who should welcome you, keep you out because you weren't born with a certain ridiculous appendage. But I do. And the one person who believed I could make a difference was murdered. Not only that, but she asked me to find out by whom.

"Yes, I care," she said, her voice stronger now, her eyes lit with determination. "Because I owe her a debt of gratitude. I had thought perhaps you did, too, but as with many things, I can see I was wrong."

She turned to go.

"You weren't wrong, damn it."

Once more, she turned back to him, her brow raised in question.

"I owe her, too," he admitted with a scowl. He thrust a hand into his hair, feeling more flustered than he could ever remember. "And I want to find out who killed her. But you have to understand, from the time I was a small boy, family loyalty has been drummed into me. And it's the way of the world. Family inherits from family. The fact that Aunt Celeste chose to leave her estate—where I and my cousins spent the best months of our childhood—to four women I'd never heard of before the reading of the will, well, it has been difficult to swallow."

At his admission, her gaze softened. "I'm not unsympathetic, my lord," she said, lifting her hand as if she'd touch him, then letting it fall. "I understand how difficult this must be. But don't let your disappointment about the inheritance keep you from finding out why your aunt died in the first place. As you say, you owed her a debt of gratitude as well. Don't make the mistake of failing the one person you should honor above all."

Suddenly exhausted, Quill let his shoulders slump a little. "Where do you want to start?"

The flash of triumph was gone from her eyes before he even realized he'd seen it.

"As we were going to before the rain set in," she said firmly, "I would like for us to pay a visit to your aunt's physician in the village, Dr. Vance. I have an actual letter home to post now, so it won't even be a prevarication when we give it as our reason for going."

"Anyone who underestimates you, Miss Wareham," he said with a shake of his head, "does so at their own peril."

Waving off the compliment, she said, "I would like to set off within the hour. Meet me in the entry hall after you've had a chance to clean up a bit."

Leaving him to stare after her in exasperation, she hurried off.

Chapter 11

"I would rather remain here organizing the collection of mathematics books," said Lady Daphne in response to Miss Wareham's invitation that the other ladies join them on their trip to the village. Quill and Ivy had decided that inviting the others to accompany them would go a long way toward alleviating any suspicions that they had any other purpose for visiting the village than posting her letter and purchasing ink. Once there, Ivy would recall that she needed headache powder and Quill would offer to introduce her to the local doctor.

"There are any number of valuable contributions to the subject, but it is impossible to find them when they are interspersed with inferior scholarship that would better be put to use as kindling." Not looking up from her position seated on the library floor where she was surrounded by uneven stacks of books, Daphne punctuated her remarks by tossing one rather thin volume in the direction of the fireplace.

Which was also where Sophia happened to be curled up in a chair before the fire, her sketchbook in hand. "Have a care, Lady Disdain," the artist said with a frown at the floor where the thrown book had landed. "Ducking from flying objects is not one my best skills while I'm drawing.

And I'll thank you to remain in the same general pose, otherwise your portrait will be a complete failure." Turning to Ivy, who stood at Lord Kerr's side, she added, "I'm trying to do a study of each of you, to commemorate our first week in Beauchamp House. Perhaps for use later as a series on the Muses. But perhaps not. I don't know that I will be able to keep Daphne still for long."

The marquess stepped forward to peer down at the sketch. "That's quite good, Miss Hastings," he said before he could stop himself. Of course it's good, he thought. His aunt would hardly have invited Miss Hastings here if she were a mere dabbler.

"My thanks, Lord Kerr," Sophia said, sharing an unreadable glance with Ivy. "For the compliment and the invitation. But I believe I'll stay here and capture Daphne while she is somewhat still. She's given me to understand that once she begins concentrating on the contents of the books themselves, she'll be a whirlwind of chalk and slate and calculations. Which does not sound conducive to being captured in pencil."

Thus far, the subterfuge they'd worked out had proved unnecessary since no one had agreed to come with them.

"Where is Gemma?" Ivy asked, scanning the chamber as if the second Hastings sister was lying prone on the library floor with a book in her hands. "No, let me guess. She's searching for fossils on the shore."

"Of course she is," Sophia said, not looking up from where her pencil flew across the page. "She was off almost before she'd finished her breakfast. Apparently the tide is out just now so she will be able to examine the cliffs without drowning. Which I must say is a prudent choice. I am not quite convinced she'd have held back from her quest even if the tide

was in. My sister on the trail of a fossil sighting is not someone you'd wish to step in the way of."

"I daresay that holds true for any of you and your chosen
field of study," Quill said dryly. "I suppose I'm fortunate
that Miss Wareham has agreed to give up her first full day
at Beauchamp House to accompany me." He turned to Ivy.
"Perhaps you'd rather remain here and explore the various
titles and fragments my aunt gathered during her trips to
Greece?"

Ivy gave him a hard look. "You won't shake me off that
easily, my lord. After the past week of rain, I am quite ready
for a long walk." Her silent glance of rebuke told him that
she was not amused at his attempt to leave her behind.

"Where are you planning to go, Miss Wareham?" inquired
Serena from the doorway behind them.

Of course Serena would choose that moment to come upon
them, Quill thought with an inward sigh. Which in the general course of things was perfectly fine. But this particular
chaperone had known him from childhood. And Serena had
suffered enough of her own tragedy that he wanted to protect her from the knowledge that their beloved aunt might
not have died of natural causes. It was bad enough to see her
stricken look every time Fanning was mentioned. He would
not add to her sorrows with the news that her beloved aunt
had been murdered until it was absolutely necessary. He'd
sent for his cousin Maitland for precisely this reason. If anyone could distract Serena it was her younger brother.

"Just a trip to the village to post a letter to my family, Lady
Serena," Ivy said brightly. "I know I could send it from here,
but I'd like to get to know the village if I'm to be here for a
year. And Lord Kerr has kindly agreed to accompany me."

Serena cast a knowing glance at her cousin, and Quill
found himself feeling guilty for things he'd not even properly

imagined yet. Not that he *would,* he reminded himself firmly. Whatever spark of attraction he might feel for Miss Wareham and her sharp wit was something that he had no intention of acting on—no matter how tempting her habit of biting her lower lip might be.

"Has he indeed?" Serena asked with raised brows. "How kind of you, Kerr. I had no idea you'd developed such a chivalrous streak."

"You pain me, cousin," he retorted with mock dismay. "I hope I have always behaved like a gentleman, which includes rescuing ladies in need. I seem to recall a couple of times in our youth when I came to your aid when you had need of a champion. Particularly when Lord Henry Threadgill snubbed you at the local assembly."

At the mention of Threadgill, Serena's eyes widened with amused shock. "What a heartless rogue you are to bring him up!" she hissed. "I was desperately in love with Lord Henry Threadgill."

"For all of two weeks when you were seventeen," Quill said with a laugh. "Didn't he throw you over for Miss Madeline Staynes?"

"Yes, the lout," she said with a shake of her head. "And she professed to be my friend. It was a particularly dreadful evening for me. But you saved it by diverting the attention of the tabbies by making a cake of yourself over some local widow."

A widow whom he'd bedded not too long after, Quill recalled with wry amusement. Not that Serena had known that.

But somehow Ivy's knowing glance at him upon the mention of the widow made Quill feel as if the whole of his youthful affair had already been revealed.

"Never let it be said that I am not loyal to a family member in distress," he said with a slight bow. "Now, unless you wish to accompany us, Serena, I think Miss Wareham and I had better set off before the day has got away from us. We don't wish to miss luncheon, do we Miss Wareham?"

"Perhaps you'd better have the cook pack you a basket just in case your trip takes longer than you anticipate," Serena said wryly. "It is already gone eleven. And I do know how you hate to miss a meal, cousin."

"An excellent idea," Quill said. "Why don't you fetch your cloak and hat, Miss Wareham, and I'll see about provisions."

"Very well," Ivy responded, looking as if she wanted to say something more. But shaking her head a little, she left and headed toward her chamber.

"I hope you know what you're doing," Serena said in a low voice as Quill moved to leave the library.

"Always, cousin," he responded. Though in this particular case, he wasn't as self-assured as he proclaimed himself to be. There was something about Ivy Wareham that set him off-balance.

And he'd better figure out a way to keep from falling, else they'd both be facing the consequences.

"You seem to be quite close with your cousin," Ivy said once she and Quill had set out away from the coast and inland toward the village of Little Seaford, a basket of sandwiches and biscuits swinging from Quill's arm.

It was impossible not to notice the resemblance between the cousins. Whereas on Quill the strong nose and dimpled chin were utterly masculine, on Serena they were muted, more delicate. And there was something else there. There was the ease that came of kinship. The same sort of bond that Ivy had with her own siblings.

"We were close when we were younger," Quill said as he assisted her up and over a stile. The path from Beauchamp House to the village crossed several fields that were sectioned neatly off with rock walls. "Unfortunately, we lost touch when she married Fanning."

Ivy noted the troubled look in his blue eyes as she stepped down and let go of his hand. "Was he as bad as I suspect?" she asked quietly. "I could not help but notice that she goes a little pale every time his name comes up. And your jaw hardens."

In her work with the women at the home she'd spoken of earlier, Ivy had become all too familiar with the signs that marked a woman as having endured some kind of abuse. Whether he'd laid hands on her or not, she suspected that the late Lord Fanning had not been kind to his wife.

"Likely he was worse than you suspect," Quill said darkly. "He took a vibrant, amusing, lovely young woman and turned her into a shrinking, tentative creature afraid of her own shadow. That he managed to get himself killed before either Dalton or I was able to do anything about it was his good fortune."

Despite her suspicions, it was difficult for Ivy to image the calm, poised Lady Serena as Quill described her. She had shadows around her, true, but she must have healed a great deal to reach her current level of self-possession.

"Aunt Celeste spent a great deal of time bringing her back to life," Quill said, guessing at her thoughts. "She invited Serena and Jeremy to stay almost as soon as Fanning was in the ground. And since Beauchamp House had always been a haven for us, she came. Thank god, for I don't think more time in the Fanning dower house, trapped in isolation, would have done her any good."

It was hardly a surprise that Lady Celeste had been instrumental in her niece's recovery. Every layer that Ivy managed to uncover of the Lady Celeste enigma seemed to reveal another way that the woman had done good. Not for the first time, she regretted that meeting her benefactor had only become possible after her death, through the recollections of others. And Lady Celeste's own written words. She had no doubt that had she met Lady Celeste in person, she would have admired her even more than she did posthumously.

"How difficult it must have been for you to stand by while she was mistreated," Ivy said, knowing instinctively that Quill would not find it easy to let anyone—even her husband—harm someone he loved.

"If I'd known half of it while he was still alive, I'd have killed him myself," Quill said grimly. "That is, I'd have killed him after Serena's brother, the Duke of Maitland, killed him first. Unfortunately, we knew nothing about it for the first several years of their marriage. He was no fool. He hid her away in Yorkshire where we would see nothing amiss. And Serena's letters were full of happy nonsense. It was only when Aunt Celeste paid a visit to them on her way to Scotland that she learned how bad things were. And by that time Fanning was on his way to the hunting trip that led to him getting shot."

"An accident?" Ivy asked.

"Only if you think it a coincidence that the bullet came from the gun of a man Fanning was cuckolding." Quill smiled but there was no joy in it. "I suppose Jackson spared us the trouble of calling him out. And because they were hunting at the time, the magistrate ruled it an accident. Though I have my doubts."

"I suppose Lady Serena was lucky to have such concerned family," Ivy said, reflecting that most of the women she knew in Oxford who suffered at their husband's hands had no such recourse for escape. "And I hadn't thought Lady Celeste could rise any higher in my estimation, but every new thing I learn makes me wish again that she had invited us here while she was still alive."

"She would certainly have liked you," Quill said with a

fond smile. "Which I suppose she knew, otherwise why leave her home to you. Though I dislike her decision, of course, I can understand it somewhat more after getting to know you a little better."

Ivy looked up and saw that he was being entirely serious. "Is it possible that Lord Kerr has decided to stop fighting against his aunt's wishes?" she asked, with playful astonishment. But though she was mocking him a little, she was surprised that he'd come around so quickly.

Not looking at her, Quill squinted across the field before them. "Not precisely," he answered, his eyes serious. "I don't believe I will ever forgive her for bequeathing the house outside the family."

At his words, Ivy felt a pang of disappointment. She'd been foolish to think that he'd change his mind so precipitately.

"I cannot ignore my aunt's decision to inform you of her suspicions about being in danger, however," he said grudgingly. "For some reason, despite the kinship I felt with her thanks to the summers I spent here as a child, she chose to tell you rather than me." His jaw clenched and Ivy felt a pang of compassion for him. It must have been hard for him to know that in her time of need his aunt had not come to him for help.

Neither had Serena, come to think of it.

She suspected he was not a man to take such matters lightly. His next words confirmed it.

"I may not like what my aunt did in leaving Beauchamp House to you all, but what's done is done. And since I was unable to help her while she was alive, I must do whatever I can to do so now she's gone. And if that means working together with her chosen one, then I will do it. I must, if I do not wish to fail her again."

Ivy was silent for a moment, the anguish in his eyes making her own burn with emotion. Not only had he failed to protect his own sister from her husband's abuse, he hadn't even known that his beloved aunt was in trouble until it was far, far too late. In his position, Ivy would have been wracked with guilt too. And with resentment for the usurper his aunt had chosen in his place.

It was a wonder he'd agreed to work with her at all.

"I'm sure she valued your relationship as much as you did," Ivy said aloud, unable to hold back the impulse to lay a light hand on his arm. At the contact, his eyes flew to hers. She felt her breath catch at the flash of fire there. But just as quickly it was gone, and by the time she'd pulled her hand back he was looking ahead of them again.

"I know she did," he said tightly as they neared another stile. "And I daresay she chose not to tell either Dalton or me about her fears because she didn't wish us to do something rash. As you might have guessed, we can be a little ferocious when someone we care about is endangered."

"I hadn't noticed," Ivy said with a wink as she glanced down from atop the stile. He stood on the other side, waiting for her to descend, and for a moment she wondered if he would catch her if she jumped. He must have read the thought in her eyes, for he extended his arms at the ready.

Before she could check herself, Ivy leapt, and found herself pulled up close against a hard male body. Closing her eyes, she inhaled his intoxicating scent of sandalwood, grass, and fresh sea air. Opening her eyes, she saw his face only inches from hers. And noted those tiny details only this sort of closeness revealed: the shadow of his beard, which was dark despite the lighter hints in his windswept hair, and the tiny lines that fanned out from the outer corners of his eyes. Eyes as blue as the sky above them, and looking at her with what she knew instinctively was not simple friendship.

"Easy," he said, his breath soft on the skin of her cheek as he pulled her closer infinitesimally before just as quickly setting her firmly back onto her own two feet. "You shouldn't take risks like that. What if I hadn't caught you?"

But she knew from the way his eyes twinkled that he would have sooner cut off a limb than let her fall. This man, for all his faults, took his role of protector quite seriously. For whatever reason, he'd decided it was his duty to protect her. And despite her innate sense of self-sufficiency, Ivy found it a little intoxicating.

"But you did," she said with a cheeky grin.

And stepping out ahead of him, she followed the path forward, able to see the village just over the next rise.

Chapter 12

The village of Little Seaford was situated to the east of Beauchamp House, farther inland. The office of Dr. Henry Vance was indeed near the blacksmith, and as they passed that establishment, they could hear the sound of metal striking metal.

"It does not look as if the good doctor is hurting for business," Quinn said dryly as he noted the newly painted exterior of the row house where the physician's office made its home. In addition, a shiny new plaque hung by the door, informing them that they were in the right spot.

A brisk knock on the door produced a mobcapped maid, who upon learning Quinn's identity informed them that the doctor was indeed in and invited them inside. If the exterior was impressive, that was nothing when compared to the interior, which boasted carpets at least as fine as those in Beauchamp House and, if Quill wasn't mistaken, a small seascape by Turner hanging prominently in the little parlor where he and Ivy were shown.

"I'm not sure what I expected," Ivy said, holding her hands before the fire burning merrily in the hearth, "but I had thought a village doctor so near the coast would be used to a more democratic clientele. I cannot imagine the local fisherman find all this finery comforting."

"I daresay he has another space for seeing patients," Quill said, examining what looked to be a primitive medical instrument hanging on the wall. "And of course his more-elevated patients he doubtless sees in their own homes, as he did with Aunt Celeste."

The walk had left Ivy with pink cheeks, and her russet hair, which had been neatly coiled around her head when they set out, was desperately trying to escape its pins. He watched, transfixed, as she rose from the fire and attempted to tidy herself, smoothing a hand over her hair, pulling down the cuffs of her hunter green pelisse.

Sensing his scrutiny, she glanced up, and they locked eyes for a moment. If possible, her cheeks turned even redder, and to Quill's anguish and delight, she bit down on her lower lip before she seemed to snap out of it and looked away. "I must look a fright," she said tersely, turning away from him to look out the window that overlooked the street below.

He opened his mouth to correct her, but was forestalled by the opening of the door to reveal the maid with a tea tray. "Dr. Vance will just be a few minutes longer, my lord," she said, curtsying once she'd set down the heavy tray. "He asked me to bring up some refreshments for you and the lady while you wait."

"How lovely," Ivy said with a warm smile. "It was a bit cooler out today than I'd anticipated and a hot cup of tea is just what I was wishing for. Thank you so much . . . I'm sorry but I don't know your name?"

Dropping a slightly shallower curtsy, the maid said, "You're very welcome, miss. And it's Daisy."

Quill stepped forward and took the cup Ivy offered him, and hid a smile as she began to question the little maid under the guise of being new to the area.

"Oh"—the maid's eyes grew round upon hearing that Ivy was one of the four heiresses up at Beauchamp House—"I hadn't thought to meet one of you so soon." Her tone implied that the four bluestockings had been much talked about in Daisy's social circles. "Is it true that one of the ladies likes to paint folks without any clothes on?" This last was said in a low whisper as if saying the words too loudly would conjure Sophia who would demand that everybody get naked at once. Before Ivy could respond, the maid continued. "Or that another one arrived with a gentleman who wasn't her husband?"

Ivy blinked, then exchanged a wide-eyed look with Quill as if to ask whether she should respond. Clearly Daisy wasn't all that bright if she were asking the latter lady about herself. But that didn't mean her inquiry wasn't alarming for Ivy. Taking pity on her, he said, "I can assure you, Daisy, that there have been no such displays while I've been up at Beauchamp House. And while it's true that Miss Wareham and I arrived around the same time, that doesn't mean we were traveling together. Perhaps one of the servants has been telling tales to make them seem more exciting. For I can assure you, all I've seen so far is a great deal of reading. And some organizing of the library shelves."

Though he said this with the same polished ease with which he would chat with any of the villagers, inside Quill was fuming. Rumors were to be expected with new arrivals, of course. It was bound to happen when so little occurred in the area to divert the townspeople that didn't involve the local fishing harvest or the rhythms of the tides. But he was furious that someone at Beauchamp House had been spreading tales about the bluestockings. It was irregular enough that Lady Celeste had chosen to leave her home to four strangers, but if they were going to be here for any extended length of time—and he was now resigned to the fact that they would be—then they would have to be welcomed into the close-knit community. Which was less likely to happen if their reputations were ruined before they even had a chance to meet their neighbors. Not to mention the fact that such tales often found their way to London. It was one thing to wish them gone from his aunt's home, but it was quite another to wish them to be utterly ruined.

At his denial of the rumors, and the revelation that he was the gentleman in question, Daisy's eyes grew alarmingly wide. "Oh, my lord!" She clapped her hands on either side of her face. "I'm that sorry. I didn't know it was you." Dropping into another curtsy, this one so low she was almost unable to get up again, she muttered another apology before hurriedly excusing herself and fleeing the room.

"Well," Ivy said staring after her. "I suppose it's comforting to know that gossip is the same wherever one goes. Though I'm rather shocked at how quickly word of our arrival has made it here. There must be quite a healthy network of gossips between Beauchamp House and the village."

"Dashed busybodies," Quill said with a grimace. He didn't like how falsely bright Ivy's expression seemed to be, as if she were hiding her true feelings on the matter. "Hopefully Daisy will set those particular rumors to rest. Though you might wish to tell Sophia that she should refrain from painting nudes for a bit."

"I was unaware that she'd painted any at all," Ivy said with a twist of her lips. "I am guessing that rumor might be just that. Unless she perhaps brought some of her paintings with her. Indeed, I rather think that must be the case, for I cannot imagine her asking Lady Daphne to pose for her. And though they are sisters, Gemma does not strike me as someone who would willingly pose for any painting, let alone a nude one."

Quill pinched the bridge of his nose, wishing Ivy would stop using the word "nude."

"Ah, I see Daisy has brought you some refreshment," Dr. Vance said, poking his head in the door before opening it all the way and stepping inside. "I do apologize, Lord Kerr. I was consulting with the local apothecary and was unable to get away."

"It's good of you to see us, Vance," Quill said, grateful for the distraction. "May I present Miss Aphrodite Wareham. As you may have heard, she is one of the four young ladies to whom my aunt left Beauchamp House."

At the mention of Lady Celeste, the doctor's face fell a little. Then he rallied and moved to bow over Ivy's hand. "It is delightful to make your acquaintance, Miss Wareham," he said with a warm smile. "I know Lady Celeste was quite eager to make her home a haven for scholarly ladies such as yourself. What a comfort it is, as her friend, to know that you are just as delightful as she had hoped."

Quill blinked. "Do you mean to say that you knew about my aunt's plans, Vance?" he demanded, unable to keep the note of annoyance from his voice. It was one thing to be blindsided by his aunt's plans if everyone else close to her had been too. But hearing that she'd confided her plans to her local physician was a little bit galling.

But if the doctor was abashed by Quill's question, he didn't show it. "Your aunt was ill for some months before she died, my lord. And as her physician I spent a great deal of time with her before she passed. Something that gave her much comfort over those weeks was the knowledge that her passing would make it possible for four intelligent young ladies to make their homes in Beauchamp House and to make their marks in a way which Lady Celeste could not."

"How wonderful that she was able to have not only her

physician by her side," Ivy said, after a quelling glance at Quill, "but also a dear friend. For I'm sure she must have counted you so if she confided her plans to you. I hope that knowing how much you helped her gives you comfort."

To Quill's surprise the other man's eyes welled and he was forced to pull an enormous handkerchief from his pocket to wipe his eyes. "I do apologize, Miss Wareham," Vance said with a grimace, his bushy gray eyebrows almost touching in his distress. "But you are quite right that I counted Lady Celeste as a friend. And it was quite hard to lose her. Especially when I still don't know precisely what caused her death."

Mindful of their reason for being in the doctor's offices, Quill spoke up, watching with narrow eyes as Ivy patted Vance's hand. "That's just why we've come, doctor. Miss Wareham and I were curious about what it might have been that took my aunt away in her prime." Improvising to explain why Ivy might have accompanied him, he continued. "Miss Wareham has a fear of illness in general and she could not rest until we confirmed with you that whatever it was that killed my aunt is not, in fact, something that could pass on to others living in Beauchamp House."

Far from flinching at his mischaracterization, Ivy nodded at Quill's description of her phobia. "Indeed, Dr. Vance. I had a rather weak constitution as a child, so I am quite careful about ensuring I don't needlessly place myself in harm's way. When I learned upon my arrival at Beauchamp House that Lady Celeste died of a mysterious illness, I could not help but fear that it might be something that even now lingers within the house. I simply cannot go about my usual business if I'm constantly worried that touching this book or wandering that corridor will bring on one of the attacks I suffered so often as a child."

On hearing Ivy's explanation, the doctor at first looked

troubled, then relieved. "I can assure you Miss Wareham that there is no indication that whatever Lady Celeste suffered from was in any way catching. No one else in the house fell ill, and indeed no one in the village did either. If it was something that might be shared between patients, then it is long gone from Beauchamp House."

"What a relief, Dr. Vance," Ivy said with a heaving sigh. "But if you don't mind my asking, what was your best guess at what might have caused her illness? I know Lord Kerr hasn't said so, but I do know how hard it is to lose a loved one. And one wants to know why, don't they?"

She was a little too good at playing the concerned former invalid, Quill thought wryly as he watched Ivy blink up at Vance with her big green eyes. She'd best be careful if she didn't wish to receive a proposal from the man. He was looking quite bowled over by her attention.

Shaking his head, Vance turned so that he could face both Quill and Ivy. "As I told your lordship in my letter," he said glumly, "I was never able to pinpoint her cause of death. I did suspect perhaps that she suffered from some sort of stomach ailment. A cancer perhaps, but that didn't explain all of her other symptoms. In the end, I fear her heart simply could not support her any longer and gave out."

"I do not wish to press you," Ivy said into the silence that followed, "but might her illness have been brought on by something she consumed? I do not like to speculate, but my dear aunt Jane fell ill after she began taking a tonic she purchased while in London. I fear she was rather too zealous about taking it and ended up quite ill as a result. It's just that Lady Celeste's symptoms as Mrs. Bacon described them to me sound so similar."

It wasn't a bad guess, Quill thought, impressed despite himself at Ivy's suggestion. Though he'd never known his aunt to be particularly prone to relying upon the sorts of tonics and tinctures that could be had in any apothecary shop, instead choosing to take whatever her doctor chose to have made up for her. But it did offer a possible means of transmitting poison.

But Dr. Vance shook his head. "I asked her, of course, about what remedies she might have been taking on her own before she consulted me," he explained with a dour expression. "But she assured me that she was taking nothing out of the ordinary. I do know that her maid was fond of giving her herbal tisanes for her headaches, but those were only occasionally, and I questioned the maid thoroughly about the ingredients. None of which would cause the kind of illness that Lady Celeste suffered from."

"If you'll indulge me, however, Dr. Vance," said Quill firmly, "is there something that in usual quantities isn't dangerous but might be if it is taken too often? Or in too large a dose?"

Dr. Vance's eyes narrowed. "Are you asking me if I think your aunt was poisoned, Lord Kerr?" he demanded, his gaze traveling from Ivy to Quill and back again.

"That is precisely what I'm asking," Quill said baldly. "My aunt suspected that someone was trying to kill her. And what I wish to know is, did you suspect it as well?"

Chapter 13

Ivy couldn't take her eyes off Quill.

Despite his wind-ravaged hair and relaxed country attire, the Marquess of Kerr was every inch the aggrieved nobleman as he waited for Dr. Vance to answer his question. And the doctor was well aware of it too, Ivy could see. Though his jaw clenched at Quill's sharp tone, he didn't wave off the question or give an easy platitude that might have worked with one of his less highly ranked patients' families.

She was always aware, of course, that Lord Kerr came from a different world than her own. But it was not difficult to imagine he was just like other men beneath the beautifully tailored clothes when he was teasing her and striding across the countryside. His posture and steely tone now told her just how much of a mistake it was to forget his privileged existence.

"I suspected it, yes," the doctor said, his mouth tight with anger. "But I had no way to prove it short of having a coroner conduct the sort of posthumous examination that I know your aunt would have despised." He looked down, clearly trying to get hold of his temper. "I knew your aunt for decades, my lord. And held her in some affection. We were friends. And I wanted more than anything to find out what was slowly killing her. For myself as much as for her own peace of mind. But she made me promise not to conduct any kind of invasive testing on her after she was gone."

He looked up and Ivy could see that, far from the coolly detached physician she had at first thought him, Dr. Vance was truly grief-stricken over Lady Celeste's death. They were of an age, she realized as she took in the doctor's trim physique and not unattractive salt-and-pepper hair. Could Dr. Vance and Lady Celeste had been more to each other than friends? If so, how painful must it have been for him to watch her wither away?

Quill must have wondered the same thing, for his next words were a bit less sharp. "But you must have tried to stop the source of the poison, surely? If you did indeed suspect that was the culprit?"

"So many stomach ailments have the same symptoms as many poisons," Dr. Vance said. "And without an autopsy there was no way of knowing for sure. So yes, I did go so far as to attempt to control what she consumed. Her maid, whom she trusted implicitly, personally oversaw what she ate and drank for the last month of her life. Which did not make her popular in the servants' hall, I can tell you. And indeed she did seem to improve for a time. But not long after she suffered what was her last attack of illness and only days later she was gone."

"And you didn't think to send for me," Quill said, clearly angry. At the situation or Dr. Vance, Ivy couldn't tell. "I might have removed her from Beauchamp House to London where she could have seen the best physicians Harley Street had to offer." He began to pace, his agitation impossible to contain now.

Though he might have taken offense at the mention of Harley Street, to Dr. Vance's credit he said, "I tried, my lord. As I said, your aunt was my friend, and I wanted to see her well. But she thought she would be able to figure out who was responsible. And by the time she was ready to admit defeat, she was too far gone to travel. Believe me when I say I did everything I could to persuade her to leave. But you know as well as I do that Lady Celeste Beauchamp was as stubborn a woman who has ever lived. And she was unwilling to listen to reason. One of the downsides of a woman with a keen intellect, I suspect."

At his last words, Ivy bristled but chose not to argue. Though, honestly, she thought, no one ever complained of stubbornness in intelligent men. Because they assumed that a smart man was always right. Indeed, when the contest was between a man and a woman, the man was always right no matter how inferior his intellect might be.

"For whatever reason," she said coolly, "Lady Celeste chose to conduct her own investigation. Did she happen to share her suspicions with you, Dr. Vance?"

He shook his head. "She refused to blacken anyone's name when she had no proof. And when it came down to it, I don't believe she had any idea who it was. She certainly had no concrete suspect, else she'd have accused them. Or at the very least dismissed them from her household, which she did not."

Seeing that there was little more they could learn from the doctor, and not wanting to overstay their welcome lest they need to question him again, Ivy was trying to catch Quill's eye to indicate they should take their leave, when a sharp knock sounded on the door.

A pretty lady, about a decade older than Ivy, stepped inside and smiled inquisitively. "I am sorry to intrude, my dear, but you've received a summons from the Granthams. Their eldest boy has fallen from a tree and broken his arm and they need you at once."

To Ivy's surprise, Dr. Vance's face transformed for a moment as he looked at his wife—for that must surely be who the lady was. Unless his housekeeper called him "my dear," which would be highly unusual. "Come in, dearest," he said with a smile that made him look years younger. "Lord Kerr, Miss Wareham, may I present my wife, Mrs. Marianne Vance. Mrs. Vance, this is Lord Kerr, the Marquess of Kerr, and Miss Wareham of Beauchamp House."

The doctor's wife made her very correct curtsy to Quill and smiled warmly at Ivy, taking her hand in her own. "You must be one of the ladies that dear Lady Celeste left Beauchamp House to. How lovely to meet you. I had no idea that any of you were in residence yet, else I'd have paid a call by now."

"Oh, I only arrived yesterday," Ivy assured her quickly. "And my compatriots only a couple of days before that. Though I look forward to welcoming you, of course."

"Perhaps once you're all settled," Mrs. Vance continued, "we can hold an assembly to welcome you all to the neighborhood. For I know the rest of our little circle will be desperate to meet you all."

At her effusive words, Ivy laughed. "I'm not sure anyone should be desperate to meet any of us, though I appreciate your enthusiasm, of course."

"Well, I must admit that we were a little worried when we learned of Lady Celeste's bequest," Mrs. Vance said with a confiding smile. "We are a close-knit community and no one knew what to make of the notion we'd be getting a sudden influx of bluestockings in our midst. But you seem like a normal young lady and not at all the sort of dour creature full of her own importance I imagined you'd be."

Ivy leaned back a little, shocked despite herself at the other lady's description of her expectations of her. She supposed villages were not as used to mixing with intellectually inclined ladies as cities like Oxford or London were. But even so, it was hard not to be offended by the assumptions Mrs. Vance had made.

"I can assure you, Mrs. Vance," said Quill, perhaps interpreting Ivy's silence correctly, "I have met all four of the young ladies my aunt left Beauchamp House to and they are all delightful. Not a hint of the radical amongst the lot of them."

This last annoyed Ivy. She didn't need him reassuring women like Mrs. Vance about her political proclivities. His words made her desperately want to spout off some outrageous philosophy or casually ask when the village anarchists held their meetings.

"Oh, I can see that for myself, my lord," Mrs. Vance said beaming. "Though I am grateful for your assurances. I should hate to think that Little Seaford was in danger of being overrun by Amazons." She laughed merrily and didn't seem to notice that Ivy didn't join in. "I am so pleased to meet you, Miss Wareham, and will definitely pay a call on the four of you before the week is out."

"Do not forget our chaperone, Lady Serena Fanning," Ivy said wryly. "She at least will lend the rest of us consequence if our own good behavior does not."

Perhaps sensing the undercurrents, Dr. Vance jumped in. "If I am to reach the Grantham farm in good time, I should take my leave. My lord, Miss Wareham, I hope you will come to me if you have any more questions."

And before his wife could ask any impertinent questions about their reasons for the visit, Ivy slipped her hand into Quill's arm and stepped back out into the street, where a glance at the sky was enough to tell her that the fine weather they'd enjoyed earlier had changed. Now a dark cloud hung low on the horizon and looked to be headed back the way they'd come.

"Damn it," Quill said under his breath. "I knew I should have sent the coachman ahead to wait here in the village for us. The weather here is apt to change at the drop of a hat. Which I well know."

"I'm sure if we hurry we can make it back to Beauchamp House before the storm," Ivy said, not necessarily believing her words but not wishing to wait it out in the village when she wanted to get back to the manor so that she could reread Lady Celeste's letter to see if there were any clues she might have missed.

To her relief, Quill seemed to agree with her. "Let's get started then before it overtakes us."

They'd only got to the edge of the village, both of them walking briskly in an effort to outrun the coming storm, when Quill heard a carriage rumbling toward them.

There was plenty of room for it to pass, thanks to the width of the carriageway at that point, but nevertheless, he said, "Perhaps we should move to the side to let him by."

Lost in thought, Ivy gave a start but allowed him to guide her to the roadside. When she glanced behind them, however, her eyes grew wide. And when Quill looked back, he saw that rather than taking advantage of the area they'd ceded to him, the driver of the cart was barreling toward them.

Without thinking, he threw himself against her, just before the horses followed by the careening vehicle sped past where they'd just been standing.

"What on earth?" Ivy gasped from beneath him, her breath coming in gasps as she tried to regain her composure. "Were his horses out of control?"

His own breath in short supply, he shook his head. "I don't know. I don't think so."

Turning to look down at her, he realized he was sprawled on top of her, and scrambled to his feet. Taking advantage of the moment, he gave her a hand up. They busied themselves in brushing off their clothes, and Quill retrieved his hat from where it had fallen in the grass a few feet away.

"Are you all right?" he asked, looking at her at last and seeing that she seemed more annoyed than hurt.

"I'm fine," she said with a frown. "But I'd like to know why that man just tried to run us over."

"I didn't recognize him," Quill said with a frown as he looked in the direction where the cart had sped off. "It was very likely just some tradesman in a hurry to reach his next stop."

"Well, I've lived in Oxford my whole life," she said, still frowning, "and it is far more congested than this village, and I've never once been in danger of being trampled by a runaway cart."

Realizing she was likely far more upset by the incident than she let on, Quill refrained from minimizing her reaction. Instead, he calmly tucked her arm into his elbow and started them off in the direction of home.

"I fear we'd best discuss this as we walk, for it looks as if this storm is about to be upon us," he said. It was a measure of how unsettled she was that she had allowed him to lead her without so much as a murmur of protest.

Despite their best efforts, the storm did, in fact, overtake them about halfway back to Beauchamp House, pelting them with a deluge of wind and rain.

"Now is not the time for missishness," he said to Ivy, who despite her shivering, was attempting to accept the shelter of his coat without touching him. "You won't give a hang about your reputation when you're dying of the ague in your solitary bed," he snapped, pulling her roughly against him even as they hurried along the path.

"I'm not . . ." she began to protest, then, perhaps thinking better of it, stopped herself. "Fine," she muttered in a voice he strained to hear over the sound of the rain, "but don't blame me if we're spotted and someone forces us into a betrothal."

Quill could think of worse things than to find himself leg-shackled to a curvaceous beauty with a sharp tongue, but wisely chose to keep his own counsel on the matter. Now was not the time to raise her ire. If his memory served, there was an empty cottage up ahead used by shepherds moving their flocks, which though likely to offend his companion's sensibilities, was at the very least dry and, if they were lucky, boasted a fireplace.

"This way," he said, unabashedly holding her against him as he led her down a side path toward the cottage, which he spotted—thank god—just as he began to think his memory had deceived him with a remembered mirage.

Fortunately, she didn't question his diversion, and when she saw the weather-beaten shack, she cried out with relief.

"I've never been so happy to see an abandoned cottage in all my life," she said as she pulled out of the shelter of his arms and began to remove her ruined hat.

Not pausing to reflect on how strangely bereft he felt at their separation, Quill removed his greatcoat and handed it to her. "Take off your pelisse and put this on while I start the fire. There should be some blankets in that chest. The shepherds generally keep a few things in these cottages for those nights when they're forced to remain here."

Relief swept through him when she did as she was told. He would never forgive himself his foolishness at getting her into this predicament if she caught her death of a cold. And a missish refusal to get out of her wet things would have risked just that. But Ivy was more sensible than that, thank god.

Confident that she was on her way to drying off, and aware that his blood was still up thanks to the near miss on the road, he knelt before the fireplace and concentrated on lighting the kindling and logs left there by the cottage's last occupant.

"How did you know about this place?" Ivy asked from behind him. "I didn't see it on our way into the village."

"I remembered waiting out rain storms here when I was a lad," Quill said, brushing his hands off on his breeches before standing. "I'm surprised it's still . . . here." When he'd turned it was to see that not only had Ivy removed her soaked outer garment, but she was seated on the little cot unlacing her boots, which revealed an impressive pair of bestockinged calves. Fortunately, she was too intent on her task to notice his hot gaze.

Or maybe she was too cold to care.

Despite his suddenly desperate wish to watch as she unrolled those stockings, Quill turned his back on her unconsciously seductive actions and began to remove his soggy coat. Once that was off, he set to work on his own boots, which he feared were beyond hope. He never traveled without extra pairs, but it almost made him weep to see Hoby's handiwork so utterly demolished.

"It's lucky you remembered it, else I know I would have crumbled in a heap on the side of the path," she said with some relief. "I can endure many things, but cold and wet is my Achilles' heel. I could withstand the heat of the desert or the tropical forests described by travelers to the southern regions of America without incident, I think. But unrelenting rain and cold I simply cannot abide."

"How unfortunate that you should be born in England, then," Quill said with a laugh. "For I do not think you could find a colder, wetter climate if you tried."

"I'm just lucky that way, I suppose," she said with an answering note of amusement.

Her laugh did something to him, Quill realized. Touched some part of him that admired her indefatigable spirit.

Despite her discomfort and distress at being drenched, she was in possession of the sort of temperament that did not allow the petty annoyances of life to dampen her spirit. He could not think of a single other lady of his acquaintance who would meet such a situation with such equanimity.

"If you wish," he said over his shoulder, "you may remove your gown and wrap up in one of the blankets . . ."

He trailed off as he saw that she was already in the process of doing just that. He swallowed at the sight of her breasts outlined by the wet fabric as she tried to reach behind to unbutton her gown.

"I am trying to do just that, but I'm afraid this gown requires the assistance of another pair of hands." In another woman he might have suspected her of flirtation, but there was a sort of shy diffidence in the way she spoke that told him she was not trying to be coy. It was a refreshing change from the cynical seductions he was used to in London.

But when he looked up, their eyes caught, and he muttered a curse. She might be an innocent, but she had a wellspring of natural sensuality that just might do him in.

Completely unaware of the direction of his thoughts, she asked, "Would you mind helping me?"

He was crossing toward her before she even finished speaking, and when he moved to stand behind her, he was almost jealous of the wisps of damp hair that kissed the nape of her neck. "Move your hands," he said thickly, unable to say more in case he'd tell her what he was truly thinking.

As he bent his head a little to see the buttons, Quill was assailed by the scent of woman mixed with rosewater rising from her warm skin. He fumbled a little as he set his fingers working against the fastenings, unable to resist dragging a little against the smooth skin of her back as one by one he pulled the bindings free. It was near impossible for him to breathe as he watched inch after inch of her gown part to reveal first the almost transparent fabric of her chemise, then neatly threaded laces of corset below.

As if she sensed his hesitation, she said quietly, "That's good enough. I think my gown bore the brunt of it."

The danger of the temptation she posed suddenly making its way into his brain, Quill pulled his hands back as if they'd been licked by flames. "I'll go have a look at the fire," he said pointedly as he turned his back to her and placed one hand against the wall beside the stone fireplace and gazed down into the actual flames below.

Perhaps it would have been safer for them both if they'd pressed on to Beauchamp House, he reflected as he tried not to listen to the rustling of her clothes as she slipped out of them. It had been years since he'd felt the sort of uncontrolled desire that held him in its grip now. It was impossible to forget every luscious detail of her. From the smooth skin of her bare back to the flush in her cheeks.

He'd also been cursed with a healthy imagination when it came to his carnal desires, which now unhelpfully flooded his mind with all the delicious ways in which two adults could put a rainy afternoon in close quarters to good use.

"You may turn around now," Ivy said finally, after several fraught minutes of him trying to think of everything but the woman undressing just feet away from him, and failing miserably.

When he turned, he saw that the thick wool blanket that covered her was about as unflattering a garment as it could be. But even that did nothing to quell the effect of her loveliness on him.

"You may sit beside me if you like," she said tentatively, her green eyes perhaps seeing more of his discomfort than he was comfortable with. "There's no other chair here, and it would be ridiculous for you to sit on the floor when there is a perfectly good seat here."

His expression must have shown his skepticism as he looked pointedly at the empty place beside her on the small bed.

"Do not be missish, my lord," she said, echoing his own words to her as they huddled beneath his greatcoat. "We are both sensible creatures. I can sit beside you without unleashing my base passions on you and offending your delicate sensibilities."

Despite his misgivings, Quill bit back a laugh. "I believe that is supposed to be my line," he said with a grin. "You must think me a poor figure of a man if you think I will collapse in a fit of the vapors." As he spoke, he walked the few steps to the other side of the cottage and lowered himself gingerly to the cot beside her.

"Hardly that," she said holding her blanket at the neck while extending her other hand toward the heat of the fire. "You looked so serious, I thought to relieve the tension a bit, that's all."

"You use humor like that frequently, don't you?" he asked, unfastening the diamond stick pin from where it nestled in the now-crumpled folds of his cravat.

Before she could respond, he said, "Let's use this to hold that," holding up the pin.

Nodding, she shifted a little to face him, lifting her chin so that he could duck his head and see what he was doing as he stabbed the pin through the thick blanket. Pulling back a little, he looked up to find her green gaze lingering on his mouth. And unable to stop himself, he gave in to the temptation that had dogged him ever since they set out together that morning.

Pulling her against him, he covered Ivy's mouth with his own, and kissed her.

Chapter 14

Ivy wasn't sure when the moment changed. Perhaps when he leaned in so close that she could feel the warmth of his body and smell the clean scent of his cologne mixed with something intoxicatingly male. Or maybe it was when he looked up at her from beneath his impossibly long lashes and their eyes met just before he glanced at her lips.

She wasn't sure because instinct made her close her eyes just before he brought his mouth up to press against hers.

And she was flooded with nothing but sensation.

His lips were soft. Softer than seemed possible. But more seductive than the most eloquent of Sappho's lyrics.

And when she kissed him back, opened her mouth and leaned into him, Quill took full advantage of the invitation, stroking into her in a tangle of tongues that was more carnal than she'd imagined a kiss could be. He pulled her closer, and Ivy slid her arms up over his chest and into the silky hair at his nape. The press of her breasts against the hard wall of his chest combined with the heat of their mouths was almost her undoing, and she moaned a little as he nipped at her lower lip. She'd been kissed before, of course.

There had been one overeager suitor who'd managed to maneuver her into an alcove during a local assembly, but that had been years ago, and she'd been more surprised than flattered since she suspected he was only using her to make another girl jealous. But she could hardly remember what it had felt like. Certainly it hadn't filled her with the sort of breathless wonder that now threatened to overtake her completely.

"May I kiss you, Aphrodite?" Quill asked, and she felt the low rumble of his voice all the way to her toes.

"A bit late for asking permission, my lord," she murmured against his mouth. "Does not lack of protest indicate consent?"

He kissed a path down from her mouth over her chin, saying as he moved, "Not always. And I have a strong desire"—he sucked lightly in a spot beneath her ear—"to hear you say yes."

"Then, yes," she said leaning back a little to give him more access to her collarbone. "Kiss me, Quill. Please."

Something relaxed in him. Ivy could feel it in the set of his shoulders as he moved against her. "Since you asked so nicely." She felt his smile as he moved back up her body and took her mouth again, this time with a demanding hunger that called out to some unnamed yearning she hardly recognized as her own. She only knew that she had to get closer, press harder, open herself to his every unspoken request. Struggling against the rough wool of the blanket, she shrugged, the stickpin holding the neck together unfastening as it fell from her shoulders onto the bed behind her.

The relief at feeling the skin of her chest and shoulders against the fabric of his shirt and waistcoat was almost palpable, and when his hand caressed her breast through the fabric of her stays, Ivy felt it in her core. The combination of the heat of their mouths and the stroke of his thumb over her hardened nipple was enough to make her jolt, and Quill pulled back a little from her mouth, whispering, "Easy, sweet. Easy."

And for reasons she could not say, she trusted him. Even as the ache his touch wrought made her move against him, seeking some relief in that restless place where only she had ever touched.

As if sensing her need, Quill pressed her back to lie on the little cot, taking a moment to glance down at her with eyes dark blue with desire just before he set his mouth over the tip of her breast beneath the thin fabric of her chemise. It was both pleasure and pain to feel the pull of his mouth on her, and when his hand slid slowly up her knee toward her aching center, it was only by biting her lip that she didn't cry out for him to move faster. But she must have made some sort of sound because he huffed out a laugh and pulled back a little to use his teeth on her sensitive breast. "Soon enough, sweet Aphrodite."

But she couldn't stop herself from lifting her hips in a silent plea for relief, and when he finally, finally stroked a finger over the bare flesh at the heart of her, Ivy's gasp of pleasure was loud over the pounding of the rain outside.

"I have to see you," Quill muttered, all amusement gone from his voice. And without removing his hand from where he caressed her, he shifted to kneel between her bent legs. Ivy widened them so that when he lifted her chemise he could look his fill of her.

She had no notion of why this man had managed to get past her defenses, but she had no wish to contemplate such things while she watched desire sharpen the lines of his austere face.

Her clothes no longer in the way, he shrugged out of his coats, and Ivy inhaled a sharp gasp of anticipation. She watched breathlessly as he made quick work of his cravat, and in one fluid motion pulled his shirt over his head and tossed it aside. Unable to look away, she only had time for an appreciative glance at his naked chest before he leaned down and took her mouth again. The sensation of skin to skin was nearly her undoing.

"Is this comfortable?" he asked after a moment, and she realized that she was clinging to him like a limpet, her hands skimming over the warm skin of his back almost without her knowing it.

Unable to find her voice, Ivy nodded, but when he stroked a finger over the sensitive flesh between her legs, she gave a gasp of pleasure. And soon she was moving restlessly against him again, only this time she felt the added sensation of his hardness through the nankeen of his breeches. Rocking against him, she brought her calves up around his hips, and pulled him closer. He mimicked their movements with the hot thrust of his tongue into her mouth.

Unable to stop herself, and driven by curiosity and a need to feel more of him, she slipped her hands between them and set to work at the buttons of his breeches. Quill hissed at the touch, and put a staying hand against hers. "I am trying like the devil to be gentle with you, Ivy," he said through gritted teeth. "If you don't release me, I can't be answerable for the consequences."

"But I want to feel you," she said, punctuating her words with a lift of her hips. She'd certainly read enough erotic classical poetry to know how the mechanics worked, but she also knew that she wanted to give him as much pleasure as he seemed intent on giving her. "And I want you to feel as good as I do."

He closed his eyes as she brushed his hand away and continued to unbutton his falls. She smiled in triumph at his surrender, and when his body sprang forth, she stroked a hand from root to tip, eliciting a groan of relief from him. And almost before she knew what he was doing, she found herself pressed back against the cot with her hands clasped above her head, imprisoned by one of his.

When she made to protest, he stifled her with his mouth. "You are undoubtedly one of the most brilliant ladies I've ever met," he said to her with a chiding look, "but I have more knowledge in this particular area. So let me lead."

She was robbed of the ability to respond by the feel of his eager body, hard and ready against the bare skin of her thigh. Suddenly she felt her chest flood with emotion as she looked up into his all too serious gaze. Kissing her softly, he said, "I'll take care of you, Ivy. I promise." It was a gentle kiss, and she trusted him despite the butterflies of nerves fluttering in her stomach. And as if they'd never paused, she felt the passion between them rise again as Quill's clever fingers stroked over her and, as she silently begged for more, thrust into her. First one, then another, which he rhythmically moved within her. The sound of their breathing rang in her ears as she shifted her hips faster and faster to meet his thrusting fingers.

She was nearing some peak she'd never scaled before when he suddenly pulled his hand away. "Come back," she ordered in a desperate voice she barely recognized as her own. "Oh, please Quill, come back."

And before she could even finish her protest, he replaced his fingers with the hot hardness of his body. And she sighed with relief as she urged him forward silently with a tiny thrust of her hips.

"Be still, Ivy," he said in a strained voice as he let go of her imprisoned hands and used his own to hold himself over her. "I'm trying to do this slowly. I don't want to hurt you."

Which was utterly noble, she knew, but her body wanted him now. "I don't mind pain," she hissed. "I just want you. Now."

And she used her heels and hands to pull him into her, gaining another delicious inch that stretched her beyond what was comfortable. Even so, she wanted more, and with another strong pull against him, she felt Quill surrender and with one swift thrust he was fully seated within her.

Ivy gasped as he moved over her.

Quill touched his forehead to hers, and asked in a strained voice, "Is it too much?" If she said yes, he was prepared to withdraw, but it was hard to imagine doing so when he was clasped in the hot, tightness of her sweet body. Still, he had no wish to give her pain, and the last thing he wanted was to give her a fear of coupling. Because he damned well intended to do this with her again. And again.

"No," she said with a little shake of her head. "No. Just . . . different."

Offering up a silent prayer of thanksgiving, he pulled back slowly then just as slowly pressed in again. This time her gasp was one of pure pleasure, and he let himself go a little, moving against her in a rhythm that pleased them both if the clench of her body around his was any indication. Soon they were both too consumed by the slick slide of their bodies against each other to speak. Dipping his head down to kiss her as he thrust, he growled out a groan as he felt her hands slide up into his hair, pulling his face closer as he moved against her. But she pulled her face away when he reached down to touch her just above where their bodies joined, and he felt some part of her uncoil with abandon as her body gripped him where he moved inside her.

"Oh Quill," she gasped as he gritted his teeth against the feel of his own completion nearing. "I. Oh. That's . . ."

Closing his eyes in relief, he felt her quicken her hips and in turn the pulsing grip of her around his cock as she gave herself over to her orgasm. And like a stallion let off its lead, only now did he give himself permission to let himself go, unable to hold back his need any longer. He pressed into her soft body with a desperation he'd not allowed himself to feel in decades, if ever. It was as if Ivy with her eager kisses and open sensuality had bewitched him into revealing some part of himself he'd long kept hidden from view. And the result was a mad hunger that made him grind into her without any thought for finesse or chivalry, but instead unleashing a raw need that had him pounding into her with abandon until finally, joyfully, he felt that telltale tingle in his spine before he gripped her buttocks and with a harsh cry went over the edge with her.

When he came back to himself, Quill realized he'd collapsed on top of her like a selfish oaf, and with a muttered apology he turned over onto his back, a barely successful maneuver given how narrow the cot was.

With the return of awareness, also came a sense of the gravity of what he'd just done. Not only had he compromised Ivy beyond repair, he'd done so after not even a full twenty-four hours of knowing her. That must be some sort of record. At least it was in his family, where as far back as he could recall betrothals had all been conducted with the attendant pomp and circumstance that accompanied marriages made within the elite circles of the beau monde.

Beside him, Ivy lay silent, and he wondered if she was regretting the rashness of their actions. If he were assessing her likely reaction to being compromised into marriage by a marquess when he'd first learned her identity yesterday, he would have assumed she'd be tickled pink. The woman he'd assumed had come to Beauchamp House with no other goal than to steal his family's inheritance out from under them would have been smiling like the cat who licked the cream as she lay beside him. But it had only taken a few more minutes' conversation with Miss Aphrodite Wareham to know that she cared only about the inheritance insofar as it would allow her to continue her studies. And even that she'd set aside today in favor of investigating the circumstances behind his aunt's death. A woman who thought only of her own well-being would have ignored the letter from Celeste and stayed behind in the library with her fellow scholars.

"It's stopped raining," she said from beside him, though she made no move to rise. "We should be getting back to Beauchamp House if we don't want them to send out a search party. I daresay the fact that we're so late will be scandal enough. Especially given the fact that I neglected to bring a maid along."

"The proprieties are a bit more relaxed in the country than they are in town," Quill responded curtly, the consequences of their missing lunch the least of his worries. In one fluid motion, he sat up and stood, turning his back to her as he refastened his breeches and bent to retrieve his cravat, shirt, and waistcoat from where he'd tossed them onto the floor. Folding his own garments over his arm, he picked up Ivy's gown and handed it wordlessly to her, not daring to meet her eye lest he see the censure he deserved in them.

He'd done a number of foolish things in his life, but this might be the worst of them. Because he knew without asking her that Ivy would not marry him without protest. And yet marriage was the only way in which he could honorably repair the damage this interlude sheltering from the storm had caused.

"I suppose you're right," she said, scrambling off the cot and taking her gown from him. From within her gown, which she had pulled on over her head, she continued, "But I don't wish to upset your cousin. She seems like such a conscientious lady, and she will see this as some dereliction on her part, I fear."

Chapter 15

Tying his cravat in as tidy a fashion as he could imagine without a mirror, he said wryly, "I think she will be less bothered by your absence from luncheon than by the fact that I spent the time waiting out the storm taking your virginity, Ivy."

Blushing, she thrust her arms into the sleeves of her gown, and turned to offer him her back. Having finished pulling on his own clothes, he stepped behind her and began doing up the tiny buttons, steeling himself not to touch the soft, pale skin above her chemise, which he'd only minutes before caressed with his bare hand.

"We need not tell anyone about that," Ivy said in a hopeful tone.

Did she honestly think he could forget what they'd just done? If so she was sorely mistaken. And not just because it had been the single most intoxicating experience of his adult life.

"There is every need," Quill said, his self-recrimination making him short. "Or rather, we needn't tell everyone the reason why. But when we return to the house we will announce that we have decided to marry. I will leave this afternoon for Oxford so that I can inform your father, and I have a friend with an uncle who is a bishop from whom I can get a special license. It will not take me above a couple of days. And I'll send a note to my secretary and have him send a notice to the papers. We can be married within the week if things are arranged properly."

He'd just finished the last button at this point, and when Ivy turned there was fire in her eyes. And not from passion.

"Were you going to consult me about this, or just issue a set of orders to me along with the rest of your minions?" she asked, her cheeks and neck flushed red with anger. Before he could respond, she continued, "I am not one of your meek society ladies who will take direction from you without so much as a by-your-leave. Has it occurred to you that I might not even believe in the institution of marriage? Or that perhaps my decision to give myself to you had nothing to do with anyone but us?"

While Quill understood her anger—he hadn't started the day with a desire to get married in a week's time either—he disagreed with the rationale behind it. "I would not have thought a lady with as much scholarly knowledge would be so naive about the way the world works. You and I might wish to keep this slipup between the two of us, but these things have a way of getting out. Certainly there could be rumors in the servants' quarters about us. I daresay they began as soon as the table was laid for luncheon and we still had not returned. Have you considered what it might do to your reputation to be dogged with such whispers? What having that kind of reputation might do to your ability to move freely in scholarly circles?"

At the mention of her scholarly reputation, Ivy's eyes widened, and despite feeling petty for it, Quill felt a stab of triumph. Perhaps he should have begun with the threat to her scholarly reputation rather than her societal one. After all, from everything he'd seen about her, she cared far more for her ability to do her work than she did about moving in society. He suspected some of that had to do with her father's estrangement from his family. It certainly wouldn't endear him to the *ton* if he'd been raised by someone who'd been purposely kept out of it.

Her jaw tight, Ivy gave a small nod. "You may be correct about scholarly circles. It is difficult enough as a woman to gain recognition for one's work. I can only imagine how much more difficult it would be to do so with a reputation for libertine behavior. It's all well and good if one is married." She gave a moue of distaste. "But as an unmarried lady I have already seen how narrow-minded male scholars can be when it comes to accepting my work without ascribing silly female illogic and foolishness to it. I'm damned for innocence when it comes to certain lyric poetry because I am unmarried, but I can guess that I'd be damned for being too knowing if I were to lose my good name."

Despite his relief that she was beginning to see reason, Quill was not so foolish as to let his triumph show on his face. Besides, were not ladies known for changing their minds? Aloud he said, "So, you agree that our marrying is the sensible course of action? I do think that you might be able to get a bit further in your quest for recognition as the Marchioness of Kerr than as Miss Wareham, if it's any consolation."

But her mouth was still tight with disapproval. "I can see the rationality behind your arguments, my lord. Indeed, I even agree with some of them, but I cannot think it will do either of us good to leap into a hasty marriage. Not only does it seem precipitate, but we are both overlooking the fact that there may be no gossip after today's excursion. It would be a shame to make such an important decision based on fears that might be unfounded."

He could see her point, but by this point Quill was already decided. It was just a matter of persuading Ivy. And if his own pleas fell on deaf ears, he had little doubt that her father would see things his way. He could not imagine that a man who had suffered banishment from the society he'd been born into would allow something similar to happen to his daughter.

Still, he had one more arrow in his quiver, and he had no qualms about using it. "Have you considered that you might already be with child?" he asked, not happy about the fact that he was the one who had put the flash of alarm in her emerald eyes, but knowing it was entirely necessary. "This is about more than the two of us, Ivy. I certainly will not countenance having a child born out of wedlock—or waiting until it becomes apparent that it's the only reason for our marriage."

"I hadn't thought of that," she admitted. "I hope you don't think I am so selfish that I would choose my own freedom at the expense of my child. Though in fairness, we do not even know yet if there is a child."

"But we must behave as if we know there is, Ivy," he said quietly. "We can avoid scandal, but only if we do the sensible thing and marry."

Seeing that she still didn't seem appeased, Quill stepped closer and took her hands in his. "I know things are moving quickly," he said, wishing he could kiss away her doubts. "But that doesn't mean we need to fight each other. And you need not think that I will be a demanding husband. I know already how much a part of you your studies are. And I would do nothing to take that away from you. I give you my word."

If he thought she would simply capitulate in the face of his gentle persuasion, however, he was quite mistaken.

Not backing down, she said, "May I have a day or two to think things over?" There was a plea for understanding in her gaze, which despite the urgency he felt about settling things between them, he could not deny.

"Of course," he agreed, with more ease than he felt. He was grateful that she was willing to consider his proposal at all, but he couldn't help a pang of impatience at her resistance. Even so, he was well aware that she was quite capable of digging in her heels and telling him to go to the devil if she chose. So he told himself to be patient and give her the time she needed. No matter how much his inner brute wished to override her objections and bend her to his will.

"Thank you," she said, her obvious relief stinging his conscience at his boorish thoughts. However he might chafe at her resistance, it was genuine and she deserved to be given some latitude in the matter.

"Now," she continued with a sheepish smile, "before we are discovered alone here, I suggest we start back for Beauchamp House. Otherwise there will be no question of which action we take. Your cousin will see to it that we're wed whether we agree to it or not."

Suddenly, he was reluctant to leave the little cottage that had served as a refuge from the rest of the world for a few short hours.

But, she was correct that they needed to get back, and the sooner the better.

With one last look over his shoulder into the little house, Quill shut the door behind them and followed Ivy toward the path back to Beauchamp House.

Far from the quiet return Ivy had hoped for, as soon as she and Quill stepped inside of Beauchamp House they were greeted as if they'd disappeared on an Egyptian expedition rather than simply disappeared for a few hours in a rainstorm.

"Oh, dear," said Sophia, giving Ivy an impulsive hug. "You look as if you could use a cup of tea and a hot bath. As soon as we saw the clouds threatening we began to worry, but I thought you would at least remain in the village until it passed." She shot a baleful glance in Quill's direction, but to Ivy's relief, he didn't betray a hint of guilty conscience. She supposed if she were going to choose a man to ruin herself over, she'd done well to pick one who would fall on his sword before he betrayed her to anyone.

Well, anyone who wasn't her father, she amended, recalling their earlier argument. Just the thought of her father hearing about this afternoon's events made her stomach flip in anxiety. She was brave enough when it came to forging her own path as a scholar, but as the eldest daughter she'd come to appreciate her father's guidance when it came to her scholarship. And she'd prided herself on not behaving like the sort of ninny she'd always thought could get herself into a situation like the one she now found herself in. The idea of disappointing her father was far worse than any fears she had about society's response to her transgressions.

"I'll tell Mrs. Bacon to have hot water brought up to both of your rooms," said Lady Serena with a cryptic glance at Quill. "I'll have some soup and sandwiches sent up as well. I daresay you're both starving after missing luncheon."

"That would be most appreciated, cousin," Quill said with a short bow. He turned to Ivy as if he wanted to say something to her, but perhaps thinking better of it, only gave her a nod and hurried up the stairs. Ivy wasn't sure if she was relieved or disappointed.

"I'll go up too," she said after a pregnant pause in which she felt as if all four ladies were staring at her.

To her dismay, Daphne, Sophia, and Gemma followed behind her and without asking permission, filed in through the door to her bedchamber.

Polly was there watching two footmen like a hawk while they filled the slipper tub in Ivy's dressing room. Turning when she heard the door though, she rushed forward. "Miss, I'm glad to see you're well. The rains came upon us sudden-like, and I just knew you were caught up in it."

Once the footmen were gone, and Ivy's fellow scholars had seated themselves around the room, the maid led her like a child into the dressing room and helped her out of her wet clothes, *tut-tutting* and *tsk-tsking* all the way when she saw how wet her pelisse and gown were, and pronounced that her boots needed a thorough cleaning. "I'll take these down, and you get into that hot bath at once."

Thanking the girl, and grateful for the chance to be alone after her ordeal, Ivy slid into the hot water, her cold skin stinging a little at the change in temperature. She closed her eyes and breathed in the lavender-scented steam, and was once more in the little cottage, Quill's warm body heavy on hers. How could a few hours have changed her whole life so utterly? For though she hadn't agreed to anything yet, she had a feeling that one way or the other Quill would get his way. From the moment they'd met she'd known he was a man accustomed to getting his way. And though she'd since learned that he didn't lack the capacity for compromise, he was certainly not quick to change his mind. Or to admit defeat.

A knock on the door broke into her reverie, and she called out for them to come in—for she had little doubt who had knocked.

"Surely you didn't think you could just hide away in here and escape us," Sophia said cheerily as she stepped in, followed by Daphne and Gemma.

"She's relentless," Gemma said to Ivy with an apologetic smile. "It is far easier to concede defeat in the face of her inquiries."

"How unloyal you are, Gem," her sister chided. "I am perfectly reasonable. I simply have an inquisitive nature. That is all."

"That is what I try to tell people about me," Daphne said, aggrieved. "But I am forever being called rude and impertinent. But why should I not ask questions when I have them? It is how one learns, after all."

Having grown up with a houseful of sisters, Ivy was used

to a lack of privacy and to being interrogated. So she wasn't particularly worried about her ability to keep her own counsel. Still, there was something familiar about being surrounded by inquisitive ladies that made her feel at home, and for that she was grateful.

While they chatted amongst themselves, she washed her hair, and finally warm and ready to talk, she said, "If you'll hand me that towel, Sophia, I'll get out of the tub and we can go see if the sandwiches have been sent up." As if to emphasize her words, her stomach gave a low growl.

"By all means," Sophia said, handing her the towel. Ivy stood and wrapped herself up in it and used another for her hair.

Once she'd dried off and wrapped herself in a thick robe, she led the other three into her bedchamber, where a pot of tea and a plate of sandwiches had been laid out on a little serving table near the fire.

Bless Mrs. Bacon, she thought as she took a seat and bit into one of the sandwiches.

Gemma, meanwhile, poured each of them a cup of the steaming tea.

"I must confess that I thought for a while on the trek back that I'd never be warm again," Ivy said after a few fortifying sips. "I've never been so happy to be indoors in my life."

"Did you get your letter posted?" Sophia asked with an ease that made Ivy suspicious. "It must have taken quite a bit of time, for you were gone for several hours."

"We looked in on the local physician so that Lord Kerr could thank him for all he did for Lady Celeste while she was ill," Ivy said in what was not precisely a lie—Quill had thanked Dr. Vance. It was just that it hadn't been *all* they'd talked about. "That took quite a bit, for his wife came to look in on us and we chatted for quite a long while."

"That was kind of his lordship," Gemma said with approval. "I gather from what Lady Serena has said, he and his aunt were quite close."

"Then one would think he would respect her wishes and not be so difficult about her leaving Beauchamp House to us," Daphne said, her lips pursed in disapproval. "It isn't as if he is destitute without this house. According to Lady Serena, the Kerr marquisate counts seven estates and manor houses amongst its holdings. And that's not counting Kerr Castle and the London townhouse."

Ivy felt her heart beat faster at hearing the extent of Quill's estates. If she were to accept his proposal, lacking in finesse as it had been, she would be mistress of all those places.

Never in her life had she longed for the sort of wealth generations of Kerrs had likely taken for granted. Oh, on occasion she'd wished her family had enough to own their own carriage or to buy some hat that had taken her fancy. But that wasn't the same as wishing she could become a marchioness and move in wealthy circles. She found most social evenings tedious and would rather speak with a hundred impoverished scholars than one society fribble. The idea of being forced to do so for the rest of her life was disconcerting to say the least.

"I suppose he has a sentimental attachment to it," Gemma said with a shrug. "I'd be the same if strangers were to inherit our family home."

"They will," Sophia said wryly. "Though we can hope that Papa will live for a very long time before Cousin Everett can even dream of inheriting."

"We can only hope," Gemma said "It's not the same as what's happened here with Beauchamp House, of course, since he has his own estate, but I can understand somewhat his reluctance to accept his aunt's decision."

"You're quiet, Ivy," Sophia said, her gaze intent. "And you've spent more time than any of us in Lord Kerr's company. What do you think about his reaction to learning we'd inherited Beauchamp House?"

Ivy blushed, hoping that her changed attitude toward Quill wasn't as obvious to them as it was to her. "I can see why he would be disappointed, of course," she said after a moment, with what she hoped was a careless shrug. "But I think he's resigned himself to it. At least, that is what he implied this afternoon. We didn't really talk much about it."

"What *did* you talk about, then?" Gemma asked, her curiosity making her eyes bright. "For I must confess I find him handsome as the very devil."

"Don't swear, Gemma," Sophia said reflexively as if used to correcting this impropriety on her sister's part.

Gemma rolled her eyes, confirming Ivy's suspicion that this was a common argument between the sisters.

Wishing she could latch onto their quibbling instead of answering Gemma's question, Ivy decided that a direct response would likely be less suspicious.

"We spoke about all sorts of things," she said breezily. "He told me a little about how he and his cousins spent childhood summers here. And he told me quite a bit about Lady Celeste and her championing of bluestocking issues."

"You must have had a long time to talk waiting out the storm," Sophia said with a speaking glance as Ivy realized that she'd been far less clever about hiding her feelings than she'd thought.

"I suppose so," she responded with a nervous laugh. "I didn't really notice."

"Hmm," Gemma said, her eyes narrowing with suspicion. "An afternoon alone, a convenient rainstorm. Just what *did* happen on the road from the village, Miss Wareham?"

Chapter 16

Ivy was saved from replying to Gemma's question by Daphne, though perhaps "saved" wasn't quite the right term.

"Your gown was almost dry when you arrived back," Daphne declared into the silence that followed Gemma's query. "So you must have waited it out somewhere. The air is far too wet for it to have done so while you walked back. Therefore, you must have got wet, gone indoors with a fire, then set out once the rain stopped. Either that or you never got wet in the first place."

Ivy bit back a frustrated sigh as she felt all three ladies staring at her with varying degrees of curiosity. So much for keeping the interlude in the little cottage a secret, she thought.

"As it happens," she said raising her chin in defiance at her companions' raised brows, "we did take shelter in a little cottage the shepherds use. It was quite rustic, but it was at least dry. Lord Kerr built a fire and that helped to dry our clothes."

"How cozy," Gemma said with a twinkle in her eyes. "I might even go so far as to call it romantic."

"I do not know why ladies are so intent upon calling what is a perfectly rational response to being caught in the rain romantic," Daphne argued. "We do not call it romantic when the wild animals seek out shelter from a storm."

"But we are not animals, Daphne," said Sophia with a tilt of her head. "Indeed, such an interlude could be called scandalous in some circles. I certainly do not think Lady Serena would be pleased to know of it. I wonder if Lord Kerr will tell her. For it behooves him as a gentleman to do so."

At this idea, Ivy sat up straighter. Surely he wouldn't. He'd promised.

"However," Sophia continued, "I suspect he will not. Unless something untoward happened while you were there."

Ivy's guilt must have shown on her face, for Gemma clapped her hands. "It did! Did he kiss you? Of course he did. A man like that would never let an occasion like that—being holed up with a pretty girl—pass by without taking some sort of liberty."

Despite herself, Ivy felt the need to defend Quill. "You must have a very poor opinion of Lord Kerr," she said with a frown.

But far from being abashed, Gemma shrugged. "Not particularly, but he is a man who seems to know what he wants. And one would have to be blind not to notice how he looked at you last night."

"And how was that?" Ivy asked, half-dreading the answer.

"As if he wanted to bed you," Daphne said baldly.

At the collective gasp from the other ladies, Ivy scowled. "It was obvious that was what he wanted. Men are quite transparent about that sort of thing at times. Ridiculous society rules mean we cannot speak openly of such things, but I thought you were all too smart to fall prey to those things."

"Daphne, dearest," said Ivy after a muffled laugh, "we might all of us think that society rules are silly at times, but that doesn't mean we should speak whatever crosses our minds. It might prove uncomfortable for one's companions. And one doesn't wish to make others uncomfortable, does one?"

"I can hardly be held responsible for how another person feels," Daphne said with a shake of her head. "For one thing, I have a very hard time knowing what others feel to begin with. But I will agree that I do not wish to make others unhappy. I simply cannot seem to figure out why plain speaking is so wrong. If we are to understand one another, why not be as precise as we can be?"

"It's all right, Daphne," said Sophia, squeezing the other girl's arm. "We are private here, so you haven't offended anyone. And your assessment of Lord Kerr's looks at Ivy is accurate. I would have put it more delicately, but that's beside the point." Turning to Ivy, she continued, "I find it very hard to believe that a man who gets what he wants most of the time would not take the opportunity to steal a kiss at the very least while you were all alone together."

Knowing that if she did not tell them, they'd continue to harass her until she confessed, Ivy sighed. "Yes, he kissed me. Are you happy now? You have winkled out my secret."

"I knew it!" Gemma said with triumph. "Especially when the two of you could barely look at each other when you returned. A word of advice for the next time this situation befalls you, my dear. Do not avoid the gentleman's gaze. It quite gives you away when you do that. You have to behave as normal no matter how much you might balk at the thought."

"I'll keep that in mind for the next time I must take shelter from a storm with a handsome gentleman, Gemma," Ivy said wryly. "I thank you for the advice."

"It is unlikely that such a thing will happen again," Daphne said. "The odds are quite steep."

Ignoring the other two, Sophia eyed Ivy with a suspicious eye. "Men have been called out for less, Ivy. Unless of course he offered to make things right."

Not liking the direction Sophia's enquiry was taking, Ivy changed the subject. "I almost forgot the most frightening part," she said, hoping that the others would forget about her confession about Quill. "We were almost run over by a runaway cart."

That had the effect Ivy had been looking for.

"In the village?" Gemma demanded, her brow furrowed.

"Was this before or after you were caught in the storm?" Sophia asked, looking concerned. "Either way, it's no wonder you were out of sorts, you poor thing."

"I was once almost trampled by a horse," Daphne offered with a sympathetic nod. "It was quite unpleasant."

Grateful that her subterfuge had worked, Ivy couldn't help but recall that the incident *had* been unsettling. "Lord Kerr was able to get me out of the way in time, but it was a near thing."

Speculatively, Sophia tilted her head to look at Ivy. "That explains the kissing, then," she said with an air of one who knows.

"What do you mean?" Ivy asked.

"Danger," Sophia said firmly. "It brings out the baser passions."

Thinking about just how passionate Quill had been in the little cottage, Ivy couldn't help but agree. Still, she didn't want to go down that conversational road again. "I find myself quite exhausted after this morning's ordeal," she said, and was then overcome by an actual sigh of exhaustion. "Do you mind very much if we discuss this later?"

Sophia shook her head in disappointment, but did not press. "I can only imagine," she said softly, and Ivy was quite certain that Sophia had guessed the truth.

Her sister, meanwhile, rose and gave Ivy an impulsive hug. "I'm quite jealous, you know," she said with a grin that removed any sting from the pronouncement. "If he weren't obviously dazzled by your beauty, I would have tried to catch his eye myself. But I don't think he would be the sort to enjoy digging around in the sand for fossils, so I'll concede gracefully."

"You are pale," Daphne said, eyeing Ivy as if she were one of Gemma's fossils. "And there are dark circles beneath your eyes. You should rest."

After Gemma's praise of her beauty, Ivy almost laughed outright at Daphne's plain speaking. "Thank you, Daphne. I will endeavor to rest so that I will look better at supper."

"Don't think this is over," Sophia said into Ivy's ear as she gave her a hug. Then, with a saucy wink, she followed the other two from the room.

Ivy shut the door behind them and fell back against it with a sigh.

It seemed years since she'd gone down to breakfast this morning. But rather than dwell on everything that had happened, she padded on bare feet over the thick carpet and climbed into her bed, which Polly had turned down for her before she had slipped out.

She was asleep almost before she could pull up the coverlet.

After he'd had a bath and changed into dry clothes, Quill made his way downstairs in search of Serena. He might not divulge the whole of what had passed in the little cottage, but he would at the very least let her know that he meant to offer for Ivy. Let her make of that what she would.

He found his cousin in her private sitting room going over the household accounts with Mrs. Bacon. As soon as he stepped into the room, however, the housekeeper rose and gathered up the ledger she and Serena had been looking through.

"I'm pleased to see you're none the worse for wear after your soaking, my lord," she said with the ease of someone who had known him since he was younger than Serena's boy. "I'll just come back later to finish up with these, my lady," she said to Serena before leaving the room with a curtsy.

"I hope that Ivy, too, is none the worse for wear," Serena said wryly after the door had closed behind Mrs. Bacon. "For I had the feeling when you both returned that something more than just being caught in the rain had occurred. Of course, that may have been my imagination. Please tell me that is the case."

Moving to stand before the fireplace, where he made a closer-than-necessary examination of a fatuous-looking shepherdess figurine, Quill was silent for a moment before turning around to meet Serena's eyes.

"Perhaps," he said with a slight shrug. "But that is between Miss Wareham and myself."

Serena's eyes narrowed. "Since I have been entrusted with her care while she is under this roof," she said with raised brows, "then I believe that is not quite true."

"And because you are her chaperone," he said calmly, "I have come to tell you that I mean to offer for Miss Wareham's hand. So the particulars of this afternoon are not the point."

But rather than being placated, Serena was so annoyed she rose from her chair and began to pace. "I should never have agreed to let her go with you this morning. I knew one of them would likely get into some scrape while I was in charge of them, but I never imagined it would happen in the first few days of their residency. In Ivy's case, it's only her first full day in Beauchamp House. That must be some sort of record!"

"Do not take on so, Serena," Quill said, stepping in his cousin's path to stop her agitated trek across the carpet. "It's no reflection on you as a chaperone. These things happen. You could hardly predict that a storm would force us to take shelter alone in an uninhabited cottage."

"Oh god," Serena groaned. "Could you be any more of a cliché? A cottage in the rain, Quill? It might have been penned in a Minerva Press novel, it's so trite. I might have expected it from you. But I thought Miss Wareham was much more sensible than to fall prey to your charms. And you, as the head of the family, know better."

Something about her dismissal rankled with him. Perhaps it was a cliché, but it had been damned cozy in that cottage. *A damned sight more than this room at present,* he thought. "I will thank you not to speak about my betrothed's sense— lacking or otherwise," he said through clenched teeth. "And I am well aware of what my duty is. Which is why I intend to marry her."

Pinching the bridge of her nose, Serena struggled to get hold of her emotions. "You are right. I apologize. I was over-set." She collapsed into the chair she'd so recently vacated. "But do you have feelings for Ivy, or is this something you are doing out of honor? For I will not force the girl into a love-less marriage. Especially when the only people who know that you were even alone with her are the two of you."

He knew all too well what Serena's own marriage had been like, and while he understood her desire to shield Ivy from such a union, he also was a little offended that she would put him in the same category as Fanning. He certainly had never raised his hand to a woman as that monster had done.

"I am not Fanning," he said, trying not to let his hurt color his voice. "And though I do not claim to love Miss Wareham, there is a certain affinity between us that I think might grow into something deeper."

At his denial, Serena reached out and touched him on the arm. "I am sorry, Quill. I know you are cut from a different cloth entirely. I just . . ." she paused, as if searching for the right words.

"You don't have to explain," he said gently. "I understand. Truly. And you needn't worry. I promise to treat her well."

"I know you will," she said with a smile. "Of course you will. I am being silly."

"You are being a mother hen, which is exactly why Aunt Celeste chose you to chaperone her girls," Quill said with an answering smile. "She knew what she was about."

At the mention of Celeste, Serena's eyes softened. "She did, didn't she. Though I doubt even *she* could have predicted that Ivy would fall prey to your charms so soon into her residence."

Quill laughed. "No, though she did tell me once that my charm would be my undoing. I daresay this is as swift a comeuppance as she'd have wished."

"Will you ride to Oxford tomorrow to speak to Ivy's father?" Serena asked, already thinking ahead to all the tasks necessary for seeing her charge settled.

At her query, Quill smiled sheepishly. "If I were pleasing myself, that is indeed what I'd do tomorrow. But I have agreed to give Ivy a few days to make up her mind about things."

Serena's brows drew together. "What is there to decide upon? She is compromised. You must marry."

He could not help but say, "Just a moment ago you were vowing to save her from a loveless marriage."

"But that was before I realized whom I was speaking of," Serena said with a wave of her hand.

"What is that supposed to mean?" Quill asked, not quite sure he wished to hear her response.

"Come, Quill," she said with a roll of her eyes. "When have you ever done anything that you didn't wish to do? Ever? I certainly cannot think of anything."

"You make me sound like a very selfish fellow," he said stiffly.

"No," she said, "quite the opposite, in fact. You are generous to a fault because it pleases you to please others. But you are hardly someone who does things out of only propriety. If not following the rules will make someone unhappy, then you will follow them. But if no one would be the wiser, you do what you want."

"And?"

"And, no one but you and Ivy knew about your afternoon together, yet you sought me out to tell me you intended to marry her," Serena said with a triumphant grin. "A man who did not wish to marry Ivy would have kept his mouth shut and prayed no one ever found out."

Which was likely true. He would not ruin his cousin's impression of his romantic nature by telling her that he'd chosen to tell her because he might need an ally should Ivy prove recalcitrant when it came to accepting his proposal. And that far from asking for Ivy's hand out of affection, though he did feel fond of her, it was the fact that she might be carrying his child that made him reveal their tryst to his cousin. Because he would not allow his child to be born out of wedlock.

Keeping his own counsel on the matter, he said instead, "You seem to know me better than I know myself, cousin."

"Of course I do," she said, beaming. "Now, I will say that I think it is a mistake to give Ivy too much time to think this over. But you must make up your mind I suppose."

"I thank you for your permission," Quill said. "Most kind."

"If that is all," Serena said with a speaking look, "I need to finish going over the accounts with Mrs. Bacon."

Knowing when he'd been dismissed, Quill took his leave of her and went in search of Aunt Celeste's brandy bottle.

Chapter 17

Ivy awoke some hours later and for a split second had no idea where she was, what time it was, or why she felt so oddly sore.

Closing her eyes again, the events of earlier in the day came rushing back in a flood of memory and awareness and for a breath she could feel Quill's weight pressing down upon her again, could smell his sandalwood and clean male scent.

This would not do at all.

She'd never been one to wallow in her emotions, and one morning's passion was hardly reason to begin now. Yes, Quill was a handsome man, and he had been all that she could have wished for in a lover. Of course she had no one to compare him to, but she had found their encounter pleasurable enough. Certainly she understood now why so many of the women in the reformatory she worked with back in Oxford fell prey to such desires. It had been a heady feeling indeed to share that nearness, that vulnerability with him.

But thankfully, Quill had agreed to give her time to decide if it warranted a betrothal. She was well aware that a man so accustomed to having his own way in everything did not generally have the inclination to grant such a demand.

That Quill had done so spoke to the inherent fairness in his nature. A sign, no doubt, that he would perhaps make for an agreeable husband.

Still, she was not going to spend every waking moment between now and two days from now thinking only of what she should do.

She'd learned long ago that the mind had a way of working things out while one did other things. And the "other thing" that was most important at the moment was discovering who had so callously murdered Lady Celeste. A woman who, as far as Ivy could tell, had never harmed anyone in her life and should be alive and well to share the finer points of her impressive collection of books and artifacts with the four young women she had chosen to share them with.

Tossing back the covers, she reached for the bell pull to summon Polly and was soon dressed for dinner.

"There, miss," said Polly, putting the finishing touches on Ivy's upswept hair. "The gentlemen won't know what hit them."

Staring at her reflection in the glass of the dressing table, Ivy had to admit that she was looking well. She would miss Polly's skill with a hairpin when she returned to Oxford. *If* she returned to Oxford, she amended, trying to accustom herself to the notion with some difficulty. Which surprised her given her eagerness to escape the little house where she'd shared a single maid with five sisters. Perhaps Pope was right and familiarity did breed contempt.

Then, Polly's words filtered through.

"Gentlemen?" she asked, turning to face the maid. "Has someone else arrived besides Lord Kerr?"

And to her surprise Polly blushed. "Oh, yes, miss. Lady Serena's brother, the Duke of Maitland, arrived in his high perch phaeton while you were sleeping."

"His grace is handsome, then?" Ivy asked with a teasing

smile. It was amusing to see the serious maid all atwitter. Clearly, Ivy thought wryly, Polly was impressed with the duke.

"It is impertinent for me to say so, miss," Polly said with a grin, "but, yes. Quite handsome. And dashing."

"And dashing," Ivy repeated. She supposed high perch phaetons were rare in this part of the country, but clearly the Duke of Maitland was something out of the ordinary to make Polly grin like a lunatic.

"Then I suppose I'd best make my way downstairs to see this paragon for myself," she said rising. She wished suddenly she'd been able to bring a better evening gown with her. She knew the deep green silk was striking with her hair and eyes, but it was hardly as fine as anything Daphne or the Hastings sisters had. When she packed her things to travel to the south coast, she'd assumed she would spend most evenings with her fellow scholars. If she'd known she would be rubbing shoulders with dukes and marquesses, she'd have been more careful about what she brought.

As a general rule she wasn't overly concerned with fashion, but she had no wish to look a dowd either.

Quill hadn't seemed to notice, and if he did mind, he'd simply have to come to terms with it, she thought grimly. She might wish for finery on occasion, but in this instance he would have to take her as she was. Outmoded gown and all.

"You're as fine as five pence, miss," Polly said to her as she opened the door into the hall for Ivy. "The duke won't be able to look away," she said in a conspiratorial tone.

But Ivy was more concerned with the gaze of a certain marquess.

When she reached the first landing, where a tall clock ticked away the minutes, she realized she was a few minutes early. On impulse, when she reached the first landing she kept going to the ground floor and made her way into the servants' hall.

If Dr. Vance's assertion that Lady Celeste's maid had brewed herbal tisanes for her mistress was correct, then the cook must have seen her doing so.

As soon as she stepped into the kitchen, however, she realized that it was not the best time to question the cook or any of the upper servants who would be involved in serving dinner. The room was a beehive of activity, but as soon as Mrs. Mason saw her, she set down the heavy tureen she carried and bowed.

"Miss Wareham," she said with a curtsy. And everyone else, from kitchen maid to Greaves, the butler, bowed or curtsied.

"Is there something you need, miss?" Greaves asked with formality.

"I am sorry," Ivy said with a shake of her head. "I've come at a bad time. I'll return later when you aren't so busy. Though I must say, this smells so delicious I look forward to sampling it at dinner."

Turning, she saw Mrs. Bacon standing behind her. Before the lady could curtsy, Ivy stepped forward and said, "Mrs. Bacon, will you walk with me a little?"

Not betraying a hint of surprise or question, the housekeeper nodded and walked beside Ivy toward the terminus of the servant's hall in the front entrance of the house.

"I was hoping you might be able to tell me where Lady Celeste's personal maid went after her ladyship died," Ivy said without preamble. She did not elaborate on why she might want such information, but Mrs. Bacon didn't seem to think it an odd question. Or if she did she did not say so.

"Elsie was able to secure a place as maid to Squire Northman's wife, miss," said Mrs. Bacon. "Mrs. Northman is a bit of a social climber, if you don't mind my saying so, miss. And I suspect she was quite pleased with herself to steal away

Elsie from Beauchamp House. Even if there was no longer a lady here for Elsie to serve once poor Lady Celeste died. Lady Serena brought her own maid, you see and there was no call for Elsie anymore. So it was a good move for her. A step down, if you ask me. Her family is from around here, though, so she was pleased to keep a situation in the same neighborhood."

It was far more than Ivy had expected from the taciturn housekeeper. And learning that Elsie was nearby was good news, indeed, since she wished to ask her about the tisanes the maid had brewed for her mistress. There were few people who controlled what a lady consumed on a daily basis more influential than a maid. From her morning chocolate to her hot milk before bed, a maid brought everything but meals served at table to a lady. It would be difficult to poison meals as a maid because a maid had no reason to go near the meals. But things served in the bedchamber were another story.

"Thank you so much, Mrs. Bacon. You have been most helpful. I had heard that Elsie was quite enterprising when it came to concocting medicinal tisanes for Lady Celeste's headaches. I was hoping to get the recipe."

At that the housekeeper sniffed. "I'm not sure she'll deign to give it to you, miss," she said tartly. "She was quite secretive about those tisanes of hers was Elsie. Wouldn't give the recipe to any of us, that's for certain."

Interesting, Ivy thought. Now she was even more eager to speak to Elsie.

Before she could take her leave of the housekeeper, Mrs. Bacon said with some diffidence, "I heard about what happened in the village yesterday, Miss Wareham."

For one brief moment, Ivy thought she was speaking of the interlude in the cottage and felt a jolt of real fear run down her spine. But Mrs. Bacon's next words made her sag with relief. "Yes, his lordship told one of the grooms about the runaway cart on the road back from Little Seaford. I am glad neither of you was hurt, Miss. I don't know what this world is coming to with such reckless drivers on the roads at all hours."

Touched by the normally starchy woman's genuine concern, Ivy thanked her.

Just then, they reached the front hall. Bidding the housekeeper good evening, Ivy headed back upstairs toward the drawing room where the household gathered before dinner. She was almost to the doorway, and deep in thought, when she collided with a hard male chest.

"Oh, I do apologize," she said as the gentleman reached out to grasp her by the shoulders. Looking up, and then up again, into a pair of twinkling gray eyes, she surmised that this must be the Duke of Maitland who had set Polly's heart aflutter.

"The fault is all mine, my dear girl," said the duke with a sweeping bow. "I am forever tripping over these feet of mine. They're quite large as you can see, and if they didn't get me from one place to another I'd get rid of them all together."

"That would be quite inconvenient, I would imagine," Ivy said wryly in response to this absurdity.

"I daresay you are right," he said easily as he walked beside her into the drawing room where the rest of the house was already gathered.

Before Ivy could step over to where the other bluestockings were chatting, the man beside her addressed Lady Serena who was in conversation with Quill.

"Serena, you must introduce me to this beautiful creature at once," the duke said to his sister. "For I nearly knocked her down just now and a proper apology demands a proper name, doesn't it?"

Ivy was quick to note Quill's scowl at the other man, and the way he looked from Ivy to the duke and back again.

Lady Serena, however, seemed accustomed to her brother's odd manners, and as Ivy and the duke stepped closer to them she said, "Dalton, I vow you are the clumsiest man I've ever met. And that includes Father who fell off his own horse I don't know how many times."

The duke shrugged, as if to ask what one could do.

"This creature, as you so suavely call her," Lady Serena continued, "is Miss Ivy Wareham, one of the four lady scholars Aunt invited to Beauchamp House upon her death."

If looks could kill, the one Quill was leveling at the Duke of Maitland would have felled the fellow in a second.

"Ivy," the duke sighed. "What a prosaic name for such a lovely lady," he said as he bowed over her hand.

"Her actual name is Aphrodite," said Lady Daphne who had wandered over along with the other ladies as if the duke were a flame and they the moths. "Which is much more fitting if you ask me."

Before Ivy could respond, however, she watched as the duke got his first glimpse of Daphne. If his response to her had been that of a puppy eager for a treat, the look he gave the willowy blonde was as full of heat as anything she'd ever seen before. And if she didn't miss her guess, Daphne was not exactly giving him the cold shoulder.

Rolling her eyes, Serena made the introductions of the three ladies, and though the duke was polite to all of them, there was a little something more in his bow over Daphne's hand. As if he were making an offering to the goddess she was named for.

Ivy, on the other hand, was not as impressed with him as Daphne seemed to be. He was handsome, she supposed. If one were attracted to blond giants with aquiline features.

She found she much preferred a certain marquess with blue eyes that could burn cold or hot as his mood changed, with a tendency toward seriousness. A humorous man like the duke would wear on her nerves after a bit, she suspected.

Just then the dinner bell rang and Quill took her arm, despite the fact that the order of precedence indicated he should be taking in Lady Serena—Daphne, of course, was on the arm of the duke.

"It's a good thing he fixed his eye on Daphne," Quill said in an undertone, "else I'd have been forced to call out my own cousin."

The rumble of his voice was enough to raise the hairs on the back of Ivy's neck in response. "I'm not so sure Daphne is such a good idea, either," she answered as he reached for her chair.

"I don't really care just now," Quill said ruthlessly. "So long he keeps his paws off you."

The look he gave was one that sent a thrill through her, and Ivy was forced to steel herself against the magnetic pull he exerted on her.

This was certainly not the sort of thing her mother would approve of for the dining table. Or at all. Ever.

Before she could reprimand the marquess however, he was taking his own seat beside her and chatting amiably with Serena on his left.

Chapter 18

Quill bit back a sigh as yet another peal of laughter rang out at some quip from his cousin. He was fond of Maitland—indeed counted the duke as one of his best friends in the world—but his easy way with the ladies was something he'd always envied. And while he waited for Ivy to make up her mind about his proposal, he was hardly eager to have Maitland, with his good looks and charm, lure her away. Though Ivy was showing no signs of attraction for the other man now, he hadn't known her long enough to assess whether she could be persuaded if Maitland got it in his head to woo her.

He'd simply have to warn his cousin away after dinner. That was all there was to it.

"Stop scowling," Serena said from his other side in a low voice only he could hear. "You look like you're going to leap across the table and strangle him. And while I sympathize with your fondness for Miss Wareham, I hardly think he will seduce her in front of a room full of people. Not to mention the fact that Ivy does not strike me as the sort of lady to give herself to one man in the morning and another in the evening."

Serena's words made Quill feel like an ass. It hadn't occurred to him how unfair to Ivy his jealousy was until she put it that way.

Taking a healthy drink of wine, he turned to her with a rueful smile. "I suppose I am being a boor, but I was hoping for a swift decision from her. And didn't count on Maitland and his charms to distract her." Before she could speak again, he raised a hand to ward off her scold. "I know it's asinine. Believe me, you can't chastise me more than I do myself."

Serena's gaze softened a little. "Have faith, Quill. If the way he and Lady Daphne are looking at each other is any indication, you have nothing to worry about. And aside from that, Ivy keeps looking at you when you aren't watching her. I don't think you have anything to worry about from my brother."

Frowning, Quill turned and caught Ivy watching him. As their eyes met, her cheeks colored and she turned her gaze back to her plate.

The reminder of what lay between them was enough to dispel any doubts he had, and Quill vowed to do as Serena asked and have more faith. Having grown up with a mother who often flouted her own lovers before his father's eyes, however, it was difficult to acknowledge that not all women were like that.

"Is the fish to your liking?" he asked, wishing for an iota of whatever it was that made Maitland so easy at conversation. "I must admit Mrs. Mason's Trout Almondine is one of my favorites."

"It's quite good," Ivy agreed, then proceeded to take another bite. "I was looking forward to it as soon as I smelled it downstairs."

At that he frowned. "Why were you downstairs?"

"I went to ask about Lady Celeste's maid," Ivy said in a confidential tone. "Because of the tisanes."

He supposed he shouldn't be surprised that she was back to looking for his aunt's murderer, Quill thought wryly. Here he'd been mooning away over her like a lovestruck school-boy, and Ivy was thinking of solving a murder.

"And what did you learn?" he asked, intrigued despite his pique. "Anything of use?"

"Apparently she was quite secretive about what she put in them," Ivy said, pausing as the footman removed her plate. When they were back out of earshot, she continued, "And Mrs. Bacon said that she took a position with Mrs. North-man, Squire Northman's wife. Do you know them?"

At the mention of Mrs. Northman, Quill felt a pang of panic. Not only did he know Squire and Mrs. Northman, sev-eral years ago when he'd been young and foolish he'd en-gaged in an illicit liaison with the bored wife of the local landowner.

Aloud, however, Quill did not betray that he was more than distantly acquainted with the Northmans. "I believe I have met them when they were here to dine a few times."

The mention of his former lover so soon after his own unwarranted jealousy of his cousin could not be a coinci-dence. At least, not insofar as the Almighty was concerned. And Ivy's next words only confirmed it. "I believe I will pay a call on Mrs. Northman tomorrow," she said firmly. "I will ask about the tisanes and see if she will allow me to speak with Elsie. Surely there can be nothing objectionable about that."

Quill could think of a dozen things to object to in the no-tion of Ivy paying a call at the home of a man whom he'd cuckolded, but he could hardly say so aloud.

He was saved from reply by Serena however, and almost laughed aloud at her words.

"Are you speaking of the Northmans? For I received an

invitation this afternoon asking all of us to dine in their home tomorrow evening. Mrs. Northman accounts herself to be a leader of local society—though to be honest, I think she will give herself more airs now that our aunt is no longer here to outrank her."

"You and I outrank this lady," said Daphne bluntly as the whole table turned their attention to Serena. "So, she has no reason for smugness, I think."

Despite his dyspepsia at the idea of sitting at the Northman dinner table, Quill couldn't help but grin at Maitland's wide-eyed astonishment at Lady Daphne's words. That young lady's plain speaking took a bit of getting used to, even if she was beautiful in her way. He himself was partial to redheads, but he could see that Daphne's willowy blonde looks were handsome enough.

Still, if Maitland meant to fix the attentions of someone like Lady Daphne, the sooner he became accustomed to her blunt talk the better. Otherwise he would live in a perpetual state of open-mouthed shock. Though come to think of it, paired with Maitland's own charm, Lady Daphne's talk might not seem so impolite.

"That is perhaps true, Daphne," said Serena with a speaking look, "but it is not the thing for you to say it aloud."

"But you are the one who mentioned that this Mrs. Northman puts on airs," Daphne protested with a frown. "I don't see what is so wrong about my own words. We do outrank her. Why is the truth so often the very thing it is impolite to say?"

Quill waited for Serena to explain, but she was forestalled by her brother who said gently, "Perhaps because the truth is so often that which hurts most, Lady Daphne."

Daphne frowned as if thinking over the suggestion. "I suppose that might be true," she said thoughtfully. "I certainly do not like being told I've made a mistake in an equation, no matter how true it might be. Is that what you mean?"

"Something like that," Maitland agreed with a nod. "Though in this case, I believe it's because to say you out-rank someone is considered impolite."

Daphne sighed. "I will never understand what is and is not considered to be polite. Why can I not simply ask where Ivy and Quill sheltered from this storm this afternoon without being shushed by Sophia? And why is it impolite of me to point out that the mud on their boots was dry when they re-turned? It was the truth. And I fail to see how mud can be polite or impolite. Mud simply is."

A silence fell upon the table as the duke eyed Quill with a gleam of speculation in his eyes. So much for giving Ivy a couple of days to sort out her feelings on the matter, he thought while exchanging a chagrined look with her.

"It most certainly is," Maitland agreed with Daphne.

"Why don't we allow the gentlemen to their port, ladies?" Serena said, rising, though some of them hadn't yet finished dessert.

Wordlessly, the other ladies followed, and though Quill wished to reassure Ivy, he let her go with them.

Once they were out of the room, he moved to sit beside Maitland who was grinning like an idiot.

"Don't say anything," he warned the other man with a shake of his head. "For you of all people have no room to cast aspersions."

Picking up the port Greaves had just poured for him, the duke raised it in a toast. "To my dear cousin, who despite be-ing the most disagreeable fellow imaginable still manages to charm the ladies."

"It's only one lady in particular I'm concerned with at the moment, Maitland," Quill said with a scowl. "And I'll thank you to stay away from her while you're here. I'm having enough difficulty convincing her to set aside her freedom and marry me without having to compete with your damned Viking charm."

But his cousin only laughed. "I wouldn't dream of it, old fellow. I'm just shocked to see you caught in the parson's mousetrap by dint of something as innocuous as a rainstorm. At the very least I hope you were able to kiss the chit during this tryst."

Quill's silence told what had happened in the little cottage more loudly than his words might have done.

Maitland whistled. "So, it's that way, is it? I'm surprised, I must admit. I always thought you were the more controlled of us two. I certainly never expected a pretty redhead to tempt you into giving up your freedom. Though she does possess the most spectacular pair of ti—"

His voice broke off as Quill's hand gripped him by the neck. "Mind yourself. That's my future wife you're speaking of."

When his cousin nodded, grin still intact, Quill removed his hand.

"My apologies," said Maitland with a huff of laughter as he straightened his cravat. "Won't happen again, I assure you. I was trying to assess your degree of affection for the girl. I think your grip on my throat speaks volumes."

"And I suppose you couldn't just ask like a normal person?" Quill groused. He didn't like losing control and he'd done so quite thoroughly twice already today. This was getting to become a habit.

"Where's the fun in that?" Maitland laughed, running a hand over top of his blond hair. "At the very least I know the truth now rather than the polite fiction I suspect you'd have given me if I asked. You like to play these things close to the vest."

"Because they're nobody's business but my own," Quill said heatedly. "You always were too damned nosy by half."

"Not nosy, cuz," said the duke. "Concerned. If I thought you'd been nabbed by a fortune hunter whom you held in contempt, then I'd see to it that she was paid well and sent on her way."

At the idea of Ivy as a fortune hunter, Quill laughed. Hard. She might be many things, but he rather thought that if she could be locked away in Aunt Celeste's library for the rest of her years, she would be happier than a young Maitland in the dancer filled green room of the Royal Opera House. If she could come to care one tenth as much for him as she did for one of her Greek fragments, he'd count himself a lucky man.

"I can see then," Maitland said with a grin, "that my fears are misplaced. You can't blame me though. These four chits with their bluestocking tendencies who were chosen by who knows what means by Aunt Celeste could all murder us in our beds tonight. From what Serena has told me, you know only what they've told you."

"And what the notes from Celeste's investigation revealed," Quill said firmly. "She was no fool, Aunt Celeste. Whatever her reasons for choosing these four, she made sure she wasn't bringing anyone likely to steal all her artifacts and burn the house down."

"Perhaps not, but I'll keep an eye out on them just the same," Maitland said with a grin. "The lovely Lady Daphne in particular."

"I'd watch myself if I were you," Quill said with a warning note. "Lady Daphne is lovely, but she could cut a man down with a word without a flinch."

"Oh, I certainly hope so," Maitland said wolfishly. "I like a challenge."

"So do I," Quill answered, "but I like my ballocks right where they are, thanks."

But his cousin waved away the warning. "You just mind yourself and your little redhead. Leave the sharp tongued Lady Daphne to me."

"With pleasure," Quill said raising his glass.

Chapter 19

"What a handsome man the duke is, don't you think?" Daphne asked the other ladies after they had retired to the drawing room.

Lady Serena had gone up to check on Jeremy before bed, though Ivy was quite sure Daphne would have said the same whether their chaperone was with them or not.

"You'd best watch yourself, Daphne," Gemma said with a hiss. "He's far too charming by half. I don't trust him one bit."

"What has trust to do with anything?" Daphne asked, puzzled. "I'm not looking to marry him, after all."

Despite herself, Ivy was once again shocked by the ease with which Daphne spoke about men. Now that she'd actually experienced what being with a man that way entailed, she couldn't imagine doing it with someone for whom she felt nothing. Though she didn't think she could call what she felt for Quill love, she certainly held him in some affection. And though her first instinct had been to ask for more time when he said they should marry, she was beginning to see that refusing to marry him might prove as difficult as marrying him would. And what if there *was* a child? She was just as unhappy at the thought of it being born out of wedlock as he was. No matter how she might believe in the institution itself, it was far more beneficial for men than it was for women.

"Don't fret, dear," said Sophia, putting a comforting arm around her shoulders. "It will work out. I promise."

"No thanks to Daphne," said Gemma with a frown at the blonde. "I thought we'd agreed not to divulge what we knew about happened with Ivy and Lord Kerr this morning."

Daphne frowned. "I don't see what the big secret is. I daresay the servants are all chattering about it as we speak."

"That's not the point," Sophia said with a sigh. "Now not only we know, but Lady Serena and her brother the duke know too."

But Ivy had a good idea that Lady Serena had known before Daphne's outburst, at least that was what she'd guessed on seeing the chaperone's lack of surprise at Daphne's words. She wondered if Quill had spoken to her or if she'd guessed on her own. It would be just like Quill to confess to her, she thought with a grimace. Despite his promise to give her time he would have felt the mark on his honor keenly. It was an insult to Lady Serena for him to have seduced Ivy, no matter how much Ivy might be loath to admit that's what it had been, and he would wish to unburden himself on her.

"And what has that to say in the matter?" Daphne asked.

"It means that Ivy will have to marry the marquess whether she wishes to or not." Sophia said.

"I don't see why," Daphne argued.

Ivy sighed. Sometimes conversing with Daphne was like beating one's head against a wall only to have the wall change direction and hit you on the back of the head instead.

"That's because they're either already married or they've got no reputation to preserve to begin with," Gemma said patiently. "One indiscretion can spell ruin for someone like Ivy."

"Oh," Daphne looked genuinely troubled by the news. Just when Ivy was ready to dismiss her as completely devoid of fellow-feeling, the mathematician surprised her with a burst of compassion. "I am sorry, Ivy."

"I don't necessarily think that Daphne's pronouncement means that I shall be forced to marry the marquess," Ivy said trying to put the best face on things. "After all, his lordship and I can refute her claim. And it's not as if anyone found us in the cottage together."

She looked at Sophia and Gemma to gauge their reaction to her words, but the pained smiles that greeted her told more than outright denials would have.

"I'm sure any number of young ladies would be thrilled to receive an offer from the marquess," Sophia said brightly. "He's a feast for the eyes, make no mistake. Have you see the legs on that man? He does justice to a pair of breeches, doesn't he?"

"Indeed he does," said Gemma fanning herself at her sister's words. "And he's quite handsome in a dark, brooding way. I can quite see him as the hero of a gothic novel, all glowering scowls and feats of derring-do to rescue his lady."

Ivy sighed, and dropped onto the nearest settee. "You can stop trying to put the best face on it," she said glumly. "I quite agree that he is handsome. And that he is doubtlessly a prize on the marriage mart. It's just that I wasn't thinking to marry him myself."

Sophia poured her a cup of tea from the tray that one of the maids had brought in discreetly while they talked, and handed it to her, taking the seat beside her.

"I daresay there is a great deal of scholarly work you'd thought to accomplish before doing anything as rash as marrying?" she asked quietly.

"Unless they are of a like mind, I've been told by another lady mathematician," Daphne offered as she settled into a nearby chair, "that husbands can be quite the impediment to scholarly pursuits."

"But that needn't be the case," Gemma offered kindly. "What of Madame d'Arblay? Her husband was quite pleased with her writing and was devoted until her death. Much more so than the lady's own father had been during her childhood." The famous novelist, known as Frances Burney to her readers had made a love match.

"That is quite true," Sophia agreed with a nod, her brown curls bobbing with her vehemence. "She did not write *Camilla* until after her marriage, and I quite enjoyed it. More than *Evelina* even. Though I still have a soft spot for Lord Ormond. So mysterious and handsome."

"Has Lord Kerr voiced any objections to your translation work?" Daphne asked, her pretty brow furrowed. "Because if he has not, then you do not know if he will do so at all. It makes little sense to bemoan something that has yet to occur, doesn't it?"

"That's the first sensible thing you've said this evening, Daphne," said Gemma with approval. "In fact, we do not know what his lordship's attitude will be toward your scholarly pursuits, Ivy. So perhaps you should put the question to him. It cannot hurt, can it?"

"Oh dear," said a deep voice as the door to the drawing room opened to reveal the Duke of Maitland and Lord Kerr. "It sounds as if they are plotting, Kerr," said the duke, raising his quizzing glass to survey each of the four ladies—lingering perhaps a shade longer on Daphne than was strictly necessary. "You must divulge all, ladies, lest you get yourselves into some scrape or other."

His pronouncement was met with four scowls from the ladies, causing his face to fall as quickly as his quizzing glass did, bouncing on its string at his side.

"What's amiss?" he asked quickly, looking to Ivy's skeptical eye like a puppy that has been chastised.

Quill exchanged an amused glance with Ivy before saying, "Perhaps that sort of thing might charm the ladies in London drawing rooms, cuz, but I think you may have insulted this lot, who were, as you well know, chosen by our aunt based upon their artistic and scholarly abilities. As such they are likely smarter than you and I put together on our best day with a fifty-yard head start."

At Quill's words, Sophia threw Ivy a speaking look. Perhaps they were right about his respect for her mind, she thought with tentative hope. At the very least he was not dismissive of her like some men were.

"I mean no offense, ladies," said the duke, eyes widened with realization. "Just being a great clumsy oaf as usual."

"I'm sure your teasing was innocent, your grace," Ivy said with a reassuring smile. "We can be a little . . ."

"Overly sensitive," Sophia finished for her as she moved to pour for the newcomers. "Force of habit really. And we've grown a bit too full of our own importance," she added with a glance at Daphne, who shrugged at her words.

"I took no offense, Duke," she said easily. "Though I do admit your words caught me by surprise. We were plotting you see . . . about—"

"Nothing at all," Gemma broke in, moving to grasp Daphne by the shoulder. "We must keep those details to ourselves, Daphne. Do you not remember?"

Ivy gave a sigh of relief, grateful that Gemma had broken into Daphne's confession. She had no wish to have what should be a private conversation between only herself and Quill with the entire drawing room.

"Did you have good weather for your travels, your grace?" she asked hoping to change the subject.

And thankfully the duke took the hint and began to regale them with an amusing story about how his phaeton had nearly collided with a farm cart on the road near Bath. And before long Daphne and the duke lapsed into a good-natured argument on the odds this year for the Royal Ascot, and the Hastings sisters were deep in conversation about some news they'd had in a letter from home that day.

When Quill took the seat beside Ivy, she felt her heart beat faster, try as she might to calm the traitorous organ.

"If nothing else it has been an eventful day," he said quietly, so close that she could see the ring of dark blue circling the lighter blue of his iris and the light tips of gold on his brown lashes. Not to mention the warmth of his thigh innocently pressed against her own.

"If nothing else," she said a little breathlessly.

"I thought I should tell you," he continued, his gaze intent on hers, "that I spoke to Lady Serena about what happened between us today."

Ivy took a beat to decide how she felt about the news. On the one hand he'd agreed to give her a couple of days to make a decision about his offer. But on the other, as a man of honor he would not wish to keep her chaperone in the dark about what he saw as a transgression against propriety on his part.

"And what was her response?" Ivy asked carefully. "Since she did not rouse me from my afternoon sleep to cart us both to the nearest minister, I would hazard a guess that she is letting us make our own decision on the matter?"

He looked down at where her hands clasped together, her knuckles white with the effort to keep them calm. This was a man who looked closely at the world around him, she thought. Who looked before he leapt. That he had so forgot himself earlier in the day was either a sign of how much he'd wanted her, or an indication that like anyone else he could behave impulsively from time to time.

"She is convinced that the best course would be for us to marry by special license," he said with a slight shrug. "But she has agreed to let us do so at our own pace. I did tell her that you are free to decline my proposal of course."

"And did she agree to keep this news from my family?" she asked, not allowing her apprehension to enter her voice. "Until we are ready to tell them, that is?"

"As I said, she will let us go at our own pace," Quill repeated. Covering her clasped hands with his own, he spoke in a reassuring voice. "It need not be a hardship," he said softly. "We rub along well enough together, I think. And I certainly appreciate that clever mind of yours. Though I cannot claim to be much of a scholar myself."

"How many languages do you speak?" she asked, suddenly, desperately needing to know the answer. She wasn't sure why, but it was the sort of thing a lady like herself should know about the man who wished to marry her. At least, that's what she thought in this moment.

Rather than annoyance, she saw him break into a grin. "I'm not a scholar," he admitted with a shrug, "but languages were something I excelled in at both Eton and Oxford. You have to know some ancient Greek and Latin in order to even be admitted to Oxford, you know."

Ivy waved her hand in the air dismissively. "It's easily enough for a peer to use his influence to get past that requirement for his son."

"Ah," he said chidingly, "but you didn't know my father. He was the least likely man ever to use his influence in such a cause."

She wanted to ask about his father, but decided that was a discussion that would keep for another day.

"So," she continued, "you have some Greek and Latin. And I daresay French, as well, yes?"

He nodded, and Ivy was aware of the fact that his gaze had dropped to her mouth. Really, it was most unfair of him to look at her like that in a room full of other people.

"And German," he said with the air of a boy trying to please a harsh schoolmaster. "And Spanish and some Portuguese."

At her questioning look, he shrugged. "I was in the diplomatic corps during the war. My father did use his influence there—but it was for his own reasons. Didn't want the heir to be placed in mortal danger, after all."

Surprised despite herself, Ivy felt her mouth gape for a second before she quickly snapped it shut.

"Do not look so surprised, my dear," he said with a grin. "I might be a useless aristocrat, but I'm not a complete simpleton. I can certainly carry on a concentration about which word is the best English translation for what I wish to do to your mouth just now."

"*Beso,*" she said in a whisper of Spanish.

"*Je voudrais vous embrasser profondément,*" he said in a tone so low she felt it in her bones.

"*Eu quero te beijar,*" she replied, the Portuguese words falling from her mouth before she knew what she was saying.

"Is there any tea left, or shall I ring for a new pot?" said Lady Serena in a cheerful tone as she stepped into the room.

Ivy nearly tripped in her haste to get to the tea tray—which she had little doubt had prompted the titter she heard from behind her.

"I'll do it," she said reaching for the bell pull. "I hope Jeremy was able to get to sleep peacefully?"

Though the look Serena gave her was searching, she answered easily enough. "Yes, thank goodness. He dislikes going to sleep when he knows there is amusement to be had with the adults downstairs. But I was able to bribe him with a visit to the shore tomorrow with his uncle. I hope you don't mind, Maitland."

"Not a bit," said the duke with a grin from where he stood before the fire. "Nothing I like more than a shell-seeking adventure with Jem. Will you come with us, Kerr? It seems to me we lads should stick together since we're outnumbered by ladies in this house."

Stretching out his long legs before him, Quill nodded. "Indeed. If the weather is fine."

"I hope it will be," Serena said with a worried frown. "Because I do not know what Jeremy's response will be if he is thwarted."

The way she spoke, Ivy would have assumed that Jeremy was the parent rather than the child. But she knew that Lady Serena was merely trying to make the boy happy. There was a hint of sadness in his eyes that told of some darker days when he was not such a big boy.

"I'm not afraid of his reaction," Maitland assured her. "Quill and I were boys once too, you know. And if we can't get to the shore we'll figure something out. At the very least the soldiers I've brought will prove a distraction."

"You will spoil him, Dalton," Lady Serena said with a smile as she lapsed into using his Christian name. "I vow he will be as tyrannical as you were as a boy before the summer is out."

"That's what happens when a boy knows he's a duke before he's out of short coats, Serena," Quill said with a wink at Ivy.

Sure enough, the duke gave a sound of mock outrage. "And I suppose you wish these fine ladies to believe you were a little angel? I could tell tales about the Marquess of Kerr's childhood crimes that would fair make your hair curl, ladies."

And he proceeded to regale them with amusing stories about the cousins' childhood together.

Before long, however, Lady Serena declared it was past time they were all in their beds. And as they filed into the hall and toward the stairs, Ivy found herself walking beside Quill.

When they reached the landing, where the ladies would go left and the gentlemen right, he said in a low voice, "Sweet dreams, Aphrodite."

And wishing despite her misgivings that he could come with her to her bedchamber, she followed the other ladies down the hall into the darkness.

Chapter 20

Though Squire Northman's manor house was not even a mile away as the crow flew, the party at Beauchamp House piled into two carriages for the drive over. One carriage conveyed the Hastings sisters, Lady Daphne, and the Duke of Maitland, while the other carried Ivy, Quill, and Lady Serena.

It did not go unnoticed by Quill that his cousin kept an eagle eye on both her fellow passengers for the duration of the journey. She'd attempted to place the four unmarried ladies in one carriage together, but Quill had insisted that he and Ivy be allowed to ride together. Since the three other ladies in the carriage with Maitland served as their own chaperones, Serena had relented to Quill's demand but then spoiled things by insisting on taking her place with them.

What she expected them to get up to in a closed carriage with her watching was beyond him. He was able, when Serena managed to glance out the window at the passing scenery from time to time, to steal several glimpses of Ivy in the deep red silk she'd chosen for the evening. It was a color that might have looked a horror with her auburn hair, but instead it showed to perfection against her peaches-and-cream skin. He would bet anything that the modest jet beads she wore were warm from her skin, and he spent a good portion of the drive pleasantly imagining what she'd look like in nothing but those beads.

"Ah, that didn't take too long, did it?" Serena asked with a cheerfulness that belied the death stare she gave Quill as the carriage rocked to a stop. Clearly he'd not been as careful at concealing his thoughts as he'd hoped.

Ivy on the other hand, seemed oblivious to them both, staring with interest out the window at the torch-lit entrance to the Northman's sandstone manor house.

Far from feeling easy about the evening to come, Quill jumped down from the carriage before the footman could open the door, and set down the step. Handing first Ivy then Serena down, he squared his shoulders and prepared to make polite conversation with his former lover in the company of his almost betrothed.

While Jem had played happily at the water's edge that morning, Quill had discussed with Maitland the possible complications tonight's supper might cause him when it came to winning Ivy over to his way of thinking when it came to marriage.

"If given a choice," Maitland had said from his seat in the sand beside his cousin, both of them barefoot despite the chill in the air, "I'd make some excuse to keep from walking into that chamber of horrors. But you have no choice. It's the damnedest thing. I don't know how you get yourself into these coils."

Quill had already explained the necessity for he and Ivy to speak with the maid, Elsie, who now worked for Mrs. Northman. The fact that his cousin had come as soon as Quill had sent for him was just one of the things he appreciated about Dalton. He might be the proverbial bull in a china shop at times, but he was a good man. And he'd loved Aunt Celeste as much as Quill had. Like Quill, Dalton and Serena hadn't had the happiest of childhoods, so they too had sought refuge in the home of their favorite aunt whenever it was possible.

But just now, he was of little help at all.

"It's not as if my younger self could guess that one day I'd have to face Cassandra across the table from Ivy," Quill said, thrusting a hand through his already windblown hair. "If I'd had that sort of prescience, I'd have left Cassandra alone in the first place."

"She is a sweet handful, though," Maitland conceded with a shrug. "I wouldn't have turned her down if she'd cast out lures to me, that's for sure."

Quill sighed. "If only I knew that she would behave herself," he said. "It's not knowing that troubles me. I know she won't be so bold that Northman will figure it out. She has no wish to give herself trouble. But if she suspects anything between Ivy and me, she might drop a word in her ear just to make things difficult for me."

"It would all be much better if you'd not ended things badly," Maitland said.

"Thank you, Duke," Quill said dryly. "That never would have occurred to me."

"Don't take out your anger on me, man," his cousin protested. "I'm just here to offer my support."

Now, some hours later at the Northman manor house, Quill couldn't miss the wink his cousin directed at him as the guests were ushered into the main entry hall.

"I am so pleased you were all able to come," said Cassandra Northman from beside her thin, taciturn husband, who nodded at the newcomers but said little. "And you too, your grace. When Lady Serena wrote to ask if you would be welcome too, I wrote her back at once. A duke at one's table must never be turned away."

To Quill's relief, Cassandra said nothing untoward as he moved through the receiving line, and soon he and the other dinner guests were milling about in a drawing room that was gilded within an inch of its life, waiting for the dinner bell.

He made pleasant conversation with the local curate, who was keen to know what news there was from London, and the wife of the local magistrate, who wanted to know if he would be around in the summer for the annual fete.

Soon enough they were all shuffling into the dining room, Quill with Lady Daphne on his arm since she was the next in precedence following Lady Serena, who was on her brother's arm.

Quill was not pleased to learn he was seated at Cassandra's left with Maitland on her right. But at least Ivy was out of earshot in the middle of the table, with the curate on one side and the son of a local gentry family on the other.

"You must tell me every little thing about the latest on-dits in London, my lord," said Cassandra as soon as they were seated, punctuating her words with a rap of her fan on his arm. "It's been far too long since I was there for the season, and I'm simply dying for news."

"You might do better to ask my cousin Maitland," Quill said with a nod in that gentleman's direction, earning him a reproachful look. "He is more lately from London than I am and I daresay his news is fresher."

"But is *he* fresher?" Cassandra said with a mischievous grin. "That is the question." Turning to the duke, she gave him a speculative look, as if weighing the possibilities. At this point, Quill didn't have any regrets about throwing his cousin beneath the wheels of the metaphorical carriage. He could not afford for Ivy to find any reason to reject his suit. Even if that meant Maitland had to take a sabre cut for the whole regiment.

To his relief, his cousin seemed happy enough to flirt with their pretty hostess, and he watched with amusement as they batted the conversational ball back and forth over the various courses. By the time Mrs. Northman rose to indicate that the ladies would leave the gentlemen to their port, Quill was feeling quite happy with the evening so far.

That sanguinity lasted until the men filed into the drawing room and a quick scan of the room showed that both Ivy and Cassandra were conspicuously absent.

"Where the devil are they?" he asked Maitland in an undertone.

"Hmm?" was his unhelpful monosyllable as he fixed his gaze on the spot near the tea tray where Lady Daphne appeared to be explaining the finer points of the Pythagorean theorem to a befuddled-looking local matron. A jab in the ribs was enough to break into Maitland's reverie however. "Hey! What was that for?"

"Use your brainbox for a moment and listen," Quill hissed. "Where are Ivy and Cassandra?"

But Maitland shrugged. "I was in the dining room with you. How should I know? Why don't you ask Serena? She appears to be attempting to get your attention." And sure enough, Lady Serena was leveling a speaking glance in their direction.

Hurrying to her side, Quill tried to look casual as he asked, "What's amiss, cuz?"

"I'm not quite sure," Serena said beneath the hum of conversation. "Ivy and Mrs. Northman left the room not long after we left you all in the dining room. I hope our hostess hasn't figured out there's something between the two of you."

"What do you mean?" Quill asked, despite the fact that he agreed with her. "What has Mrs. Northman to say to it?"

"Well," Serena said tartly, "there is that fact that she was your lover some years ago."

Despite himself, Quill gasped. "How did you know?" he asked in a low voice.

Serena rolled her eyes. "You were one and twenty and as full of your own importance as any young man I've ever known—with the notable exception of my brother. I would be very surprised if everyone in the next county didn't hear of your conquest."

Wincing, Quill recalled that her assessment of him at that time was painfully accurate. "So you think it has something to do with Cassandra wishing to scupper things between Ivy and me?"

"I cannot know," Serena said with a slight lift of her shoulders. "They didn't seem to be at daggers drawn if that helps."

It did. A very little.

"I'm going to intervene," he said firmly. "Ivy is stubborn enough without Cassandra giving her more reasons to reject my proposal."

But it was Serena's turn to gasp. "You cannot simply go blundering around the house looking for them. It's possible there is an innocent explanation for their absence."

"If that is the case," he said grimly, "then they will have no reason to be surprised at my intrusion."

Serena's expression told him they would have every reason, but Quill couldn't afford to let her scruples keep him from the truth.

As unobtrusively as possible, he slipped out of the drawing room and into the hallway. Spying a footman standing at the ready, he strode over to the man. "Do you know where I might find your mistress and Miss Wareham?" And to his shame the man didn't look surprised at all. Instead, he laid a finger alongside his nose and winked.

Good god, he thought in spite of his anxiety. *How many*

lovers had Cassandra had assignations with under her own husband's nose?

Still he followed the directions the man gave him and hurried up the stairs to the hall leading to Cassandra's bedchamber. When he reached the door, he heard the sound of conversation within and, taking a deep breath, he gave a brisk knock and strode inside, as if he had every reason in the world to enter his hostess's bedchamber without invitation.

Instead of Ivy and Cassandra deep in conversation about *him,* however, he found Ivy with a woman he recognized as Elsie, his aunt's former personal maid.

He closed his eyes at his folly.

Of course that was why she'd come up here. His own damnable guilty conscience had made him suspect the worst, when it was all part of the plan he and Ivy had put into place before they even left Beauchamp House earlier in the evening.

"My lord?" she asked, her eyes wide as he walked over to where she and the maid were standing beside Cassandra's writing desk. "What are you doing here?"

"I thought you might be ill," he said with a slight shrug. "I noticed you were gone from the drawing room."

Her raised brow told him what she thought about this explanation. But she clearly thought they should discuss his perfidy once they were alone, because she only said, "Well, as you can see, I am quite well. . . . Go ahead and tell him what you told me, Elsie," she said with a reassuring nod.

Looking from one to the other, Elsie seemed to relax a little. "Begging your pardon, my lord, but I was just telling Miss Wareham here that the recipe for the tisane that Lady Celeste liked for the headache, it wasn't my own." The maid looked sheepish, and even colored a little at the admission.

"My mam was friendly-like with the Rom hereabouts. And she was the one who suggested I go to the old woman there. She gave Mam a tonic that was helpful with me gran's rheumatism. So when her ladyship was struck down with the headache, I went over to where the camps was and I asked the old woman."

"But Elsie didn't mix the powder herself," Ivy said with a speaking look. "She got the powder from the gypsies and added water to it."

Which, Quill realized, meant that the poison was likely added before Elsie even had the powder in hand. This was a significant breakthrough, and he saw the truth of it in Ivy's eyes.

"You've been most helpful, Elsie," Ivy said to the maid, squeezing the girl's hand. "I cannot thank you enough. And remember, please don't speak to anyone about what I've asked you."

The girl nodded. "I never thought it was right the way Lady Celeste died. But if I'd known it was the tisanes, I never would have given them to her." Tears filled her eyes. "I was only trying to make her feel better. Not kill her."

"You could have had no notion that the curative was poisoned, Elsie," Quill assured her. "I saw your years of loyal service to my aunt, and am sure you meant her no harm."

She nodded miserably, then in a soft voice as if reluctant to continue, she said, "I hate to mention it, but if there was any way you could keep from telling Mrs. Northman about my dealings with the encampment? It's just that Mr. Northman doesn't hold with the Rom. 'Specially not since they been known to steal 'is sheep from time to time."

"He won't hear about it from us," Ivy said with a warm smile. "Will he, my lord?"

"Certainly not," he agreed.

Then, the conversation over, there was nothing to do but to step back out into the hallway and brace himself for a scold.

Which was not long in coming.

Ivy's eyes flashed with exasperation as, once they were out of earshot of Elsie and safely ensconced in an alcove near the second-floor landing, she turned on him. "What on earth were you thinking? You might have ruined everything!"

Chapter 21

"You are the most exasperating man," Ivy continued without allowing Quill to speak. "Elsie might very well have refused to tell us anything because of your intrusion. You do realize that, do you not?"

She had been pleasantly surprised when Mrs. Northman proved so amenable to allowing her a few minutes with Elsie on the pretext of asking for the tisane recipe. It hadn't been expected. Especially not when she saw how the other lady's gaze lingered on Quill at dinner. But not one to look a gift horse in the mouth, she'd followed her hostess upstairs and entered her bedchamber eagerly, and had been rewarded with Elsie's confession about the gypsies. If Quill's arrival had ruined that in any way, she would have been hard pressed to keep from boxing his ears.

To his credit, however, he did seem to realize the gravity of what he'd done. "I walked into the drawing room and found that both you and Mrs. Northman were nowhere to be found," he admitted, rubbing a hand over the nape of his neck. "I was concerned."

"Because you thought she'd taken me away to regale me with tales of your affair?" Ivy asked with raised brows. She'd guessed at their former relationship almost as soon as they entered the house. There was something predatory about the way the older woman watched him, and she had little trouble adding up the clues.

"It was a long time ago," Quill said, his cheeks hot with color. "Years before I even knew of your existence."

His sheepishness went a long way toward assuaging her anger. She had been racked with jealousy when she first noticed Mrs. Northman's proprietary hand on his arm. But it hadn't taken a few minutes before she recognized Quill's own discomfort with the other woman's overtures. Which had gone a long way toward making Ivy feel better about the matter.

Of course, there was still the fact that she'd had to guess at the thing rather than hear it from his own lips.

"I should have told you," he said quietly, as if reading her mind. "I didn't want to give you a disgust of me so soon into our relationship," he admitted. "Especially since you were still thinking over my proposal. And the fact that she is now Elsie's employer, and we needed her permission to question the girl, well, I thought it best to keep my own counsel."

Stepping closer, he crowded her into the little alcove until Ivy felt the wall at her back. "You forgive me, don't you?" he asked, before kissing her gently on the mouth.

It was difficult to stay angry when he was so sweetly apologetic.

Drat the man.

"I'm still thinking it over," she said with a dignified sniff. Which earned her a kiss in the soft spot beneath her left ear. A kiss that made her toes curl and caused a throb of longing deep within her.

"I'll just have to make it up to you," he said before taking her mouth again, this time all sweetness gone as he slipped his tongue inside and caressed her in a stroke of hot need.

Ivy slid her arms up over his shoulders and clasped him to her, her fingers threaded through the silken hair of his nape.

If there were ever a means of building heaven on earth, she had little doubt that it would be constructed from kisses and sighs and aches the likes of which she'd never imagined were even possible between a man and a woman. The vibration of her groan as he slid his hands up to cover her breasts where they ached within the prison of her stays felt loud to her own ears. But she was too far gone to care. Especially when Quill—clever Quill—tugged down the bodice of her crimson gown and bared her nipple to the cool air. And when his hot mouth closed around it, she would have cried out with the joy of it if he hadn't placed a hand over her mouth to quiet her.

"Well, isn't this interesting."

The sound of an amused voice behind them made Ivy and Quill still at once. Ivy opened her eyes to see Quill's mouth tight with annoyance, his expression grim. Was he angry at getting caught, or at getting caught by Mrs. Northman, she wondered, her heart still pounding with un-slaked lust.

He braced himself on the wall behind her and took several deep breaths as he stared down at the floor. She wanted to push him off of her, but a glance down indicated his own excitement at their passion was plainly evident in his evening breeches.

At least she didn't have to deal with *that,* she thought wryly. How uncomfortable it must be to be a man sometimes.

Still, their interruption was still there. Which she made plain with another conversational sally. "I did wonder if there might be something between you and one of the young ladies, Quill," said the Squire's wife. "But my money was on Lady Daphne. She seems more like your type. I certainly would never have guessed this one would pique your interest. What with her carroty hair and, shall we say, *buxom* figure? I do dislike to call a spade a spade, but really my dear, if you do not push away from the table you'll be as fat as Prinny."

Ivy shoved Quill's chest so that she could get a closer look at her accuser, but he turned and spoke before she could draw breath. "Jealousy doesn't become you, Cassandra," he said coldly. "And I will thank you to keep your opinions about my betrothed to yourself. They are, like the rest of you, unwanted."

The other woman's eyes widened as his words hit their mark. But she fired back easily enough. "Not entirely unwanted," she said with a cat-in-the-cream-pot smile, "unless I miss my guess about your delightful cousin, Maitland. One can only hope all of him is built to proportion." She gave a shiver of anticipation that made Ivy's gorge rise.

"I can assure you, madam," the duke drawled as he prowled up behind her, "I would sooner bed a she-wolf than the likes of you. And I daresay the she-wolf would be more affectionate and less grasping." He surveyed her with his quizzing glass, then added, "I can assure you it is proportional, and I know how to use it. More's the pity for you."

Ivy would have laughed at Mrs. Northman's expression if the situation weren't so utterly mortifying. Not only had she been discovered in an embrace by Quill's former mistress, but now his cousin was there to see the whole contretemps. It was worse than the time her sister had callously revealed Ivy's crush on her father's prize pupil. A young man of twenty to her thirteen, and who had laughed heartily upon learning of it. At least there had been no fear of losing her reputation then. This incident had every possibility of making her a byword amongst the neighborhood as well as the *ton*.

"If you were hoping for my silence in this matter," their hostess said in a hostile voice, "then you are sorely mistaken, Lord Kerr. It will take only one letter from me to my sister in London for the rumor of what I just saw to spread far and wide within the *ton*, not to mention what I will do to this slut's reputation here on the coast. There will be nowhere for her to go when I'm finished."

The vitriol in the matron's voice sent ice dancing down Ivy's spine. Quill, however, was having none of it. Stalking over to where Mrs. Northman stood with her hands fisted and her lip curled in anger, he bent so that his face was level with hers. "If I hear so much as a hint of scandal where Miss Wareham is concerned," he said in a silky tone that might have come from the devil himself, "then I will see to it that you are never admitted into another genteel entertainment again. Not a London drawing room. Not Almack's. Not the local assembly. Not the subscription ball in Bath. Not even the taproom at the Fox and Pheasant."

"It is never a good idea to anger my cousin, Mrs. Northman," Maitland said pleasantly from her other side. "He might not look it, but he can be quite as ruthless as one of them pagan gods in the classics Miss Wareham knows so much about. And I suppose I should mention, I'll lend my own social capital—my being a duke and all—to his campaign as well. Cousins, you see. We're loyal that way."

Without a backward glance at their hostess, Quill turned and offered his arm to Ivy. "Come, my dear. I find the company here quite beneath our notice. Much better to get back to Beauchamp House where the air is purer."

In a daze, Ivy allowed him to lead her away.

"What a coil," Quill said as they strode down the hall away from Mrs. Northman.

They'd only got as far as the first landing, with Maitland

close behind, when just as they passed a large bronze statue of Pan displayed prominently on a faux Greek column, a hidden door behind it opened abruptly, toppling both.

"Oh, I am sorry," Elsie gasped from where she stood in the doorway. "I didn't know—" Her eyes widened as she saw the fallen ornaments. "Why was that there?"

Quill, who had just missed bearing the brunt of the heavy piece, frowned. "Is it not usually kept here, Elsie?"

She shook her head. "No, my lord. It's kept just to the side." She pointed. "There. One of the housemaids must have moved it today to clean for the party tonight."

She turned to Ivy. "You weren't hurt, were you miss?"

"No, it missed me." Ivy shivered. She turned to the others. "Quill? Maitland?"

"Right as rain," Maitland said with a shake of his head. "It would take more than a chap in cloven hooves to damage this hard head."

Grateful for the duke's bit of levity, Ivy smiled. "You may go, Elsie. We'll tidy this up."

She watched the girl go, and waited as Quill and Maitland lifted the column and placed the statue back atop it.

"The carpet is depressed here where it's usually kept," Quill said as he stood up from where he'd moved to examine the floor. "Elsie was right."

"If you don't mind, I'd like to leave now," Ivy said, starting for the stairs. "I've had about all that I can endure of surprises for one night."

Wordlessly, Quill and Maitland followed.

Quill's mood on the drive back to Beauchamp House was much darker than it had been on the journey out.

The fact that Serena had separated him and Ivy into separate carriages did nothing to improve things either. Though they'd not told her about what had happened with Cassandra, the fact that both he and Ivy, and later Maitland, had disappeared from the drawing room for an extended period of time had alerted her to the fact that something was amiss, and she'd hurried Ivy into the first carriage with the Hastings sisters, leaving Quill to ride back with Lady Daphne and Maitland, who flirted shamelessly all the way.

By the time the carriage stopped in the drive of Beauchamp House, Quill was ready to throttle anyone who so much as breathed in his direction. And his humor was not improved when he stalked into the entrance hall to find Serena waiting for him, her mouth a line of impatience.

"I would like to speak to you, please," she said without preamble as he brushed past her toward the stairs.

"In the morning," he said in a tone that brooked no objection. "I need to speak to Ivy."

Now that they were back on home territory, he didn't care who heard him.

"She's gone up to bed with a headache, Quill," Serena said hurrying after him. "I think you'd better get some rest too. You've got a long journey ahead of you tomorrow."

"Where are you going, my lord?" asked Daphne as she and Maitland followed behind them at a slower pace. "I don't suppose you'd wish to bring a few things back from London for me if that's your destination. I left some very important books, and I'd like to—"

Quill heard Maitland's low voice telling her to hush and was grateful for that at least.

When they reached the landing at the third floor, he turned to Serena and took her by the shoulders. "I know my duty. I will do it. But I beg you will leave us alone for now."

He saw a flicker of understanding in Serena's eyes as she took his meaning. And though she squared her jaw, she gave him a reluctant nod.

Not caring if Maitland or Daphne saw his intention, he strode down the hall and without knocking opened the door to Ivy's bedchamber and walked in.

To find it empty.

A frisson of panic ran through him before he realized Ivy and her maid were likely in the dressing room.

In for a penny, in for a pound.

When he opened the door to the dressing room he found Ivy being unbuttoned from her gown by her maid.

"Get out," he said to the wide-eyed girl. Bobbing a curtsy, she was gone before Ivy could even turn to give him the full force of her scowl.

"You have no right to come into my dressing room and order my maid about," she said with a huff of anger. "You get out."

"Not until we've had a conversation," he said curtly.

When he didn't begin at once, she raised her brows in exaggerated annoyance. "Well? You're so keen to talk to me. Then talk."

He noted the shadows beneath her eyes and the traces of dried tears, and cursed himself for being a scoundrel.

In a gentler voice he said, "Come, let's go into the other room where you can be comfortable."

"I would have been a great deal more comfortable if you'd let Polly finish getting me out of this corset," she said in a harassed tone.

Wordlessly he moved behind her and began undoing the buttons that ran down her back. The action so reminiscent of their afternoon in the little cottage that he found himself swallowing back a groan of desire.

But that was what had got them in this mess in the first place. So he steeled himself against the sight of the vulnerable skin of her back and let her step out of the gown before going to work on the lacing of her corset.

With a modesty that was somewhat amusing given what they'd been to each other, she refused to turn around when the corset was unfastened and said in a cool voice, "Please hand me the robe on the hook there."

He glanced around and saw the one she meant and held it as she slipped first one, then the other arm through the sleeves and allowed the stays to drop to the floor before cinching the belt of the cotton wrap. Turning to him with a glower, she turned with hauteur and stalked out of the tiny dressing room into the bedchamber beyond.

Where the candlelight and the turned-down counterpane loomed large.

Swallowing, Quill followed her, unable to keep from noticing how her hips swung from side to side as she walked.

But if Ivy was in any mood to continue what they'd started in the alcove at the Northman house, she was giving no indication of it. In fact, if he didn't know for a fact that she was the same woman he'd held in his arms, he would never have guessed it.

Clearly he was going to have to do some persuading if he wished to gain entrance into the bed behind them.

"Well," she said with a tilt of her chin, "you have something to say, I gather. Say it then get out."

The coldness in her tone might have made him back off if he hadn't seen the pulse beating in her neck. Or the way her eyes darkened when their eyes met. She might be angry. As she had every right to be. But she wasn't completely done with him.

At least he hoped not.

"I apologize for not telling you about Cassandra before we went to her house this evening," he said firmly, deciding that straightforward explanation would be his best strategy. "I should have let you know that you might be facing some jealousy from that quarter. And for that I am deeply sorry."

But to his discomfort, her gaze only grew stonier.

"Do you think I give a damn that you bedded that horrible woman years ago when you were little more than a boy?" she asked, a flash of something he couldn't interpret in her eyes. "My own experience with you tells me that you learned how to be so seductive somewhere, my lord. No man is born knowing exactly what he's about in that arena, I think."

"What do you know about it?" he asked, surprised at her candor despite himself.

"Have you forgotten that my father lets university boys run tame in our household?" she asked, a hint of impatience in her tone. "They will kiss anything that moves at that age," she said with a shake of her head. "And a number of things that don't, I wager. Though I've never seen it, thank heavens."

"Did they kiss *you*?" he asked, annoyed at the thought of her in the arms of someone else—even if it was a passel of damned schoolboys.

"No," she said with a lift of her chin. "But that doesn't mean I am ignorant," she added, some of the bravado dissipating at the admission.

"Oh." The monosyllable was an inadequate expression of his relief, but it was all he could manage at the moment.

"My point is not that I've been kissed before," Ivy said in a softer tone. "It's that I know how little a kiss can mean. But that's clearly not the case with you and Mrs. Northman. It's not the idea of her that I mind, so much as what she meant to you. And that you failed to tell me suggests that you wished to keep that a secret."

It was something that hadn't even occurred to him, the notion that she feared he might still be holding a torch for Cassandra.

"God no," he said, truly appalled at the idea. "I hope you don't think I could ever cherish tender feelings for a woman with so little human charity that she'd say what she did to you."

The relief in her eyes was enough to make him step closer. "I did fancy myself in love with her in my salad days," he admitted with a wry smile. "But almost as soon as I declared my undying love for her she laughed so heartily as to make it impossible for me to ever fancy her again—well, not quite that, I suppose; at one and twenty I was little more than a walking cock-stand with eyes, so it was impossible not rise to the occasion."

Her eyes widened at the crudity, but she also laughed, which had been his intention.

"You're incorrigible," she said with a shake of her head.

"She's not much different now than she was then," he continued, slipping his arms around her waist and pulling her closer. "I've matured and she's remained the same. Which is sad when I think of it. But I suspect our sympathy is wasted on her. I doubt she would thank us. And I know that I can think of other things I'd much rather be doing."

Ivy didn't resist when he kissed her then, and Quill set himself to prove to her with his every touch that he meant every word he'd said about Cassandra.

If truth were told, he'd been a little repulsed by her when he first saw her tonight. Seeing her with the eyes of a man rather than a boy. And he'd known with the certainty of a man that Ivy on her worst day was worth ten of Cassandra.

"Ivy," he said, his voice husky with wanting her, "yesterday in the cottage was an impulse, a moment out of time. Will you let me make love to you now, in a proper bed, when there is the promise of marriage between us?"

She pulled back a little, her eyes searching, and Quill hoped that she could read the affection for her in his face. If not love yet—it was far too soon for such a heady emotion between them—then at the very least, there was genuine friendship there. And there were far worse foundations for marriage.

Whatever she saw in him must have given her reassurance, for she gave a little smile, her green eyes bright with emotion.

"Yes," she said on a breath. And he knew that it was more than just in response to his request just now. It was an assent to follow him into far more than one night.

Unable to contain his relief, he scooped her up into his arms with a whoop, startling a little shriek from her.

"Put me down, you silly man!" she protested. "I'm far too heavy."

But he liked the feel of her in his arms. The solid weight of her, and the warm press of her against his chest. It evoked a primitive emotion he'd never imagined himself capable of. But then, Ivy had been wringing emotions from him from the moment they met.

"You're as light as a feather," he said with a grin as he pulled her closer. "I'd be a poor sort of man if I couldn't carry my lady to bed."

"I do not doubt your ability, my lord," she said primly, "but your wisdom."

Reaching the bed, he gently placed her down on the soft mattress, enjoying the play of candlelight through the thin fabric of her robe.

"You'll forgive me, I trust," he said, shrugging out of his coats, and unwinding the cravat from around his neck, "if I disagree. I quite think this is wisest decision I've ever made."

"Then we will simply have to agree to disagree," she said watching from beneath her lashes as he tossed his cravat to the side and pulled his shirt over his head in one fluid motion and dropped it.

He couldn't help but notice the appreciation in her eyes as she scanned his bare chest. "Will we?" he asked in a purr.

"Perhaps you're right," she amended as he put one knee on the bed, and shifted to prop himself over her.

"Of course I'm right," he said, leaning down to kiss her on the nose. "Wisest decision I ever made."

And to his surprise, he meant it.

Chapter 22

Ivy's breath caught in her throat as she saw the predatory gleam in Quill's eye as he held himself over her. She was keenly aware of the fact that beneath her robe she was wearing nothing at all. And the heat of his big body curled around her like the tentacles of a spell meant to bind her to him forever.

"Are you quite comfortable?" she asked politely, as she tried to find somewhere to look besides into his all-too-knowing gaze. For some reason the easiness of the little cottage was scarce here and she felt her inexperience in carnal matters far more keenly now than she had before.

He smiled, and she noticed a single dimple in his left cheek. It gave him an impish air, so different from the serious nobleman whom she'd first met in the taproom of the Fox and Pheasant. "I am quite comfortable," he said, raising his brows. "In fact, I would count myself quite content if I never moved from this spot. Do you think it would be feasible?"

His absurdity was the very thing to set her at ease, and relieved she considered his question. "I don't know," she said with mock seriousness. "It might be difficult to take all our meals in this position."

"Or, I could feed you," he said with assurance. "In fact,

I'd insist upon it. It would be the least I could do for your allowing me to rest my . . . ah . . . self against your sweet. . . . self for the rest of our days." He punctuated his pauses with tiny thrusts that made Ivy well aware of just how much he was enjoying their current position.

"In fact," he continued, dropping his head to tug on her earlobe with his teeth, "I think I might be getting a little hungry right now."

"Oh," Ivy said, breathless at the sensation of his mouth making its way down her neck. "I'm sure I could send for something from the kitchen. It's late, but Polly would bring something if I asked." She continued to babble as he untied the knot at her waist and opened the robe to reveal her nude form. Her breasts budded in response to the chill air. Almost painful in their tautness.

"I'll just make do with what we have here," he said, closing his lips around first one, then the other peak, sucking each one into the moist heat of his mouth. The sheer carnality of it making Ivy writhe with pleasure. "So pretty." His breath on her wet skin made her shift beneath him.

While he caressed her with his mouth, his hand slipped down, down, over the slight round of her belly, pausing to tease a fingertip over the dip of her navel, and resting at the top of her pubis. The memory of his hands on her in the cottage, combined with the suckle of Quill's mouth on her breast had Ivy almost bucking beneath him, searching, aching to the feel of his touch on the sensitive skin between her legs. Where even now she could feel the damp proof of her desire.

But she needn't have worried. The hardening of his erection against her hip was enough to tell Ivy that he was just as eager as she. The hiss of his breath when he slipped first one, then another finger into the moisture told the tale far more eloquently than words.

"So wet for me," he crooned into her ear, as he teased over her hot flesh, always staying just shy of that spot where she needed him most. Making her search him out with her hips, even as he danced a finger over the sensitive bud near the top.

"Please, Quill," she murmured, aching for something more. More pressure, more heat, more . . . just more.

And when he thrust his fingers inside her she nearly came off the bed in her relief. Not knowing or caring how she looked, she followed her body's lead and lifted her hips, following his hand as it moved in and out, stroking into her just like she needed.

"That's it," he said, kissing her with open mouth, mimicking the motion of his fingers with his tongue, before shifting downward.

When he removed his hand she almost wept at the loss, and for a moment she was puzzled to see him press her knees wider with his shoulders.

"What are you . . . ?" she began, only to gape as she met his eyes. With deliberation, he leaned in and licked her. And though she was shocked, she couldn't have told him to stop if her life depended on it.

"Just relax," he said, his deep voice vibrating against her sensitive core. And she let her head fall back, and reveled in the sensation as he used lips and tongue and fingers to bring her to a writhing need that had her crying out with the ache of it. Until without warning, the thrust of his fingers coupled with the suck of his mouth sent her hurtling over, her body no longer hers to control.

She could taste herself on his mouth when he moved up to kiss her sweetly before coming into her with a strong thrust that reignited the sparks she thought had been doused.

Quill pressed his forehead against hers and watched her as he moved in her, his hot gaze igniting a fullness in her heart even as his body stoked the fire at her core. It was the most intimate moment of Ivy's life. More even that the afternoon in the cottage, when they'd both kept parts of themselves hidden from the other. From self-preservation or unconscious distrust she couldn't guess. All she knew was that this, now, was as binding as any marriage ceremony. She gave herself to him then, body and soul, and she knew with a certainty that he gave himself to her.

Clutching him to her, the strong heat of his back beneath her fingers, Ivy's body was all too soon gripping him in a heartbeat rhythm all its own, and when she felt the explosion of feeling this time, she felt him follow her, his cry only seconds after hers as he let his weight come down on her.

Ivy was still asleep when Quill slipped out of her bed the next morning.

Leaving her naked and warm, one breast exposed by the sheet tangled beneath her body, had been one of the most difficult things he'd ever done. Soon, he told himself, he wouldn't have to leave her at all. He just had to get to Oxford to speak to her father, and then to London for a special license. And there was also the matter of Aunt Celeste's killer to catch.

But first, he told himself as he washed and dressed for the day beneath the exasperated eye of his valet, they needed to find that damned gypsy woman.

He would have left Ivy to find her on her own—or at the very least with Maitland and the other ladies—but he disliked the idea of her traipsing about the countryside without him by her side. They were all but convinced that his aunt had been murdered. And once someone chose to take a life, the decision to take another was but a stone's throw away.

Though he would have preferred to make the trip to the gypsy encampment with only Ivy, that was not to be the case. Once the others got wind that they were planning to visit a gypsy, fortune telling fever had taken hold. Over the break-fast table it was decided that the Hastings sisters, Daphne and Maitland would go along with them.

"I'm desperate to know what the future holds," Sophia said with a grin. "It's thrilling to guess what might happen."

"It's pure nonsense," Daphne asserted with a tone that brooked no argument. "I daresay this woman you're seeking employs the same sort of tricks and gimmicks as they do at a country fair. Only with more skill and more flowery language."

"I think you are far too quick to dismiss it," Ivy argued. "Who are we to say what is and is not possible? I am not ashamed to admit that there are some things in this world beyond my understanding."

"But you're both being romantic," Gemma said, her scientific nature aligning with Daphne's mathematical one. "Daphne has a point that fortune tellers are notorious for spinning tales out of nothing. You remember the one we visited in the village back home, Sophia? The one who said that we would soon go on a journey over water? As far as I know neither of us has done so. It was a fiction she told so that you would give her more coins, nothing more."

"That is patently false, Gemma," Sophia retorted. "We crossed several streams and a river on our journey here, didn't we?"

"Perhaps we should wait to see what this particular gypsy fortune teller has to tell us before we make a decision," Quill said diplomatically. "After all, this one might be the one who is entirely sincere."

"We'd best be off if we don't wish to miss the good weather," Maitland said, wisely refraining from engaging in the discussion. "After all," he said with a wink at Quill, "we don't wish to be caught in a storm like Miss Wareham and Kerr were the other day."

Quill and Ivy both sighed as a collective titter rose from the table. The rest of the residents of Beauchamp House, with the exception of Serena who was still a bit incensed about the whole thing, had been remarkably unfazed by the scandalous behavior of the linguist and the marquess. But that didn't stop them from taking every opportunity to tease them about it.

Not waiting to see if they would comment, Ivy pushed her chair back and rose. "I'll go get my wrap."

The other ladies soon followed, leaving Quill and Maitland to wander from the room in their own time.

"You look chipper this morning for a man who was caught in the parson's mousetrap last night," Maitland said with a grin as he rose from the table. "One would almost imagine you're happy about what happened."

His good mood was far likelier due to the hours he'd spent in Ivy's bed, but Quill was hardly going to tell his cousin so. "Perhaps the means was not what I would have wished for," he said with a shrug, "but I cannot say that I am entirely displeased with the outcome. Though I do not look forward to informing Ivy's father of what happened."

"You utterly outrank the man," Maitland argued. "The fact that you, a marquess, wish to marry his daughter at all should have him worshipping at your feet. It's a far better match than the daughter of a disinherited duke's son and a social nobody could have ever hoped for."

"Don't be an ass, Maitland," Quill said in exasperation. "I am well aware of the difference in our social rankings. But the fact remains that I have compromised the man's daughter not once but twice—the second time publicly in the house of my one-time mistress. It is hardly the most auspicious of occasions upon which to ask for the hand of the woman I . . . hold in esteem."

If Maitland noticed the pause—where Quill had just

stopped himself from saying he loved Ivy—he didn't mention it. The slip was likely the result of lack of sleep, Quill assured himself. After all, though he was fond of Ivy and resigned to marrying her, he couldn't possibly have fallen in love with her. For one thing, it hadn't been long enough; and for another, he wasn't even sure he believed in the sentiment. Much like the power of the gypsy woman to tell the future, love was a thing he'd believe when he saw it. And it was unlikely he'd see either anytime soon, if ever.

"You're far too nice about these things," Maitland said as the two men strode into the entrance hall to call for their greatcoats. "In the good old days you'd have thrown the fellow's daughter over the pommel of your saddle and taken her over his protests. And marriage wouldn't have even been a part of the equation."

"So you think I should just dispense with visiting the man altogether and simply send him the sheet's with Ivy's virgin blood, then?" Quill asked dryly in a voice low enough to thwart eavesdroppers. "I look forward to watching you deal with your own in-laws when the day comes. I suspect you will have a rude awakening."

"The thing of it is," Maitland said with a laugh, "you care too much what others think. I get the sense that you consider the responses of those around you before you make the least little step. I've learned to live my life without giving a damn. And I've managed well enough so far."

"Yes," Quill argued, "but you've had no one to answer to but your mother since you were in short coats. Having a father with a sharp tongue and a cane at the ready will make a man learn to think before he acts."

"From what I've heard, my father was just as headstrong as I am," the duke said cheerfully. "So it's doubtful he'd have been the steadying influence you think. Like Lady Daphne and Miss Hastings on the subject of fortune tellers, however,

I suspect we will never reconcile our opinions on the matter, so let us dispense with this talk of fathers and discipline."

"With pleasure," Quill said, taking his hat from Greaves. "Though I will add that I plan on striking out for Oxford this evening and I would ask that you keep a watchful eye over Miss Wareham. She has proved to be levelheaded thus far, but the quest for Lady Celeste's poisoner may prod her into acting rashly in my absence."

"You think there's danger afoot, then?" Maitland asked, frowning. "I thought poisoners were generally too timid to strike out physically."

"I suspect that's the case," Quill agreed, grateful that he could speak openly about Celeste's murder with at least one member of his family, since he'd yet to inform Serena about the real cause of their aunt's demise. "But I cannot think that the questions we've been asking will go unnoticed. And if I'm gone, that will leave Ivy alone."

Maitland had only the chance to nod before they were joined by the ladies filing down the stairs, having added hats and coats for the cross-country walk.

Chapter 23

"I missed you this morning," Ivy said in a low voice as she and Quill walked behind the others along the path leading to the field where Elsie had claimed to find the gypsy fortune teller. "Though I suppose it would not have done for Polly to find you in my bed."

It had come as a shock to her how painful his absence had been to her. Whether it was because of the vulnerability she felt after giving herself to him so fully, or simply because she was beginning to want him with her whatever the circumstances, she didn't know. The stark reality had been that she woke alone in her bed, and hadn't liked it one bit.

"Not that we haven't created enough scandal in the household to last a year's time," Quill said with a grin, "but, yes I did not risk having your maid find me. It may take only a day or two for the news from the Northman's dinner party to travel to the staff at Beauchamp House, but by that time, I hope to have settled things with your father and have a special license in hand."

"So you will travel to Oxford?" she asked, her stomach twisting at the notion of how her father would response to Quill's arrival. Alton Wareham might have been born as the son of the Duke of Ware, but he had little respect for the aristocracy, an institution he declared an affront to the common people. He didn't use his courtesy title, and he would greet the news that Ivy was to marry a marquess as nothing short of a disaster.

His response would be more cheerful if she announced she were to marry a bootblack.

"Is that strictly necessary?" she asked Quill, not quite knowing how to bring up the subject of her father's feelings about the peerage. "After all, isn't it customary to use the special license, *then* announce the marriage to the family?"

Quill frowned. "I'm not sure it's wise to use the word 'customary' when it comes to situations like ours. I rather think it changes from circumstance to circumstance." He searched her face. "Is there some reason why you would rather I not speak with your father? I must admit it is not something I am looking forward to, but I assumed that was part of my penance."

"Penance?" Ivy asked frowning.

"For ruining you," he said simply.

Of course he thought in those terms, Ivy fumed.

"I am not a side of beef or a keg of small beer to be ruined," she said through clenched teeth. "And I will thank you for not speaking of me as if I am."

A flicker of impatience crossed his handsome face. "I do not think of you like that," he said. "But it is how the rest of the world will speak of it. Especially if they learn about what happened in Northman's hall last night. I understand your dislike of the way the world discusses such things, but it is pointless to argue about wording when we must focus on practicalities."

"My opinion on the subject," Ivy said coldly, "is not pointless. Words like 'ruined,' and 'compromised' reinforce the idea that ladies are commodities, and I ask that you do not use them around me. Or at all, if we are being frank. It only perpetuates these archaic notions, and the sooner men in power—men like you, as a peer of the realm—begin changing how you speak of it, the sooner such things will cease to matter."

"But they do matter, Ivy," he argued. "I understand why you object to the terms, but you would sooner force the moon to go round the sun than convince a father that his daughter's innocence is worth nothing. It's why there are dowries and laws of succession for God's sake."

Understanding dawned in Ivy. "So it's because you think my father will offer a dowry that you wish to see him?" she asked, aghast.

"Don't be absurd," Quill said dismissively. "I don't need your father's money. But if you wish to have a widow's portion or provisions for our children, it would do some good for us to sit down and make some decisions. Not that I don't mean to speak to my man of business about that regardless. But it would be good for you to have a man there to look out for your interests besides me."

"Well, excuse me for forgetting who I'm dealing with," Ivy snapped. "I forgot to whom I was speaking. Of course you have no need of my father's money. But he will likely accept whatever bride price you choose to pay him. He might reject the notion of the peerage in theory but he is not above taking their money. Even when it means giving it to the man who 'ruined' his daughter."

"Ivy," Quill said, thrusting a hand through his hair, "be reasonable. If you do not wish me to meet with your father before the marriage, then I will not do so. But I don't understand why you are so angry about this. So far as I can tell, my sin is that I used a word you do not like—which you just used by the way—and I dared suggest that your father might ask for a settlement on hearing of our impending marriage. Is that the whole of it?"

"That was *sarcasm* you silly man," she hissed. "And stop making me sound like the one at fault here."

He shrugged as if to say "but you are," and Ivy wanted to shriek. Why were men so obtuse?

"I'm going to go up ahead and speak with the other ladies," she said curtly. "We will finish discussing this later."

Not caring what his response to that would be, she hurried up to join the others, leaving Quill to stare after her.

"That looked unpleasant," said Maitland, who had lingered so that Quill could catch up with him. "In your lady's black books already?"

"Nothing so dire," Quill responded thoughtfully. *I hope,* he added silently to himself. He wasn't quite sure where Ivy's ire had sprung from, but he had little doubt it stemmed from her feelings about her father. As a man whose relationship with his own father had been strained at best, he could relate. But he'd been unable to even mention it thanks to her tirade about commodities, and kegs of beer, and all that rot.

"Maitland," he asked now, watching as the four women up ahead leaned their heads together and spoke in low voices—doubtless talking about the perfidy of men and plotting for ways to have him roasted on a spit before nightfall, "have you ever considered that by calling a lady 'ruined' when she's been . . ." He searched for a word that conveyed the meaning of ruined but could come up with nothing that worked so well as it did.

"Breached?" his cousin asked, eyebrows raised. "Sullied? Tupped? Prematurely drunk?"

"Compromised," Quill said tightly. He should have known better than to ask Maitland's opinion. He lacked the gravitas necessary for such a conversation. Though to be fair, he suspected most men would make the same sorts of quips. Men simply didn't take the matter as seriously as women did. But he pressed on because he had to talk to someone about it. "Did you ever consider that by using those terms, it unfairly places ladies in the same light as beef and corn and other commodities?"

"I'm not sure how unfair it is," Maitland said with a shrug, "but if you ask any man who's been forced to pay through the nose for the honor of marrying the lady he's . . . compromised, then I suspect he'd say it's accurate enough." He glanced at his cousin with a frown. "Why, has Miss Wareham been smarting over the fact that she's no longer . . . ah . . . as she once was?"

"She just flew into a rage because I mentioned my intention of speaking to her father before I get the special license," Quill said pettishly. "As if the man didn't have the right to at least hear it from my own mouth that I took her innocence. Not in so many words of course. I don't have a death wish. But you would have thought I told her I was going to bring the bloody sheets as you said earlier. She was livid at the idea there was anything to tell beyond that we're marrying. As if a father hasn't got a right to know."

"Not to mention the effect it might have on her sisters' chances," Maitland said practically. "Though that's something her mama is more likely to cut up rough about."

"Right," Quill said, feeling a much-needed sense of vindication. Perhaps Maitland wasn't the wrong man to speak to about this after all. "I thought it was perfectly natural that I would explain to Mr. Wareham what I intended to do right by her despite the fact that we'd anticipated the vows, and instead I was met with fury and recriminations. Then when I brought up the dowry. Well, you can guess how well *that* was received."

"I am sorry old chap," Maitland said, clapping him on the back. "I thought Miss Wareham was a sensible creature, but you can never tell with bluestockings. They get their backs up about the queerest things. Lady Daphne ripped up at me last night because I confused Pythagoras and that other maths chappie. You know the one, the Greek one who's not Pythagoras?"

"Euclid?" Quill asked, amused despite himself.

"That's the one." Maitland beamed. "You would have thought I'd said up was down, day was night, and the moon was made of Christmas pudding to see Lady Daphne's reaction. I thought she'd never speak to me again."

"But she did?" Quill guessed.

"Of course," Maitland said with a shrug, and a gesture from his head to his toes, as if to say, "Who could resist this?"

What must it be like to live such a charmed life, Quill thought wryly. If he didn't realize just how seriously his cousin took his ducal responsibilities despite his savoir-faire, he'd be green with envy. Though there was the fact that he and not Maitland had won Ivy. Despite their spat, he was as infatuated with her as ever. And despite the ease with which they'd got along so far, it was not unexpected that they'd disagree about something. Couples bickered. It was the way they solved their disagreements that mattered.

They'd reached the edge of a clearing by now, and beyond the four ladies who walked ahead of them he could see a colorful gypsy caravan in a little copse of trees.

So much for a gypsy encampment.

This appeared to be a gypsy camper.

Singular.

The ladies waited for them near a horse chestnut tree that was sporting a few bursts of green in honor of the chilly spring.

"It's much smaller than I expected," Sophia said with a pout as Quill and Maitland reached them. "I was hoping for a carnival at the very least."

"Or some handsome gypsy men," Lady Daphne said with a frown. "Since the fortune teller will be useless for anything practical."

"I wish to get the recipe she used in Lady Celeste's tisanes," Ivy reminded her with a roll of her eyes, which to Quill's relief, she shared with him. Like a joke that only they shared.

"I know," Daphne said with a wave of her hand. "But that seems just as foolish as seeking your fortune."

"You would not say so, I think, Lady Daphne," Quill said, happy when Ivy slipped her arm through his, "if you suffered from the same headaches my aunt did. And indeed that Miss Wareham does."

They had agreed upon the fiction that Ivy needed the recipe for her own personal use. Since she'd known the other ladies for a couple of days, they could hardly dispute the matter.

"Poor Ivy," said Gemma with a sympathetic smile. "I know how horrid they can be. I suffer from them myself at times. So I'm just as eager for the recipe. Even if I do agree with Daphne about the fortune telling."

"Well none of you will make me ashamed to ask her for my fortune," Sophia said with a dignified sniff. "For I wish to know what's to come even if the rest of you don't."

"And I'll join you, Miss Hastings," said Maitland with a grin as he took her arm.

Quill couldn't help but note that Lady Daphne's eyes narrowed at the way his cousin was making so free with Sophia's arm. If they weren't careful, Maitland would have the two ladies fighting over him. Though if he didn't mistake his guess, Miss Hastings was only being friendly. She had a romantic nature, but there seemed to be nothing beyond friendship in her manner with the duke.

They approached the caravan and soon saw that an old woman sat in a little chair just outside the red-and-green-and-yellow-painted house on wheels, laddered steps leading into the interior just behind her.

"What brings you to Madame Albinia?" she asked, rising with some difficulty as they approached. "A fortune for the ladies? A tonic for the gentlemen?"

As they got closer, Quill saw that she was older than he'd first thought. Her wizened face had seen many years in the sun, and her fingers were twisted with arthritis. But her black eyes were bright enough, and if he didn't miss his guess she'd not failed to notice that Sophia at least was eager to have her fortune told.

"We were told by the maid at one of the manor houses nearby that you have a tonic for the headache," Ivy said with a smile as she stepped closer to the woman. "I was wondering if I might speak to you about what goes into it?"

"That is valuable knowledge, lady," said the old woman with a wave of her hand. "Some pay me well to give them the secrets of my years of potion-making and physicking."

Wordlessly, Quill flipped a half crown in the woman's direction, which she caught with an agility that belied her age. "The ladies would like to have their fortunes told as well," he said with a nod that indicated the coin included that as well.

After biting the coin to ensure its value, the woman nodded. "Fortunes first, then tonic."

Resuming her seat by the fire, she had the young ladies approach her one by one—even Daphne, who despite her earlier derision appeared to be just as eager as Sophia had been—and told them things that Quill suspected were calculated to be both probable and vague. Daphne would soon search for a very valuable thing, but to find it she would risk her greatest love. Sophia would meet a handsome stranger who would make her choose between love and happiness. And Gemma would go on a great quest where she would best a strong man.

Each of the ladies heard her fortune with what looked to Quill like genuine excitement. And there was something otherworldly about the way the old woman held each girl's hand in hers and closed her eyes as if summoning some invisible spirits to her side, who then whispered each fortune in her ear.

When Gemma stepped back and Ivy stepped forward, however, the woman raised her hand and stood.

"You wished for the tonic, yes?" she said with a nod, as if answering her own question. "You will come into the vardo." As if the matter were settled, she turned and began to make her way slowly up the steps leading into the colorful wagon.

"No," Quill said, staying Ivy with a hand on her arm. They had no notion of who had poisoned his aunt yet. For all they knew the tonic had been poisoned when the old woman had given it to Elsie for her mistress. "She can bring it out here."

But Ivy waved away his concern. "You're right here. It's not as if she's taking me across the sea. And if it will make you easier, I promise not to ingest anything while I'm inside."

She made sense, but he still felt a pang of uneasiness at the idea.

"Do you come, lady?" the old woman asked from the doorway of the caravan where she stood waiting.

Ivy squeezed his hand then stepped forward to carefully climb the laddered stairs.

Chapter 24

The inside of the caravan, or vardo as the old woman had called it, was just as colorful as the outside, with gilded scrollwork and decoration on every surface. There was a neatly made bed on a platform at the back and shelves on either of the long walls that Ivy could see were stacked with all sorts of things, including what looked like herbs and various powders.

She expected the old woman to take out a bottle of the tonic before giving her the same sort of vague fortune as she'd given the others. But instead, almost as soon as she stepped inside, Madame Albinia took her hand and scowled down at it.

"Is there something amiss?" Ivy asked after a few minutes passed during which Madame Albinia muttered words in what Ivy guessed was the Romani language.

As if she were being brought out of trance, the old woman looked up, blinking, her eyes still lit from within. Finally, shaking like a dog after being caught in the rain, she said in a fervent voice, "You are in great danger, lady. Great danger. You must leave this place at once. Take your man and go. Do not come back."

Perhaps because she'd asked about the tonic, and Ivy expected the old woman might wish to rattle her, Ivy had prepared herself for something dire. Or at the very least, something mysterious. But something about the old woman's pronouncement chilled her to the bone.

"What do you mean?" she asked dumbly, staring down at her palm as if it would tell her what the gypsy woman was talking about.

"From the moment you speak," Madame Albinia said with a frown, "I see the light around you. But many people, they have the light. But I bring you here, into the *vardo* to see for sure. And for the tonic." As if reminded of the request for the tisane ingredients, the woman began to gather items from the various bottles and jars on the shelving.

When she'd finished gathering the ingredients, she named them off as she added them into a jar. "Lemongrass, feverfew, chamomile, and mint."

Momentarily distracted from the dire fortune the woman had given her, Ivy asked, "That's it?"

Despite her seriousness, the old woman grinned. "Did you expect magic beans? The Rom have the gift, but we use the fruits of the earth too. There is nothing otherworldly about the tonic. Only knowing what herbs to put together."

Ivy smiled ruefully. "I suppose I was expecting some sort of special quality that would explain its effectiveness."

"And its poisonous effect, as well, lady?" Madame Albinia asked with a keen look. At Ivy's shocked sound, she gave a slight smile. "I hear things. And when Albinia's tonic is used as poison, it angers her. This one, the one you seek, they are not what you think."

"What do you mean?" Ivy asked, desperate to know anything that might help them find Lady Celeste's killer.

"I do not know exactly," she said, "but the reasons for

killing the Lady Celeste, they are from long ago. And they know you seek them. It is why you are in danger. If you wish to remain safe, you should go with your man away from here."

Ivy's gaze sharpened. "Who are *they*?"

But the seer only shook her head and repeated, "You should go."

Before Ivy could repeat her entreaty, they were interrupted by Quill, who stepped up onto the ladder and peered inside.

"Almost finished in here?" Quill asked with a cheerfulness that didn't meet his eyes. Clearly he'd sensed something was amiss.

As if she'd expected him, Madame Albinia nodded. Turning to Ivy she said aloud, "Remember what I say. Or there will be great heartache."

With a speaking look, she handed the jar of tonic ingredients to Ivy and waved her away, as if she no longer had the energy to talk to them.

Quill's mouth was tight as he listened to the fortune teller, but he said nothing until they were out of the *vardo*. "What did she mean 'heartache'?" he asked with a scowl.

But Ivy wasn't sure she wished to share what Madame Albinia had told her yet. At least not until she'd had a few minutes alone to think about it. As if she feared speaking the words aloud would give them power. Seeking to reassure him, however, she said, "Of course it was nonsense. All danger and long journeys, just like she gave the others."

"Then why did you look so stricken when I came in?" he asked with suspicion, clearly sensing that she was prevaricating. "Your face is ghostly white."

But she waved that away. "Oh, I felt a little faint. It was quite warm in there."

She could tell he didn't want to let it go, but was saved from further discussion by their arrival at the horse chestnut tree where the others had gathered.

"Did you get your tonic ingredients?" Lady Daphne asked with a raised brow. "I was afraid for a moment that she'd cast some sort of spell over you and we'd need to rescue you. Lord Kerr was happy enough to go in after you, however, so you were saved from a stampede."

"What do you know of stampedes?" asked Maitland with a snort. "And what *is* a stampede if it comes to that? Something with a lot of people, I can guess, but what?"

Daphne rolled her eyes as the rest of the party laughed.

"I did get them, as it happens," Ivy said once they'd settled. She held up the jar. "Would you believe it's nothing more than common herbs we could have gathered ourselves?"

"I am shocked," Gemma said with mock surprise. "Shocked I tell you. That a gypsy woman would pass off a healing potion as something magical when it is in fact ancient and easily known. Why, next you'll tell us that our fortunes were untrue."

"Come over here by me, Gemma," said Daphne with approval. "We who hold logic and science in high regard should stick together."

"Oh, don't be smug, ladies," Sophia said slipping her arm through Ivy's. "Just because Ivy and I are more interested in art and language than in your boring old numbers and rocks doesn't mean that we are simpletons. It takes a great deal of skill to look at a painting and know if it is any good, just as I imagine it takes skill for Ivy to examine a few lines of Greek and determine if they came from a famous poet or a simple fishmonger."

"It is doubtful that a fishmonger would've been able to write," Ivy said with an apologetic smile, "but I think the spirit of your argument holds true."

The chatter of her friends did much to dispel the aura of ill portent that had seemed to follow her out of the little caravan. And as they walked back toward the path to Beauchamp

House she let their wordplay punctuated by the occasional quip from the duke distract her from what Madame Albinia had told her about Lady Celeste's murder, as well as the warning that she herself was in danger.

Soon, however, she fell back and before long—just as they had done on the way to the clearing—she found herself walking alone with Quill, some distance behind the others.

"What did she really tell you, Ivy?" he asked, his blue eyes shadowed with worry. "Because I don't believe it was just the same sort of claptrap she told the others. Was it something to do with the person who killed Aunt Celeste?"

"Perhaps it wasn't strictly as innocuous as I told the others it was," Ivy said reluctantly. "But I was hoping to think it over for a bit."

"So that you could twist it into something innocuous?" he asked, with brows drawn.

"Not in so many words." She bristled. "But more that I wished to think about it. To make sense of it. Because it might not be as dark as what I interpreted it to be."

"You'd best just say before you truly worry me," he said gently. "Because at this point I'm suspecting the worst. And I don't even truly believe in such things."

"She said that I was in—"

And almost as soon as the words left Ivy's mouth she heard a loud report from the trees on either side of the path, and she felt a sharp pain in her upper arm just before Quill threw her to the ground.

All of Quill's senses were on alert as he crashed to the ground, shielding Ivy with his body. He scanned the trees on either side of the path, trying to determine where the shot had come from. The windy day made it impossible to tell which of the moving branches was from human motion and which from the breeze. Up ahead he could hear the whimpers of the other ladies, and Maitland's order for them to stay down.

Beneath him, Ivy was breathing heavily, but she kept silent, either too shocked to talk or sensing that he needed quiet to tell where the bastard was.

When several minutes passed without another shot, Quill eased off of her. "I think it's safe now," he said, still scanning the area to ensure that he hadn't been premature in his assessment. "Are you all right?"

"I think so," she said, her face pale, but standing easily enough when he gave her a hand up. Wordlessly, he brushed the leaves and twigs from the skirt of her gown, using the contact to reassure himself that she was, indeed unharmed. "Please tell me that was just a hunter making a wild shot."

He wished that he had the words to erase the stricken look in her green eyes, but Quill didn't think lying would make things any easier for her. "I'm afraid that's unlikely," he said, pulling her to him in a quick hug. "This is not precisely an area known for good hunting."

"Were either of you hit?" Maitland demanded as he and the other three ladies backtracked toward them.

"No," Quill said, glancing up at them. "You?"

"No," Maitland said, his usual lighthearted expression replaced with grim anger. "Not for lack of trying. Who the hell would be out shooting on a commonly used footpath?" His question didn't need an answer. They all knew that no one with any sense would.

"We need to get back to the house at once," Quill said, reaching for Ivy's arm. But her cry of pain made him stop. "Did you hurt yourself in the fall?" he asked, moving to get a look at her upper arm, which she was probing it with her fingers.

"I don't know," she said frowning. "I did feel something,

but it happened so quickly I'm unsure of whether it happened before or after I fell."

Her hand came away covered in blood, and Quill uttered a low curse. "You're hit, damn it."

And even as he spoke, she swayed on her feet, whether from blood loss or pain he could not tell. In one swift move she was in his arms. "We have to get her to the house at once."

"Here," Maitland said, pressing his handkerchief against the wound, which was bleeding slowly but steadily now. "I'll run ahead and send for the doctor. Do you want me to send the carriage?"

"It will take too long," Quill said, his mind entirely focused on the task at hand. "We've only half a mile or so to go."

With a nod, Maitland headed in a jog toward Beauchamp House.

"She said I was in danger," Ivy said, resting her head against his shoulder as Quill carried her past familiar landmarks but seeing none of them.

"Who said, Ivy?" Sophia asked, from where she hurried along beside them, flanked by Daphne and Gemma.

"Madame Albinia," Ivy said in a weak voice. "Told me I was in danger. They know I'm looking for them."

"Whom are you looking for?" Daphne asked, her voice puzzled. "I think her mind is disordered. She's not making any sense."

But Quill knew precisely whom Ivy was looking for.

A murderer who would not hesitate to kill again.

He should never have let her go into that gypsy caravan alone. He'd suspected the old woman was up to something, but if he'd guessed she would've put Ivy in real danger, he would never have allowed the visit at all. Hell, from the start he should have told her *he* would search for Celeste's killer. He'd been blinded by his attraction to her. His sense of fairness had told him she deserved to be in on the hunt since

Celeste had asked her personally to see to it in her letter. But fairness be damned, he fumed. He had gone against his instincts as a gentleman and look where it had got them.

"It hurts, Quill," she said, moving her head restlessly against him. "So much."

That the stubborn woman he'd argued with that morning was admitting as much was an indication of just how much the wound must be paining her.

"I know, darling," he said softly, all but running now, grateful that the path was so deeply ingrained in him that he could have walked it blindfolded. "We'll be at the house in a few minutes and we'll give you something for the pain."

"Should have listened to her," she muttered, her breath soft against his throat. "Told me they're after me, but I didn't believe her. Thought it was gypsy piffle."

"I'll keep you safe, Aphrodite," he said in a low voice. He hadn't managed to today, but that was because his guard was down. But he'd be damned if he'd let the blackguard who killed his aunt harm Ivy again. If that meant finding him and beating him within an inch of his life, then so much the better.

She laughed in a soft whimper against him. "Only one who calls me that," she said in a wavering voice that ended in a moan of pain.

"Because you are a goddess," he said gently. "My love."

He didn't care if the others heard him. And if they did they gave no indication as they trudged on behind him.

Finally, he saw the roof of the house come into view and, buoyed by the sight, he increased his pace. And when Maitland came hurrying toward them, directing a pair of footmen with a litter, he shook his head. "I've made it this far with her," he said in an impatient tone. "I'll get her into the house."

"Dr. Vance has been sent for and should be here soon," Maitland said, walking at a fast clip beside him. "Serena has the maids bringing hot water to her bedchamber, and her maid is ready to help as needed."

"Thank you," he said to his cousin, knowing he could have asked for no better man to assist him in this situation.

Soon they were bounding up the stairs and into the house. Moving past gawking servants who seemed to overrun the hallway, he took Ivy up the main staircase and finally into her bedchamber.

"Here, Quill," Serena said, waiting at the bedside. "Put her down here."

His arms and back were aching like mad, but he didn't feel them until after he'd gently deposited Ivy onto the bed. If it weren't for Maitland following close behind him, he'd have sunk to the floor.

"Come on, old chap," his cousin said in a soothing voice. "She's safe now. Let's get you a chair."

"I'm not leaving her," Quill said in a harsh voice, though he was too weak to break way from the other man's steadying arm.

"Just come into the dressing room for a moment while they undress her," Maitland said as he led him to the doorway leading into the small room. "We all know you intend to marry her, but one mustn't flout convention before the servants. Shameful lack of imagination they've got."

Maitland prattled on in similar fashion as he shut the door behind them and—from where Quill didn't stop to wonder—produced a decanter and two glasses and proceeded to pour.

"I find there's nothing like a jot of brandy to ease the nerves in a situation like this," he said, handing Quill a generous helping. "Drink it up like a good lad."

Doing as he was told, Quill swallowed the fiery liquid and found himself reviving a little, though his legs chose that moment to let him know they needed a rest. Dropping into a chair that was far too small for a man of his size, he brushed a hand over his forehead, the enormity of what had happened suddenly threatening to crush him.

"Someone tried to kill her, Dalton," he said, reverting to his cousin's given name, as he'd called him when they were boys. Closing his eyes against the memory of the shot and his immediate instinct to get Ivy down as quickly as possible, he said in a hoarse voice, "What if I'd lost her?"

Unbidden, the memory of the near miss on that momentous journey back from the village rose in his mind. And what of the bronze statue that had almost hit her at the Northman dinner party?

He'd marked them down as accidents, but now he wasn't so sure. Had someone been trying to kill her all this time? The very idea chilled him to the bone.

Sighing, the duke crouched before him. "But you didn't lose her. She's well. In no small part because you had her out of harm's way before another shot could hit her."

"Wasn't fast enough," Quill said, shaking his head. "She's hurt because of me."

"She's hurt because some idiot with a pistol decided to take aim at her," Maitland said firmly. "If you weren't there she would very likely be dead now. Instead she's got a flesh wound that will likely hurt like the devil for a week or two and then will be forgotten. That's because of you."

Quill tried to get his mind around the idea that he'd saved her, but he could only think of how his decision to let her investigate had nearly got her killed.

"I'm going to find him, Dalton," he said grimly. "And he will pay for what he did this day. And what he did to Aunt Celeste."

"And I'll be by your side when you do it," Maitland agreed with a nod. "I'll even help you bury the damned body. But right now, your lady needs you to keep a level head. And to keep from getting yourself killed."

Brushing his hand over his face, he knew his cousin was right. He drained his glass and set it down on a nearby shelf.

"Do you think they're finished yet?" he asked, staring at the door as if trying to detect what was happening on the other side through sheer force of will.

"There's one way to find out," said Maitland, rising to his feet and draining his own glass.

Quill stood too and opened the dressing room door.

Chapter 25

Ivy hissed as Serena and Polly tried to ease off her pelisse.

"I am sorry, miss," the maid said in a stricken tone, "but the ball pushed the cloth into the wound. I'll fetch a scissors to cut around it."

Soon, after some further moments of pain, Ivy was dressed in a clean shift, with the bedclothes pulled up over her bosom for propriety's sake, as Dr. Vance inspected her upper arm. "The good news, Miss Wareham," he said as he gestured for Serena to place the lamp he'd used to better see the wound on a nearby table, "is that the ball went straight through. So, while I know it hurts quite badly, at least there is no need for me to dig around in your arm to retrieve it."

At that description, Ivy felt the room spin a little.

"Unfortunately," Dr. Vance continued as he opened the black bag he'd carried into the room with him, "there is the matter of the fabric in the wound. I'm afraid removing it will be quite painful. So, be a good girl and drink this laudanum and you won't feel it a bit."

But Ivy shook her head, though the motion made her feel a little ill. "No laudanum," she protested. "It makes me violently ill."

"But my dear girl," the doctor chided, "the pain will feel a great deal worse, I can assure you. Come now, be sensible."

"If she says she doesn't want laudanum, doctor"—Quill's voice broke in—"then she shan't have it." The relief Ivy felt was so great, she sank back against the pillows with the force of it. Her agitation gone now that she knew Quill was there to fight for her.

"Lord Kerr," said Dr. Vance, his usually pleasant face pinched with annoyance, "I will thank you to let me know what's best for my patient."

"I will instead let Miss Wareham be the one to know what's best for her, sir," Quill said firmly. "She is surely the one who knows how laudanum has affected her in the past. Why can't she get roaring drunk instead? I daresay it may make her feel ill too, but its aftereffects will be of a much shorter duration."

The doctor's expression said he thought this was a foolish notion. Yet, he was a man who knew which side his bread was buttered on.

"Very well, my lord," he said with a supercilious sniff. "If that is how you wish to handle the matter, I shall leave you to it. I will be downstairs enjoying a cup of tea. When Miss Wareham is, as you so eloquently put it, 'roaring drunk,' send for me and I will clean the wound."

"He is a good physician," Serena said from where she sat on the other side of the bed, "but Dr. Vance can be a bit of an old woman at times."

"Thank you," Ivy said, reaching for Quill's hand with her uninjured one. "I would probably have allowed him to sway me if you hadn't intervened."

"I doubt Serena would have let him dose you against your will," Quill assured her, kissing her forehead gently.

"I'd have tried," Serena said wryly, "but I suspect the good doctor is not very fond of having his wishes contravened by ladies."

"Well, we've routed him regardless," Quill said in a tone that sounded falsely cheerful, but Ivy was too distracted by the throbbing in her arm to make mention of it. "Maitland, bring the brandy if you please."

And as if Quill had conjured him from the air, the Duke of Maitland appeared bedside, holding a decanter of amber liquid up high. "At your service, your grace," he said, making an exaggerated leg to his cousin before handing him the liquor and a glass.

Seating himself beside her, Quill poured a generous glass of brandy and put it to Ivy's lips. "Sip it so that you don't choke," he told her in a gentle tone. "There's no rush."

The brandy burned at first, but the trail of warmth as it slid down into her felt comforting, and soon Ivy was feeling much more the thing. "This is really quite pleasant, isn't it?" she asked after she'd finished the first glass. She wasn't generally one for strong spirits, but if this was how they made her feel, perhaps she should start drinking them more often.

"I think she's well on her way," Serena said from what to Ivy seemed like very far away, though she was sure Serena was standing only a little behind Quill.

"One more glass I think," Quill said, giving Ivy another sip. But when Ivy felt herself hiccup, he pulled the glass away. "Or perhaps she's had enough now."

"I'll go get Vance," Maitland said.

When did he get here? Ivy wondered, her fuzzy brain trying to make sense of the scene.

"He accompanied us upstairs when I carried you inside," Quill said patiently, as he patted her uninjured hand. *Oh, that's right,* she remembered as if through a fog, *I'm injured.*

"Someone shot me," she said, her voice sounding slurred to her own ears.

"They did, indeed," Quill said, and she could tell that he was angry. Was he angry at *her*? She must have said the words aloud for he assured her, "No, sweet, I'm angry at who-ever shot you. But you rest now. And concentrate on healing. I'll keep you safe from danger."

Danger. Danger. There was something in the back of Ivy's mind trying to catch her attention. But the fog was so thick now, she couldn't quite get to it. *Danger.* She could hear an old woman saying the word. And other things too. Things she needed to tell Quill. But just as soon as the thought occurred to her, it was gone again.

"Ah, I see she's all but insensible," Dr. Vance said from where he appeared behind Quill. "I hope this works as you think it will, Kerr, else Miss Wareham will be in a great deal of pain."

Ivy heard the doctor as if he were speaking from a very long way away. Then she heard Quill respond, but couldn't make out the words. Just the familiar deep rumble of his voice.

*I'll just close my eyes for a minute,*she thought, . . . *and take a little nap . . .*

And then she knew no more.

Though Dr. Vance strongly suggested that Quill leave the room while he extracted the bits of cloth from Ivy's wound, Quill had answered in no uncertain terms that either he re-mained at her side, or it was the good doctor who could leave.

Perhaps knowing when he had been bested, the physician muttered something about high-handed aristocrats, but did not further object.

Holding the hand of her uninjured arm tightly, lest she awaken and need him, Quill took up the position on the other side of the bed from the physican, and watched with grim anger as the doctor used a pair of tweezers to pluck bit after tiny bit of cloth from the oozing wound in Ivy's upper arm. Though she flinched, and groaned in pain from time to time, she did not awaken fully, and by the time the doctor was finished, she was snoring softly.

"I know you will not believe it, as worried as you are, my lord," Dr. Vance said as he sprinkled basilicum powder over the wound before pressing a clean bandage over it, "but this is not, as these things go, all that bad. Your lady was incredibly lucky it only struck her arm. Do you know who was out shooting today? Has anyone come forward?"

In one thing, the doctor was correct, Quill thought, staring down at Ivy's sleeping form: he didn't wish to hear how much worse her wound could have been. The fact that she'd been injured at all was something he would rue to the end of his days.

"It was no accident," he told the other man with a scowl. "You know as well as I do that the hunting in this part of the county is all but nonexistent. And no one with any sense would practice his aim so close to the footpath."

"But that's impossible," Dr. Vance said, his mouth opening and closing like a trout on a line. "Who would wish to harm Miss Wareham for God's sake?"

Caution kept Quill from revealing too much of his suspicions about who had reason to wish Ivy dead. He might wish to, but now was not the time. Instead he shrugged. "I have no idea. For a sweeter, more innocent lady you're not likely to meet."

The doctor's jaw clenched. "You don't suppose whoever it was that poisoned your aunt . . ."

Not wanting to give the other man a hint either way, Quill shrugged. "I have no idea. But if I find out who harmed her, he will rue the day he decided to go after the woman I love."

Swallowing in the face of the marquess's vehemence, the doctor set about putting his instruments back into his black bag. Placing a small vial on the table, he said, "I'll leave the laudanum just in case she has more pain that the brandy can manage." Turning to Serena, who just returned from emptying the basin of dirty water, he said, "Keep her wound dry and clean. And make sure to use plenty of powder on it. If she begins to turn feverish, send for me at once. Make her comfortable, and don't let her out of bed for several days at least. And give her beef broth to replenish the blood she lost."

Despite his anger with the man, Quill said a grudging thanks as the doctor opened the door to leave. Turning, his eyes shadowed, Vance said, "I am sorry, my lord. If I could go back . . ." He left the unsaid words hang in the air for a moment before stepping out and shutting the door behind him.

Quill could feel Serena's gaze on him like a tangible thing from where she stood behind him.

"Why didn't you tell me that aunt was poisoned?" she demanded quietly. "Or that you and Ivy were trying to determine who did it?"

He did her the courtesy of not denying that he and Ivy had been looking into the matter.

"Do you recall the letter Aunt left for Ivy," he said tightly, "the one I presume you left for her in her bedchamber that first night?"

"Yes," Serena said, her brows drawn. "I remember it."

"Aunt told her she suspected someone was trying to kill her. And as it happens, she was being poisoned," he said, feeling exhausted all of a sudden. The events of the day, the long journey back from the scene of Ivy's shooting, were finally taking their toll now that Ivy was resting comfortably.

But Serena had just learned now why it had even happened. And she wanted answers. "Why would she tell a stranger and not one of us?" she demanded, the hurt in her voice evident even through Quill's fatigue. "She'd never even met Ivy. And why Ivy of all the ladies?"

"I don't know," Quill said wearily. "Perhaps Aunt didn't trust us to look at the thing with the necessary lack of emotion?" Though even as he said it, he knew it wasn't fair to Ivy. She'd been affected greatly at the knowledge her benefactress had been murdered. She just hadn't had decades of memories to go along with it. "Who knows why she did it, Serena?" he asked with a sigh. "The simple fact is that she did do it, and because Ivy didn't quite feel she should go about investigating it alone, she told me. And here we are."

"All this time," Serena said with a shake of her head. "I thought the two of you were conducting a love affair. But you were merely conspiring to find who killed Aunt. And now you've compromised her, so you'll have to marry her."

That started a huff of laughter from him. "Oh, the affair is quite real," he admitted with a weary grin. "But, yes, what initially had us putting our heads together was an attempt to discover who poisoned Aunt Celeste."

"Ivy might have been killed," Serena said, her voice tight with emotion. "*You* might have been killed."

He could see that she was just as upset by the news as he'd feared she would be. But to her credit, her back was straight, and his cousin seemed ready to do battle.

The fact that he might have lost Ivy to a murderer today was something he wasn't ready to think about just yet. But something he could do was reassure his cousin. "We are well. All of us. And of all people, Aunt Celeste wouldn't have wanted us to hide ourselves away in fear. And I will do what it takes to protect Ivy and the rest of this family."

Serena shook her head. "Stubborn man," she said softly. "When will you learn that we can take care of ourselves?"

Her eyes softened. "But we do appreciate some assistance from time to time."

She reached out a hand to touch his arm. "I am glad you're both alive. See that you remain that way."

Giving her a crooked smile, he said, "I plan on it."

She was silent for a moment as she looked at the sleeping Ivy.

Quill had leaned his head back against the headboard when Serena's peeved voice broke through his exhaustion. "You told Dalton, didn't you? That's why he suddenly appeared out of nowhere."

At his nod, she muttered a word he'd not heard her use since they'd first learned it as children from one of the grooms.

"I'm going to rip him to shreds," she said, striding across the room to the door, the purpose in her gait spelling imminent doom for her brother.

"Don't kill him," Quill called after her.

"I haven't yet," was her tart reply. "Though lord knows he's given me reason enough over the years."

Quill heard the door close behind her with a snap, and giving in to the demands of his body, he closed his eyes and slept.

Chapter 26

Ivy awoke the next morning in pain. Both in her head, which informed her in no uncertain terms that it was not fond of strong drink, and her arm, which was throbbing in concert with her head.

She thought at first that she must have slept on it wrong, but that was before she felt a heavy masculine arm draped over her middle and the events of yesterday came rushing back to her. The morning light made her close her eyes again at once, but when she raised her lids more slowly, she saw Quill lying on his stomach beside her, his handsome face looking younger somehow in sleep.

His morning beard shadowed his jawline and, as if approaching a wild thing, she reached out tentatively to brush her fingers over the prickly stubble. She gasped when, without opening his eyes, he brought up his large hand to cover hers. Bringing her palm to his mouth, he kissed it.

Then, as if he too had just remembered why he was there, his eyes flew open and he scrambled into a sitting position.

"How are you?" he asked, his brow furrowed. His hair was sticking up at odd angles, but to Ivy's mind he was looking far more handsome than he had any right to at this hour of the morning. She certainly suspected she paled in comparison. "Is your arm paining you? Were you able to sleep?"

He stood and hurried over to the other side of the bed to pour her a glass of water. "I'll ring for some tea, shall I?" He rang the bell pull, then sat down on the edge of the bed and made as if to hold the glass to her mouth.

"Stop," Ivy said, pushing his hand away. "I can hold it myself, Quill. I'm not incapacitated." She tried to sit up and, despite her impatience, was grateful when he helped her by adjusting the pillows. After taking a long sip of the water, which felt like heaven on her parched tongue, she handed the glass back to him.

"Why are you here at this hour anyway?" she asked, as she watched him put the water back on the table. "Where is my maid?"

He blew out a breath and ran a hand through his hair, only making it worse. "I stayed in here with you last night because I wasn't convinced that a footman outside the door would be enough to keep out whoever took a shot at you yesterday."

"And Lady Serena allowed this?" She was rather shocked since the chaperone had seemed earlier to not want to add further flames to the fire of gossip surrounding her relationship with Quill.

"I gave her no choice in the matter," Quill said with the air of a man used to getting what he wants. "Someone tried to kill you yesterday, Ivy. I'm damned if I'll let him make another attempt while I'm here to prevent it. Serena knows better than to cross me when I'm protecting what's mine."

That declaration should have set her back up, but Ivy was strangely reluctant to call his words into question when he was so intent upon keeping her safe.

"And Polly?" she asked, referring to the absent maid.

"I told her to let you sleep as long as you needed to," he

said. "I'll ring for her if you'd like to have her take care of you while I dress."

Since she'd very much like to relieve herself, she nodded. "I wonder if any of my gowns will work with my bandage," she said thoughtfully as he slipped on his waistcoat and picked up his coat from where it lay draped over a chair.

"You won't need to worry about that for a couple of days at least," he said pulling his cuff from the sleeve.

"With the exception of a headache from the brandy I drank," Ivy said reasonably, "I am quite well enough to go downstairs."

His expression turned mulish. "No you are not," he said firmly. "It's very likely that your wound will cause a fever, and you must rest as much as possible to reserve your strength."

"But that's nonsense," Ivy argued. "I see no reason on earth why I should remain cooped up in this bedchamber when I can be looking over Lady Celeste's collection of relics and artifacts. Or looking over some of her translations. I've been so intent upon finding out who killed her that I've not spent even an entire hour in the library. Surely that is unobjectionable. It's not as if I'll be out combing the countryside in search of a killer."

"It's only nonsense if you discount the importance of your health," he said, not looking appeased by her explanation. "You might be carrying my heir, I'll remind you."

If anything could have been more calculated to set her back up, Ivy could not have imagined it.

"Ah," she said with a scowl. "I see now why you are suddenly so interested in my health. I might have known it was only because you see me as a brood mare."

"Don't be absurd," he retorted mildly. "Of course I see you as much more than that, which you should know by now. I only meant to remind you that if you will not rest for your own sake you might do so for the sake of the child." He leaned forward and kissed her, taking care to avoid touching her injured arm.

"The child we aren't even sure exists," Ivy said, exasperated. Though his reassurance made her feel a bit more sanguine about his admonition for her to rest, it didn't dismiss the fact that she'd be stuck alone all day.

Standing upright, he gave a put-upon sigh. "If you must go to the library, then I suppose you must. Have one of the footmen there to fetch things for you, though. I don't want you to make your arm worse with overuse."

"Where will you be?" she asked. Somehow she'd hoped that he would come with her to look over the collection. Though he'd never expressed a particular interest in translation, she'd perhaps foolishly expected him to be there when she first looked at his aunt's books. Or perhaps that was just a wish on her part to read some of the more salacious bits of poetry to him. She couldn't be sure.

His face hardened. "I'm going to see the magistrate, who in this case is Squire Northman, about the attempt to kill you yesterday. I hold out little hope that he'll be able to do anything to find them, but I wish to follow proper procedure in case I do find the miscreant." He didn't say what he'd do if he found them, but it was implied that he wanted it on the record that he'd reported the crime before he meted out his own brand of punishment for the attempt on her life.

At the mention of Northman, Ivy blanched. "Do you really wish to risk seeing Mrs. Northman again so soon?"

But if the idea bothered him, Quill didn't let on. "I'm not ashamed of you, Ivy," he said with a quizzical look. "If anything, the fault lies with Cassandra for being so histrionic about it. And since we are betrothed now, I don't think it's an issue. I doubt I'll see her today anyway. It's far too early in the day for her to have risen. She keeps London hours even in the country."

Ivy wasn't quite sure his lack of worry was warranted, but she supposed it was too late to worry about reputations—hers or his—at this point. And his dismissal of Mrs. Northman went a long way toward quieting any fears she might have had that he nursed a lingering affection for the lady.

"Shall I fetch you something from the village while I'm out?" he asked her, moving back so that Polly, who had just entered with a bowl of hot water, could place it on the side table.

"No, nothing," she said with a smile at his sweet offer. "Just be careful yourself. You seem convinced that yesterday's shooter was after me, but it's entirely possible that you were the target. You were standing right next to me, after all."

But he waved away the suggestion. "I wasn't the one who'd just been warned by a gypsy fortune teller that I was in danger."

When she opened her mouth to counter his argument, he shook his head. "But nonetheless, I will take care. At this point, I suppose we cannot afford to discount any theory about the shooter."

And with a wave, he stepped out of the room, leaving Ivy to Polly's tender care.

After ensuring that Maitland would keep close watch over Ivy in his absence, Quill set out on horseback for Squire Northman's house. But when he arrived, he saw Dr. Vance's familiar carriage waiting at the door. A pang of foreboding ran through him.

"Is someone in the house ill?" he asked the groom who stood waiting to take the horse's reins.

The young man winced. "One of the maids, my lord" He looked around as if to see who was watching them. "Took her own life, like."

With a curse, Quill sprinted up the stairs of the portico

and when the door opened, he didn't wait for a greeting from the butler. "It was the maid Elsie, wasn't it?" he asked the man, who looked aghast at Quill's lack of decorum.

"I'm sure if you will wait in the drawing room, my lord, Mr. Northman will explain in due time what has happened," Watson said in a dignified huff.

But his lack of reply to the question told Quill all he needed to know. Brushing past the indignant servant, he hurried through what looked to be the servants' hall and followed the sound of weeping and murmured whispers to a small group of servants standing near an open door.

"My lord," the butler called out from behind him. "I'm sure if you will just come with me Mr. Northman will be happy to—"

"It's all right, Watson," said Northman himself, as he stepped out from the door where the crowd was gathered. "I'll speak to his lordship here."

Quill glanced back at the butler, who looked perturbed at the breach of protocol, but was silent.

Northman, who looked grim, gestured for Quill to come forward. "You lot should go down to the kitchens and have some tea. I'll let you know of any news as soon as I'm able."

Watson came forward and ushered the servants, a couple of footmen and three weeping maids, back toward the other end of the hall.

"I don't suppose you know why my wife's maid, whom you and Miss Wareham questioned only days ago," Northman said with a scowl to Quill as they stepped into the grim little bedchamber where Elsie had drawn her last breath, "would wish to take her own life?"

Quill was silent for a moment as he looked to where Dr. Vance stood over the body of Elsie, which was lying stiff on the floor. It was obvious from the posture of the corpse that her death had not been a peaceful one. Her face was contorted in a rictus of agony, and her hands were tightly fisted against her chest. He wondered suddenly if this is what it had been like for Celeste and was assailed by a renewed sense of determination to find out who had done this to her. To them both. For he was sure now that whoever had killed his aunt had also killed her maid.

The doctor, who had been making notes in a small bound book, turned and met Quill's eyes. It was clear that the other man had come to the same conclusion.

To Northman, Quill said, "I have a suspicion that the same person who killed my aunt might have killed Elsie."

If the magistrate was shocked by the news, he didn't show it. Instead he scowled. "What makes you think that Lady Celeste was deliberately murdered? I thought we'd decided that she likely died of a wasting disease, Vance."

That he and Vance had discussed the possibility that Celeste's death may not have been from natural causes was evident from Norman's words, and Quill would have demanded an explanation, but Vance spoke up, cutting him off. "I told you at the time, Northman, that I could not be sure without sending the body to London for autopsy. And that was not what the family wished. Now, thanks to some pointed questions from his lordship and Miss Wareham, I have decided that it is likely that Lady Celeste was poisoned by the tonic Elsie was giving her for her headaches."

The squire looked grim. "Has my wife been in danger this whole time?" he demanded with icy calm.

Vance had the good grace to look abashed. "I would never have allowed her to come here if I'd suspected the maid at the time of Lady Celeste's death," he said defensively. "It was not until Lord Kerr began asking questions that it occurred to me that the tisanes were the likely source of the poison."

That didn't seem to reassure Northman much, but he did not belabor the point. "So, Elsie has also been murdered?

What about this indicates that she didn't simply take her own poison in a fit of conscience?" He gestured to the overturned teacup on the floor beside the body, the dregs of the last sip clinging to the bowl of the floral-patterned porcelain.

"Aside from the fact that there are far less agonizing ways to die," Quill said, stooping to pick up the cup and sniff it. As he'd suspected, there was no strange odor. No indication that it was been laced with anything other than tea. "There is the fact that the amount of poison needed to kill her so quickly would be all but impossible to drink in such a concentrated source as a single cup of tea."

"Would it not depend upon the poison?" Northman demanded. "Surely they all cannot taste foul."

"I suspect in Lady Celeste's case," Dr. Vance said, taking the cup from Quill and sniffing it with diffidence, "that the culprit was aconite. Since the visit Lord Kerr and Miss Wareham paid me earlier in the week, I have done some research into substances that might cause symptoms that mimic those of a wasting disease or cankers of the bowel, and aconite seems to be the most likely source. And it could easily be masked in a brewed tonic of the sort Lady Celeste was in the habit of taking."

"But if there was no sign of aconite in Elsie's tea," Northman said, his mouth tight, "then how the hell did she ingest it?"

Quill stooped and pulled a small box—the sort that was often used by confectioners to preserve sweetmeats and other sweet delicacies—out from beneath the bed, where it lay on its side. The lid was off, and Quill looked inside before showing it to the other two men. At the bottom there was both greasy residue and some crumbs.

"Did Elsie receive any gifts in the past several days?" he asked Northman. "Anything unexpected or perhaps a surprise to mark her birthday or some other special day?"

Northman pokered up. "I am not in the habit of keeping track of the personal lives of my household staff, Lord Kerr. I couldn't even tell you when the damned woman's birthday was, much less whether she received any gifts on the occasion."

"Then we should question your housekeeper," Quill said, not bothering to ask whether it would do any good to speak to Northman's wife. Cassandra was also not the sort to show an interest in the lives of her servants. Even one so personal as her own maid. "I suspect the poison was delivered over the course of a few days, which would be easy enough to do if it were used as an ingredient in a pastry or sweetmeat."

Vance nodded his agreement. "Aconite might have been unpalatable in a single cup of tea, but spreading it out over several pieces of candy or biscuits would make it less noxious."

Cursing, Northman shook his head. "I would have liked to know there was a madman poisoning people in my district before he struck in my own household, Vance."

"And shooting," Quill said, not wishing to lose sight of his original reason for seeking the magistrate out. "Yesterday someone made an attempt on Miss Ivy Wareham's life as we walked back to Beauchamp House from the gypsy fortune teller's caravan."

Looking as if he wished himself anywhere but the Sussex coast at that very moment, Northman cursed again. "I guess you'd better come up to my study so that I can take down the details and have my investigator look into it." Turning to Vance, he said, "I'd like for you to testify at the inquest, doctor, so please ensure that your report is as thorough as necessary."

The physician shot a look of sheer loathing at the magistrate's back as Northman turned and dismissed him. Quill filed that away for future reflection, and with a look of commiseration with the doctor, turned and followed Northman from the room.

Chapter 27

A bit of toast and tea in her room was all Ivy could stomach thanks to yesterday's pain-relieving dose of brandy, so she arrived in Lady Celeste's magnificent library before any of the other ladies.

Once again she was hit with the wish that she'd been able to meet the woman with the diverse scholarly knowledge who assembled such a collection. Not to mention the artistic sensibility that had directed Lady Celeste to design the room itself, with its gorgeous inlaid ceiling and rich mahogany and gilt-edged shelving. The visual effect was breathtaking, and Ivy was certain that it had been her benefactress's intent to overwhelm each visitor who stepped into what had clearly been a labor of love for the lady.

But with the thought of Lady Celeste's life came the thought of her premature death. And even as she took in the details of the room that had been Celeste's personal domain, Ivy wondered for the first time if there weren't some clue to the identity of who had killed her hidden here. The thought was overwhelming given that the collection, according to Greaves, contained some seven thousand volumes. If Celeste had thought to secrete some message in one of the books, it would take more than Ivy working with her uninjured arm to find it in enough time to catch the killer before he struck again.

With a sigh, she stepped over to the shelves behind the massive desk Celeste had used for her own personal studies. If Ivy were going to hide something, it would definitely be near where she spent the most time. And the books on these shelves, if the wear on their spines was any indication, were amongst Lady Celeste's favorites. Unlike the rest of the shelves, these few behind the desk seemed to be arranged in some order that only their owner had understood. Multi-volume novels were sandwiched between mathematical treatises and philosophical works.

For instance, she thought with a smile for the happy disorder of it, here were two volumes of Samuel Pepys diaries beside the third volume of Madame d'Arblay's *Cecilia*. Whether Lady Celeste had simply shelved them as she finished or she kept them there to reread favorite passages, Ivy had no idea. It was one of those circumstances of day-to-day life that was lost along with Celeste. And like so many details of that lady's thoughts, the reason for it was impossible to learn now that she was gone.

If only Lady Celeste had, like Pepys, kept a record of her . . . Ivy stopped, her hand reaching out toward the shelf in question, arrested by her train of thought.

What were the chances that a woman who so valued philosophy and scholarship and the life of the mind would not have kept some sort of record of her studies or, if not her scholarly pursuits, then at the very least of her thoughts? It was hardly uncommon for a lady to keep a journal, but for a woman of Lady Celeste's proclivities to *not* do so would be positively unheard of. Especially if she knew, as her letter had indicated, that she was not long for this world.

Thus it was that when Sophia, followed close behind by Daphne and Gemma, wandered into the room after breakfast, it was to find Ivy balanced on the rolling ladder along the shelves on the wall behind the big desk using her good hand to remove a single volume at a time to see if there was anything behind it.

"What on earth are you doing out of bed?" Sophia asked aghast, hurrying to stand gaping up at where Ivy seemed to hang upon the library wall. "You were shot yesterday, Ivy. You should be resting."

"Or at the very least refraining from climbing ladders when you've only one hand to save yourself with," Gemma said from beside her sister. "You might have waited until someone else was in the room before you decided to tempt fate and gravity by taking your life into your own hands."

"Fate and gravity have nothing to do with one another," Daphne said staring up at Ivy with interest. "One is an abstract concept that relies upon supernatural beliefs to sustain it that cannot be proved or disproved, while the other is a natural law that can easily be proved by dropping any common object from a height equal to or greater than the length of said object. I doubt it is possible to tempt either because they do not possess human feelings."

"Yes, thank you, Daphne," Sophia said with a small sigh. "I believe that was one of those 'figures of speech' we were discussing yesterday. I doubt Gemma meant literally that fate and gravity would be wracked with the desire to make Ivy fall from this ladder."

Ivy could see from her elevated height that Daphne wished to argue the point, so she spoke up. "I am looking for Lady Celeste's private diaries, and since you have come in at just the moment when I was considering the folly of my decision to climb this ladder, I will thankfully accept your help in descending."

With Gemma holding her waist and Sophia holding the

ladder, Ivy carefully made her way, step by step, down from her perch.

Daphne spoke up almost as soon as her feet were on the floor again. "I believe I saw some journals in Lady Celeste's bedchamber last evening when we were playing hide-and-seek with Jeremy."

"Why were you in that part of the house?" Sophia asked, her pretty face scrunched up in puzzlement.

"Why were you playing hide-and-seek on the night I was shot?" Ivy asked, cutting to what, for her, was the more pertinent question.

Gemma smiled sheepishly. "Jem overheard his mother and Lord Kerr speaking about what happened and he was frightened that whoever shot at you might try to get into the house. So the duke thought a game of hide-and-seek might prove a useful distraction."

On hearing that young Jeremy had been frightened, Ivy felt a pang of distress for the boy. From what she'd heard, he'd already had what wasn't a particularly uneventful childhood, so hearing that someone living in the same house had been shot must have been upsetting.

Gemma, however, was distracted by something else. "Speaking of the duke," she said, her eyes narrowed on Daphne, "both you and he were missing for quite a long time while the rest of us played. You didn't see him somewhere near Lady Celeste's diaries, did you?"

To Ivy's astonishment, Daphne blushed. Something Ivy hadn't been sure was possible.

"I may have run into him in the vicinity," she said, looking just past them into the room beyond, her usual habit of not making eye contact seeming more intentional than usual, though Ivy knew that was absurd. "We hid together for a while before realizing that no one would be coming to find us there."

"I'll bet you 'hid,'" Gemma said with a smirk. "I suspect you two have been doing quite a bit of 'hiding' over the last day or so."

Daphne frowned. "Of course we haven't. At least, only while we were playing hide-and-seek. It would be odd to hide during the normal course of a day."

Ivy shared an amused look with the Hastings sisters. "I think what she meant, Daphne," she said with a grin, "was that you and the duke have been spending some time together. Alone time."

The cloud lifted and Daphne nodded. "Oh, yes. We have. He is quite good at kissing. Though I haven't been able to convince him to take me as a lover. He is convinced that it would not be proper. And no amount of convincing on my part will sway him on the matter. It is really quite frustrating."

Ivy, Sophia, and Gemma all stared at her.

An uncomfortable silence descended upon them.

"I've shocked you," Daphne said with what sounded to Ivy like disappointment. "I don't know why I cannot seem to tell what will and will not shock my acquaintances. I do not wish to distress you all. Certainly not while Ivy is still recovering from a gunshot wound."

Her innate sense of fondness for the other girl made Ivy push past her surprise at her declaration about the Duke of Maitland, and she moved to touch Daphne on the arm. She'd sensed from their first meeting that anything else would prove uncomfortable for her. "We are surprised, dear, by your plain speaking, but not distressed. Pray do not become distressed yourself. It's just that we are not used to hearing such things, and well, as perhaps your mother has told you, it's not quite appropriate to speak of such things in public."

"But you're my friends," Daphne said, looking even more puzzled. "We are not in the middle of a ballroom. I know well enough not to speak of such things in drawing rooms, or in mixed company, or at the mantua-makers." The way she listed off the locales where she knew not to speak told Ivy that these had been where she'd done so in her mother's presence.

"She's right," Gemma said with a rueful smile. "We are her friends, and we are alone in here. So she's technically correct."

Before Daphne could tell them that technically was the only way to be correct—something she'd done on a previous occasion when Gemma used the term—Ivy spoke to the issue at the heart of their discomfort. "Daphne, I realize that it is frustrating for you to be rejected by the duke, but he is quite correct that it would be quite improper for him to ahh . . ." She searched for a word that was explicit enough for Daphne to understand, but not so graphic as to offend the other two ladies.

"Engage in sexual congress with me?" Daphne supplied, not betraying with so much as a blush that the term embarrassed her. Ivy wondered what must it be like to be so comfortable with speaking about such things. It had to be difficult, of course, since her plain speaking often landed Daphne in trouble, but on the other hand it would be such a relief not to be constantly afraid of saying the wrong thing.

"Yes, that," Ivy agreed with an apologetic smile to Sophia and Gemma. "Lord Kerr and I were only found kissing at the Northman's house and we are now betrothed because of it. If you wish to, ah, do *that* with the duke, then he would of course, need to marry you."

"First of all," Daphne said patiently, "the duke and I would not engage in sexual congress anywhere where we might be seen by anyone. That would be quite odd." Before Ivy could respond to that, she went on. "And secondly, why is it that men are allowed to do it without marrying their partners but ladies are required to? It is highly illogical that ladies cannot f—"

Sophia placed a finger to Daphne's lips to stop her words. "We understand, dear. It does seem wretchedly unfair that ladies are required to marry the men they do *that* with. But nevertheless, it is the way of our world. And as your mother has explained to you I feel sure, those who do it without benefit of marriage risk any number of problems. Bearing a child out of wedlock, for instance, or being ostracized from society. Poor Ivy will be the subject of a great deal of talk, I suspect, thanks to her interlude with Lord Kerr in the Northman hallway."

"In point of fact," Daphne argued, "my mother died when I was only a small child, so I was left to learn about such things from books. There is a quite interesting pamphlet called *Aristotle's Masterpiece* that contains all sorts of ridiculous notions—that a child conceived out of wedlock, for instance, will be born covered all over with hair. Truly ridiculous stuff—especially when one considers how many children of the aristocracy are born on the wrong side of the blanket. I believe that—"

"Oh, I am sorry, Daphne," Ivy said, latching onto the news about the other lady's mother, hoping to divert her before one or all of them broke down in tears of exasperation. "It must have been quite difficult to lose your mother at such a young age." It also went a long way, in Ivy's opinion, toward explaining why Daphne was so ungoverned in her conversation.

But much as she would like to discuss the matter more, it was the death of Lady Celeste that was foremost on her mind at the moment.

"Perhaps we can continue this discussion later?" she asked hopefully. "After we've gone to find Lady Celeste's journals? For I truly fear that if we do not find out who killed her, someone else will die very soon."

She'd known her interruption would perhaps upset Daphne, at the very least, but all three of the other ladies gasped. And Ivy realized what she'd just done. In her effort to soothe Daphne she'd let the truth slip out.

"Lady Celeste was murdered?" Sophia demanded, her eyes pinning Ivy to where she stood.

"How long have you known?" Gemma asked with a stricken expression.

"So that's why you were shot," Daphne said as if something had finally clicked into place.

Ivy's mind raced, searching for some way of explaining things that wouldn't make them more annoyed than they already were.

But she was saved from reply by Quill, followed by Maitland, striding into the room.

"Elsie is dead," Quill said without preamble. "Poisoned, and likely by the same thing that killed Celeste."

When Quill arrived back at Beauchamp House, he was displeased to find that instead of keeping by Ivy's side in the library as per his request, Maitland was instead seated in a chair outside the door of that room.

"Why the devil aren't you watching over Ivy as I requested?" he demanded of his cousin, who stood as soon as he saw Quill approach.

Northman had listened with mounting frustration as Quill told him about the letter from Lady Celeste that had prompted his and Ivy's investigation into her murder, their suspicion that the medicinal tisanes had been the means by which the poison was administered, and their visit to the gypsy woman the day before. When he got to the point at which Ivy was shot at, the magistrate had cursed.

"I hope you're happy now, Lord Kerr," Northman had spat out. "Not only should you have reported this business about your aunt as soon as the letter surfaced, but you've very nearly got your lady killed because of your damned aristocratic notion that you can handle all of this on your own."

Quill had forborne from pointing out to Northman that while he was a magistrate, it wasn't as if he had a stable of men at the ready to seek out criminals as was the case with Bow Street. This was a relatively rural locale and as such had been run by the landowners and aristocrats who lived there for centuries. And he was quite able to take care of himself and those whom he cared about. Ivy included. Instead, he had accepted the admonishment without replying and took his leave. Promising without really meaning it, that he would let the other man know of any further developments.

He had felt the need to report Ivy's shooting, of course, because it was the right thing to do. But now that another life had been taken, Quill knew that there was no time to wait for the wheels of local justice to find the killer. He would simply have to do that himself. And if Northman disliked it, he'd simply have to live with his anger.

Now, however he was back at Beauchamp House facing Maitland, who contrary to Quill's request had seen fit to sit outside the library rather than at Ivy's side. "Well? Why aren't you bloody well in there?"

Maitland's jaw clenched and his cheekbones reddened. "The other ladies are in the library with Miss Wareham. And if there were anything untoward happening I would have heard them cry out."

That his cousin would not meet his eye made Quill's brow furrow with suspicion. "What aren't you telling me?" he demanded. "Are you hiding out here?"

When Maitland's face only turned redder, Quill knew he had his answer. Diverted momentarily from the murders, he tilted his head. "What happened? I thought you were smitten with Lady Daphne?" It wasn't like his cousin to leave off pursuing a woman so soon after catching her scent. "Has she given you the heave-ho already?" It was rare that the duke, with his golden good looks and sunny personality, was rebuffed, but it did happen on occasion. And Quill knew that when it did, Maitland wasn't happy about it.

"If you must know," the duke said with a dignified sniff, "it is I who have chosen to back away from Lady Daphne. For the time being at any rate."

This was novel. "I know she can be outspoken, but surely that's nothing you can't handle. After all, it's not as if you don't put your own foot in your mouth from time to time."

Maitland glanced to either side, as if ensuring that they would not be overheard, then in a low voice hissed, "She wants me to sleep with her, Quill!"

In spite of his cousin's very serious distress, Quill couldn't help himself. He laughed.

"It's not funny," the duke said, reaching up to grip his blond locks in frustration. "I am not in the business of debauching innocents. I am a gentleman. If she were a widow, or a bored wife, perhaps, but I won't touch an unmarried lady without some kind of understanding between us and you damned well know it. Not only is it beyond the pale, it goes against my code as a gentleman."

"And what was her response to this?" Quill asked, his interest piqued by this unusual turn of events. He'd known Lady Daphne marched to her own drum, but this was a surprise even for her.

"When I said that she'd have to marry me first, she told me I was being foolish," Maitland said, his eyes wide with outrage. "I'm a duke of the realm, by god, and she behaved as if a proposal from me was utterly unnecessary!"

That his cousin had, in fact, asked the chit to marry him

told Quill just how far gone he was over her. To his knowledge, Maitland had never before asked a lady to marry him. And since he knew well enough how sharp the pain of rejection could be, he bit back his amusement and clapped the other man on the shoulder. "Perhaps she'll come around," he said, despite the fact that he suspected Lady Daphne could be quite as stubborn as Maitland when she felt like it.

"Well, she'll have to if she wants me to give her the benefit of my legendary lovemaking skills," Maitland said, in a not-altogether-joking mode. He'd always been a bit full of himself when it came to that, Quill thought with a roll of his eyes. "I won't settle for anything less than marriage, and she'll simply have to capitulate or miss out."

It would have been quite satisfying for Quill to point out to his cousin, who had only recently been taunting him over his own fall into the parson's mousetrap, that he himself was about to dive in headfirst. However, there were other more pressing matters to attend to.

"Much as I would love to continue this discussion of your 'legendary lovemaking skills,'" Quill said dryly, "there is the matter of a murderer on the loose that needs my attention right now. And if you are too frightened to go into the library with me to discuss the goings-on at the Northman house with Ivy and the other ladies, then I suggest you make yourself scarce."

But despite his earlier refusal to enter the library, the duke had never been one to back down from a challenge from his cousin, so he indicated to Quill that he should proceed. Opening the door, the marquess stepped inside to find the four ladies clustered together behind Aunt Celeste's enormous desk.

"Elsie is dead," he said knowing that the other three ladies were not even aware that Celeste had been murdered but deciding it was high time they all spoke openly about the entire matter. "Poisoned, and likely by the same thing that killed Celeste."

To his surprise, however, neither the Hastings sisters nor Lady Daphne seemed particularly shocked by the news that their benefactress had been murdered.

"I told them about Lady Celeste," Ivy said in response to his questioning look. "I thought it was time to enlist the aid of three of the most intelligent ladies of my acquaintance in our search. Besides, who is to say that this person will not make an attempt on their lives next."

"Not if I have anything to say about it," Maitland said hotly as he shut the library door behind him. "It's time we put this monster out of commission once and for all."

"I agree, cousin," said Quill with equal ferocity. "And since all the ladies are now aware of the situation, perhaps we should discuss our next move in this deadly game."

"First tell us about Elsie," Ivy said moving to take a seat at one of the large library tables, and waiting for the others to follow suit.

Once he had taken a chair beside her, Quill explained what had happened to Elsie, including the details of the poisoned confectionary and his discussion with Northman. "Though I know the magistrate would like us to sit back and let the authorities find out who is doing this," he said in conclusion, "the fact that he is brazen enough to kill beneath Northman's own roof, in addition to the fact that he took a shot at you, Ivy, while we were all there to see it, tells me that the killer is desperate now. And I, for one, am not willing to just sit by and let him try to kill you again."

Ivy gave a shiver and, not caring about the impropriety of the gesture, he covered her free hand with his own.

"Something occurred to me while you were gone this morning," Ivy said into the silence that followed. Quickly she outlined how she'd come to think about the possibility that

Celeste kept a journal. "And since Daphne recalled seeing some journals in Lady Celeste's bedchamber last night, we were about to make our way up there."

Feeling like a fool, Quill shook his head. "Of course, she kept journals. Don't you remember that she was always scribbling away in them when we were children, Maitland?"

"Yes," his cousin said, his voice rising with excitement. "I don't know why I didn't think of them either. I suppose that after a certain time she never let us see her with them, and I simply forgot altogether."

"Then let's go upstairs and get them," Ivy said in a firm voice. "Because Lady Celeste deserves to have justice."

Chapter 28

Though it felt a bit ridiculous for them all to go upstairs to Lady Celeste's bedchamber at once, that is what they did. Ivy and Quill led the way with the others following close behind. When they arrived in the darkened chamber, however, all eyes turned to Daphne, who said, "They were stacked on the little shelf behind the writing desk, there."

Sophia and Gemma went to open the curtains to let in the daylight, and Ivy took a moment to look around the room where Lady Celeste had lived for most of her adult life. It was decorated in the colors of the sea—light greens and blues with a burst of white here and there in the trimmings of the bedclothes and on the valances over the windows, which looked out, as it happened, on the sun-dappled waters of the channel. There was a hint of rosewater and lavender in the air, almost as if Celeste had only just walked through the room, leaving her scent behind.

Crossing to the writing desk, where Quill had taken a seat and was scanning the low shelves that ran along the wall behind, Ivy picked up the lamp he'd just lit and held it so that he might see the rows of books better. "Here," he said tersely. "There must be decades worth of diaries here. This may take longer than we'd hoped." He began pulling out the volumes in stacks of three and piling them onto the surface of the desk.

"There are six of us," Ivy said with a practical air. "Perhaps we can each take a decade to look over."

"We should go back to the library where we can take notes," Gemma said, grabbing a handful of volumes and not waiting to see if the others would follow.

It was a good idea, so Ivy tried to gather up a few of the diaries into the crook of her good arm, but ended up dropping one.

"I'll carry yours," Quill said, edging her out of the way as Sophia, Daphne, and Maitland picked up the rest of the books and filed out leaving Ivy and Quill alone.

"I hope she knows we are trying," Ivy said in the suddenly quiet room. "That we appreciate what she did for us and will try to avenge her."

Slipping an arm around her shoulders, Quill said against her hair, "I think if Celeste is watching us now at all, she's having a very hearty laugh at how quickly her favorite nephews have succumbed to two of her chosen bluestockings."

At his words, Ivy looked up at him with wide eyes. "Did Maitland tell you about Daphne then?"

"More like whined," Quill said with a laugh. "I was not very sympathetic, I'm afraid. It is far too amusing to see the tables turned on him for a change."

"I must admit to feeling some sympathy for the poor man," Ivy said with a shake of her head. "I think anyone would be flummoxed by such a direct request from a lady as beautiful as Daphne. We did try to explain to her that it's not quite proper to tell a gentleman in those terms what she wants from him. Though I do see your point about the whole marriage bit. If it's good for the goose, why wouldn't it be good for the gander?"

Well, it will be a while before Aunt Celeste sees any

resolution on that front, I fear," Ivy said wryly. Then turning serious, she added, "But I do hope we will succeed in finding her poisoner. I do dislike the idea of her spirit being restless because this thing is unresolved. I certainly know I will not be able to rest easy until he's caught."

"Then I suppose we should join the others and see if we can find some clue in the journals," Quill said, snuffing out the lamp, then gathering the remaining journals in his arms and following Ivy from the room.

When they reached the library, they found that Serena had joined them and had taken a stack of journals to go through as well.

"I believe you have the earliest years there," Gemma said, looking up from where she'd opened the first of a stack of six books. "Just call out if you find something that might be useful." She gestured to a slate and a bit of chalk. "I'll make notations as we go. Even if you're unsure, tell us. It will be better to have too much than too little information."

Resuming the chairs they'd vacated earlier, Ivy and Quill sat side by side and began to go through their diaries.

The room was silent for a long while as everyone scanned the diaries.

As they went through the journals, Daphne, who had been reading the past ten years of entries, had mentioned when Lady Celeste began to search for the four ladies she would leave her estate to. Quill hadn't considered that the decision to leave Beauchamp House to a quartet of women outside the family was anything but caprice. But the passages Daphne had shared revealed that, far from whimsy, Celeste's decision had rested on a genuine wish to see that her collection was put in the hands of scholars—lady scholars like her—who would put it to best use.

Only about a quarter hour had passed before Daphne issued a most un-Daphne-like noise.

Frowning, Ivy looked up and saw that everyone else was also staring at the blonde, too, "What is it? Did you find something troubling?"

When the mathematician looked up, Ivy was startled to see tears in her eyes. "My goodness," she said, moving to sit beside her. She exchanged a wide-eyed look with Sophia who seemed just as puzzled as Ivy. "You must tell us, my dear. If it can help us find the killer, no matter how awful, we need to know it."

Accepting the handkerchief that Maitland had wordlessly handed her, Daphne blew her nose loudly and said, "It's not so much a clue as it is just something that . . ." She seemed at a loss for words. "Well, I suppose it moved me. That's all."

"Are you going to keep it to yourself then, dear?" Serena asked with a raised brow when Daphne didn't elaborate.

"What?" Daphne looked up as if she'd just noticed they were all there.

She was behaving very oddly, Ivy thought, surveying her friend. Perhaps her interactions with the duke had set her off-balance. Interesting.

"Oh." Shaking herself a little, as if emerging from a trance, Daphne blinked. "It was just this passage in one of the later journals. From about three years ago, I think. She talks about her reasons for choosing us, and why she wished to ensure that female scholars benefitted from the collections she'd amassed over the years. It just struck me a little, I suppose. That she felt so strongly about it. That she chose you all. And me."

Picking up the journal she'd been reading, Daphne opened it and began to read aloud:

I know my family will think me mad for it, but I am determined that my life's work will not go to waste. That the books and artifacts and art I so painstakingly purchased, piece by piece, in an effort to expand my own knowledge of the world, will serve to further the education of women with the good sense and intelligence to put their minds to good use. I am confident that the young ladies I have my eye on will only be a credit to their sex and their chosen disciplines. It is my hope that once they realize how important this is to me that my nephews and niece will understand and let my heirs do what they were put on earth to do without causing them grief for it.

Perhaps because the way in which my own pursuit of scholarship was discouraged by my parents, I know all too well how difficult the way can be for those of us who were gifted with intellectual ability, but had the misfortune to be born women. One day I hope that it will be possible for anyone with the requisite talent—be they rich or poor, male or female, aristocrat or serf—to pursue her true calling. But until that day, I will do my part to open the door for these four, whom I hope will prove themselves worthy of my gift.

The silence in the library was so thick you might have heard a feather fall. And Ivy found that her own eyes were damp. "Oh, I wish I could have met her just once," she said, feeling the loss of their benefactor more keenly than ever. "If only to thank her for choosing me. Though I cannot imagine what set me apart from the countless other lady scholars out there."

"Me too," said Sophia, also a little misty.

"I want to find whoever killed her," Daphne said, her earlier sentiment gone now, leaving in its place a grim determination. "Not only did he rob us of the chance to meet Lady Celeste, but he also took her from the place she loved best in the world. Against her will." Her fists clenched. "I dislike it above all things when a woman is forced to do something against her will."

Ivy got the feeling that there was something more than just mourning the loss of Lady Celeste behind Daphne's declaration, but she decided to speak with her about it later.

She was about to suggest that they get back to work, when Gemma spoke up. "Why didn't she send for us? When she knew she was dying, I mean?" The younger Hastings sister, who was generally the least likely of the quartet to take something to heart, seemed to be particularly upset at their benefactor's decision. "I know it can't have been pleasant," she went on, "but we would not have cared about that. So long as we'd been able to meet her. To thank her."

Serena, who had been silent up to now, cleared her throat. "I think I might be able to shed some light on that," she said sadly. "I think it's easy not to guess, when all you've known of her has been her hopes and dreams set forth in these journals. Or the individual messages she left for each of you upon your arrival here. But I knew Aunt Celeste, as did Maitland and Kerr, from the time I was little. And despite her intelligence, and zeal for reform, she was, in point of fact, a bit shy."

"You aren't telling us that she didn't call us to her because she was afraid of meeting us, surely?" Sophia looked skeptical in the extreme. "Because I won't believe that the same woman who defied her family and left her entire estate to four strangers was too timid to actually see them at least once."

But Serena shook her head. "No, not in so many words. It was more that meeting people—even those she knew she would enjoy getting to know—was hard for her. After a dinner party once, she took to her bed for a week. 'Refilling the well' she called it. And as much as she would have loved meeting you, I think in those last few weeks she was using every bit of strength she had to fight off her illness.

And then, by the time she knew it was hopeless, it was too late."

"It did take a lot out of her," Quill confirmed, his eyes reflecting his own sorrow at the loss of his aunt. "Meeting people. She could be as animated and witty as can be, but she didn't have an endless supply of energy. And I can well imagine her thinking she had all the time in the world to meet you only to find out she was wrong."

"I want to know who it was," Gemma said fiercely. "I want to know who killed this remarkable woman."

Ivy agreed. "I think we all wish to find out who did this. So, let's dive back into the journals and find something. There has to be some clue here that will tell us something useful."

With murmured assent, they all got back to perusing their portions of the journals.

She was nearing the end of the volume from the summer after Celeste's debut when Ivy reached a notation that had her heart quickening with excitement. Celeste had fallen in love with a man named Ian. And when Ivy moved on to the next journal, she found another mention of Celeste's passion for Ian, followed by a lament about the unfairness of the parents who wouldn't let them be together. But it was the description of their thwarted elopement along with vague but unmistakable descriptions of what had occurred between them on their single night together that had Ivy convinced that she'd discovered something that could be the clue they were looking for.

She read the tear-stained words of the page Celeste had written some three months after the elopement:

My dearest love has been sent away, but God has given me something to remember him by. If only I can manage to convince Mama and Papa to let me keep the child. Surely

even they cannot be so cruel as to wrest a babe from its
mother's arms—especially when it is entirely their doing
that its father is rotting away in some country parsonage
in Yorkshire.

Then, ten months later, again in tear-stained script, she'd
written:

It is done. They have taken the only real things I've ever
loved from me. I only hope that my dear little girl will have
a happier life than the one I've been given. I will never forgive Father for his perfidy. He might have agreed to give
me Beauchamp House outright as a peace offering, but
there will never be peace between us again. And I will
never be happy again.

Ivy brushed away her own tears at the thought of what
Celeste had endured at such a young age. That she'd been
separated from the man she loved—a clergyman it sounded
like, so likely not smart enough for the Duke and Duchess of
Beauchamp to allow to court their daughter—was one thing,
but to also have the child born of that love torn from her very
arms? Well, Ivy would not have blamed Lady Celeste a bit if
she'd become a bitter, cold, unfeeling woman after that. And
yet, from all appearances, she'd gone on to make a name
for herself in scholarly circles and to amass one of the most
impressive collections of books and artifacts in Europe, let
alone England.

"Lady Celeste had a child," she said aloud, eliciting gasps
and shocked sounds from her fellow readers. "A girl who was
cruelly taken from her when it was but a month old."

"Oh, poor Celeste," Serena said, her lovely features contorted with sadness. "I knew our grandparents were cruel, but
I had no notion they'd do such a thing."

"What makes you think they were responsible?" Maitland asked his sister. "I'm not disagreeing about their character, mind you, I just wish to know what makes you think it was they who did this."

"I always had the sense from Aunt Celeste," Serena explained with a sad smile, "that she'd once had a great love but for some reason they'd been separated. She never came right out and said so. But she told me when I was foolish enough to elope with Fanning that I must follow my heart. That she'd tried to do so herself but had been cruelly thwarted. Of course, it turns out that eloping with Fanning was far from the great love story I'd wished it to be, but that's neither here nor there."

"You never told us this," Quill said, looking hurt that his cousin hadn't taken him or her own brother into her confidence.

"I forgot about it after Fanning," Serena admitted with a sigh. She'd confided in the four bluestockings about the horrors of her marriage, so it wasn't surprising to Ivy to learn that her attention had been focused solely on her own safety and that of her child during that period. That Quill's cousin had managed to regain a sense of her own self-worth and power after the way she'd been treated was a testament to Serena's strength. And it was something Ivy admired about her wholeheartedly.

"He had a way of demanding all my attention," Lady Serena continued. "Then when Jeremy was born, and Fanning died, Celeste was adamant that I should come to her. And she said something the first time she held Jeremy that should have told me, but again I was awash with my own thoughts. She said that it had been over twenty years since she'd held a baby. I thought she meant any child at all, but of course she meant her own."

"But who was the father?" Quill demanded. "I always

thought Celeste never married because she preferred going her own way. I dislike the thought of her alone and lonely for all those years."

Ivy pointed them to the mention of the vicarage in Yorkshire. "It seems to me that if the daughter of a duke were to fall in love with a clergyman—perhaps one who wasn't from a particularly prosperous family—that would be something her noble parents would make every attempt to nip in the bud."

"Only they were too late to stop an elopement," Maitland said quietly. "But if they were away long enough to consummate the thing, why in God's name didn't grandfather allow them to marry? If I were Celeste and this vicar fellow, I'd have calculated that being away for an entire night together would seal the deal, so to speak. Instead grandfather had the vicar sent away and forced Celeste to give up her child?"

"We knew he was a cold, unfeeling man," Quill said with a shake of his head. "You only have to look at the fact that of their six children, not one visited unless he or she was summoned. And not even then in the case of your father, Maitland and Serena. My own mama would only ever say that they were not very kind people, and leave it at that. I suppose we were lucky that they both died before we were of an age to interest them."

"But what happened to the child?" Sophia reminded them. "What did Celeste's parents do with it?"

Ivy scanned the pages before her. "It doesn't look as if she knows," she said after a few moments of reading. "She asked, 'begged' was her word, to have the baby returned to her, but her parents refused."

"Poor Celeste," Serena said, closing her eyes in distress. "I don't think I'll ever be able to forgive my grandparents."

Sophia interrupted. "We must find this vicar. What if he

blamed Lady Celeste for his banishment and decided to kill her for it?"

"But why do so over twenty years later?" Gemma asked, puzzled. "It's hardly what one would expect from a vicar in any case."

"Which is why we need to learn who he was and find his location," Ivy said with a nod. "What if he only found out where she was recently?"

"I think I know someone who might be able to tell us," Serena said suddenly, her eyes bright with excitement. "Because I think Ivy is correct that he only found Aunt Celeste a short while ago."

"What do you mean?" Daphne asked, frowning.

"Our local vicar has only been in the village for a little over a year," Serena said. "He's around the same age as Aunt Celeste, and more importantly, his Christian name is Ian."

"I do wish you'd let us come too," Serena protested as Quill lifted Ivy into his curricle. He was momentarily diverted from his cousin's words by the feel of Ivy's curves against him. *Soon,* he told himself. *Soon we'll be able to hide away from the rest of the world and not worry about murder and such.* Ivy's sharp intake of breath and the darkening of her green eyes told him she was thinking along similar lines.

She, however, seemed better at holding a conversation at the moment.

"It would look odd for all seven of us to appear on his doorstep," Ivy said as she settled herself onto the carriage seat. "And we don't wish to frighten him away if he is indeed the man we're seeking."

"God knows there are plenty of vicars named Ian," Maitland said wryly. "We are likely jumping to conclusions over this odd coincidence."

"We'll learn something soon enough," Quill said, taking his seat beside Ivy and grasping the reins in one hand. "Finish looking through the journals for some further mention of the child. It's possible that the father sought her out at some point and perhaps can shed some light on who would wish to kill Celeste."

With a wave, he set the horses into motion and they were off.

"The girl would be thirty-two years old by now," Ivy said over the sound of the horses' hooves on the road. "Lady Celeste must have found it impossible not to mark her birth date every year. I wonder if she ever saw her."

"We don't know that my grandfather even let her know where the child was placed," Quill said, unable to imagine the pain his aunt must have suffered over this whole affair. "Knowing how he wished to punish her, I cannot imagine he would."

"But once she was on her own," Ivy said, her voice echoing his own sorrow, "surely she tried to find her. Or at least had someone search for her."

"I don't know," Quill said. "The others read those later diaries, but no one made mention of any kind of search. Nothing beyond her quest to find the four of you."

He felt a little ashamed for so misconstruing his aunt's motives when he'd first learned of her decision to leave Beauchamp House to the bluestockings. Like the rest of the family, he realized, he'd not really taken his aunt seriously as a scholar. But the insight into her character he'd gained from the journals reminded him that she was, once upon a time, a young woman with hopes and dreams and that even into her later years she wanted to make her mark on the world.

The fact that one of her choices had turned out to be Ivy, well, that was more than serendipity. There was no way

Celeste could have known that he would find one of her beneficiaries irresistible, of course, but he liked to think that she would have found their mutual attraction pleasing.

"A penny for them," Ivy said into the silence. "Though I can guess you're thinking, as I am, about Celeste and her heartache."

"Indeed," Quill responded. "I can't help but imagine what I'd have done in Ian's position. I simply cannot fathom letting the father of the woman I loved keep her from me. It's impossible for me to think that if your father told me to leave you be, that I'd listen. Nothing would keep me from your side, Ivy."

Ivy slipped her hand into his free one. "I feel the same," she said. "But you must consider that Ian was likely a younger son who relied upon the patronage of men like your grandfather for his living. Perhaps we shouldn't judge him too harshly. You are a marquess with wealth and property. Would you be able to stand it if your decision to defy my father meant living in reduced circumstances in a hovel, with no prospect of any means for keeping your wife and child fed and sheltered? You've always known you would inherit the marquisate, have you not? You don't know what it is to live from one week to the next not knowing where your next meal would come from."

He knew she was speaking from experience, and felt a pang of dismay at the thought of her in such circumstances. "Your father was cut off from his family for marrying your mother, was he not?"

"Yes," she said with a nod. "And when I was small I do remember there were days when Mama wept over our lack of funds. But soon after, Papa was able to secure a position as outside tutor to several tradesmen's sons who needed the help to gain entry into university. And one job begat another and he was able to earn a decent living. But for a time there, when he was unable to secure work at the University, and had no way of doing so, we were in difficulties. It is no easy thing to defy your family. Especially when one's father makes sure that none of your erstwhile mentors will give you a reference. When you're cut off from the world you once knew. And anyone who says it is easy hasn't really had to face the consequences up close."

"Perhaps I spoke too soon," Quill agreed, trying to see Ian's defection in a different light. "But I still do not understand how he could have left his child. At least he could see that Celeste would be cared for by her family. But once the child was given away, there's no telling what happened to her. What sort of family took her in."

"But who is to say your grandfather even let him know there was a child?" Ivy argued. "Celeste certainly was unable to speak to him after their ill-fated elopement. I daresay young Ian was trundled off to Yorkshire within hours of their being found on the road and never saw or heard from Celeste again."

"Until recently," Quill said thoughtfully. "If this Ian is indeed the same one from Celeste's letters."

They'd reached the drive leading to the little church where Quill remembered many a Sunday service in the front pew with Aunt Celeste. He tried to imagine what sort of man was the pastor now. If he was indeed Celeste's Ian, what a shock it must have been on that first Sunday when she arrived at the door. Had he remembered her at once? Had she remembered her? It was impossible to imagine being able to simply greet the love of one's life as if nothing had ever passed between them.

"Oh look," Ivy said as they neared the vicarage. "There is Mrs. Vance. I suppose she's come to visit the vicar, too."

And sure enough as he pulled the curricle to a stop, Quill saw that there was a gig with a piebald horse tied up to a nearby tree just to the side of the house. Mrs. Vance, her face composed, stood in the doorway of the vicarage.

"I'm afraid if you've come to see Reverend Devereaux," she said with a brief smile, "he's away at the moment. He just left to go to a deathbed. My husband sent me to fetch him."

Ivy's disappointment was evident in her voice as she said, "Oh how sad. We were hoping to speak with him. I suppose you don't know when he'll be back?"

"I'm afraid not," Mrs. Vance said with a shake of her head. "I don't know how much experience you have with sickbeds, but sometimes these things take days. I don't anticipate that the vicar will stay there for that long, of course, but it could be tomorrow before he's able to see you. I presume you're here to request the banns to be read?"

Quill nearly rolled his eyes at her ill-concealed attempt to get some gossip from them. But Ivy spoke before he could. "News does travel fast in this village, doesn't it? I see you've been speaking with Mrs. Northman."

But the censure in Ivy's tone didn't cow the inquisitive matron. "I hope you won't think too poorly of me, Miss Wareham. I only knew Dr. Vance for a matter of days before I decided he was the one for me, so I'm hardly one to cast aspersions," she said with a smug smile that seemed more proud than abashed. And I do love a love story, so do let me know your plans."

There was something about the woman's smile that made Quill feel a bit of sympathy for the good doctor. And he didn't like the comparison she drew between herself and Ivy. Both couples might have made hasty betrothals, but he had a feeling that Mrs. Vance had been the one doing the chasing in her relationship.

"Oh, you'll be the first to know," Ivy assured her with a sunny smile that was, if Quill guessed aright, just as sincere as Mrs. Vance's.

"I suppose we'll be off, then," he said, eager to get away from the doctor's wife before she attempted to wheedle more information from them. "Have a pleasant afternoon, Mrs. Vance."

And before she could reply, he'd given the horses a little flick of the reins and they were on their way back the way they'd come.

"You didn't need to flee her," Ivy said once they were out of earshot. "She's simply a childless matron with nothing to occupy herself with but other people's news. Quite sad really."

"Sad for those who fall prey to her tattling tongue, you mean," Quill said sourly. "I daresay she had the whole of the tale of our run-in at Northman's the other evening before we'd even arrived back home. That sort has ears everywhere. She's likely known Aunt Celeste was murdered from the day she died."

"You're probably not far off there," Ivy said with raised brows. "She did seem a bit gleeful when she asked about the banns. As if she knew good and well that we'd have to be married by special license."

"I suppose we should be glad, then," he said, "that she didn't cut us. Though I can't imagine she'd ever turn her back on a marquess. No matter how scandalous his behavior."

"You've a high opinion of yourself, don't you?" Ivy asked with a grin.

"It is more that I have a low opinion of others, my dear," Quill said with a shrug. "It takes a great deal of scandal to put off a true social climber. And I fear Mrs. Vance, for all that she's a country doctor's wife, would dearly love to be more than that."

"I suppose we're going to have to wait to meet with Reverend Devereaux now," Ivy said, changing the subject. "I confess

I'm disappointed. I thought we might be able to solve at least part of the mystery this afternoon."

"It will keep for another day," Quill said, patting her on the hand. "Perhaps the others will have learned something else from the journals by the time we return."

"I hope so," Ivy said with a little sigh. "Because I begin to fear we'll never find out who killed Celeste."

Chapter 29

They'd only gone a mile or so when Ivy realized that Quill wasn't following the way back to Beauchamp House.

"Where are we going?" she asked. "I thought we were going to see what the others might have learned."

"I apologize," he said, looking pensive. "I should have said something, but it only occurred to me while we were talking that I saw something in my portion of Celeste's journals that I may have misread."

He turned down a lane that seemed to lead toward the seafront.

"Well, I'm listening," Ivy said, impatient for some explanation. "I do admit if we're going to the shore, I'm excited by the prospect. I've wanted to go since we arrived but haven't yet found the time. What with getting compromised, and shot and so forth."

Quill laughed. "If you'd only said something I'd have been happy to take you. Dalton and I took Jeremy the morning after we arrived."

"So, what did you remember?"

"Celeste made mention of a visit to St. Clement's, which I read before your revelation that she'd had a lover," he said, directing the horses to a clearing near the portion of the

Beauchamp House property that led to the chalk cliffs overhanging the sea.

"A church?" Ivy asked. "Could it have been one of Ian's parishes perhaps?"

"Not knowing the context, of course," he said, "I thought as you did, that it was just a visit to a local church—for it appeared that her visits were made from Beauchamp House, not on some journey to another county. But, the entries seemed rather . . . floridly described. Ecstatic."

Ivy looked puzzled. "What, you mean as if she were having some sort of religious experience? Like a saint?"

"Aunt Celeste wasn't particularly devout," Quill said dryly. "So, when I recalled the other St. Clement's in this area it made a bit more sense."

"What did?" Ivy made an impatient noise. "Really, Quill, you are being quite vague about this."

"St. Clement's is also the name of a series of caves along the coast here," he said patiently. "One of which is just here on the stretch of land that's part of the Beauchamp property."

It took Ivy a moment to process what he was saying. Religious experience, cave, Beauchamp House.

"Oh!" she said softly when she realized what he was implying.

"Yes," he replied. "Oh."

"She met her lover there," Ivy said, realizing that she too had read references to the cave in her sections of the journals. "I thought she was simply having qualms of conscience about her defiance of her father. That she was simply going to church frequently. Though I admit to not knowing if there was a St. Clement's church in the area."

"There have always been rumors that one of the caves had a tunnel leading up to Beauchamp House," Quill said before jumping down from the curricle. Jogging over to the other side, he reached up for Ivy and held her close for a moment before setting her down on her feet.

"Do you think they're true?" she asked, a little breathlessly, wishing they could just leave off their investigation for the afternoon and be together. It felt a very long time since he'd kissed her properly.

"I think we're going to go find out," he said, slipping his arm through hers after he'd secured the horses on a nearby tree. "There are stairs over here leading down to the beach. And if I remember correctly, the cave is only a few feet away."

"You must admit," Ivy said as they walked along the path leading to the stone stairs, which she could see from this vantage point, "it must have been dreadfully romantic for her to meet him here. Their own little place along the shore. Far from the prying eyes of the village—and her disapproving parents. I cannot help but sympathize with Celeste. What an awful heartbreak for her to endure at so young an age. It's no wonder she never married."

"I had always wondered why she remained unwed," Quill admitted as they reached the top of the stone steps. "Though I suppose I believed my mother when she said that Celeste was far too demanding to ever think of marrying. She was quite envious of her I think. All that freedom to do whatever she liked. Mama didn't have an easy time of it with my father. I believe my grandfather Maitland chose him for her because they were cut from the same cloth."

"Do you remember him? Your father I mean?" Ivy asked, curious about the late marquess. Quill seemed to be close to his mother, but he hardly ever mentioned his father.

"Only a few times when I was small," Quill said, keeping a tight grip on her hand as he let her precede him down the cliffside. "He wasn't very interested in me, to be honest. I was a child and therefore beneath his notice. He called me into his study a couple of times to make sure I was able to recite my letters and numbers and that sort of thing. But he died before I was old enough to go to school, so I don't recall much more than that."

Ivy, who was quite close with her own father, felt a pang of sympathy for him. She had a hard time imagining what her life would have been like if she'd had the same sort of parents as Lady Celeste, or a father like Quill's. Despite their restricted means and the house full of sisters, she realized she'd been rather luckier than she'd previously thought.

"And yet," Ivy said squeezing his hand, "you've turned into a decent man. I suppose your mother is to congratulate for that?"

"She and Celeste." Quill smiled. "I actually spent more of my formative years here than at Kerr Castle. Which is why I was so dead set against you and your fellow bluestockings inheriting it. I see the error of my ways now, of course."

They'd reached the bottom of the cliff, and Ivy leapt from the last step onto the rocky ground. The sun had come out and dappled the sea as it lapped peacefully against the shore. She could smell salt on the air, and a brisk wind threatened to take her hat from her head.

Sucking in a deep breath of the fresh air, she smiled at Quill. "I should hope so," she said, slipping her arm through his as he followed her down. "At the very least I think you should know we're not the social-climbing upstarts you once thought us."

"Well," he said with a lopsided grin, "perhaps the other three aren't . . ."

"Beast," she said with mock anger. "You know you love me."

Her words hung between them for a moment, like a feather caught up in the breeze.

She saw his eyes darken, and he slipped a hand up to tuck

an errant curl behind her ear. "I do indeed," he said, leaning in to kiss her. "More than I ever thought possible."

Ivy felt her heart speed up as Quill's words sank in. He loved her.

She slipped her uninjured arm up around his neck and gave herself over to the desire she'd been holding back all day. Opening her mouth under his, she welcomed the invasion of his tongue as he pulled her closer, let her feel the hard press of him against her aching body.

His kiss was everything she'd never thought she'd needed. At twenty-three, she'd long ago begun to suspect she'd never find her other half, that she'd be doomed to the same kind of solitude that Lady Celeste had endured. But she knew now that Quill was the one she'd been searching for.

"My sweet love," he whispered against her, his breath hot against her ear, making Ivy shiver. "I would desperately love to follow this to its natural conclusion, but I'm afraid we are not alone."

And turning, Ivy saw that there was indeed a party of fishermen farther down the shore.

"Drat," she said in a low voice.

"My thoughts exactly," he said with a wry grin. "But I suppose that will keep us on point. It's not as if we're here for our own amusement, after all."

At the mention of their true reason for being on the shore, Ivy felt a pang of conscience. "You are right, of course. Let's see this cave and mayhap we can find some other clue to Ian's identity."

With a regretful sigh, Quill led her to where an indentation in the cliffside was almost hidden by the rocks on the near side of it. If Ivy hadn't been searching for it specifically, she'd never have guessed the mouth was there.

"I remember coming here as a boy," Quill said as they

neared the entrance, which was just high enough for Ivy to step inside, while Quill was forced to duck his head. His voice echoed off the walls of the cave's interior, which opened up into a higher, more spacious area than Ivy would have imagined from the outside.

"I wish I'd known to bring a lamp, or a candle or something," Quill said. "The back is quite dark, isn't it?"

"What's this here?" Ivy asked, as she stepped over to where she'd seen something that looked far more square than one would expect of a natural formation. Sure enough, as she stooped she saw it was a wooden box. "Look, it's a casket of some sort." Opening it, she found a candle and a few small sticks.

"They're lucifer matches," Quill said, taking one from her and striking it against a bit of rock lying beside them. To her surprise, a flame lit the air, and Quill used it to ignite the wick of the tallow candle. "Whoever has been using the cave recently must have left these for convenience's sake."

"It's certainly convenient for us," Ivy said with a smile. There was an unmistakable sense of excitement running through her. Not just because she was here with Quill, alone, but because of the cave itself. It was hard not to feel the sense that this place had been the den of smugglers and lovers and any number of adventurers who had found refuge in the snug rock room.

"I wonder if we can find the door leading up to Beauchamp House," Quill said as he moved farther into the darkness.

"I thought you said that was just a legend," Ivy said, following along behind him. "You sound as if you believe it."

"There were definitely smugglers here during the war," he said, raising the candle to throw the light farther back. "I remember Maitland and I found a couple of brandy bottles down here once. And if Celeste was meeting Ian here, then it would be easier to do so if there was a way for her to get here without being seen."

"It makes sense," Ivy agreed, her eyes darting around them as they moved farther from the cave's entrance and the natural light it let in.

"Maybe you should wait here while I go up ahead," Quill said when she stumbled on a rock behind him. "You're so damned ready for anything that comes your way, I forget you're still recovering from your wound."

Ivy wanted to protest that she could handle herself, but she was indeed feeling rather tired. And perhaps just a bit light-headed from the closeness of the cave. "I dislike admitting as much," she said wryly, "but I do think I'll go back closer to the entrance. I have never been particularly fond of tight spaces, and the farther we get from the entrance, the more constricted I feel."

"My brave girl," Quill said kissing her on the forehead. "Why didn't you say so as soon as we stepped inside? I'd not have made you come this far. Come, let's go back the way we came and I'll get you back to the house."

But Ivy wasn't willing to let her weakness stop them from finding a possible way into Beauchamp House through the cave. "No! You must go ahead. I'll wait just outside for you to return. It's a lovely day out and I could use a bit of sun on my face and fresh air."

"Are you sure?" he asked, his eyes worried in the candle-light.

"Yes," she said, giving him a little shove. "Now go. I'll be waiting for you. And maybe I'll be able to find something else hidden away near the entrance. Maybe some artifact from Celeste and Ian's time here."

He nodded. "All right. But call out if you need me. With this echo I'll hear you at once."

With a peck on his cheek, she sent him off and turned back

toward where the sunlight shone into the cave. Picking her way carefully over the stone floor, she was soon stepping out into the open air, unable to hold in the deep breath of relief at no longer being trapped in the enclosed space.

"Well look what we have here," said a cool voice from the large rocks on the side of the entrance.

Ivy looked up, startled to find she wasn't alone. "Mrs. Vance?" she asked, surprised to find the doctor's wife here. "How odd to see you here."

"Not particularly," the woman said, sliding off the rock where she'd been seated. "There's a tunnel from the vicarage that leads into the cave. I could hear his lordship's deep voice booming against the cave walls. He's got quite a deep one, hasn't he? Not at all like poor Vance's nasal twang."

A hint of unease ran through Ivy. There was something . . . off . . . about the way the doctor's wife was speaking to her. A lack of emotion that gave her a sense of foreboding. "Why were you in the cellar at the vicarage?" she asked, recalling that the vicar himself had been called away. And how did she know that there was a tunnel there? Something was not right here.

"That's where I had to put the vicar, of course," Mrs. Vance said patiently. "I could hardly lock him up in the front room where anyone could see. My father and I have a great deal to catch up on, don't you know? Which we'll have to do in a bit of a rush thanks to you."

"Mrs. Vance," Ivy said, trying to keep her voice steady as she spoke. "What have you done?"

"Surely you've guessed by now, Miss Wareham," the other woman said with a small smile.

And before Ivy could cry out, Mrs. Vance struck out with her hand, which Ivy registered with horror, was clutching a large stone.

Then the world went dark.

Chapter 30

Quill had gone several hundred feet farther into the cave when the glint of metal in the candlelight alerted him to the hinges of a cleverly crafted door built into the cave wall. He considered going back to tell Ivy, but remembering how much being in the interior of the formation had upset her, he decided to ensure that the passageway did indeed go to Beauchamp House before retracing his steps back to the entrance.

Fortunately, there were sconces built into either side of the tunnel walls and he lit them as he went, ensuring that his journey back to Ivy would be less daunting than the one in. He'd never been particularly afraid of the dark, but there was something eerie about wandering deserted passageways that had likely been used by smugglers for hundreds of years. He knew there was a tendency amongst some to think of the men who evaded the excise tax as heroes, but he was not one of them. There had been too many stories of men who crossed them being struck down, of homes set ablaze, for Quill to ever mistake them for anything but the criminals they were.

When he finally reached a set of stairs leading upward, he held his breath a little with hope, and the sight of a wooden door had his heartbeat quickening. When he pushed against it, and saw that he was in the wine cellar of Beauchamp House, his sigh of relief was genuine.

Hurrying up into the kitchens, he ignored the odd looks from the kitchen maids, and made his way to the library where he found Maitland, Sophia, Gemma, and Daphne poring over the diaries, just as they'd been when he left.

"What did you learn from Reverend Devereaux?" the duke asked, putting a finger in the book he was reading. "And where is Miss Wareham?"

Quickly, Quill related what had happened when they arrived at the vicarage, and how he and Ivy had discovered what they suspected had been Celeste and Ian's trysting place. "I'd like you to come back with me through the tunnel," he told his cousin. "Just in case you see some clue I might have missed. And I daresay Ivy, Miss Wareham that is, is growing impatient."

Looking more than eager to leave the journals behind, Maitland stood. "I remember searching for the smugglers' tunnels when we were boys," he said ruefully. "I suppose we weren't very good detectives if we couldn't find them given how many hours we spent looking."

"I think that was likely because Greaves kept the wine cellar locked," Quill said with a quirk of his lips. "He knew better than to leave it open with curious boys running about."

"What about us?" Sophia demanded as the two men began to walk toward the door. "We would like to see the tunnel too. I've spent the past four hours reading these journals, and aside from a few mentions of Lady Celeste's investigations of us four, they have been sadly mundane. I need some fresh air."

Daphne and Gemma echoed her frustration.

"And I am quite good with noticing details," Daphne added hopefully.

"And as a fossil hunter," Gemma said with a chiding tone, "I really should be allowed to examine the cave. There may be some important findings there."

Quill exchanged a look with Maitland, who opened his hands in a speaking gesture.

"Fine," Quill said with a sigh. "But you must all do precisely as I say. This is serious business, not a day adventure. And I would not like it if one of you was to be hurt while I'm in charge of you."

One of the ladies gave a whoop of triumph, and they all three hurried from the room to fetch their hats and coats.

"You're a more patient man than I," Maitland said, clapping Quill on the shoulder. "They'll likely take a half hour at least to decide which hats to wear."

"Lady Daphne will not, I daresay," Quill said with a wink. "She seems quite sensible except for her unaccountable wish to bed you."

Before Maitland could respond to that, they heard the noise of approaching footsteps and turned to see Serena hurrying toward them.

"Dr. Vance's wife has disappeared," she said without preamble. "I've just had a visit from one of his servants asking if we'd seen her. And now the doctor himself is in the drawing room."

"Ivy and I just saw her at the vicarage," Quill said with a frown. "She had gone to fetch the vicar to a sick bed. On Dr. Vance's orders, no less. Why is he not there himself?"

Something about the situation made him uneasy. And without waiting to hear Serena's response, he hurried away from them toward the drawing room.

When he entered, he found the doctor there, pacing back and forth, as if under the weight of some great worry. Upon seeing Quill he stopped and said, "She has lied to me, my lord. And now she's gone."

The unease in Quill's gut turned into full-blown panic. "What do you mean, man?"

"I was searching for a pen knife in her sitting room this afternoon," Dr. Vance said. "And I found a bottle of aconite powder hidden in one of her desk drawers. As well as a journal containing all sorts of details about Lady Celeste—her interests, her direction, and any number of personal details about her life. There was also a description of Reverend Deveraux and the name of his wife, his children. And each church where he'd been posted over his career."

"Why was she keeping a journal about Aunt Celeste?" Maitland asked. "And what the devil is aconite powder?"

"The journal entries were dated two years before I ever met her," Dr. Vance said, his mouth tight. "I think she may have married me to get close to them."

"And aconite poisoning shares many of the same symptoms with the illness that killed Celeste," Quill stated. "You weren't called out to a sickbed today were you?"

"No," the doctor said, looking puzzled. "Why?"

"The last I saw your wife," Quill said curtly, "she was at the vicarage, saying she'd just come on your orders to send him to a deathbed in the village."

Turning to his cousin, he said, "Maitland, you should go with Dr. Vance to see if she's still there."

"Where are you going?" his cousin asked, even as Quill walked away

"To get Ivy," Quill said over his shoulder, beginning to run toward the wine cellar.

Because his gut was churning now with very real fear. Fear that Mrs. Vance might get to Ivy before he did.

And that lady was a stone cold killer.

Ivy came to back to consciousness with the feeling that the earth was shifting under her. She would have moved, but she found her limbs uncooperative and her head aching as if it had come into contact with something quite heavy. A grunt of exertion made her open her heavy eyelids, and she saw Mrs. Vance's face contort as she tried to move something heavy.

That something heavy was Ivy.

She tried to feel beneath her with her hands, but found to her dismay that they were tied together. And her gunshot wound hurt like the very devil. It felt on fire. And if she wasn't mistaken, it was bleeding again.

And though there were lit candles along the walls, she saw that they were in a dark tunnel. The memory of the cave, of Quill, came rushing back. Could they be in the same tunnel he'd told her about? The one leading up to Beauchamp House?

Deciding that her best chance at freedom lay in feigning unconsciousness, she closed her eyes again, and soon felt the cart, or whatever device Mrs. Vance had used to move her, come to a stop. A hinge squeaked loudly, and soon she was being trundled forward again, over a threshold of some sort and through a doorway so narrow she could feel the scrape of it against her shoulders.

"There," said the doctor's wife with a sigh of relief, letting the cart drop down onto the floor.

Ivy was unable to keep from crying out at the sudden movement.

"So," said Mrs. Vance with mock cheerfulness. "Someone is awake. Look, Father, I've brought you a visitor."

Not bothering to continue pretending to sleep, Ivy opened her eyes and looked around. They were in a damp-smelling chamber with no windows. A quick scan of the room revealed a man she presumed was the Reverend Ian Devereaux judging by his collar.

The vicar, who was tied to a chair with a handkerchief stuffed into his mouth, only moaned in response to his long-lost daughter's taunt.

"You haven't met yet, I don't think," Mrs. Vance continued, "but this is Miss Ivy Wareham. She's been making things difficult for me, these past few days. Putting her nose into things that don't concern her."

"I should think the deliberate murder of two women and an attempt upon my own life is just cause for concern," Ivy said, her voice scratchy from her dry throat.

"None of it concerned you." Mrs. Vance was pacing now, with a frenetic energy that told she was feeling threatened by the presence of someone who talked back. Ivy considered her options and decided that it might be best to placate the woman rather than challenge her. A calm Mrs. Vance was less likely to kill her prisoners, she thought.

"You are right, I suppose," Ivy said, trying to infuse her voice with apology. "I was simply concerned about Lady Celeste's untimely death. I should have left it alone and applied my interest to my studies."

"Yes, you should have," Mrs. Vance said smugly. "Now look at where you are. You might have simply gone about your business, and married that handsome marquess of yours, but instead you're here. And I'm afraid I'm going to have to kill you along with my father, here. Because I can hardly let you live now that you know I'm the one who killed Celeste and that fool Elsie."

Ivy blinked at hearing the confirmation so clearly from the murderess's lips. "You cannot know how much I wish I'd kept to my own affairs," she said with feigned regret. She might not be in this predicament if she'd not decided to listen to Lady Celeste's letter, but she could not in good conscience have ignored her benefactress's request that she find her killer. She could only imagine what that lady's response would have been to the knowledge it was her own daughter who had poisoned her to death. Poor Lady Celeste.

"But why did you do it?" Ivy asked, truly wanting to know what had prompted this woman, who seemed to have a comfortable life as the wife of a prosperous country doctor, to kill her birth parents. "They certainly did not give you up because they wished to, Marianne." She used the woman's Christian name in an attempt to build a bond between them. Anything that might make her see Ivy as less of an enemy and more like a friend.

A flicker of unease passed through Mrs. Vance's eyes. "What do you mean they didn't wish to? They did it, didn't they? This hypocrite has spent his life preaching godliness to people while he himself is a fornicator who didn't even deign to marry my mother when she fell pregnant. I hardly think running away from responsibility is the action of a man doing his Christian duty." She shook her head in disgust. "And Lady Celeste, a wealthy duke's daughter, who was so ashamed of me that she didn't even deign to place me with a family befitting my rank as her daughter—she doesn't deserve my sympathy. If anything I hold her more accountable than this miscreant." She gestured toward where the vicar was looking at her through eyes that were at once horrified and mournful. "At least he didn't give me up after carrying me for months inside his body. It takes a very despicable sort of woman to give away her child."

"But Lady Celeste wanted to keep you," Ivy insisted, though she knew there was little chance Marianne Vance would believe her. She was far too accustomed to the narrative of her abandonment that she'd built up in her head. "It was her parents, the Duke and Duchess of Maitland, who insisted that you be given to the couple who raised you.

And it was they who sent your father away to Yorkshire to a church on the Earl of Moreland's estate. They were powerful enough to have him banished from this part of the country. And they did."

"How do you know any of this?" Marianne spat out. "You never even met the exalted Lady Celeste. And yet, you and those other three ungrateful bluestockings came here to take possession of her house. Her home. The place I should have, would have, inherited if I had been given my birthright."

Ignoring the jibe against her and the other bluestockings, Ivy said, "Because I've read her journals from that time. She was devastated by what her parents did. And she even went so far as to search for you for several years. But the duke and duchess were quite good about erasing all traces of you. It was as if you'd never existed." She had no proof that Lady Celeste had, in fact, looked for her child, but Ivy had a feeling that the woman she'd come to know through her journals would not have sat idly by while her child was raised by strangers.

"Yes," Mrs. Vance said with contempt, "that's because the couple they gave me to were rotten to the core. They were cold and unfeeling. And they forced me to work like a dog on their farm from the time I could walk until they had the good grace to die when I was seventeen. The only good thing they did was leave that despicable farm to me so that I could sell it the first chance I got and use the money to set myself up in Bath. Which is where I lived for nearly a decade before I met the good Dr. Vance."

Curious in spite of herself, Ivy asked, "How did you know that he worked in the same village Lady Celeste lived in?" Shifting her weight to ease the discomfort of her arm, she felt the bonds around her hands were looser than she'd thought before. Maybe she could get them off herself?

Not daring to show what she'd discovered, she turned her attention on Marianne Vance and listened to her answer while she pulled against the rope behind her back.

"I didn't, not at first," Marianne said with a laugh. "I had found several letters from the old Duke of Maitland in my father's papers, and he had mentioned Celeste and the vicar, here. It was really just a matter of serendipity that Dr. Vance mentioned the grand lady in his county—Lady Celeste Beauchamp. And I knew I had to get there. Vance was already taken with me, so it was just a matter of making myself pleasing to him before he was falling all over himself to marry me. That the recently widowed Reverend Devereaux had only just moved into the area was a happy coincidence I discovered when Dr. Vance brought me to my new home."

"But why did you decide to kill Celeste?" Ivy asked, aghast at the cold calculation that had led Marianne to marry a man she didn't love for the sole purpose of getting close to the mother who abandoned her. "If you had only told her who you were she would have welcomed you with open arms. She loved you. She looked for you for years."

"Not. Hard. Enough," Marianne said coldly. "And why should I introduce myself to the woman who let me be taken from her when I was a defenseless babe? That sort of person doesn't deserve sympathy, certainly not mine. By the time I met her, I was already planning her downfall. The couple who raised me died of a stomach complaint, or so the doctor believed, shortly after Serena's husband died in hunting accident. So I already knew how much easier it was to put a dose of aconite into an herbal tisane, when compared with engineering lying in wait with a gun—though both have their uses. And when my dear husband mentioned that Lady Celeste suffered from dreadful headaches, it was only a matter of suggesting to her that she try the tisane recipe that I'd used for my own dear mother to set things in motion. I made sure to tell her that Elsie should get the ingredients from the gypsy woman, of course. After, I'd given the maid herself my own little powder to add to the mix, telling her that Dr. Vance had given it to me expressly for Lady Celeste's use. Vance is too much of a snob to speak to the likes of Elsie, so I knew he'd never find out, and I knew that adding the gypsy woman to the mix would throw suspicion her way before it ever came back to me." She smirked. "And I was right of course."

"But how did you know Lady Celeste would even drink the tonic?" Ivy wanted to know. She kept her gaze focused on Marianne while she tried to work her hands against the ropes. She'd crush her own fingers if it meant getting out of this cellar with her life intact.

"I didn't," the doctor's wife said with a shrug. "But fortunately for me, her headaches got worse. And by that point she was willing to try anything that promised to give her relief. If she'd continued being recalcitrant, of course, I'd have had Elsie give her something to make them worse. I know any number of herbs and powders that could have done the trick."

"But why kill Elsie?" Ivy asked, wondering what could possibly have got the maid killed. As far as she knew there was no reason for Mrs. Vance to wish her dead.

"Because once Lady Celeste died and you began asking your questions," Marianne said grimly, "she figured out that I'd been the one to help Lady Celeste along the road to her demise. After you and Lord Kerr visited her on the night of the dinner party, she sought me out to let me know what she suspected. And demanded that I pay her to keep quiet. I couldn't have that, could I? So I sent her some pastries I'd laced with rat poison—far more efficient than the slow death I'd devised for Lady Celeste. Fortunately, I knew Elsie had a sweet tooth. The sugar disguised the taste of the poison quite nicely. At least I suspect it did since she was found dead the next morning."

The dispassionate tone Marianne Vance used to relate the details of her crimes was more chilling to Ivy than outright glee would have been. There was something amiss with the other woman. Some lack of feeling for her fellow human beings that made her lack the capacity for empathy. A woman like this would not feel even a flinch of conscience at taking a life. And she certainly would not be talked out of her plans.

Still, Ivy knew she had to keep her boasting about her own cleverness if she was to survive this. Quill had surely got back to the cave entrance by now and discovered she was missing. Hopefully he would recall how odd Mrs. Vance's behavior had been at the vicarage and go back there for answers.

She was making some headway with the ropes, and had managed to get one hand out almost to the palm. But she was beginning to lose hope.

"And what of the gypsy fortune teller?" she asked aloud. "Surely you didn't pay her to tell me I was in danger."

Marianne laughed. "No, not at all. She was just being her own foolish, gypsy self. And I'd never even spoken to her, so I knew if she mentioned anyone it would be Elsie. It was good of you to tell the servants at Beauchamp House that you all were going to visit her caravan that day, though. My dear friend, the kitchen maid, was able to get word to me as soon as you set out, so I was able to hide along the path."

"You're the one who shot me?" Ivy demanded. She's thought perhaps Marianne had hired someone—a local man, or a lover—to shoot at her. The news that she'd done the deed herself was startling somehow.

"Do not sound so surprised, Miss Bluestocking," said the doctor's wife with a laugh. "For someone who is a champion of the female sex, you sound quite skeptical that a lady would be a good enough shot to wound you. I learned to shoot on the farm. Got quite good at it, though it was never my favorite sport. Too bloody for my taste. I much prefer the safe distance poison provides. Not to mention that it makes the victim suffer for quite a bit longer."

As she at last managed to get one hand free, then the other, of her bonds, Ivy couldn't help but say to her would-be killer, "And yet you missed, if you wished your shot to take my life." She was careful not to let her triumph at freeing her hands show in her face. It would do little good to alert Marianne to the fact that she'd worked her way loose before she had a chance to do anything with her newfound freedom.

Marianne's eyes narrowed. "Your damned marquess was in the way," she spat out. "Or I'd have hit your chest, which is what I was aiming for. And I'll soon finish what I started." She lifted her arm and Ivy saw, to her horror, that her captor held a pistol in her hand.

Mrs. Vance scowled at her over the gun, taking aim. Ivy prepared herself to leap to her feet, which Marianne had left untied in her haste to get Ivy into the cellar.

But they were both startled by a loud banging on the front door of the vicarage.

Taking advantage of Marianne's diversion, Ivy made her move.

Chapter 31

There was no sign of Ivy when Quill made it back through the tunnel and out to where the cave opened onto the rocky shore. Calling out to her in the hope that she had just decided to walk a bit along the waterfront, he almost tripped when his booted foot became entangled in something.

His heart leapt into his throat when he saw it was Ivy's hat—a straw and ribbon confection that framed the heart-shaped face he'd come to love so well. He stooped to pick it up and was shocked to see a smudge of crimson just where the crown of her head would be. He broke into a run and was up the cliffside stairs in a trice. His horses were just where he'd tied them up what seemed like days ago, and in minutes he was driving like a madman along the road to the vicarage.

He had no doubt now who had injured Ivy and who had taken her away.

It was Dr. Vance's wife, who had so cheerfully lied to them earlier when they inquired about the Reverend Deveraux's whereabouts. Who had been so welcoming that day in the doctor's offices, and who had mourned the loss of Aunt Celeste.

He did not allow himself to wonder what sort of woman

could do those things. Because she now had Ivy. Smart, sensible, sensual Ivy. Who had stolen his heart that first day in the Fox and Pheasant with her wry humor and her love for books.

There was no question he would get to her in time.

To imagine anything else was to give up.

Torquil Beauchamp, Marquess of Kerr, never surrendered.

And he was damned if he'd let Marianne Vance be the one to make him start now.

He had too much he needed to say to Ivy.

With a curse, he cried out for the horses to speed up.

As luck would have it, he reached the vicarage before Maitland and Dr. Vance did.

The exterior of the little house looked as benign as ever. With its picturesque climbing roses budding in anticipation of spring and its cheerful green door, it looked like what it was—the home of a widower of middle years who served the community and lived alone.

There was no sign that Ivy or anyone else had been here since they'd come hours earlier to pay a call on the vicar. Mrs. Vance's horse and cart, however, were still where they'd been tied up earlier. If she'd used the cart to move Ivy, she'd done a remarkable job of placing it exactly where it had been before.

He leapt down from the curricle, tossed the reins over a post, and hammered on the vicarage door.

"Mrs. Vance!" he shouted. "Mrs. Vance, I've come for Miss Wareham. I know you have her. Let me in."

Whether from the force of his pounding or the fact that it wasn't locked, the door swung inward, just as he heard Maitland and Dr. Vance approach in the doctor's open barouche.

Cautiously, he stepped into the dark interior and heard someone shouting from the back of the house. Caring only that Ivy might need him, he all but sprinted to the kitchen and followed the high-pitched cries to an open door at the top of a staircase leading down into darkness.

Following the steps, he was almost to the bottom when he heard a cry of triumph.

Please God, let that be Ivy.

The light became brighter as he made his way down, and when he reached the damp room he saw at once that Ivy was standing over Mrs. Vance, a dueling pistol leveled at her with a hand that was steady as a summer rain.

"You won't do it," Mrs. Vance sneered. "You don't have the bottle. I doubt you've ever held a pistol in your whole sheltered existence. You're just like she was. A pampered, ungrateful dabbler. You think you're so brave for studying things that no one but your kind care about. While girls like me were working just to stay clothed and fed, you were weeping over life's unfairness. You don't know the first thing about unfairness. Unfair is when your aristocratic parents give you up so that you have no chance of gaining your birthright. Unfair is when your mother gives away her price-less collection and her home to a quartet of spinsters with no claims on her."

Neither of them noticed where Quill stood silently, his heart in his throat as he watched Ivy glaring at her erstwhile captor.

"Try me," she said to the woman on the floor. "You've killed who knows how many people now. And you intended to kill both your father and me just now. If you make a sudden move, make no mistake, Marianne, I will shoot you. I might not have practiced as you did, but we're quite close now. I should be able to hit you somewhere."

Without turning around, she said to Quill, "Darling, would you please get the rope from the cart there and tie her up. Then you'd best see to the vicar."

He shouldn't have been surprised she'd known he was there, Quill realized with a grin, but he was. Clearly he needed to learn that Ivy was up to any rig. Even capturing murderers.

"With pleasure, my dear," he said as he stepped farther into the room and retrieved the rope that had been used earlier to subdue Ivy.

When Mrs. Vance was trussed up like a Christmas goose, Ivy lowered the pistol with a sigh and would have collapsed if Quill hadn't been there to catch her. Taking the gun and placing it on a high shelf where it would do no harm, he carried Ivy to a nearby chair.

The sound of boots alerted them that Maitland and Dr. Vance had arrived on the scene.

"Good god!" Dr. Vance cried out. "It's true, Marianne You tried to kill Miss Wareham and Reverend Devereaux. And *did* kill Lady Celeste and her former maid, Elsie."

"See to Devereaux, Duke," Quill told his cousin, who had looked to him for guidance on what to do. "He may need Dr. Vance's attention."

With a nod, Maitland crossed over to where the vicar was tied up.

Quill turned his attention back to Ivy. He crouched before her, and when their eyes met, she launched herself into his arms, throwing them both to the cellar floor.

"I was so afraid," she whispered against his neck, the solid weight of her in his arms a relief after the terror he'd felt when he found her hat. "She would have killed us both. Even you, if you'd come a few minutes earlier. I was only able to overtake her thanks to your pounding on the door. Oh, Quill. I thought I'd never see you again."

He didn't even know what he said to her, crooning reassurances and words of love and devotion that bubbled up out of him like a newly discovered sweet water well finally set free from where it was hidden underground. And he let her cry. Which he knew even the strongest of ladies—and men— needed to do sometimes. Especially when they'd endured the sort of hell Ivy had.

"I love you, Quill," she said, moving her head back so that she could look him in the eye. "I love you so much. And I was so afraid I'd never see you to tell you how much."

"I love you too," he said kissing her eyelids, then her cheeks, then her nose, then, finally, her lips.

They were kisses of love, but also promises.

That no matter what else happened, he loved her. And she loved him. And they would be together.

"When I realized she had you, Ivy," he said against her cheek, "I thought all was lost. But I should have known better. My sweet, brave, bluestocking. You are made of sterner stuff than that. And I should have trusted you to save yourself."

He felt her thumb softly stroke beneath first one, then the other, of his eyes, gliding in the moisture there. "My sweet marquess," she said with a smile in her voice. "You *do* love me." There was affection in her voice, but also wonder. As if she couldn't quite believe it.

"More than life itself," he said solemnly. "Which is why we will leave for London tonight so we can be married by special license at once."

"What about asking my father for permission?" she teased, a little breathlessly.

"All respect for your father, my dear," he said pulling her closer, "but he will just have to wait."

And there, on the floor of the vicarage cellar, he kissed her properly.

Until, that is, the sound of a throat clearing broke the spell.

"I do not like to interrupt," Maitland said, clearly lying. As Quill well knew, his cousin *loved* to interrupt. "But we're taking the vicar and Mrs. Vance upstairs now. And I thought perhaps you'd like to, I don't know, take yourselves back to Beauchamp House so that you can continue this"—he made a gesture in the air with his hand—"there."

Sighing, Quill knew that any continuation would have to wait until the other bluestockings and Serena were informed about what had happened here.

Pushing up to her feet, Ivy offered him a hand, which he took with a smile.

"We'll be gone by the time you get back," he informed his cousin, who rather than looking surprised simply nodded. "See that all of this is taken care of."

"Northman will wish to question you both," Maitland said as they started up the cellar stairs.

"Northman can bloody well wait until we get back," Quill called back over his shoulder.

He and Ivy had important business to attend to.

Chapter 32

Some few weeks later, having been assured by a beaming Greaves that the residents of Beauchamp House were assembled in the library, Ivy and Quill stood in the doorway of the now-familiar chamber and saw, to their surprise, the Duke of Maitland lecturing the others.

"I think it's highly likely that my man will find evidence of more crimes when he visits Marianne Vance's childhood home next week," he said with a flourish. "I've been reading Bentham on the criminal mind, and it seems to me that—" Seeing Ivy and Quill in the doorway, he broke off with a wide grin.

"I see you've taken up a new hobby since our departure," Quill said as the assembled household gathered around the newlyweds to welcome them.

Grinning, Maitland shrugged. "Beauchamp House is full of books, would be a shame not to take advantage of it."

"Don't be modest, brother," Serena said with a roll of her eyes. "You'd think he was on the verge of becoming a Bow Street Runner with the amount of attention he's devoted to explaining what made Marianne snap."

"I suspect we've all found our own ways of dealing with what happened," Ivy said quietly as she accepted a hug from her erstwhile chaperone. "Perhaps Maitland's is just different from ours."

"Always so wise, Ivy," said Serena with a warm smile. "We've missed your level head these past weeks. I'm glad you're back."

"So am I," the new Marchioness of Kerr said, a feeling of contentment settling over her at being back amongst the inhabitants of Beauchamp House. "It was lovely to be away for a while, of course. But I found I missed you all." She raised a saucy brow. "Even you, Jeremy," she said as she spotted the boy lingering behind the sofa.

"You did?" he asked, looking pleased with himself.

"I did." She confirmed with a nod. "Quill and I even brought you back a present."

The boy's eyes grew wide. "You did?"

"Is there an echo in here?" Quill asked, striding over to the boy and lifting him into his arms. "Let's us gentlemen leave the ladies together so that they can gossip. I have a feeling Maitland will enjoy your gift just as much as you will, Jem."

Leaning down, he gave Ivy a quick kiss and the men left, shutting the doors behind them.

A few minutes later, a tea tray between them, the four bluestockings and Lady Serena were deep in conversation. "He's smitten, I think," Serena said with a grin as she looked to where Ivy and the rest of the bluestockings had gathered at one of the library tables. "And so are you," she continued. "Lady Celeste was quite brilliant to throw the two of you together."

"I hardly think it was that calculated," Ivy said, though in some moments she did wonder if her benefactress had anticipated Quill's strong objection to the way she left her estate. "Surely not?"

"She asked you to find her killer," Serena reminded her.

"And you did. She chose correctly. And she knew Quill better than anyone. She always lamented that he was so remote. So alone. I think she must have hoped one of you would catch his interest."

"I suppose we'll never know," Ivy said with regret. She had so much to thank Lady Celeste for. If only they'd been able to meet. Even if only for a moment.

"No. Thanks to her daughter, we won't," Serena said sadly. Then, brightening, she smiled. "I'll just go have a word with the cook about dinner, since there will need to be two more places at the table. I'm so glad you've returned, Ivy."

And without waiting for an argument, she slipped out of the room.

Now, surrounded by the other ladies whom she'd come to love as well as her own sisters, Ivy continued relating the story of how Quill met her father.

"I don't know that Papa was surprised I'd married so much, but that I'd married the son of his childhood crony," she said with a grin. "Neither Quill nor I knew it, but apparently Papa, as the younger son of the Duke of Ware, had visited Kerr Castle any number of times and even played at soldiers with Quill's father. He remembered the late marquess as a bit of a tyrant, which Quill found not at all surprising. But Papa was quite pleased to note that Quill seemed to have taken more of his temperament from his mother than his father."

"How romantic," Sophia said with a happy sigh. "It's almost as if you and Quill have righted some old quarrel between the two families. Like Romeo and Juliet, only without all the dying."

"I'd call it inevitable," Lady Daphne said with a frown for Sophia's sentiment. "There are only so many aristocratic families in the kingdom. That the grandchildren of dukes fell in love and married is hardly a great surprise. If anything, it's to be expected. If Ivy had been the daughter of the late marquess's valet? Now, *that* would have been romantic."

"Oh, Daphne," Ivy said, giving her a quick hug, which Daphne clearly did not enjoy, "I've missed you."

"Thank you, Ivy," Daphne said, pulling away from the embrace as quickly as possible. "I admit that I have missed you and the marquess in your absence. Especially when Sophia and Gemma are teasing me about the duke."

At the mention of Maitland, Ivy exchanged a wide-eyed look with the Hastings sisters. "And how goes your friendship with the duke, Daphne?" she asked carefully. When she and Quill had left, the duke was still avoiding Lady Daphne as if she were wearing a noxious perfume.

"There is nothing of note," Daphne said with dignity. "I have given up my quest to make love to him. He is not the carefree gentleman I thought when we first met. He is instead just as hemmed in by the ridiculous rules of society as any other man. Though as a duke he could quite likely ride his horse naked through Hyde Park without risking social ostracism, he cannot bend his moral code enough to engage in a simple, straightforward affair with me. I am disappointed, naturally. But resigned."

It was a long speech for Daphne, who tended to speak in short sentences. And Ivy felt a pang of sympathy for her. It cannot have been easy to accept Maitland's rejection. She was a lovely woman, and had likely not suffered such a fate much in her life.

"I have turned my attention to other matters," Daphne continued, with a spark of enthusiasm that soothed some of Ivy's worry for her friend. "There are far more intriguing mathematics books here in the library than I'd formerly thought. So I have immersed myself in reading the journals of Sir Isaac Newton and have been reacquainting myself with the *Philosophiae Naturalis Principia Mathematica*. It is quite a brilliant achievement not only for mathematics but also for England. No matter what that plagiarist Leibniz had to say about it."

"We shall have to take your word for it, dearest," said Sophia patting the other lady's hand. "For I must admit, I don't even know who those men are."

Daphne looked as if she would tell them, so Ivy spoke up again. "I presume Mrs. Vance has been taken to the gaol in Brighton by now?"

"Yes," Gemma said with a nod. "I must confess that it was a great relief to know she was taken away from here. I know she was unable to do any more harm from where she was being kept in Squire Northman's cellar, but just knowing such an evil person was nearby made me feel a little ill."

"The duke has determined that she likely killed her parents—her adoptive parents, that is—as well as Lady Celeste and Elsie," Sophia said with a shiver. "I know it must have been upsetting to learn that but for the intervention of the old Duke of Maitland she'd have been born into a much higher social class, but I cannot understand how it would turn her mind so."

Ivy thought back to that day in the vicarage. "I don't think she is mad," she said thoughtfully. "Or rather, not mad as we understand it to be. She wasn't ill, or unable to care for herself. She is, rather, prosaically efficient. I daresay if Lady Celeste hadn't left her letter telling me what she suspected, Mrs. Marianne Vance would have kept on killing."

"What of the vicar?" Ivy asked. When she and Quill left for London, the Reverend Devereaux had still been unconscious. She would visit him at the first opportunity, if only so that she could tell him how sorry she was that he'd lost Lady Celeste. It had been difficult to forget his silent, stricken gaze at her as they both listened to Marianne rant.

"He has recovered," Sophia said sadly, "but I think he will not be able to forget what happened for a long, long while."

"To know that his own daughter killed the love of his life," Gemma said aghast. "If only the old Duke of Maitland hadn't been so determined to keep Lady Celeste and the reverend apart all of this might have been avoided."

"He has gone to live with his sister in Scotland," Sophia said. "I can't say I blame him, really. It would be painful to be so close to where Marianne's crimes occurred."

"Did he and Lady Celeste ever meet after he came back to this area?" Ivy asked. "Surely they must have. Serena said that she attended the little church regularly."

"We'll never know," Daphne said. "Unless there was some mention of it in Lady Celeste's journals."

But none of them could recall reading anything relating to the vicar in their benefactress's diaries.

"So much heartbreak," Ivy said with a shudder. So easily, she and Quill could have ended up dead along with Marianne Vance's other victims.

Which reminded her. "What of Dr. Vance?"

"He was quite overwrought when he came to speak to the duke," Daphne said with an air of disdain. She hadn't quite been able to forgive the doctor for not realizing he was married to a killer it would seem.

"I suppose he was here to discuss his wife's prosecution?" Ivy asked, curious about the doctor's condition. Now that she was married herself, she understood just what a betrayal it had been for the physician's wife to lie to him about her every motive.

"Yes." Sophia set her empty brandy glass on the table. "He looked as if he hadn't slept in days. I must confess that I think the crime against him is as horrible as any Marianne committed against her murder victims. At least they do not have to live with the consequences."

"To spend your whole life helping people only to realize that you're harboring a disease in your own house," Gemma said grimly. "It has to have him going over his marriage with a fine-tooth comb to see if his wife left any more victims in her wake."

"At least she's finally caught," Ivy said. The other ladies echoed the sentiment.

Epilogue

Sometime later, after the ladies had taken tea and caught up on all the other news Ivy had missed while she and Quill were away, the subject turned to living arrangements.

"Where will you and Quill make your home, Ivy?" Sophia asked, stretching a little. "At Kerr Castle or the London townhouse?"

Ah, Ivy thought with a bit of trepidation, *the moment of truth.* She had a proposal for the other ladies, but there was no guarantee that they'd agree to it. After all, the house belonged to all of them equally so long as they remained here for a year. She didn't want to risk her stake in it.

Especially since Quill had such fond memories of his childhood here.

"Would you all mind terribly if we made our home here for the rest of the year?" she asked, tentatively, hoping against hope that they'd agree to the idea. If they didn't, she and Quill could, of course, go to any of his numerous homes. But she'd only scratched the surface of the collection of ancient Greek and Latin texts in the library. And she wished more than anything to use Lady Celeste's bequest to her to the fullest. It was the sincerest way she could give thanks to the woman who had given her more happiness than she'd ever imagined. "I understand if you object, of course. We were supposed to be a sort of bluestocking refuge, and there was never any plan for gentlemen to reside here too. In fact, I know what you'll say. Just give me a short time to let the marquess know, and we'll be on our way back—"

"Will you please be quiet, you ninnyhammer?" Daphne said in a loud voice after each of the ladies had attempted and failed to put a stop to Ivy's monologue.

Her eyes wide, Ivy hushed.

"Why would you think we would wish you gone?" Daphne continued, her puzzlement clear in her eyes. "Lady Celeste left Beauchamp House to the four of us. There is no rule that says you must leave if you marry. Or that one is no longer a bluestocking upon marriage—I have a feeling Madame D'Arblay, the former Frances Burney, would have some strong words at that notion."

"She's right, Ivy," Sophia said with a warm smile. "Besides, I thought we'd agreed when we first arrived that since Maitland, Lady Serena, and the marquess had all but grown up here, it would be cruel to bar them entry now. We can hardly eject you while allowing your husband to remain. It would be a breach of the bluestocking code!"

"Besides all that," Gemma said wryly, "Maitland has all but set up housekeeping here. Why would we toss your husband out on his ear? Lord Kerr can hardly be any more disruptive than the duke, who puts Daphne to the blush at every opportunity and in general makes her impossible to live with."

At a speaking look from her sister, Gemma gave a rueful laugh. "More impossible than usual, then."

"I am not impossible," Daphne protested. "And it is not my fault that the duke will not forget about my indecent proposal to him at the beginning of our acquaintance. It's almost as if he thinks I set my cap at him. When, in fact, it couldn't be farther from the truth. I didn't want to marry the man, I just wanted to f—"

"We understand you perfectly, dear," Ivy interrupted before Daphne could finish her thought.

"If only Maitland did," Daphne sighed.

"So you see, Ivy," Sophia said, returning the discussion to its original subject, "we need you both here—you to give Gemma and me someone besides each other to gossip about Daphne with, and Lord Kerr to give the duke a sobering influence."

Ivy felt a wave of relief wash over her. She had hoped the others would not object to her living here with Quill, but since they'd begun their tenure here with his vocal objection to their presence in his aunt's home, it would have only been fair if they chose to banish him.

"I promise we will not be one of those annoying pairs of newlyweds who makes everyone feel ill with our constant billing and cooing," she assured them. "You'll hardly know we're here."

"Speak for yourself, wife," said Quill stepping into the room followed by a sheepish-looking Maitland and Lady Serena with Jeremy in tow. "I will bill and coo from sunrise to sunset. And there's nothing you can do to stop me."

Unable to resist him, Ivy turned up her face to his to accept his kiss, which was a bit more heated than strictly proper.

"Oh dear," she heard Serena say. "I am a very poor sort of chaperone, am I not?"

"Thank God for that," Quill whispered into Ivy's ear. "It took a scandal to make me realize I loved you." But Ivy knew deep in her bones, that even if Serena had been a dragon, she and Quill would have found a way to come together.

Scandal or not, they were meant to be together.

And Lady Celeste, who had herself been denied a happy ending, had all but ensured Ivy and Quill had theirs.

The only question now, she thought as her speculative gaze fell on Daphne—who was pretending to ignore Maitland—was which bluestocking would fall next. She knew which of the three she'd place *her* bet on.

And from the looks of the duke, he would not wait long before he set that adventure in motion.

Amid the chattering of the others, she felt a calm wash over her.

Thank you, she said silently, sending up a little prayer to her benefactress.

"What is it?" Quill asked her in a low voice from where he'd taken a seat beside her. "Is something wrong?"

"Nothing." She kissed him softly, her heart full of love. "Everything is just as it should be."

And Ivy knew, from wherever she watched them, that the redoubtable Lady Celeste approved.

THE END

Duke with Benefits

To Vince, Kate, and Adair. Your little family, born from love, is the essence of everything I'm writing about. (Without the murder, obviously.) Love you guys so much and I'm proud to say we're family.

Prologue

You will soon embark on a quest for something very valuable, but along the way you will risk losing your greatest love.
MADAME ALBINIA'S FORTUNE FOR LADY DAPHNE FORSYTH

Lady Daphne Forsyth's boots crunched over the gravel of the drive leading up to the entrance of Beauchamp House as she walked behind the group of men carrying her wounded friend.

Someone had shot Miss Ivy Wareham.

It would have been impossible to believe if she hadn't seen it with her own eyes, but even now the sight of a clenched-jawed Lord Kerr, Ivy's betrothed, walking beside her make-shift litter told her it was all too real. As did the drawn faces of the others who had gone with them today.

It had all begun when the party from Beauchamp House had set out to visit Madame Albinia in the gypsy encampment near Little Seaford.

At first Daphne had assumed Ivy, who along with Daphne and the misses Sophia and Gemma Hastings had inherited Beauchamp House from Lady Celeste Beauchamp, had wished to visit the fortune teller for all the usual reasons. To hear some silly predictions about her future or the like. But as the four ladies, accompanied by Lady Celeste's nephews, the Marquess of Kerr and the Duke of Maitland, had walked to the edge of the village, Ivy had confided that her reasons for the visit were far more serious.

Lady Celeste had been poisoned to death, and the vehicle for the poison had been the tisane recipe supplied by Madame Albinia to Lady Celeste's maid.

That her benefactress had been deliberately poisoned was a shock, and it had been the main topic of conversation as they made their way along the path to the village.

All four ladies had been the unexpected heiresses of the late Lady Celeste Beauchamp, who as a scholar herself wished to see her home and extensive library collection go into the hands of those who would make best use of it. The bequest had come as a shock. None of them had met before their arrival at Beauchamp House, and each had dedicated themselves to different scholarly endeavors. But somehow in the time since they'd arrived, they'd managed to become friends.

Daphne had enjoyed the fresh air and the company despite the revelation about Lady Celeste's death. And if she were honest, she'd also enjoyed the chance to converse with the Duke of Maitland away from the watchful gaze of his sister, who took her job as chaperone quite seriously now that Ivy had been compromised by Lord Kerr.

That is, until on their journey back some unknown person had actually shot at them and wounded Ivy.

As luck would have it, their return had been spotted by young Jeremy Fanning, the son of their chaperone, Lady Serena. At the sight of the injured Ivy, the boy's eyes widened and he clung to his mother's skirts. "Mama, what happened?"

"Ivy had a bit of a mishap, old fellow," said the Duke of Maitland before Lady Serena could respond. Stepping forward to lift the small boy into his arms, he continued, "But she'll be right as rain in no time. Won't she, Mama?" This last he addressed to his sister who threw him a grateful glance before rubbing the little boy's back.

"Of course she will, Uncle Dalton," she said brightly. "Jem, will you stay with your uncle and the other ladies while Quill and I see to Miss Ivy?"

The boy, whose watchful blue-gray eyes were very like his uncle's, nodded. "Can we play hide-and-seek, Uncle Dalton?"

"Of course, we can, lad. Ladies, will you join us?"

"I don't suppose there's much else we can do at the moment," Sophia said with a worried glance toward upstairs, where Ivy had been taken.

"And I do love a good game of hide-and-seek," Gemma said, her cheery tone echoing Lady Serena's of a moment earlier. "Though if you don't mind, Jem, could we ladies have a cup of tea before we get started? I think perhaps we can convince cook to send up some tarts as well."

The mention of treats did the trick with the child, and they all retired to the drawing room for tea and something stronger for those who needed it.

Now some time later, Jem had gone off to hide, while the others set off in separate directions to look for him.

As she turned the corner, lost in her thoughts, Daphne caught her breath as she slammed into a hard male chest.

"Caught you," said Maitland with a grin as he grasped her by the elbows. But as soon as he saw her face, his smile faded.

"What is it, my dear?" he asked, still holding her arms.

Unwilling to admit her residual upset, Daphne shook her head. "It's nothing. And may I remind you, I'm not the one you're meant to be seeking."

When he didn't let her go, she continued, "Let me go, Duke. I am quite well. And don't need anyone to fuss over me."

He let go of her but didn't step away. He was close enough that she could smell the scent of his shaving lotion and see the glint of lamplight on the blond stubble of his beard.

"Why do I get the feeling you're pretending to be more sanguine about this than you actually are?" His perceptive gaze was narrow, as if he was trying to see into her thoughts.

Not for the first time, Daphne was grateful for the fact that mind-reading had never been perfected. She had a difficult-enough time dealing with the fallout from her spoken words. If her thoughts were subject to the same sort of scrutiny, she'd find herself in a difficult spot indeed.

Since the moment he arrived at Beauchamp House, the handsome duke had drawn Daphne's interest. Not only because he was a fine specimen of masculine beauty—though he was certainly that with his broad shoulders, tall build, and twinkling blue eyes—but also because of something intangible. It had been there from the moment she'd spied him across the drawing room. Some spark of attraction between them that was unlike anything she'd ever felt before.

And that afternoon, she'd almost asked him about it. Daphne was nothing if not plain spoken and to her mind, the most sensible thing to do about the attraction between them was to talk about it and decide if they wished to pursue it.

Of course, her own ideas about what was and was not an appropriate topic of conversation had never been entirely in keeping with what the rest of polite society decreed. Since her arrival at Beauchamp House, Ivy, Sophia, and Gemma had taught her a great deal about what she should and should not say aloud.

Her mother had died when she was only four years old, and the series of nurses and governesses who had been hired by her father had only lasted a short while before they each gave up in defeat. Only the male tutor—an expert in mathematics—had managed to stay for any length of time. And that was perhaps because he saw her not as a young lady, but as a mathematical genius. A mind to be molded rather than a prize to be auctioned off in the marriage mart.

And so, her lessons in gentility had been abandoned in favor of higher maths. Which left her with the ability to solve complex equations more quickly than most Oxbridge fellows and almost no sense of how to speak without setting up the backs of those around her.

The walk to the gypsy encampment had seemed like the perfect opportunity to lay her case before the Duke of Maitland. They might be relatively private without fear of being overheard, and there was no danger he'd mistake her words for a marriage proposal, which was the furthest thing from her mind. But despite her determination to speak, Daphne had found that, once the opportunity presented itself, she was reluctant to broach the subject, her usual sangfroid replaced with a rare shyness. So she'd kept to less-volatile topics and had enjoyed herself immensely on the walk.

Now, however, she was surprised by just how easily Maitland could see past her mask of calm. "I might still be a bit overset," she admitted. "But I will recover."

Looking down to where his hands still grasped her arms, she repeated, "You may let me go."

He let go of her but didn't step back. "Perhaps I haven't regained my balance yet, Lady Daphne."

But that was nonsense.

"Of course you didn't lose your balance. A man of your size is hardly going to be knocked over by me, tall though I am for a lady."

Moving to her side, Maitland slid her arm into his. "You are of course correct." She could hear the smile in his voice, and she was relieved he hadn't been annoyed by her correction. Sometimes conversation was a trial for Daphne, who wished people would simply say what they meant instead of using metaphors and the like. Turns of phrase made life very frustrating for her.

"Shall we continue down this hall to look for Jem?"

After the events of the day, she was glad to have the company. And perhaps now that they were truly alone she'd be able to speak to him frankly.

"That's what I was doing before I ran into you," she said allowing him to lead her past the bust of Mary Wollstonecraft that marked the passage leading to Lady Celeste's private rooms. "But I shall enjoy the company. Especially after what happened to Ivy."

"It was distressing, wasn't it?" he asked, as he moved to open the door to a small sitting room. "Jem?" he called out.

From behind him, Daphne could see that the room was dark and there was no fire in the hearth. None of the heiresses had been willing to take over the mistress of the house's rooms. Daphne hadn't had the courage to enter them, so strong was the feeling that Lady Celeste had only gone out for a walk and would return at any minute.

But Maitland, who had run tame in Beauchamp House from childhood, had no such diffidence. He lit the lamp nearest the door and moved to light the other two as well. Soon the cozy room was bright and the shadows that had made it seem gloomy were vanquished.

Daphne could see now that it was a charming space, with butter yellow walls, a pair of comfortable chintz chairs before the fire, and when she stepped closer to look, she saw a basket of mending beside the farthest chair. Something about the needle still plunged into the chemise Celeste had been repairing was more poignant than any of the testaments she'd heard thus far from the people who'd known her.

"This was her inner sanctum," she said, and it wasn't a question. She knew, as she moved to look at the shelf of books beside the window, that though the library had been the place where Celeste had placed the books and artwork that would be valued by the world at large, the items here, in this room, were those that meant something to her personally.

"It was," Maitland said as he moved to stand beside her as she scanned the shelves. "I can remember when I was a boy she would give me adventure novels from these shelves and tell me never to forget that reading was first and foremost for pleasure."

And indeed, most of the shelves here were the sorts of things that engendered criticism from a certain element of society for whom words were meant only for edification. There were the familiar bindings of Minerva Press, and many other four-volume sets of popular novels as well as what were likely Celeste's personal copies of Wollstonecraft, Mary Shelley, and other greats.

"I do wish I'd have been able to meet her," Daphne said, reaching out to touch the gilded spine of what looked to be a private journal. "I wonder if she'd have found fault with my blunt talk." It was something she hadn't meant to reveal—certainly not to the man who made her body tingle whenever he was within arm's reach, as he was now. But there was something about being here in this room that put her off guard.

"She'd have loved you," Maitland said, his voice much closer than she'd expected.

Swallowing, she dared a look up at his face and saw that his blue eyes were dark with an emotion she couldn't name.

"She would have found your forthrightness refreshing," he continued, reaching out to touch his thumb to her cheek. It was a light caress. A whisper of skin over skin. "And so do I."

The words hung in the air between them as Daphne tried to process what was happening.

"Do you?" she asked, turning so that she was facing him now, too. "I'm not too rude? Too blunt?"

To her surprise, she found she wanted to know. For some reason, it mattered—mattered desperately—what he thought of her. Whether he was truly not bothered by her tendency to put everyone to the blush.

"No," he said, his golden head lowering to hers. And just before he pressed his lips against hers, he whispered, "I like it."

Daphne had been kissed before, but never like this. And never by someone she'd felt such an overwhelming degree of attraction for.

She felt her heart leap up in her chest at the gentle pressure of his mouth, and instincts had her slipping her arms around his neck and pulling him down to her. In answer, he groaned and slipped his hands around her waist.

It was heady, this moment that was at once surrender and vanquishment. And when he pulled her more closely to him and his kiss grew more heated, his mouth opening over hers, she gave herself up to the sensations engulfing her.

But almost as soon as it had begun, he was pulling away from her, and putting a foot of distance between them.

Trying to make her brain work against the flood of emotion that threatened to overwhelm her, she asked in a breathless voice, "Did I do something wrong?" It had seemed as if he was enjoying himself very much. And goodness knows she'd had no objections to the feel of his strong body pressed against hers.

Taking in a gulp of breath, Maitland thrust a hand into his golden curls, already disarrayed from her hands. "No, you were perfect. It's just that I can't . . . that is to say, it wouldn't be appropriate . . ."

Ah, this she understood. "Of course, you are worried about the proprieties. It makes sense for a man in your position. But I can assure you that I won't insist you marry me or any such nonsense. It is perhaps unusual for unmarried young ladies of the *ton* to take lovers, but hardly unheard of. And

I think the attraction between us is unusual enough that it shouldn't be ignored."

But far from agreeing with her as she'd hoped—indeed expected—the duke looked shocked.

The one thing she'd never considered, in all her imaginings of this conversation, was that the object of her desire would have his sense of propriety wounded.

"Lady Daphne," he said, his deep voice almost hushed, as if he feared they'd be overheard, "I don't know what sort of man you think I am, but I am not in the habit of deflowering virgins. And I certainly would not do so without doing my duty and paying the consequences for my actions."

Daphne frowned. "But I just told you that there will be no need to do so. I don't intend to marry. And I certainly don't wish to trap you into a marriage simply because we acted on what is a perfectly natural attraction between us. What harm can there be in the two of us indulging in our desires? There's no one who can be hurt by it as you have no wife. And besides that, I have given you my word I won't trap you. I don't see the problem."

His handsome features twisted in disbelief. "I thought I liked your plain speaking, my dear," he said, shaking his head, "but I fear I may have been too quick to say so. For there is so much to object to in your little speech that I don't know where to begin to dispute it."

Daphne blinked. She hadn't thought is possible that such a short acquaintance would make her vulnerable to being hurt by anything he said. But by taking back his assurance that he enjoyed her plain speaking—something that was as intrinsic to her as her mathematical abilities—he had hurt her more than she'd ever imagined he could. She hadn't realized how much she'd come to value his opinion. And she'd certainly never imagined he had the power to wound her in this way.

Not wanting to prolong the discussion, she took a deep breath, and with one last quick glance at his lovely face, she straightened her spine.

"I apologize for offending you, your grace. Please think no more of it."

Brushing past him, she hurried from the room, wanting to sprint, but refusing to make a cake of herself any more than she already had.

Behind her, she could hear him hurrying after her. "Daphne, wait. You didn't offend me, it's just that . . ."

But before he could catch up to her, Jem came hurtling around the corner.

"Uncle Dalton!" the boy cried as he threw himself into the duke's arms. "I hided and Miss Sophia found me!"

Daphne could feel Maitland's gaze on her, but she dared not look at him fully. Her cheeks burned with embarrassment at her miscalculation.

"Where are Miss Sophia and Miss Gemma, Jem?" she asked the little boy, hoping that the distraction of her friends' conversation would help her forget what had just transpired.

"They're back in the drawing room," Jem said from where he sat perched in his uncle's strong arms. "They were looking for you. And Uncle Dalton, too."

"We were looking for you, sport," said Maitland in a cheerful tone. Clearly he hadn't been as upset by their disagreement as she had been.

"Excellent," Daphne said, adopting the same upbeat tone. "I'll just go find them then."

"I still would like to speak with you further, Lady Daphne," she heard the duke say from behind her.

But that was a conversation she would avoid with every last fiber of her being, Daphne thought as she hurried down the stairs toward the drawing room.

As she reached the landing, the words of Madame Albinia

came back to her. *You will soon embark on a quest for something very valuable, but along the way you will risk losing your greatest love.*

She stopped mid-stride.

No, it was too ridiculous to consider, she chided herself. While technically, she had been searching for something valuable, i.e., Jem, a game of hide-and-seek was hardly what one would call a *quest*. And though she was attracted to the Duke of Maitland—correction, while she *had been* attracted to the Duke of Maitland, she would hardly call him her greatest love. Her mind was simply falling into the trap that thousands before her had succumbed to, twisting the vague words of a fortune-teller into a self-fulfilling prophecy that had no basis in reality.

Just as her assumption that the duke would simply agree to a liaison with her had no basis in reality.

She had made the mistake before, and it had left her with more than simple wounded pride, as this afternoon's encounter had done.

With this hard-won determination in her mind, she went off in search of the other ladies.

Chapter 1

THREE MONTHS LATER

Lady Daphne Forsyth would rather listen to a thousand lectures on decorum from her chaperone than listen to another word from the Marchioness of Kerr about her husband's thoughtfulness. Or his loyalty. Or his humor.

Or any of a myriad of qualities about which the former Miss Ivy Wareham—once a quite sensible classics scholar, capable of conversation on any number of interesting subjects—now extolled morning, noon, and night to anyone who would listen.

At this point, even young Jeremy Fanning, the six-year-old son of the aforementioned chaperone would be a more intriguing conversationalist.

She kept her own counsel, however, as she, Ivy, the Hastings sisters, the Marquess of Kerr, and the Duke of Maitland walked along the cliffside path running from Beauchamp House inland toward the village of Little Seaford.

It had been several months now since she'd received the news that the celebrated bluestocking leader, Lady Celeste Beauchamp had left her beautifully appointed manor house—complete with one of the most impressive libraries in the country—to a quartet of young ladies with their own artistic and academic *bona fides,* the mathematics prodigy, Lady Daphne, among them.

The letter from Lady Celeste, forwarded by her solicitor, had been effusive in its praise, but that hadn't been what convinced Daphne to pack her bags and travel from London to Beauchamp House. If praise was all she wished for she could sit down for a hand of cards in any drawing room or gaming hell in Mayfair—though admittedly the praise would be peppered with envy and anger over lost fortunes. No, it had been the promise in the carefully worded letter that the library at Beauchamp House contained more than first editions and scholarly tomes.

> You will find Romance and enough intrigue to Riddle even the most unschooled of ladies with envy among the Treasure of my collections.

Any other reader would have supposed Lady Celeste merely had an odd habit of capitalizing random words in her writing—it was common enough among the ladies of the *ton,* who were hardly the most educated of creatures. But to Daphne, who was able to see beyond the set order of letters to the pattern beneath, her benefactress's words had been a message intended just for her. Without needing a pencil, her mind rearranged the letters of Romance into Cameron. And the rest of the clue was hidden in plain sight.

Cameron Riddle Treasure

It had been the promise that the library at Beauchamp House contained the famous Cameron Riddle, which legend said would lead the one able to decode it to a treasure hidden away by the leader of Clan Cameron in the days of the last Jacobite rebellion, that led Daphne to travel south to take her place among the four Beauchamp Heiresses. That and the hope that she could separate herself at last from her father's clutches and would never have to play cards for money again.

But in the time since she came to the coast, she'd found no trace of the promised puzzle, and she'd searched nearly half the contents of the admittedly impressive book room's collection. She'd told the rest of the household that she wished to familiarize herself with the collections before she began any in-depth research on the maths books, but the other ladies knew she found other subjects tedious at best and she'd begun to catch them exchanging amused glances when she started her methodical searches each morning.

Of course, their amusement might have been because many of these sessions included the "assistance" of the Duke of Maitland, who was inexplicably still on an extended stay at Beauchamp House. He claimed it was to spend time with his sister, their chaperone Lady Serena Fanning, and her son Jeremy. But Daphne was no fool. She saw the way he looked at her from beneath his criminally long eyelashes.

"A penny for them," said the object of her thoughts as they reached the signpost that marked the outskirts of the village.

This was what came of woolgathering, Daphne thought wryly, unable to stop herself from giving her companion a sidelong glance as the rest of their party walked along ahead of them.

With his sun-burnished hair, tall athletic frame, and dimpled grin, Dalton Beauchamp, the Duke of Maitland, was certainly no hardship to look at. And yet, after a few weeks of enjoyable flirtation just after he arrived, he'd begun treating her more like a sister than a potential lover. She'd made the mistake—only once, mind you—of suggesting that they conduct an affair, such as she'd seen were commonplace among the London *ton*, and he'd acted like a scandalized maiden. Given his reputation as a bit of a rogue in London, she had been disappointed at his response. She had hoped he would be less conventional, but his rebuff had been plain. If he was holding out for marriage, however, he wouldn't get it from her. She would never, after being used as a means of gathering income by her father for so many years, willingly enter the institution that would give another man control over her. She found Maitland attractive, and so far as she could tell, he found her intriguing as well. Why did they need to bring marriage into the equation at all?

Since he insisted on remaining in residence at Beauchamp House, she was forced to interact with him. And if she was honest, she enjoyed some of his nonsense. He was no scholar, but he was amusing and kind. And he hadn't chosen to shun her, as she knew many men in his situation would have done.

"If you must know," she said, knowing her confidence was safe with Maitland, "I was debating whether a gag or a muzzle would be a more appropriate means of silencing Ivy on the subject of her husband's every waking thought."

This startled a bark of laughter from the duke, who quickly turned it into a cough when the others turned to see what had caused it.

"Carry on," he said with a wave at them. "Nothing to see here."

"I know it is churlish of me," Daphne admitted once they were relatively private again, "but even a paragon among men would not measure up to Ivy's praise. Certainly not the Marquess of Kerr."

"Still haven't forgiven him for the way he arrived on the scene calling for the lot of you to be tossed out on your collective ear, eh?"

Maitland hadn't been there for Kerr's first meeting with the heiresses, but he'd no doubt heard about the ugly encounter from his sister.

"It's not just that," Daphne said, though admittedly it was a large portion of it. She'd learned to judge people based on first impressions from an early age, and with a few exceptions she'd come to find that more often than not they held true. "It's Ivy. She's turned into just the sort of besotted fool I learned to avoid like the plague in London. You can hardly get two words of sense from her these days without the other three being about her darling husband or some other nonsensical tale. A line from Catullus the other day sent her into peals of laughter and all she would say was that it reminded her of something Kerr had said. I want my sensible friend back."

Even as she spoke, Daphne knew she was exaggerating the degree to which Ivy had changed since her marriage. But even if there was a bit of envy in her assessment of the pair, she'd hardly admit as much to Maitland. He'd never let her hear the end of it.

When he remained silent, she looked up to see that he was biting his lip.

"What?" she demanded. Really, it was as if everyone in the house had gone mad.

Looking rueful, Maitland said with a grin, "It's just that Catullus is known for being a bit . . ." He paused, clearly searching for the right word. "Ribald," he finally settled on.

Which meant that Kerr had likely said whatever had so amused Ivy in bed.

Daphne felt her cheeks redden. This was what came of neglecting one's classical education in favor of a diet of only maths.

She wasn't accustomed to embarrassment over such things. She'd been privy to conversations unfit for most adult ears before she reached her thirteenth birthday, and could swear in three languages thanks to the card rooms of the *ton*. She'd long ago schooled herself to ignore such things as just another coded language. One that she herself had no desire to partake in.

That had been before she lay eyes on the superior physical specimen who walked beside her now.

Of course, he'd rejected her one and only attempt at seduction almost before the words were out of her mouth. Which was just as well, Daphne thought wryly, since she'd not long afterward discovered that Maitland wasn't quite the most bookish of men.

The idea that Ivy was now sharing libertine jokes, and more, with her new husband, though? That gave Daphne a pang of loneliness she'd not experienced since she'd first met the three ladies with whom she'd share Beauchamp House for at least the next year.

It was perhaps silly of her, but in the other bluestockings she'd thought she'd found kindred spirits. They might not understand much of her conversation about the finer points of trigonometry, but they understood what it was to be the best in a field dominated by men. And Ivy, it would seem, had traded in her bluestocking hat for a matron's cap.

"If it's any consolation," Maitland said, breaking into her thoughts once more, "Kerr is just as besotted. Serena and I have taken to adding a penny to a jar every time he extols one of Ivy's virtues. We've not counted yet, but I suspect there's at least ten pounds in it by now."

"But he was never a man of sense. He's like you in that reg—" Daphne stopped because she'd learned from her friends that speaking her mind as truthfully as she would like sometimes led to hurt feelings. And she had no wish to insult Maitland. Tardy though her judgment was.

If the duke was insulted, however, he didn't show it.

"Oh, I'm well aware of the gulf that exists between you ladies and the rest of us," he said with a staying gesture. "At least when it comes to intellect. We're not simpletons, mind you, but neither are we great minds. My old nanny told me that you've got to know your good points. I'm a likable fellow. I can sweet talk a spooked horse like nobody's business. And I'm not too awful to look at. But you and the other bluestockings can think rings around us."

At his tone of understanding, Daphne heaved a sigh of relief. "Yes, that's it precisely. I'm so glad you understand, Maitland, because I wouldn't like to think I'd said something hurtful. The others have taught me, I think, finally, that my plain-speaking sometimes makes others unhappy."

What was he thinking? she wondered, as the duke gave her a long look. She'd always had trouble guessing what feelings lay behind a person's words. When she said something, it was exactly what she meant.

But before she could ask for his thoughts, she heard the others greeting a pair of gentlemen as they entered the village.

"No harm done," was all Maitland said as they caught up with the others.

The two newcomers were dressed in what Daphne assumed was the current country fashion. She had little use for such things, but she'd grown accustomed to seeing Maitland and Kerr and the gentlemen of the neighborhood at large dressed in boots and breeches and more casual neck cloths than were required in town. The taller of the two men looked up as she and the duke approached, and Daphne felt a constriction in her chest.

"Lady Daphne Forsyth, as I live and breathe! Is it really you?"

Through narrowed eyes, Dalton examined the man who greeted Daphne, only just resisting the urge to remove his quizzing glass and subject the fellow to his most ducal glare. He might have a reputation for being affable to a fault, but even Merry Maitland had his limits. And, he thought wryly as Daphne greeted the newcomer with a cry of recognition, it seemed that seeing another man look at Daphne like an oasis in the desert was his.

Daphne, on the other hand, did not seem quite so pleased. "Mr. Sommersby," she said, her expression unreadable as she stopped in her tracks.

Maitland would be the first to admit she wasn't the most effusive of women, but something about her reaction to this fellow put him on alert. Perhaps it was the way she didn't advance to take his outstretched hand. Or maybe it was the slight pallor that overtook her when she recognized him.

Daphne wasn't overly emotional, it was true, but neither was she devoid of emotion.

Maitland knew very well that she felt some things strongly. One only had to hear her wax rhapsodic on one of her mathematical bits to know she was capable of great joy. It was just that she wasn't demonstrative with people. Perhaps because she had difficulty gauging what response they would have to her unpolished conversation. He had only been in her company for a short while before he recognized that she deeply regretted the fact that much of her plain-speaking led to hurt feelings, but she knew of no way to curb her errant tongue.

She was feeling some strong emotion now, however. If only he could read her well enough to know what it was.

"Why on earth are you in Little Seaford?" Daphne asked Sommersby, her eyes narrow with suspicion. "The last letter I had from your father said that you were in Egypt." It was almost an accusation. As if he'd broken some oath by leaving the land of the Pharaohs for England.

At the mention of Egypt, however, Maitland bit back a groan. Of course, this fellow had just returned from Egypt.

He looked exactly the type. Right down to the tanned skin and slightly rumpled coat.

"Mr. Sommersby and Mr. Foster were just telling us why they're in the area, Lady Daphne," said Lord Kerr. He had a possessive arm around his wife's waist.

Maitland's cousin was no fool. He saw that these fellows were not to be trusted just as well as he did.

"They're on the hunt for lost treasure, if you can believe it," the marquess continued before quirking a brow in Maitland's direction.

Treasure hunters? Really? his cousin seemed to ask.

Maitland gave a slight shrug. It was as likely a scheme as any, he supposed. He might also have guessed that the two men were riverboat gamblers, if they'd happened to be in the Louisiana territory of the Americas. They just had that look about them.

Up to no good.

"You always were one to dream of riches and treasure, Nigel," Daphne said tartly. "Your father would be attempting to teach us both some new mathematical principal and you would be attempting to read a penny dreadful about some lost jewel or the like under the table."

"And I always got caught," Sommersby said with a laugh. "Because you always told my father."

"So this is the son of your tutor, Lady Daphne?" asked Ivy with a raised brow.

"Indeed," Daphne said with nod. She seemed less than pleased at meeting him here. At first Maitland had thought she was just surprised, but there was something else at play here.

Something darker.

But that was likely his imagination, he chided himself. He had no reason to think badly of a man he'd only just met.

Still, when Sommersby said, "We grew up together, you

might say. Though not as brother and sister," he saw Daphne's spine stiffen. There was definitely something about the fellow she didn't like.

If Daphne didn't trust him, then neither did Maitland.

She didn't say as much however, instead turning the conversation to Sommersby's reason for being here. "What lost treasure are you searching for hereabouts?" Her tone implied that there could not possibly be treasure or anything like it within five hundred miles of Little Seaford.

Foster, who up until now had been silent, chose that moment to speak up. "We've actually heard a rumor that the lost Cameron Cipher is in a library collection in the vicinity."

Some niggle of memory from his childhood fired in Maitland's mind, but he could not recall any specifics. But the cipher was better known to Daphne if her sharp intake of breath was any indication.

Her next words only confirmed his assumption. "That is impossible. There is no Cameron Cipher. It is just a myth."

Poor Daphne. She didn't have a dissembling bone in her body. And it was evident that whatever she thought about the Cameron Cipher, it wasn't that there was no validity to Foster's claim. Rather the opposite. Though she was trying in her way to convince him otherwise.

"You weren't so skeptical when we first heard the legend, Daphne," said Sommersby with a grin. "You were the first one to get out the map and trace the likely route Cameron took on the way to Dover with the chest of gold in tow."

Before Daphne could retort, Miss Sophia Hastings broke in. "But what is this Cameron Cipher? I must confess I've never heard of it. I am woefully ignorant about such things."

"I'm sure that's not true, Miss Sophia," Foster assured her. "The Cameron Cipher is a coded message that holds the secret of where the leader of clan Cameron hid the Jacobite gold meant for the Pretender in 'forty-five. He was on the way to

France to deliver the gold when his party was set upon by the English army, and he took safety somewhere along the coast. He hid the gold nearby and trusted the coded message telling where it was hidden with someone hereabouts. Or, as the alternate theory goes, hid it somewhere nearby where it was subsequently found, but proved too difficult to decrypt. A letter was found among the papers of Cameron's wife that said it was somewhere safe, but it was no more specific than that. And thus, a legend was born."

"That's right," Maitland spoke up as the memories flooded back to him. "Don't you remember we used to search for it in the caves when we were boys, Kerr?" He and his cousin had spent countless summers hunting for the cipher without success. "I haven't thought about it in years."

"Nor I," the marquess said with a grin. "Those were fun days."

"Why wasn't I included in these searches?" Serena asked crossly. "I should have enjoyed treasure hunting."

"Because you were a girl, Serena," Kerr said with a roll of his eyes. "It was just us lads."

"I want to hunt for treasure," young Jem piped up from beside his mother. "Will you take me, cousins?"

But Daphne it seemed, was still determined to dissuade the men from their quest. Over the sound of Quill assuring Jem that they would indeed go search the caves for treasure soon, she spoke up. "I am sorry you both came all this way for nothing. But it is highly improbable that the cipher exists in any of the libraries hereabouts."

"I had heard that the library at Beauchamp House is quite impressive," Sommersby said with what to Maitland's eye looked like calculation. "You wouldn't care to allow us to examine it, would you, Kerr? Just for our own amusement if nothing else. You are no doubt right about the cipher not being there."

"You'll need to ask all four of these ladies," Lord Kerr said amiably. "My wife, Lady Daphne, and the Misses Hastings inherited Beauchamp House from our aunt. But you likely know that already."

"Indeed, I do," Sommersby said with a grin, making no attempt to hide the fact that he'd just dissembled. "It was the talk of town for weeks. The four bluestocking heiresses of Beauchamp House. Congratulations to all of you."

"I'm afraid it will be quite impossible for us to allow you to search the library," Daphne said before any of the others could speak up. "We are all quite busy with our respective studies. I'm sure you understand."

A hard expression flitted across Sommersby's face before he masked it with one of affability. "We understand perfectly, of course. Perhaps one evening after you've finished your studies for the day, then?"

Something about this fellow was putting Maitland's back up. And it wasn't his ingratiating manner with Daphne. At least, that wasn't all of it. Aloud he said, "Perhaps you both can come by tomorrow evening for dinner, gentlemen? I, for one, would enjoy hearing about your travels. And I know Kerr will wish to question you about them."

At his words, Daphne gave him a glare. But the duke wanted to know more about Sommersby, which he would prefer to do when the man was on familiar territory. Besides, he was curious about the man's relationship with Daphne. And he could hardly seek him out at the local inn and demand to know what he'd done to make her distrust him so.

Of course, he could just ask Daphne outright, but they weren't exactly on the easiest of terms at the moment. He thought back to that moment in his aunt's bedchamber with a pang of regret. He couldn't have handled it worse if he'd tried.

"Capital," said Sommersby, his triumphant grin, showing he was unaware of the direction of Maitland's thoughts. "We'll see you all tomorrow then."

And after making their farewells, the two continued on their journey to the beach.

"Why were you so rude to him, Daphne?" Sophia asked with a frown as they began walking again. "He seemed quite friendly. And I should think you of all people would be intrigued by this Cameron Cipher. You're just the person to unravel its code, I'd think."

Daphne looked as if she would simply refuse to respond for a moment, but finally she said with a sigh, "Because I do not wish him to find the Cameron Cipher."

"That much was obvious, I think," Gemma said wryly.

"But why, Daphne?" Ivy asked, her expression concerned but not angrily so.

Maitland watched as Daphne blinked several times. *Were those tears?* His own chest constricted at the very idea.

"Because it's *mine*," she whispered. "Lady Celeste promised the Cameron Cipher to me."

Chapter 2

Daphne felt the ribbon of her hat brush against her cheek in the wind as she listened to the others' silence following her announcement.

All were silent but Jem, that is.

"What a Cam'rn Sife, Mama?" he whispered loudly from where he skipped along the path to Little Seaford beside Lady Serena.

"Hush, Jem," she said in an undertone. "Why don't you see how fast you can run to that dandelion up ahead?"

With a squeak of delight, the boy lifted his legs and ran ahead of them.

"When were you going to tell us this?" Ivy asked, once the child was out of earshot. "We've been here for three months, and this is the first I've heard of this cipher."

"Is that what you've been searching for in the library every day?" Sophia asked, her head tilted in exasperation. "You told us you were especially interested in the mathematics volumes, but I knew you had been through the art books, too."

"Well, I don't blame you a bit," Gemma said firmly. "I know very well how difficult it is to maintain your credibility in the sciences as a woman. If it got out you were treasure hunting, your academic reputation could be ruined.

Unless, of course you were keeping this quiet because you didn't wish to share your gold with us, in which case, I am quite put out."

But it was obvious from Gemma's grin that she was nothing of the sort.

"Perhaps you would like for Maitland and me to leave you ladies to discuss this on your own," said Ivy's husband with a speaking look at Maitland. The duke, Daphne was relieved to see, looked only concerned for her, which she couldn't quite fathom after how she'd been treating him.

"No," she said with a wave of her hand, not meeting any of their gazes—not that she was particularly fond of eye contact at the best of times. "You should stay, since Ivy will tell you whatever I say anyway. And then you'll tell Maitland, who'll tell his sister."

Since none of the named gossips denied the accusation, she took that for their agreement with her assessment.

"Perhaps we should wait until we reach town and can safely sit down to a nice cup of tea in a private dining room at the inn?" she asked. It was illogical, she knew, but she feared Sommersby might somehow overhear them out here in the open.

"If that's what you wish," Maitland said, taking her arm in his and leading her past the others and toward the village, which they could now see as their party approached.

A more subdued group, they made the short trek into the village and had little trouble procuring a dining room at the Pig & Whistle. Serena, aware that what Daphne would say was perhaps not something Jem should overhear, made an excuse and took him back to Beauchamp House.

Once they were seated around a large table, full teacups before the ladies, pints of beer for the gentlemen, and two plates of sandwiches and an assortment of cheese and fruit for all of them, Daphne began her story.

"There isn't all that much to tell," she said staring into her teacup. "Like the three of you, I received a letter informing me that I'd inherited a quarter of Lady Celeste's estate, and telling me that per the terms of the will I needed to remove to Beauchamp House at once and remain there for a year or I'd forfeit my share."

The other ladies nodded. This was information they'd exchanged before.

"But I also received a letter from Lady Celeste herself, which I didn't tell you about."

The fact that only the gentlemen expressed surprise at this news told Daphne that they had also received personal letters from their benefactor.

"What did it say?" Maitland asked. He'd refrained from peppering her with questions on the way to the inn, as would have been his usual wont. But now that they were enclosed and away from prying eyes and ears, he seemed more relaxed. At least his posture seemed so to Daphne. She wasn't very good at reading his expressions.

Quickly, she told them about the line of the letter that was pertinent to the discussion at hand. They didn't need to know the other parts of the letter, where Lady Celeste talked about how lonely she had guessed Daphne must be, and hoped that she could find friends among the other bluestockings at Beauchamp House. That was personal. And for once, Daphne stopped herself from blurting out exactly what she was thinking. "So," she concluded, "I knew she was telling me that the Cameron Cipher was somewhere at Beauchamp House. And since she mentioned the library several times in the letter, I guessed that it was probably hidden there. It's taken me longer than I thought it would however, because I keep getting distracted by the other treasures there."

"All those summers of searching for the blasted thing and it was in the library all along," Kerr said with a shake of his dark head. "Aunt must have known what we were up to but she never said a thing."

"She would hardly have put the things into the hands of a couple of grubby schoolboys," Maitland said with a shrug. "And it was the chase that was fun. I sincerely doubt either of us would have been able to decipher a code like that. Try though we would have done."

"It's possible that she didn't find it herself until later on," Ivy said reasonably as she peeled an orange. "Or perhaps she acquired it from someone else and then secreted it in the library herself."

"She did spend a great deal of time in the library," Kerr said thoughtfully. "I always thought she was reading or writing letters or whatnot. But since I had an active boy's loathing for staying indoors, I never joined her there if I could help it."

"Nor did I," the duke agreed. "She might have been trying to solve the puzzle herself for all we know. Though I suppose she wouldn't have told Daphne about it if she had done so."

Daphne gave a nod of thanks to Gemma, who had just poured her another cup of tea. "She gave no indication one way or the other in her letter. Though my guess is that she was unable to unravel the cipher because if she had done so, she would likely have told someone about it. She knew as well as anyone how much of a coup being the woman who solved one of the greatest puzzles in a generation would be. Woman being the operative word. As someone who valued women's contributions to scholarship and the arts, she'd have found a way to use the accomplishment as a means to further the cause."

"That is my thinking as well," Sophia said, her dark brown hair showing chestnut highlights in the light from the window. "I knew who Lady Celeste Beauchamp was long before I received my own notification that I was one of her heirs. And it was always in reference to some way she was celebrating the accomplishments of other women. Perhaps I misinterpreted her actions, but despite her own modesty, I think she'd have felt duty bound to report her feat if it meant shining a light on just what sort of things women were capable of."

"So, she chose to leave it to the one person she knew would be able to solve it," Ivy said with a nod in Daphne's direction. "The winner of the *Ladies Gazette* editor's prize."

Two years ago, the editor of a prominent ladies' magazine had printed a series of ciphers in its pages, promising a free year's subscription to the person who could solve them. Though not a reader of the publication, Daphne had been unable to resist the opportunity to use her ciphering skills to unravel the puzzles. She'd always been fascinated by codes and secret messages and had studied some of the more famous ones with her tutor. She'd quickly dispatched her solutions to the editor and had won the contest handily. According to her letter, Lady Celeste had taken note. And so she had chosen Daphne to inherit the Cameron Cipher.

"So." Kerr sat his now empty pint glass on the table. "If we're agreed she didn't solve the thing herself, why didn't she just tell Daphne in her letter where to find it so that *she* could decipher it? Why go to the trouble of hiding it again?"

"I think I know," Daphne said, grateful that none of them seemed angry with her for keeping her own counsel on the matter up to now.

Because there was something else Daphne was keeping from her friends. There had been another note waiting for her once she reached Beauchamp House. And its contents she would keep to herself. Not only because its contents were somewhat personal. But also because they pertained to another member of their party.

In full, the second note had read:

> *My dear Lady Daphne,*
>
> *I cannot tell you how pleased I am to welcome you to Beauchamp House. I have long admired your intellect, and mathematical genius, as well as your facility with solving equations of other sorts, like the ciphering contest in THE LADIES GAZETTE. What joy it gave me to see an intelligent young woman do that which scores of men could not, by solving their nonsensical coded phrases. I knew I had to include you amongst my Bluestockings in that moment. And I hope you will sharpen your ciphering skills for a much more difficult task now that you're here.*
>
> *You will find Romance—and enough intrigue—to Riddle with envy even the most unschooled of ladies among the Treasure of my collections. And as you peruse them, I hope that you will accept the assistance of my dear nephew, Maitland.*
>
> *His father, my sister's husband, was a devilish creature and I am happy to say that not one drop of the scandal attached to his father's reputation has splashed onto dear Dalton. His happy disposition might make you question his intellect, my dear, but do not be fooled. He is quite as clever in his way as any man. (Though not, of course, as clever as you—but who among us is, dear Daphne?)*
>
> *I hope you will do your benefactress the favor of allowing him to provide any assistance you might need as you begin to plumb the depths of mystery to be found within the many wonderful shelves of my library.*
>
> *You see, I think as much as adventure, you need a friend. I've seen too many brilliant minds brought low by the more emotional toll of loneliness. And if nothing else,*

I think dear Dalton's sunny humor can give you a bit of light.

I have every faith that you are the special one I've hoped for. And I know you will dazzle the world when your quest is complete.

Yours in intellect,
Lady Celeste Beauchamp

Now, feeling a pang of conscience over her deception, she tried to explain the contents of the note without actually disclosing its existence. "I believe all that Lady Celeste wished was to make an adventure of it. A sort of real-life puzzle, as it were, to lead me to the cipher. She told me as much in her letter."

That the lady had also wished for her to let the Duke of Maitland be her assistant in the matter was something that they didn't need to know. Besides, after *her* indecent proposal, and his perfectly respectable one, she considered that she'd done a creditable job of attempting to let Merry Maitland ease her loneliness. Perhaps they were even friends now. Whatever the case, it was not a matter for the ears of the whole of Beauchamp House.

"There is a certain logic to it," Gemma said with a nod. "A puzzle that leads to a puzzle."

"And Aunt Celeste was fond of mazes, riddles, and all sorts of games," Maitland said with a grin. He turned to Daphne. "You rather remind me of her in that way."

"I can see that," Kerr said with a tip of his head to his cousin.

"Then why are we waiting?" Gemma demanded with excitement in her eyes. "We need to get back to the house at once and start looking for this cipher!" It was ironic how quickly she'd turned from skeptic to true believer, Daphne thought with an sigh. Which was quickly followed by another as she thought about the consequences of having their entire household pawing through what she'd come to think of as her own territory.

But, there was no time to waste. Sommersby was here now, and he was going to find a way into the Beauchamp House library whether she liked it or not.

The walk back to the house seemed to pass more quickly than the one into the village.

Maitland had watched Daphne as she carried on a lively conversation with the other ladies, an unruly blond curl bouncing against the sensitive skin of her neck. He'd never really considered the back of a woman's head to be particularly enticing before, but he supposed there was a first time for everything.

To his relief, Kerr left him to his own thoughts and when they filed into the front entrance of Beauchamp House, he managed to separate Daphne from the others without being seen.

She must have recognized the need for discretion, because she made no protest as he led her by the arm into the small antechamber his aunt had used as a waiting room for unwanted guests.

With its dull gray walls and mismatched furniture, it was hardly the appropriate setting for a proposal of marriage, but with the arrival of Sommersby that afternoon Maitland had realized that he couldn't abide the notion of Daphne going to the other man because he'd been too principled to bow to her wishes.

"What did you wish to speak to me about?" she asked, her lovely face tight with impatience. "I should like to have another look at Lady Celeste's letter before dinner. Especially now that Sommersby has arrived to search for the cipher."

Her thoughts were a million miles away, and Maitland was suddenly determined to bring her back here to this room. With him.

Pulling her against him, he lowered his lips to hers in a soft, seductive kiss, full of all the pent-up desire he'd been fighting against since their first encounter weeks ago.

She was surprised, but it took only the barest moment for Daphne to catch him up. And when she opened her mouth to his, and slipped her arms around his neck, he hummed with satisfaction. Whatever might have passed between them, whoever might have arrived to distract her, the spark between them was still there.

Coming up for air, he leaned his forehead against hers, and looked down into her half-lidded eyes. "Marry me, Daphne. So that we can explore what's between us."

When she didn't reply at once, he realized his mistake.

Shaking her head, she pulled away from him, and reluctantly, Maitland let her go.

"I won't marry you simply so that we can lie together, Maitland," she said with exasperation. "It's too high a price. If I were already married, or a widow, you wouldn't even feel obliged to offer at all. Why can you not afford me the same courtesy as you would a willing widow?"

At her words, he huffed out a startled laugh. "You do realize that you're probably the only unmarried lady in the country who doesn't wish to become the next Duchess of Maitland?" He thrust a hand through his hair, disheveled from her hands. "I vow, Daphne, you are the most frustrating lady it has ever been my misfortune to meet."

"If it's such a misfortune," she retorted dryly, "then I wonder at your wanting to spend the rest of your life with me."

"You would try the patience of a saint, madam, and make no mistake about it," he said with a sigh. "And no, that is not a contradiction of my wish to wed you. It is rather a statement of fact."

He stepped close to her again, looking down into her defiant green eyes. "Another statement of fact is that there is unfinished business between us, and I will not insult either your or my honor by attempting to bed you without an understanding between us. You might wish to be treated like a different sort of woman, but the truth is that you are not. And a gentlemen would not, could not, forget that."

"Then I fear you will be doomed to disappointment," Daphne responded with a shrug. "Which is a shame. For I think we'd get on well together."

How she could be so hot in his arms one minute and cool as a cucumber the next, he couldn't know. But he couldn't deny it added to his desire for her. Even now his fingers itched to pull her against him and persuade her to change her mind.

He wondered suddenly if others were tempted by her in the same way. And was beset with a rare fit of jealousy. "I won't stand by and let this Sommersby chap take advantage of your friendship, either," he warned her.

But rather than the irritation he'd expected, he saw instead a shadow pass over her eyes. He realized at once that he'd mistaken her feelings for the other man. Whatever was between her and her former tutor's son, it wasn't the sweet tale of young love's dream he'd conjured in his imagination. If he wasn't mistaken, it had been fear he'd seen in her eyes.

"What is it, my dear?" he asked, noting that the hands he pulled into his own were trembling. "Daphne, what has that blackguard done?"

But she took a deep breath and pulled away. "Nothing," she said with a hollow laugh. "We simply knew each other in our youth. That's all. And I do not wish him to find the Cameron Cipher before I do."

But Maitland couldn't let her get away so easily. "Simple acquaintance does not explain the way you paled when you set eyes on him. Nor the way you trembled just now."

She looked as if she would speak for a moment, then stiffened her spine and gave a slight shake. "Do not be absurd, Duke," she said with a sunny smile. "I fear you are letting my rejection go to your head. But please do not repeat your proposal again, for I do not know how many times I can tell you I have no wish to wed."

"You will have to do so one day," he warned her. "I doubt your father will simply allow you to do whatever you wish."

Daphne's lips curled into a genuine smile. "You'd be surprised, Duke. Very, very surprised."

He watched her, trying to guess what she was thinking. Finally, he shook his head. "I'm going to wear you down, you know. I can be very persuasive."

"I'm sure you can be," she replied with a catlike smile. "And so can I."

Lifting his chin, he said, "Then may the best man, or woman, win."

With a nod, she accepted his challenge. And without a backward glance, she sailed with head held high from the room.

Watching the sway of her hips as she went, Maitland knew he had his work cut out for him.

And more than ever he wanted to know what had passed between Sommersby and Daphne. Because judging from her response to the man, it hadn't been anything good.

After dinner that evening, the ladies—clearly eager to discuss matters they did not wish to share with male ears—headed upstairs to bed, while Kerr and Maitland retired to the room they still thought of as Aunt Celeste's study, though she'd been gone for months now.

"What did you make of him?" the duke asked his cousin as he settled his large frame into one of the oversize chairs his aunt had purchased expressly for her nephews. "I didn't believe his story a bit."

Kerr, who had been pouring them both generous snifters of brandy, looked up, his brow furrowed. "Who?"

If Daphne was frustrated with her friend Ivy's recent lapse into absent-mindedness, then Maitland was equally put out with Kerr, who spent most of his time away from his wife gazing off into space with a vague smile on his face. "That Sommersby fellow, of course. He looked at Daphne like she was a prize calf at the cattle show."

His cousin nearly dropped the glass in his extended hand. "You'd better not let her hear you describe her thus. Or any of the ladies, actually. They would flay you alive."

"You know what I mean," Maitland said pettishly as he took the brandy. "That chap is up to something, make no mistake about it. And he has designs upon Lady Daphne as sure as the sun rises in the west."

"It rises in the east," Kerr corrected absently, "but I suppose I agree about your point. He did seem a bit . . . calculating."

"East, west? What does it matter when there is a wolf on the doorstep?" Maitland had never been particularly interested in such things. But he was interested in Daphne, who had clearly not been pleased to hear of her old friend's reasons for being here. Whether the man wanted her for romantic reasons, or strictly because he knew her agile mind would far more easily unravel the Cameron Cipher once it was found, Maitland was unsure. Hell, it might be both.

"You really are enjoying the animal metaphors this evening, aren't you?" Kerr quirked a brow at him. "Though the wolf one does seem apt."

"Well, this is one wolf who will not catch his prey.".

Maitland would allow the fellow near Daphne again over his dead body.

"You can hardly bar the door to him when he arrives for dinner tomorrow," Kerr said reasonably, crossing one booted foot over his knee. "Aside from the fact that the house doesn't belong to you, you really have no claim on Daphne aside from friendship." He narrowed his eyes at his cousin. "Unless of course, you've changed your mind recently and allowed her to have her wicked way with you. You haven't, have you?"

"Of course, I haven't." Maitland scowled. "Not that it's any of your business. But, no, my mind is made up on the subject. I will not besmirch her honor. Even if she is willing to let me do so."

"You're a stronger man than I am," Kerr said, shaking his head. "If Ivy had approached me with such an invitation . . ."

"She'd have to have done so before you even met in order to beat you to the mark, cuz."

It was no secret that Kerr had compromised his now wife only a few days after their arrival at Beauchamp House.

"I think you've proven your inability to control your baser urges around your wife, else you'd not now be married." Maitland gave his cousin a speaking look. "Though I will admit to a certain amount of envy at your situation. It's certainly no easy feat to get through every day around her knowing that she'd be mine for the taking if I only agreed to her terms. But I am not in the habit of seducing innocents. And bold though Daphne might be, she is no wanton. I won't bed her without at least the promise of marriage. It's as simple as that."

"I'm not saying it's not noble of you," the other man said. "It's just that not many men would be able to resist temptation like that."

"Not many men were raised by my father," Maitland

said, his mouth tight. "I will not repeat his sins, no matter how strong the urge. He was a rake and a scoundrel and is likely somewhere in hell beside himself with laughter over my priggishness. But I will not relent. I saw what havoc his dishonor did to not only my mother, but also to the women who were unlucky enough to fall prey to his charms."

Kerr nodded solemnly. "I know, old fellow. I shouldn't have teased you on the matter."

Maitland only nodded in response.

"It was rather a shock to hear Sommersby mention the Cameron Cipher," Kerr said, changing the subject. "I haven't thought of it since we were boys. And I certainly had no idea that Aunt Celeste knew anything about it other than the legend."

"I begin to think there was a great deal that Aunt Celeste knew but didn't share with us," Maitland said wryly. "The identity of her heirs, the secrets of her youth, and now the fact that she knew the location of the infamous Cameron Cipher. I wonder if we knew her at all."

"It's no secret that she disliked mysteries," Kerr said with a shrug. "And it would appear that she's left two at least as part of her legacy to the four heiresses. I wonder what the Misses Hastings are keeping back from us."

"For now, let's concentrate on the Cameron Cipher," Maitland said, more concerned with Daphne than the Misses Hastings, fond though he had grown of them. "Daphne has been searching the library for it since her arrival, it would seem. And has thus far had no luck finding it. Which, given her intellectual abilities leads me to believe that it isn't there."

"Or it's somewhere she hasn't looked yet," Kerr retorted. "It's one of the largest libraries in England. One lady searching for three months is hardly going to find it quickly. No matter how brilliant she is."

"You have a point, I suppose," Maitland said with nod.

"What I want to know is how Sommersby learned that it was hidden in Beauchamp House. Or that there was a connection at all."

"Someone must have told," Kerr said reasonably. "Perhaps we can learn from him at dinner tomorrow. Aunt certainly had innumerable friends and acquaintances. She might have hinted at the cipher's presence at Beauchamp House to any one of them."

"She clearly chose Daphne as one of her heirs because of it," Maitland said. "I wonder if she feels any discomfort over that. That she was picked because of her ciphering abilities."

"I can't imagine Lady Daphne is the sort to dwell too much on such things. She seemed eager enough to find the thing. It's Sommersby's arrival on the scene that's set the cat among the pigeons. For all that they're old friends, she didn't seem particularly happy to see him."

Maitland thought back to her response earlier when he'd brought up Sommersby's name. There was definitely something from the past between them. And on Daphne's side at least, it was an uncomfortable memory. If he judged Sommersby aright, he thought Sommersby had some sort of an in with Daphne. There had been no mistaking the proprietary way the man's eyes had roamed over her.

He'd proposed tonight because he thought perhaps Daphne would turn to her old friend in the face of his own rejection of her advances, but the way her hands had trembled at the mention of the man told him she'd sooner proposition a snake.

He looked down to see his hand clenched tight around the brandy glass. When he glanced up, he saw Kerr was watching him knowingly.

"I don't think there's anything particular between them, you know," his cousin said. "If there were, Sommersby would have looked far more smug than he did. He was trying to win back her trust, I think. Ingratiating himself with her."

"Perhaps," Maitland said, not wanting to speak of his suspicions regarding the newcomer just yet—at least not with any specificity. "Regardless, I will continue to keep an eye on him. Until he proves otherwise, I don't trust the man."

"What did you make of his friend? Foster?"

"Most of my attention was on Sommersby," Maitland admitted. "But Foster seemed a nice enough chap. He didn't strike me as anything but what he seemed. Certainly not like Sommersby did. There's just something about the fellow I cannot like."

"Foster didn't look familiar to you at all?" Kerr asked, his eyes troubled. "I could have sworn I knew him from somewhere, but I cannot think of where for the life of me."

Maitland thought back to the scene on the path to Little Seaford. Sommersby, he could recall with exact detail. His companion, however, was less clear. He had an impression of reddish hair and a medium build. But he'd not lied when he said he wasn't focused on the fellow. Kerr was usually good at recognizing faces, however, so he didn't dismiss the other man's words.

"Perhaps you saw him somewhere in town? Or at university?"

"Maybe," his cousin replied. "Doubtless it will come to me as soon as I stop trying to remember."

"If you'd stop mooning over that wife of yours, you'd probably remember quickly enough," Maitland said, setting down his now empty brandy glass and stretching. "You were a rather clever fellow before Ivy came into your life."

"I was a rather *lonely* fellow before Ivy came into my life," Kerr corrected him with a wink. "And you cannot blame me for being a besotted fool when I have such a prize."

Despite his jest, Maitland could see that his cousin was happier than he'd ever been. It was as if Kerr had become lighter somehow. As if the cares of the world had lifted from his shoulders and been replaced with a mantle of joy. Or something. He was no poet. He only knew his cousin was a different man since he'd married Ivy. And the duke couldn't help but be a wee bit envious.

Aloud he said, "I won't agree too heartily, because I do not wish to be called out."

"Now, who's the clever fellow?" Kerr asked with a wink.

And on that note, the cousins made their way upstairs. Kerr to his own room where he would likely share every syllable of their conversation with his wife, and Maitland to his bachelor bedchamber, where he would lie awake for some time mulling over the events of the afternoon.

Chapter 3

"Why didn't you tell us you were searching for the Cameron Cipher?" Sophia demanded once the ladies were safely ensconced in the sitting room they shared upstairs near their bedchambers. "We could have helped!"

"I knew you weren't simply cataloging the books," Gemma said with a scowl.

Ivy only looked at Daphne with disappointment.

Daphne could tell that the other ladies were hurt by her deception, but she could not regret her decision to keep her own counsel on the matter of the cipher. Not only had Lady Celeste chosen to share the presence of the puzzle in Beauchamp House with Daphne alone, but some sense of inner caution had warned her that once the others knew, the secret would not be secret for long. News like this had a way of getting out. And given the number of people who had traipsed in and out the house following that business with Ivy's search for Lady Celeste's killer, Daphne knew she had made the right choice.

"You know now," Daphne said aloud. "And that is what matters, is it not?"

Sophia opened her mouth to object but closed it again.

"What matters is that we find it before your Mr. Sommersby does," Ivy said briskly. "For he seems quite determined. And unless I mistake the matter, he will arrive on our doorstep first thing tomorrow morning rather than waiting until the dinner hour."

"He did have the look of a man on a mission," Gemma agreed. "I was rather surprised he didn't invite himself along with us on our trip into Little Seaford. He certainly wanted to spend more time with you, Daphne."

"Yes, he did." Sophia's shrewd gaze rested on Daphne's, as if assessing her response. "If I know men, and I believe we'll all agree I do, then he wants more than just the Cameron Cipher from you, Daphne."

Daphne felt her cheeks heat. She had, once upon a time, thought Nigel Sommersby the most handsome gentleman of her acquaintance. And for a fleeting moment that afternoon, her old feelings had come to life again, like the reanimated being in Mary Shelley's novel *Frankenstein*, which she and Nigel had devoured in the schoolroom.

But, like the monster, her feelings were not something that could be allowed to flourish. There had been a moment, years ago, when she thought perhaps . . . but those fanciful notions had been snuffed out almost as soon as they'd come to life.

"Do not be absurd, Sophia," she said aloud. "He's desperate to find the Cameron Cipher since he was a youth. If he has any thought that it could be in the vicinity, he will stop at nothing to retrieve it."

"Those are rather strong words," Gemma said with a frown. "Are you saying he has no thought for the law? Or that he would physically harm someone to get to it?"

Daphne swallowed. It was possible that Sommersby was not at twenty-eight the same man he'd been at eighteen. But there had been a glint in his eye that afternoon that told her he was still capable of the sort of ruthlessness he'd demonstrated to her all those years ago. Back then she'd been unable to protect herself, but now, she knew better than to let herself be caught alone with him. Still, it would not do to let her friends think he was harmless either.

"I am saying that if you can help it, do not allow him to maneuver you into a corner," Daphne said, looking down at her hands, knowing that if she showed her friends her eyes they'd read her true feelings in them. "Do not allow him to charm you with his words or to physically cow you. He is not a nice man, for all that he appears so."

The other ladies were silent for so long that Daphne wondered if they'd even heard her.

Finally, Sophia asked softly, "Daphne, did Mr. Sommersby hurt you? Perhaps press you to do something you did not wish to do?"

But Sophia's words brought back the memory of that night in her bedchamber at her father's house, and it was all Daphne could do to breath, much less stop herself from trembling.

Though she did not as a general rule encourage other people to touch her, Ivy's hand on her arm gave her comfort.

"I c . . . c . . . can't t . . . t . . . talk ab . . . b . . ."

"Shh, it's all right," Ivy soothed. And she tried to calm herself as she listened to Sophia and Gemma kneel before her on the floor, just touching the skirts of her gown lightly. "You needn't talk about it if you don't wish."

In some faraway part of her mind, Daphne was mortified at appearing thusly in front of her friends. She was not given to outbursts of emotion. Nor was she one to wear her cares on her sleeve. What must the other ladies think of her?

She only thanked the heavens that she hadn't behaved like this earlier when she'd first seen Sommersby. For a brief moment, she'd even felt her old affection return. The mind was deceptive that way, allowing you to feel two opposing things about the same person at the same time. Fortunately, that old affection was soon pushed aside by fear and loathing.

"I will have a word with Quill," Ivy said to her. "He will not let this cretin within a stone's throw of Beauchamp House. If I ask it, he and Maitland will usher him out of the county."

At the mention of Maitland, however, Daphne's head snapped up. "No," she said in a strangled voice. "Under no circumstances is anyone to tell Maitland about this. You must all promise me."

The idea of the Duke of Maitland knowing even a hint of what had been the most shameful moment in her life was anathema to her. She could bear many things in this life, but a look of pity from him was not one of them. Or worse, disgust. For she was not entirely blameless in the matter. And most men would lay the blame not where it belonged, on the man who did the debauching, but instead upon the woman. She knew Maitland was not most men, but she didn't wish to risk the odds.

"We promise," Gemma said, placing a hand on her arm. "No one will tell him. But that does not mean that he and Lord Kerr shouldn't see to it that Sommersby is ushered out of the area. We needn't tell them the reason. Just that he makes you uncomfortable."

"Or we could say that you do not wish him to get near to the Cameron Cipher," Sophia said practically. "That is also true, is it not? And there will be no need to raise either gentleman's suspicions about anything else."

By now, Daphne had stopped trembling, and she was able to breathe easily. She had not been this overset by memories of Sommersby's assault on her—because that is what it had been, even if he hadn't been able to get all of what he wanted from her—in a long time. Not since she'd learned from his father that he was bound for Egypt. And now that she had regained her composure, she refused to allow him to upset her for a minute more.

Even so, she craved the calm that only putting things in order could give her. She hadn't been completely deceitful about organizing the library. While she'd been searching, she'd also been rearranging things in what she thought of as the proper order. None of the other ladies had complained thus far, so she supposed they agreed with her arrangement.

She'd thought removing herself from her father's house, where she was subject to his insistence that she use her skills at the card tables for his own financial gain, would be such a relief that she would be able to overcome her sometimes uncontrollable urge to tidy. But despite her fondness for her new friends, there was quite a bit of anxiety associated with her new surroundings. And now that Sommersby had arrived on the scene, she was even more fraught with nerves.

Aloud, she said, "I suppose that will work. Though I wish it were not necessary to tell them anything at all."

Unable to stand one more minute of scrutiny from the other three, she stood abruptly, and said, "I need to go to the library now." And supposing they would want some more explanation, she added, "To think." Surely thinking was something one was allowed to do alone. And if anyone should understand such a need, it would be these particular ladies, who also prized contemplation as a worthy pastime.

And without waiting for a response, she fled.

After an hour or so of tossing and turning, Dalton threw back the counterpane and pulled on a pair of breeches, a shirt, and a pair of slippers. If anyone was scandalized by the sight of him wandering the house in shirtsleeves, then they would simply have to endure it. He was in a bit of a mood, and surely a trip to the library for something to occupy his mind and perhaps lull him to sleep was not so objectionable. It wasn't as if he were going about in the altogether.

A scowl on his face as he contemplated his earlier conversation with his cousin, the duke stalked down the corridors of Beauchamp House until he came to the library door, which was ajar. And there was light shining from within.

Well, whoever it was would just have to excuse his state of undress. Because he wasn't going back upstairs.

But when he stepped inside, he could see no one amongst the mahogany tables and floor-to-ceiling walls of books, although several of the lamps throughout the room were lit. And he could see that several books on the far side of the room had been removed from their shelf and were stacked haphazardly on a nearby table. And to his surprise, the French doors leading out to a balcony overlooking the gardens were wide open.

Something was wrong.

With a low curse, he hurried over to the open balcony doors, but a quick scan of the parapet showed that no one was there.

"What are you doing here?"

Startled, he turned and saw Daphne glaring at him from inside the book room.

"I asked what are you doing here?" she repeated. "And why are you on the balcony? Surely you can find some other place to enjoy the evening air."

He was on the brink of telling her that he didn't answer to her, when the sound of a pistol firing sent him into motion borne of instinct. Careless of her temper, he threw himself at her, bringing them both crashing flat onto the thick Aubusson carpet.

They lay there breathless for a moment and listened for another report, but after some moments of quiet, it was clear whoever it was had finished his assault.

Gradually, Maitland became aware of the fact that the body underneath his was distinctly female and that Daphne's soft curves fit with aching perfection against his own hardness. Moving back a little, he scanned her face, noting a hint of pink in her cheeks as she stared at his mouth.

"Are you all right?" he asked, his voice hoarse to his own ears. "I didn't hurt you, did I?"

"N . . . no," she said, her breath soft against his cheek. He waited for her to continue, but the usually talkative Daphne was unusually quiet.

"We'd best wait for a minute or so more," he said, knowing the decision was justified, but feeling like a cad all the same as he felt her breasts rise and fall with each breath. "Just to make sure there are no more shots."

"He shot at us," Daphne whispered. As if whoever it was could hear them from his coward's hiding place out there in the dark. "Why would he do that?"

"I don't know," he said, closing his eyes against the scent of the lemon verbena she must use to wash her hair. Then what she'd just said sank in. "What do you mean 'he'?" Maitland demanded. "Do you know who this is? Is it that Sommersby fellow? Why would he shoot at you?"

At the mention of Sommersby, she stiffened and pushed against his chest. She was no match for his superior strength, but he pushed away from her all the same. He sensed the panic in the gesture as she scrambled away from him, scuttling backward across the floor like the crabs down on the beach below.

"Why would you say that?" she demanded rising swiftly to a standing position. "What makes you think he'd have reason to shoot at me?"

Taking his time as he got to his feet, Maitland thought back to their encounter with Sommersby that afternoon. At the time, he'd thought Daphne was merely annoyed with the other man because of his interest in the Cameron Cipher. But this response now was something else. Something darker.

He shut the French doors firmly and pulled the curtains so that they couldn't be seen from outside.

Turning, he surveyed her. Taking in her clenched hands and downcast eyes.

"Daphne," he said softly, "are you frightened of this man?"

Though her answer was clear in her expression, she said, "No, of course not. He's an old friend. That's all."

"Is he?"

The question seemed to give her pause. He could see worry, and something else in her face. Fear?

He was assailed with a sudden, intense urge to find Sommersby and beat him into a bloody pulp.

"We were friends once," she said stiffly. "And now he is here. He wants the cipher."

While that might be true, Maitland thought, it didn't mean Sommersby was only here for the cipher.

He would have liked to question her further about her relationship with the treasure hunter, but he could see that she was eager to leave the subject.

"Is he willing to kill someone to get to it first?"

"I don't know," she said in a hoarse voice. "I don't know what he's capable of."

With a strangled sound, she hurried over to where the stack of books had been removed from the shelves and began sorting through them. Then, as if just realizing what she looked at, she said, "Why were you looking at Scottish histories?"

There was a frown in her eyes, and she was clearly unsettled by the idea.

"I wasn't," he said, wondering why it mattered. "Those books were off the shelf when I came in here this evening.

And all the lights were lit. I thought one of you ladies had done it."

Turning, Daphne scanned the shelf behind her, where one shelf was empty of its contents, like the gap in Jem's smile where he'd lost his two front milk teeth.

She slid her hand over the underside of the shelf above, then down over the inside of the box created by the four sides. "Will you bring that lamp, please?"

Wordlessly, Maitland took up the flickering light and carried it over to where she stood staring into the dark space of the empty shelf. "Hold it just there," she requested, tilting her head to the side, as she looked at something on the inside of the left-hand border of the shelf. He complied, and she squinted as if she wasn't quite sure what she was seeing. Then with a nod, she stood up straight and said. "Step back, please."

He obeyed, and watched as she pressed against the side of the shelf where she'd been looking and gasped in amazement as the entire shelf, from floor to ceiling, swung inward silently, revealing a chamber beyond.

"I'll be damned," he said with a shake of his head.

Then, recalling just how they'd been alerted to the presence of this hidden room, he said, "Let me go in first. Whoever was here earlier might have set some kind of trap in there."

Though she looked as if she'd like to argue, Daphne nodded, and stepped back so that Maitland could pick up the lamp and slide into the narrow doorway.

Almost as soon as he stepped inside, he was hit with a foul smell. And a quick glance at the floor told him it's source.

"Daphne," he said calmly. "Go get Kerr and Ivy."

"What? Why?" she asked, coming up to stand behind him and trying unsuccessfully to see around him. "What are you hiding from me? And what is that awful smell?"

And before he could stop her, she'd wiggled around him and stopped in her tracks beside him with a gasp.

"Oh!"

Quickly, Maitland pressed her face into his shoulder so she would not see any more of the horror on the floor.

It was Mr. Nigel Sommersby. A small trunk lay on the floor beside him, open, and empty. And he was quite, quite dead.

Chapter 4

"And you say this Sommersby fellow was looking for the Cameron Cipher?" Squire Northman, the local magistrate asked, his bushy brows conveying his opinion of those who engaged in such frivolous behavior.

After the initial excitement had died down, Maitland had instructed the two sturdiest footmen to remove Sommersby's body to the icehouse for the night. Mindful of the empty box they'd found with the man's body, he himself had searched the body for any sign of the Cameron Cipher, or any other clue to who might have done him in. But he'd found only a set of what looked to be lock picks. No purse or papers of any kind. He'd returned to the house exhausted, and the household had decided to get what rest they could before the coming day.

Kerr had summoned Mr. Northman before breakfast and now the four heiresses, and the Beauchamp cousins—with the exception of young Jeremy—were all assembled in the library answering the man's questions, while his private secretary scribbled down their every word in a book with a lead pencil.

"That is what he told us when we met him on the way into town yesterday," Kerr agreed with a nod. "He and his friend, a Mr. Ian Foster, were staying at the Pig & Whistle in Little Seaford, I believe."

Northman nodded, and said to his secretary. "Write that bit down. We'll need to talk to this fellow Foster at once."

"I sent one of the footmen to inform Mr. Foster first thing this morning," Maitland said, "but he was told that the fellow had traveled on his own to visit friends in Pevensey for a few days. The innkeeper didn't know their name, so he will get the bad news when he returns I'm afraid."

Daphne, who had enjoyed the first restful sleep she'd had in years last night, felt a pang of guilt over the relief she felt at Sommersby's death, given how upset his friend Foster would be when he learned of it. Not to mention how his father, her mentor, would take the news. It wasn't that she'd wished the man dead. She might have wanted him to never set foot in the same vicinity as her ever again. But she hadn't wanted him to die a horrible death.

And his death had been horrible. That she'd been able to see from the quick glance she'd managed before Maitland pushed her face into his shoulder.

Nigel's expression had been one of pure agony, and his hand had been clasped uselessly around the dagger protruding from his chest.

"How did he get in?" Northman asked, scanning all of them, as if he could extract the information with the power of his gaze alone.

"As I said earlier," Maitland said, with barely repressed exasperation, "the doors leading out onto the balcony were open when I entered the library. As Kerr and I know from when we were boys, it's quite easy to climb the yew tree near the balcony and gain access that way."

"And you're sure you didn't find the fellow there in the hidden room, your grace?" Northman's brows were intent now. "You didn't perhaps struggle with him over the knife and accidentally kill the man? It would be well within your rights, your grace. After all, this Sommersby was an intruder. You were protecting your family." He paused, giving a speaking glance at Daphne and the Hastings sisters. "And your friends."

"That would be quite impossible, Mr. Northman," said Daphne, unable to stop herself from leaping to Maitland's defense. "Because as we have told you once before, I was the one who found the latch for the secret doorway, and the duke and I were together when he discovered Mr. Sommersby's body. It would be quite impossible for him to have stabbed the man to death without my witnessing it."

"But Lady Daphne," the squire said slowly, "you might have reason to lie. To protect his grace. Especially if he was protecting you."

Daphne, however, had had quite enough. "If anyone had reason to wish Mr. Sommersby dead it was me. And yet, neither I, nor the duke, was responsible for the man's death. We found him in the very way which we have already described to you more than once. I am sorry if you were not gifted with a great deal of intellect, but even you can understand that we do not wish to respond to the same question repeatedly while you do nothing to search for the person who shot at Maitland and me last night, and very likely murdered Mr. Sommersby."

Northman's mouth opened and closed a couple of times, like a newly caught fish.

Daphne felt herself flanked on either side by Maitland and Kerr.

"I think that's enough for today, Northman," said Lord Kerr in a tone that brooked no argument. "As you can see, the ladies are quite overset by the events of last evening and are in need of rest."

Though he looked as if he would like to argue, Northman

rose, his secretary popping up to his feet beside him like a jack-in-the-box. "I'm not finished with my questions," the magistrate said ponderously. "And I will wish to speak with Lady Daphne in particular. She knew him from before, I believe you said. Perhaps this had nothing at all to do with this Cameron Cipher."

Daphne opened her mouth to speak but was silenced by a not-so-subtle squeeze on the arm from Maitland, who then stepped over to usher Northman bodily from the room.

Once they were gone, Daphne sank onto the nearest chair.

"What were you thinking, Daphne?" Ivy chided from where she'd gone to stand beside Kerr. "You cannot antagonize the magistrate like that. He could have decided to throw you into the nearest gaol."

"I said nothing that wasn't true," Daphne said, puzzled. "He must know that he's not as clever as any of us. That is why he kept asking the same questions again and again. And it is highly unlikely that he would have had me put in gaol. He has no proof that I killed Sommersby. And even so, I am the daughter of an earl. He could probably be bought off with a promise from my father to stand him membership in one of his clubs."

"She's likely right about the latter," Kerr said with a grimace. "Northman is a dreadful toadeater."

She was spared from reply by the reappearance of Maitland, who stalked over to her and glared. "What did you mean that you had a reason for wishing Sommersby dead? Because I know very well you weren't speaking about the cipher. There's something else between you that you aren't telling us. What is it?"

"You needn't be such an ogre about it, Maitland," said Lady Serena, coming to stand beside Daphne, much to her relief. "Anyone can see that she's overset by what happened last evening. And aside from that, I believe she was standing up for you when she dressed down the squire. Who is a boor, without question. He was quite rude to keep us for so long."

"You'll forgive me for not stepping back, sister," the duke said. Daphne could feel the heat of his gaze on her as he continued to speak. "But, last night I found a dead body in a house I've run tame in since I was a child. The body of a man who has some connection to Lady Daphne. Something more than just their mutual quest for a cipher telling the location of lost Jacobite gold. She said it herself when she was defending me to Northman. I am merely asking her to elaborate."

He was angry. Daphne could see that. But she wasn't sure why. He hadn't known Sommersby before yesterday, so it couldn't be grief. And there was really no other reason for him to be upset.

Surely he wasn't jealous? The very idea made her heart beat faster.

"You do not need to say anything you do not wish to, Daphne," said Sophia stepping up to stand on the other side of her. Daphne swallowed, feeling perilously close to tears. "I think she's had quite enough interrogation for today, your grace."

"Come on, man," Kerr said, stepping up to clasp Maitland by the shoulder. "Leave it be for now."

Daphne peeked up at him from beneath her lashes and saw that though his jaw was set, his eyes were troubled. She was able to recognize that, at least. For the barest second, her gaze locked with his, and she felt a jolt of emotion surge through her. Breathless, she quickly looked away.

With a sigh, Maitland said, "Fine. But this isn't over, Daphne. You will tell me whatever it is that gave you reason to want him dead. Because if you had a reason, then it's likely someone else had the same one. And that's why he's dead."

A chill ran down Daphne's spine at the thought. Could Sommersby have forced himself on some other young lady? Had he perhaps been killed by an angry father or a vengeful brother?

She had thought it was simply someone else who wanted the cipher. There had been no sign of it in the hidden room, so they'd thought the killer had taken it with him. But what if it had had nothing to do with the cipher at all?

What if Sommersby had been killed by someone just like her?

Deciding she couldn't remain indoors for a moment more lest she say something she'd regret, Daphne muttered her excuses to the other ladies and slipped out the back door and followed the well-worn path to the stone stairs leading down to the little beach below.

She breathed deeply, taking in the salt-tinged air, and let the wind whip through her hair, disarranging the tidy chignon her maid had worked so hard on that morning. The sea was rough this morning, churning up wave after wave before surging forward to break on the pebbled shoreline, which was in keeping with her tumultuous emotions.

Daphne was not generally the sort of lady who flew into fits of emotion at the least little thing. But in the past two days she'd found herself grappling with such dark feelings as she'd not endured since Nigel Sommersby's betrayal years ago. She'd long ago learned not to trust her father. And though she felt great affection for the elder Mr. Sommersby, indeed considered him something of a father figure, she had never been made to question his loyalty to her. Not in the way her father and Nigel Sommersby had done.

It occurred to her now, as she perched on a large stone there where she could watch the sea, that it was not until she'd come to Beauchamp House that she was able to know what

real trust was. She may have been skeptical of the other ladies and their immediate offer of friendship at first, but in
the months since they'd arrived here, and perhaps thanks to
the events leading up to Ivy's marriage to Lord Kerr, she
had come to realize that though their acquaintance might
be short their offers of friendship were genuine. She would
trust Ivy, Sophia, and Gemma with her life if need be. And
though she was not as close to Lady Serena or Lord Kerr, she
sensed in them a genuine decency that she hadn't often en-
countered in her relations with the *ton*.

The Duke of Maitland? Well, her feelings regarding him
were more complicated. The one time in her life she'd had
the courage to ask for what she wanted, he'd rejected her. And
that still stung. She'd thought perhaps that taking someone
like him—someone she liked and chose for herself—to bed
would exorcise the demons of her encounter with Sommersby all those years ago. She would have given her virginity, of course, but she had thought the price worth it if she
could replace the memory of Nigel Sommersby's degrading
advances with more pleasant ones. Because despite the fact
that he would never be able to compete with her intellectually, Maitland was a decent man. And he would never—she
knew this instinctively about him—take from her that which
she did not want to give.

Unbidden, her mind recalled the feel of his taut, muscular
body covering hers on the library floor. Despite her genuine
fear at being shot at, her heightened senses had seemed to
revel in the weight of him. In the warmth and masculine
scent of his skin. Even as she listened for another shot, some
part of her had yearned for him to bend his head just the tini-
est bit forward and take her mouth with his. She closed her
eyes at the memory, remembering that sense of urgency as
the brisk wind whirled around her.

"The tide is coming in."

As if she'd conjured him from memory, Maitland's voice broke into her thoughts, making her jump.

He squinted against the brightness of the weak sun on the sea, and she could not guess what he might be thinking. Not that she ever could. Reading faces was far more difficult for her than reading equations.

Uninvited, he dropped down onto the beach beside her rock, and stared out at the churning water for a moment. She was keenly aware of him there next to her. Especially given where her thoughts had just been.

"Quill and I used to spend nearly every summer day at this spot," he said easily. "Playing at pirates and sailors. Whatever make-believe game that might whisk us away for a while. Away from responsibilities and the demands of our parents. Away from worries."

She tried to imagine him as a boy, and had little trouble conjuring a tow-headed child, a little tall for his age, with fine almost girlish features. Funny how such a pretty man might yet be the picture of masculine strength.

"It's a good place for thinking, too," he continued, never turning to look at her. "I have an idea of what you might be thinking about."

She felt her cheeks heat at his words. She doubted very much he would guess the direction of her thoughts. At least, she hoped he could not.

"I apologize for being so hard on you earlier," he said. This time he did turn to look at her. His blue eyes were bright with some emotion she could not name. She allowed herself to sneak a look at them before she looked away, her heart pounding at the connection, almost as if they'd touched hands rather than gazes. "It's just that I . . ." He paused, as if searching for the right word.

"I don't like the idea of a connection between you and

him," he admitted, looking away from her again. "And my imagination is quite adept at conjuring reasons why you might wish him dead. None of them particularly palatable."

She wasn't sure what he meant by that—one didn't eat reasons, after all.

"Why should that bother you?" she asked instead, focusing on the part of his confession she did comprehend. "That we knew one another before, Sommersby and me?" She did not speak of what he might imagine her reasons for wanting to kill her former friend. That was too tender a subject.

At her question, Maitland stared at her for a moment and then burst out laughing. "You really are the most fascinating lady," he said softly.

Her stomach gave a flip at his words. It wasn't so much what he said—she knew she was not fascinating, unless one were considering her mathematical and ciphering abilities—but how he said it.

Like an endearment.

Still, the memory of Sommersby's death lingered. And she suddenly felt the need to tell him just why she had reason to stab her oldest friend, innocent of the crime though she might be.

"He tried to force me," she said in a low voice. So low she could barely hear herself over the wind.

But Maitland had heard her. She could sense it in how utterly still his normally active countenance grew. In how his hand, which had been in the process of thrusting itself through his windblown hair, halted there atop his head as if he were a debutante striking an attitude: Arrested Gentleman.

Then, everything woke up again. The wind continued to blow, and Maitland dropped his hand to rest, fist clenched, on his muscular thigh.

He muttered a very foul word, one that Daphne had only ever heard stable hands utter. And that only when they thought she was out of earshot.

"When?" he asked, his voice vibrating with some emotion she could not name.

"It was years ago," she said, feeling strangely relieved to have told him. No, she corrected. Not strange at all, because this was just how she'd felt when she told the other ladies the night before. "Long before I came here. Before he embarked upon his travels."

"I daresay that is *why* he embarked upon his travels," Maitland said in a growl. He seemed to be taking this far more badly than she could have imagined. It had happened to her, after all. Not to him.

But, he had a point. *Had* Sommersby left England because of what had happened between them? She remembered shouting that night, after her maid had saved her by arriving unexpectedly to stoke her fire for the night, sending Sommersby rushing out of her room. It had never occurred to her that the girl would have told someone. Daphne certainly hadn't. And yet, Sommersby had been gone the next morning.

"Perhaps," she admitted. "He was gone the next morning, so it's a possibility."

"You told your father, of course?" Maitland asked, though it didn't sound like a question.

"Certainly not," Daphne said, aghast at the idea. "He would have ordered Nigel's father to leave, too. And I was at a critical stage in my studies. Besides, the son was gone the next morning. There was no need to tell Papa."

She didn't say that her father would likely have placed the blame upon her instead of on Nigel Sommersby. Oh, he would have told both Sommersbys to leave immediately, since he'd been looking for a reason to be rid of the tutor and his son for years. But once they were gone he'd have found a way to use the incident as a means to force Daphne into doing his bidding. He had always done so. Used her own weaknesses against her. To get his own way at her expense.

Maitland cursed again.

"He never came back," Daphne assured him, thinking that his anger was because he perhaps thought it was an ongoing problem. "I hadn't seen him again until yesterday on the path to Little Seaford."

"And he did not . . . succeed in forcing you?" the duke asked, his fists still clenched where they rested on his thighs. "I believe your words were that he 'tried to force you'?"

"No, he only touched me a bit," she said, though she knew that made it sound much less traumatic than it had been. She swallowed, remembering his hot breath on her face, his hand rucking up her skirts. She must have made some noise, because Maitland turned to her and placed a comforting hand on her arm. Only that, his hand. But it did what he'd no doubt intended.

Though she was not generally a demonstrative person, she felt compelled to place her hand over his. Seeking comfort from the feel of his warm skin beneath her fingertips.

"So, you see," she said, calmer now, "I did have reason to want him dead. Or at the very least to harm him. But you know I did not. We were together when we found him. As you told the magistrate."

He was quiet for a minute. So long that Daphne wondered if he'd fallen asleep, though a peek told her his eyes were open.

"The devil of it is, Daphne," he finally said stroking his thumb rhythmically over her arm, "I might know you didn't do it, and the others at Beauchamp House might believe us both, but there is no guarantee Northman will do so. You admitted to him that you had reason to want the blackguard to die, and he was found in your residence. In Northman's position, I might find myself considering you a suspect."

"But you aren't in Northman's position," Daphne said, frowning. "And you don't consider me a suspect."

"That is right," he agreed. "Which means we need to find out who actually murdered Sommersby. Because if we do not, Northman might just decide to prosecute you for it."

Chapter 5

The next morning, Maitland was still thinking about his conversation with Daphne as he made his way downstairs for breakfast.

He wasn't quite sure what to do with what she had told him about Nigel Sommersby's attack on her. What could be done, after all? The man was dead, and it wasn't as if Maitland had any claim on Daphne beyond that of friendship. The knowledge had put her awkward proposition not long after they met into some sort of perspective, however. And he wished he'd known about her past before he'd rejected her with so little finesse. One thing was clear, however. They had to learn who had actually killed Sommersby. Not only because of Northman's suspicions about Daphne, but also because despite what he'd said earlier that day in the heat of the moment, it was all too likely that whoever had killed the man had done so because of the Cameron Cipher.

There were simply too many elements that pointed in that direction. First that Sommersby and Foster were in the area expressly to search for the cipher. Secondly, that the man had mentioned, and then been found murdered in, the library at Beauchamp House, where Daphne had been told by Lady Celeste the Cameron Cipher was hidden. It was too much of a coincidence that the man would be killed while in the midst of searching for the thing.

Was it also coincidence that had Foster away on the night of Sommersby's murder visiting friends whose existence no one could verify? The innkeeper had seemed to think Foster would return, but what if he'd simply disguised his flight by inventing the story of a quick journey? He'd just stepped onto the first-floor landing, when Serena came hurrying toward him, her familiar countenance flushed with anxiety.

"What is it?" he asked his sister, knowing she didn't upset easily. Especially not after the hard life she'd lived with her now mercifully dead husband. "Is Northman back?"

A gasp sounded behind him, and he turned to see Daphne, looking pale. "Is he here to arrest me?" Clearly she was more worried about the magistrate's suspicions than she'd earlier let on.

"No, no," Serena assured her with a strained smile. "I'm afraid it's a different visitor, though. And I am not sure whether it will be a happy one for you."

Maitland's brows drew together. It was likely Sommersby's father. Though how he could have gotten here so quickly was a mystery. Still, when family was involved, speed was possible.

"Who is it?" Daphne asked, frowning.

Serena bit her lip. "I'm afraid it's your father, dear. And he does not appear to be in the best of tempers."

This didn't lighten the other lady's expression. If anything, she looked even more troubled.

"What can he be doing here? I expressly told him that I was not to be disturbed during my time here at Beauchamp House." She rushed forward, leaving the siblings to trail after her as she headed for the drawing room. "If he has need of funds then he will simply have to win it at the tables himself."

Maitland exchanged a look with his sister as they followed the somewhat windblown Daphne. Surely she hadn't meant that *she* had won money for her father in the past. Though God knew she was a gifted card player. She showed no particular fondness for whist as a general rule, but it had only taken a few hands with her to know she possessed exceptional skill there. Likely because of her extraordinary memory.

It might have been more discreet for him to leave her to speak to her father alone, but Maitland found himself pushing past Serena, who seemed reluctant to go back into the drawing room where Daphne and her father were closeted.

"There you are, my dear," said the Earl of Forsyth with a beaming smile that didn't quite reach his eyes.

Maitland saw at once that Daphne favored him. Her green eyes were the same shade as his, though there were lines of dissipation bracketing the earl's. And though his expertly cropped blond hair was shot through with silver, what remained of its original color was the same shade as hers. But whereas Daphne's gaze was focused off to the left of whomever she conversed with, like a bird hovering just over a branch, Forsyth's speared one with cold calculation. As he did to Daphne now.

"You are looking well, Daphne," the earl continued, stepping forward to embrace his daughter, who looked as uncomfortable with the contact as Maitland had ever seen her. "The sea air agrees with you. As I knew it would."

"The sea is very beautiful," Daphne replied woodenly. "Why are you here, Father?"

"Is that any way to greet your Papa?" the earl chided, stepping back from her and wandering farther into the room, standing to stare out at the gardens below through the window. "I've traveled all the way from London to see you. And this lovely estate. I must admit that when I first learned of your inheritance, I thought it was all some sort of trick. But you would have your own way and leave the loving bosom of your family no matter what I said. Now that I'm here, though, and see it in person, I must admit that it's a lovely spot. And your chaperone, Lady Serena, is quite beautiful, isn't she? A widow, I take it?"

His jaw clenched at the man's mention of Serena, and Maitland thought perhaps it was time to announce himself. Daphne seemed not to realize he'd followed her in, and the earl was too busy waxing rhapsodic over the beauties of Beauchamp House.

"I don't believe we've met, Forsyth," he said forcefully, stepping up to stand side by side with Daphne. He gave a slight bow, perhaps not quite as deep as was warranted, but not caring. "The Duke of Maitland. I am a friend of your daughter's, you might say."

What he meant by that last, he could not say, but the man made every bit of protective instinct within him go on the alert. He was her father, but all the same Maitland knew that Daphne was no safer with him than she would have been with Sommersby if he still lived.

At the sound of the duke's voice, Lord Forsyth turned with almost comical haste from the window and stared. For the barest flicker, he looked angry. Well, if he were upset at the knowledge that his daughter was not without friends, then he would simply have to swallow it. Because Maitland was damned if he'd leave her alone with the fellow.

"Duke," Lord Forsyth said with a tilt of his head, "I am pleased to make your acquaintance. I was a friend of your father's, and had little notion I'd be meeting you here. He was a good man, your father."

His father had been nothing of the sort, but Maitland was hardly going to discuss it with Forsyth.

"I am here visiting my sister, Lady Serena," Maitland said coolly, letting the other man know in tone rather than words that he had not appreciated the older man's speculative words about her earlier. "And of course my cousin, Kerr. He only recently married another of the heiresses here, and resides here with her."

Forsyth's eyes narrowed at the implication that Daphne was well protected should her father wish to cause trouble. At least that was the message Maitland was endeavoring to send. And by the looks of it, Forsyth read him loud and clear.

"Capital, capital," the earl said with false cheer. "A merry party you must all make here. I had no idea you were in such fine company here, Daphne. No notion at all."

"Because we have not spoken since I left," Daphne said, looking from her father to Maitland then back again, as if wondering what went on between them. "And now, father, I really must ask you to leave. I have a great deal of work to do and . . ."

"Don't be absurd, Daphne," her father said with a shake of his head. "I only just arrived. And there is something very important I must speak to you about." He turned to Maitland with a raised brow. "I'm sure you'll excuse us, Duke. I'm afraid what I need to tell my daughter is private family business."

Maitland was opening his mouth to tell the man he would leave Daphne alone with him when hell froze over, when Daphne did it for him.

"Maitland stays," she said, reaching out to grasp him by the arm. It was as much of a cry for help as he'd ever thought he'd see from her. Wordlessly, he slipped her arm into his, as if they were about to promenade round the room. He covered her hand with his, keenly aware of the thread of tension in her.

Once more, the earl's eyes narrowed, and he turned an assessing gaze on Maitland, perhaps realizing for the first time the threat coming at him from that direction.

His jaw clenched, Forsyth said grimly, "Very well. If you wish your *friend* to witness our dirty linen, so be it."

As if needing to be in motion in order to speak, the earl began to pace the area between the window and the fireplace. "You know, Daphne, you left me without any obvious means of recouping what I lost from years of paying that tutor of yours, old man Sommersby."

"You agreed to pay him," Daphne said tightly. "After I threatened to expose . . ."

Hastily, Forsyth continued, "And I am currently in need of funds. As such, I must insist you return to London with me for the time being and meet a particular gentleman who has expressed interest in marrying you. Though his birth is not as high as yours, he's quite wealthy and will make you a good husband, I trust. He's assured me he has no concern about your odd ways, if you're as beautiful as your portrait."

Before Maitland could burst out with the string of invectives the other man's pronouncement inspired in him, Daphne said, "I cannot marry this person. I've never even met him. You promised me that I would not have to marry someone for money as long as I won enough at the tables. I did so. You promised me, father."

"I never actually promised, Daphne." Forsyth said with a shake of his head. "If you chose to interpret it as such, that is not my fault. Now, go pack your things."

Daphne's hand on Maitland's arm gripped him tightly. And before he even knew what he was doing, he said, "I'm afraid that's impossible, Forsyth. Daphne is staying here."

"I don't know who you think you are, Maitland," said the earl through clenched teeth, "but I am her father, and I am well within my rights to take her back to London. Now, kindly take your hands off of her and let her go pack."

"It might once have been your right, Forsyth," Maitland

said coldly, "but Lady Daphne is my betrothed now and as such, she will remain here. With me."

"Maitland, what are you . . . ?" Daphne could barely articulate the question she was so flummoxed. Why on earth would he say such a thing?

"Hush, dearest," he said in a chiding tone, while his hand that covered hers squeezed in some sort of signal. "I know we did not wish to make our betrothal public yet, but you must admit that your father has a right to know. Especially in light of his reasons for coming here."

Which gave Daphne pause. She might be of age, but he was still her father, and could if he so chose remove her from Beauchamp House and force her to marry this fellow he had waiting in London. It had happened twice before, that he'd tried to force her into matrimony with some wealthy man with no more sense than hair. She'd thought that by leaving him with the small fortune she'd managed to win at the tables before she left to the coast, she would be safe from his importuning for a while. But clearly, she'd underestimated the amount of time it would take him to blow through twenty thousand pounds.

Glancing at her father's face now, she saw that he was calculating how he might squeeze as much or more money from Maitland than he'd have gotten from the prospective suitor in London. His next words told her she was right.

"What a charming surprise," said the Earl of Forsyth rushing forward to kiss her on the cheek and pound Maitland on the shoulder.

"I should have guessed it as soon as you entered the room together," he continued, beaming at them. "It was as plain as the nose on your face."

Daphne couldn't help reaching up to touch her nose. She'd always rather liked it. But, there was no accounting for taste.

"So," Maitland was saying, "you can understand why I should not wish her to go back to London with you. Aside from the fact that she truly does have work to do here, I shouldn't want her to catch someone else's eye while she's in town. You understand, of course."

Except that her work would need to be put aside for the time being because she needed to find out who had killed Sommersby, Daphne thought. Which reminded her, she'd not told her father about that.

"Of course, my boy, of course," Forsyth said jovially. "And I suppose you wish to be married just as soon as the banns are read? She's not getting any younger, is she, eh?"

"I'm only one and twenty, Father," Daphne said defensively. "Besides which, I can marry at any age. What's that to say to anything?"

"And I would marry you at any age, my dear," Maitland said in a soothing tone. "Perhaps you can leave me alone with your father for a bit so that we can discuss the business details. Marriage settlements and the like."

"But we aren't act—"

To her shock, Maitland stopped her words with a quick kiss. In a low voice, he whispered, "Stop talking. Trust me."

Too startled to gainsay him, she nodded, and with one last glance at her father, she hurried from the room, shutting the door firmly behind her.

Once they were alone, Maitland turned back to Lord Forsyth. "Let us speak plainly, Forsyth."

"By all means," said the earl, indicating with a flourish of his hand that Maitland could have a seat if he wished. A gesture the duke found amusing considering the man had only just entered the room for the first time a little over half an hour ago. "I cannot say I understand what reason you might have to want my daughter, considering she has only the small marriage portion left to her by her mother's side of the family, but I daresay you wish to keep Beauchamp House in the family."

Could the man really have no notion of just how beautiful and intriguing his own daughter was? Maitland had thought the man was more clever than that. Clearly he was wrong.

As if reading his thoughts, the older man waved a hand in the air. "Oh, I know she's lovely enough. But she's got no conversation to speak of. Unless one wishes to discuss maths all the day long. Or worse, to be told to one's face the innumerable ways you fall short. It's a high price to pay for a bit of skirt, which I should know since her mother was just the same way, though she brought me enough of a dowry that I was able to overlook her strange ways."

Disgusted at the man's callousness, Maitland bit back a sharp retort. "Let's just get down to business shall we? How much to make you leave for London on the next mail coach?"

"How eager you are to get me away from her," Forsyth murmured, his eyes searching. "One would almost think you didn't wish to know your future bride's family. What if I have a wish to remain here for a little while? To meet my daughter's new friends? Or would that put a crimp in your plans, Duke? Are you enjoying the benefit of her favors before the banns are called? If that's the case, then I shall expect to be compensated."

"Thus making you your daughter's panderer," Maitland spat out. "I thought it was impossible for you to fall in my estimation but I see now I was mistaken. Though I suppose I should not be surprised given how little you did to protect her from Sommersby."

At the mention of Sommersby, Forsyth's anger turned to puzzlement. "What has the old tutor to do with anything? She had no need of protection from him. If anything, it was the other way round. I thought she'd exhaust him with how she demanded more and more lessons from him."

"Not the elder Mr. Sommersby," Maitland said with a shake of his head. "The younger. Nigel Sommersby."

Forsyth rolled his eyes. "There was nothing to protect her from there either. He was a weakling. Barely strong enough to lift his boots. If you're telling me he posed some sort of threat to her, you're sadly mistaken. He was enamored of the chit, of course. But he left when she was fifteen. There was nothing between them."

"Then you will perhaps be interested to know he was found murdered in this house night before last," Maitland said coldly. He wasn't sure why he wished to see the earl's response to the news that Sommersby the younger was dead. Perhaps it was the fact that Daphne's father had shown up unexpectedly on their doorstep so soon after Sommersby's death. Or maybe it was because he wished to be the one to tell him that the fellow had attempted to rape her and he'd done nothing to stop it. Or avenge it.

That, however, was Daphne's secret to divulge, much as he'd like to cram the news down her father's throat.

Forsyth's response to the news of Sommersby's murder, however, was all that Maitland could have wished.

"Nigel Sommersby?" the older man sputtered. "Dead?" Gaping, he looked as if he would collapse, but in a show of determination, he soon recovered his composure.

"What was he doing here of all places?" he continued, his face a mask of mild interest. "And what sort of protection are you offering my daughter if you would allow a man to be murdered beneath the very same roof where she sleeps? I cannot like it, Duke. I cannot like it at all."

It was somewhat reassuring to see Forsyth react like a father—even as tepid as his indignation was. Of course, he ruined the effect with his next words. "Perhaps I should remain here for the time being. Just to ensure her safety, you understand?"

Or to use as an excuse to extort more money from his supposed future son-in-law, Maitland thought wryly. He had to give it to the earl, he was up to every rig.

"I do not think that will be necessary," he assured Forsyth. "I simply thought you might wish to know, given that the man once resided in your London residence. I also thought you might know how we might contact the elder Mr. Sommersby. He will wish to know at once what's happened."

Daphne might know the fellow's direction, but Maitland would spare her the necessity of contacting him if he could.

"It isn't as if I spend time with these men, for heaven's sake," Forsyth protested. "We barely spoke. The tutor was there to perform a service. And his son was of no consequence to me. As for the whereabouts of the elder Sommersby, I have no idea. Once he left the house without notice, I never heard from him again."

"Without notice?" Maitland was startled despite himself.

Forsyth shrugged. "It was of no matter. Between you and me, I was glad he was gone so I no longer had to pay him."

Which didn't surprise Maitland in the slightest.

"It was Daphne who was overset by it. And I can't say I blame the gel," Forsyth continued, "for she spent nearly all her time with the man for years. Excepting of course those occasional evenings out when I encouraged her to accompany me. She was far too good at the tables to leave at home, you understand?"

Maitland would have liked to speak a few home truths to Daphne's father about that, but he knew it was no use. Men like Forsyth were unrepentant. Maitland knew that well enough from dealing with his own father.

He ignored the question and asked one of his own. "The man simply packed his bags and left without telling anyone where he'd gone?"

"That's the long and short of it," Forsyth agreed. "I don't know if my daughter's strange ways got to him or if he found a better position or what. But he left, and there was no way to know where he'd gone."

Daphne hadn't mentioned any of this. Perhaps she knew more about the tutor's disappearance than her father did. He would ask at the next opportunity.

"Is she upset by it, the death of Nigel Sommersby?" Forsyth asked, looking troubled for the first time since Maitland had met him. At this rate, Maitland didn't know if the man was coming or going. "I don't think she was fond of him in the same way he was fond of her, if you get my meaning, but they were friends, I suppose. It can't have been easy to know he died here while pursuing her."

"Pursuing her?" Maitland echoed.

"That has to be why the fellow was here, after all." Forsyth shrugged. "He must have got wind of Daphne's inheritance somehow and come to ingratiate himself with her."

Just as *you* have done, Maitland thought, scowling.

Able to stand no more of the earl's scheming, he clapped the other man on the back. "Let's discuss the marriage settlements now. Of course, I will be more than happy to give you something to tide you over until the marriage."

Chapter 6

"Maitland just announced our betrothal to my father," Daphne announced baldly as soon as she stepped into the library, where the other three heiresses were busy searching every nook and cranny for the Cameron Cipher. "And I let him!"

Ivy spoke first, leaping from her kneeling position before the volumes of Greek poetry—perhaps she wasn't looking for the cipher after all?—and hurrying to take Daphne's hands in hers. "My dear, this is wonderful news! If you only knew how much we've all been hoping this would happen."

"He's been smitten with you from the moment he first laid eyes on you," Sophia agreed, her skirts whispering over the carpet as she moved to join them.

"He's no fool," Gemma agreed. "Any man with sense would wish to stake his claim before some other chap entered the picture. I'm only surprised it took him this long."

They must have lost their minds, Daphne thought shaking her head. "I do not know what you have been conjuring amongst yourselves," she said hastily, "but this was most assuredly *not* something I was anticipating. And Maitland certainly did not speak to me about the matter before he told my father."

She suddenly felt weak in the knees and collapsed into a nearby overstuffed chair. "Papa was attempting to whisk me back to London, you see. And though I thought he'd given up the notion of selling me off to the highest bidder, it would seem that my surmise was premature. He has some plump-pocketed cit eagerly awaiting my arrival so that he can marry me with my father's blessing."

All the pleasure in the other ladies' expressions turned to horror. "Oh, Daphne," Ivy said. "I suspected your relationship with your father was not a good one, but I had no idea that he was this awful."

"It is worse than awful," Daphne said with a sigh. "Things were different when my mother was alive. At least what I can remember of her. She was clever like me. And was always encouraging me to learn more. I think Papa would have paid me more attention if I'd been a boy. As it was, he didn't notice me until long after Mama had died. But from the moment he realized my skill with numbers and memory might be used to his own advantage, he's used me as his very own prize horse, only instead of races, he's had me playing whist in drawing rooms all over the *ton*."

"But he must have had some care for your education," Ivy said with a frown. "After all, he hired your tutor, Mr. Sommersby, did he not?"

Daphne wished that were true. That her father had been supportive of her activities of the mind, as Ivy's had been. And no doubt Sophia's and Gemma's had done. "I blackmailed him into hiring on Mr. Sommersby," she said wearily. "I told him that if he did not hire me a competent tutor from whom I might learn the level of mathematics suited to my superior intellect, that I would expose his schemes to the *ton*. The only thing Father values more than a night at the tables is his social standing. Despite the fact that he owed money to almost every peer in the realm, he was still received in all the best houses, and did not relish being exposed as the sort of man who would use his own daughter for profit."

"And he did as you demanded?" Sophia asked, clearly impressed with Daphne's maneuver.

"He did," Daphne said with a nod. "And he did not insist that I accompany him to card parties so frequently after that. It is one thing for a father to trade upon his daughter's virtue in exchange for marriage settlements, but it's quite another to openly be known to take her winnings at cards. So long as there was the pretense that he was using his own funds, his friends overlooked the irregularity of it. But a public accusation? Well, that would have offended his cronies' delicate sensibilities."

"And I suppose when you left for Beauchamp House your father was left without a ready means of earning money?" Ivy asked.

None of the ladies seemed to question the fact that despite his earldom Lord Forsyth was frequently pockets to let. It was not uncommon among peers of the realm for all of their funds to be tied up in their country estates. Thus, they lived on credit and were frequently cash poor. Lord Forsyth, Daphne knew, was more in need of blunt than most since he spent whatever he received from the estate at the gaming tables.

"Yes," Daphne said. "Though I left him with tens of thousands of pounds, thinking it would last him the year, he's run through it only three months in."

"So when he announced he wanted you back in London, Maitland told him you were already betrothed?" Sophia asked, "I must say, that's quite the most romantic thing I've ever heard. He's your knight in shining armor."

"But I didn't need a knight," Daphne protested. "I've dealt with my father's ridiculous demands for years now. And I might have done so again, if only Maitland hadn't stepped in. Now that Papa thinks he's got his hooks into a wealthy duke, he'll never give up. I daresay when Maitland and I attempt to dissolve this farce of a betrothal, Papa will sue him for breach of contract. He is just that sort of man!"

Daphne fought the urge to push away from where her friends were crowded around her and move to the other side of the room, where she might rearrange the shelves devoted to novels. (They were at present arranged alphabetically by author, but she thought perhaps they might work better organized first by publisher, then by author, then by title. Just pondering the possibilities made her feel calmer.)

"Maitland won't give a damn about that," said Lord Kerr, who had slipped in a few moments earlier. "He obviously thought you needed his protection and so offered it. He has armies of solicitors. Enough to stall your father's breach of contract suit in the courts for decades. Though hopefully it will not come to that."

"I don't see how it cannot," Daphne argued, all the calm she'd gained from her organizational thoughts evaporating with Lord Kerr's observation. She did not wish Maitland to be forced to fight her father in court. If he'd simply stayed out of it, none of this would be an issue. "We cannot remain betrothed. I do not wish to marry. Especially since as soon as I reach my majority I will be able to escape my father's influence forever."

"But Maitland is hardly cut from the same cloth as your father," Ivy soothed. And when Daphne started to argue, she held up a hand. "I know, I know. Marriage can be just as much of a prison as any gaol. But perhaps we needn't solve all of these problems today? After all, it's been a busy few days. What with finding Mr. Nigel Sommersby in the secret room, then your being questioned none-too-gently by Squire Northman, and now your father's arrival. Any of these things alone would be enough to send the most sensible lady into a decline."

"Are you saying I am not strong enough to deal with all of this?" Daphne asked, not knowing whether to be insulted or relieved to be let off the hook.

"I most certainly am not," Ivy said, patting her on the arm. "But I am saying that we can perhaps deal with these issues one at a time. And I mean 'we'—you are not alone anymore, Daphne. You have friends who are willing to help you now."

"But I am quite able to take care of myself," Daphne protested.

"Of course you are, dear," Sophia said with a gentle smile. "But perhaps you misunderstood Ivy. What she means to say is, you have no choice in the matter. Our help is not negotiable. That's what friendship is all about."

Daphne was silent for a moment, processing what Sophia had just said.

She'd never had a true friend before, it was true. Many acquaintances, but aside from Nigel—and look what a bounder he'd turned out to be—she'd not had anyone to rely upon besides herself. Perhaps it was time she accepted a bit of help here and there. Just to see how it felt.

"Very well," Daphne said. "It would appear I have no choice." Though she could hear the hint of pride in her voice. Curious.

"If you are all finished giving Daphne the rules of friendship," she heard Maitland say from behind her, "then I would greatly appreciate it if you would give us the room."

Turning, she saw that he appeared none the worse for wear despite what must have been a most trying conversation with her father. She might have known Maitland would emerge unscathed from such a meeting.

Without protest, her newly sworn friends all slipped away from her and out the door, closing it behind them while Maitland moved to sit on the edge of the library table just across from her chair. So close he was able to cross his booted feet only inches from where her skirts rested just above the thick Aubusson carpet.

"Your father is quite an interesting man," he said without preamble. "I had thought perhaps the tales I'd heard about him in town were exaggerated. But only a few minutes in his company was enough to tell me they were likely toned down for credibility's sake. Any description of him as he is would be dismissed as utterly outlandish."

"Interesting is one way of describing him," Daphne said, not knowing whether she should apologize for her father's behavior or scold Maitland for telling the lie to Lord Forsyth that would surely cost him both money and a bit of his reputation. "Greedy is another, though not one I would use in polite company. At least he's asked me not to on more than one occasion."

Maitland laughed softly. "I'll wager he did not like having his own daughter tell the truth about him amongst the tea things after dinner."

"It was actually at Lady Beresford's dining table," Daphne said with a frown. "Though you are correct that he did not like it. Rather the opposite, in fact. I thought perhaps he would strike me when he scolded me later. One is never quite sure, you know, if verbal violence will turn to physical. But he never did."

The duke's amusement evaporated at that, and when Daphne dared to look at his face, his mouth was tight. "I only did it that once, you understand."

"I am not angry with you, Daphne," he said moving to kneel before her, which should have made her uncomfortable, but instead made her heart beat faster. "I am angry with him. For making you feel threatened. For using you to make money because he was too damned lousy with a hand of cards to make it for himself. But I am most enraged at him because he forced you to blackmail him in order to protect yourself from being sold like a brood mare to the highest bidder."

She was silent. Her father had done all of those things. And she was angry about them. But the notion that someone would feel angry on her behalf was so foreign she couldn't quite comprehend it.

"Is that why you told him we were betrothed?" she asked, wondering if those reasons he'd just named added up to his declaration before Lord Forsyth. "Because you were angry with him and wanted to thwart him?"

He dipped his head so that she had no choice but to look at him. As she'd noticed before, eye contact with Maitland did not fill her with the kind of anxiety as it did with other people. Still, her heart pounded harder.

"I told him we were betrothed," Maitland said in a low voice that vibrated along her spine like a struck tuning fork, "because I wanted to."

She blinked at that. Because he wanted to? But why?

As if he'd spoken the questions aloud, he continued. "Because I couldn't bear the thought of some rich social climber with piles of money but no appreciation for how special you are to have you."

She didn't know what to say.

And didn't need to, because he said finally, "I did it because I wanted you for myself, Daphne. I wanted you to be mine."

As he spoke, he moved his face closer to hers. So close

that by the last word, she felt his breath on her lips. And a whisper of anticipation ran through her.

Just before he kissed her.

It wasn't as if Maitland had awoken that morning with the notion of proposing to Daphne before the day was through.

He'd actually been awakened by his nephew Jeremy—who had escaped his nanny's leash—jumping on the bed beside him asking if he'd come play soldiers with him. But almost as soon as he'd opened his eyes, the duke had recalled the moment when he'd seen Nigel Sommersby's dead body on the floor of the secret room.

Reluctantly, he'd told Jem he would come visit him in the nursery later, and dressed to go downstairs. If he was going to ensure that Northman's pursuit of Daphne as a suspect in Sommersby's murder went nowhere, he would need to get to work at once finding an alternative theory of the crime.

As it was, he'd been thrust almost immediately into that awful scene where Lord Forsyth had tried to bully his own daughter into giving up her inheritance at Beauchamp House and return to London with him.

Not mind you, so that she could return to the loving bosom of her family, but instead so that she might marry some strange fellow with little more to recommend him than the fact that he was possessed of enough funds to give Forsyth enough to pay off his debts and live in the style to which he'd become accustomed. Ironically, Daphne's father had confided all this to Maitland as they'd discussed terms for his own—that is, Maitland's—marriage to Daphne.

All of this was running through his head as he knelt before her in the library, trying to explain his reasons for making that impetuous pronouncement to Lord Forsyth.

But then he'd looked up into her big green eyes and lost all capacity for talk.

Knowing her history now, and wanting to give her comfort, his kiss was gentle.

With just the slightest pressure, he leaned into her. Closing his eyes, he breathed her in, inhaling the lemony scent of her and the warmth of her skin. Giving himself up to the feel of her.

And when he deepened the kiss, licking at her with the tip of his tongue, she welcomed him in. Opened to him in a way that told him everything he needed to know. And then he was lost to the sensation of the moment. Of knowing just who it was he held against him, just whose lips he kissed.

Daphne, he thought with a flicker of satisfaction, sliding a hand up to cup her face in wonder. Daphne, whom he'd wanted from the moment he saw her. The beautiful, maddening, creature who shocked and amused him at every turn.

Her mouth was hot and soft and sweet, and as their kisses grew more intense—as she slipped her arms around his shoulders to pull him against her—Maitland had to fight his growing need to feel her hands on other parts of him. He'd meant to keep this kiss sweet, chaste even, but with each stroke of her tongue, he was growing more mindless.

He'd only just reversed their positions, settling Daphne in his lap so that he might kiss his way down her neck, when a knock sounded at the library door.

With a jolt, he realized just how close he'd come to taking her here in the library, and reluctantly, pulled back a little. Breathless, he buried his face in her neck, inhaling the sweet scent of her for the barest moment before lifting his head and resting it against the back of the chair. Daphne, who was also out of breath, rested her cheek against his shoulder.

"A moment if you please," he called out loudly, hoping that whoever it was would give it to them.

"Sorry old fellow," came Kerr's voice, sounding amused,

"but Mr. Sommersby's friend, Foster has come. And he wishes to speak with Daphne. You won't be disturbed further. I just wished to let you know he was here." A sound that was suspiciously like laughter disguised as a cough followed. Then silence.

Daphne flattened her palm against where his heart was still pounding. "I knew I had chosen wisely," she said with the tone of one who had been proved right. "We are very compatible. Amorously speaking, I mean."

He huffed out a laugh. "My apologies for denying you, madam. I see now I was harming us both by refusing your offer the first time."

It felt as if decades had passed since that first awkward suggestion she'd made that they become lovers. He hadn't wanted her any less then. He saw now that his rejection had sprung from shock more than anything else. And bruised pride. Clearly it took him some time to get used to the force of nature that was Lady Daphne Forsyth.

"I accept your apology," she said regally. Then, sobering, she said, "I suppose we cannot stay here forever."

"I'm afraid not," he said, kissing the top of her head.

Reluctantly, she climbed off his lap, and righted her skirts. Her hair, he noted, was mussed from his hands. But he said nothing. In some primitive part of him, he liked that she looked as if she'd just been thoroughly kissed.

Straightening his own cuffs, he ran a hand through his own no doubt disordered hair.

When they were as tidy as they could get given the lack of professional assistance, he offered her his arm, and they left the sanctuary of the library and made their way to the drawing room.

Still a bit breathless from her interlude with Maitland, Daphne walked into the drawing room on his arm not knowing what to expect from Sommersby's traveling companion. Having only met him for those few minutes three days ago, she'd had little time to assess his emotional state. Though he'd seemed civil enough. If he was like other men, he was likely having a glass of brandy while he waited.

Mr. Ian Foster, however, was doing no such thing.

Instead he was pacing before the low fire, and muttering under his breath. Lord Kerr and Ivy stood together by the window and looked relieved when Daphne and Maitland walked in.

Foster, on the other hand looked aggrieved. "I was beginning to think you had fled the country, Lady Daphne." While his words might have been considered a jest from some men, in this one, they were deadly serious.

"Of course, I did not, Mr. Foster," she said, puzzled at his suggestion. "Why would I do such a thing?"

She felt Maitland's comforting hand on her lower back and was grateful for it. Something about Foster's demeanor made her nervous.

"Perhaps you'd best tell us why you're here," the duke said once Daphne had taken a seat on the settee. He took up a perch on the arm, a protective hand on her shoulder as if reminding her he was here if she needed him.

"Yes, do, Mr. Foster," said Sophia, who was seated with Gemma near the windows overlooking the garden. "He wouldn't tell us a thing until you got here," she said to the newcomers with a speaking look.

"I should think that was obvious," Foster said with a scowl. "My friend was found dead in this house three nights ago. And no one saw fit to inform me of that fact. I had to learn of it from the innkeeper when I returned from Pevensey. Surely it would not have been too much trouble to send a messenger for me?"

"Oh, I do apologize, Mr. Foster," Daphne said, knowing

that in his situation she would be overset, too. "I had supposed that Squire Northman would do so, since he is the magistrate and was here to question us. And then . . . well, as you can imagine things have been rather at sixes and sevens, so we must have overlooked you."

"Well, Squire Northman did not, in fact, send for me," Foster continued, his face still red with pique.

"Lady Daphne has apologized, Foster," said Maitland firmly. "And we are all sorry for your loss. But I believe some of the blame for this must rest on you. It's not as if you left details of your direction with anyone. We will, of course, do what we can to assist the magistrate in his investigation of the murder. But I believe that is all we can do. Now, if you will excuse us, Lady Daphne has had a trying time as you can well imagine, and. . . ."

"I wish to see the room where he was found," Foster interrupted, his fists clenched at his sides. "I know he was here searching for the Cameron Cipher that night, and I wish to see the room where he was murdered. I daresay one of you might have done the deed because he found it when you yourselves could not."

"Of course, we didn't kill him," Daphne said in an aggrieved tone before anyone else could speak. "And though I know he was your friend, so it might pain you to hear it, but Mr. Sommersby was not nearly as clever as he thought he was. Or really, as any of us gathered in this room. It's true he was no simpleton, but he was hardly the sort of mind capable of finding the Cameron Cipher. And even if by some miracle he did find the cipher, it would have been useless to him. He was terrible at unraveling ciphers. Always was."

Then, thinking to soften her words, she added, "Though he was quite good at geography, if that's any consolation."

Foster gaped.

Thinking that his silence denoted agreement, Daphne continued, "Perhaps you didn't know, but someone shot at the Duke of Maitland and myself the night Sommersby was killed. Perhaps the same person who killed him. I hardly think we would be capable of shooting at ourselves."

By this time, however, Foster had regained some of his composure. "He told me you had reason to wish him dead, Lady Daphne. So do not think to draw suspicion away from yourself with this tale of being shot at. If you are as clever as you say you are, then you would doubtless be smart enough to hire someone to shoot at you."

"You are offensive, sir," Maitland said coldly, his hand hard on her shoulder, which she interpreted to mean she should stop talking. "And I will remind you that you yourself are without anyone to verify where you were the night of your friend's murder. How do we know you weren't simply hiding out here with the intention of killing him while everyone thought you were out of town?"

"What is offensive, your grace," said Foster, "is the way you aristocrats stick together. Sommersby warned me it would be this way. That you would do whatever you could to discredit him. I simply didn't guess that it would mean you'd murder him."

"You are overset, Mr. Foster," said Lord Kerr, who had come to stand on Maitland's other side. "Perhaps after you have had time to grieve, you will come to realize how wrong you are. In the meantime, pray accept our condolences for your loss. Mr. Greaves will see you out. I'll be sure to let Squire Northman know you've returned so that he may question you about your whereabouts three nights ago."

And as if he'd been waiting there listening, the butler Greaves appeared and took Ian Foster by the arm and led him from the room.

As soon as the door closed behind them, Maitland turned to Lord Kerr. "What do you mean exposing the ladies to that fellow? Especially after everything that's happened to Daphne. She's had quite enough to upset her for the time being."

"It's hardly Quill's fault, Maitland," said Ivy coming to her husband's defense. "Mr. Foster seemed amiable enough when he arrived. But the longer he waited, the more overset he became. But the time you both arrived, he was showing signs of agitation."

"It was bad of us not to let him know what had happened to Sommersby," Daphne said ruefully. "I didn't even think of him, though we met him on the trail with Sommersby."

"None of us did," Maitland reassured her. "But that still doesn't make his accusations against you appropriate."

"I wonder what he wished to see in the secret room," Sophia asked, rising to stand before the fire, her sketchbook in one hand, as if she'd forgotten she had it with her. "It was almost as if he thought he'd find the cipher there."

"Well, he'd be out of luck there," Daphne said with a scowl. After the body had been removed from the inner chamber, she and Maitland had searched the recess from floor to ceiling, as well as the small chest that had been lying open on the floor beside Sommersby's body. But they'd found nothing. Whoever had killed Sommersby had likely taken the cipher as well. "We certainly didn't find it. And not for want of trying."

"Perhaps we weren't looking in the right place," Maitland said thoughtfully.

As if in response, Daphne's stomach growled. Loudly. Thanks to her father's surprise visit, she'd missed breakfast.

"It's time for luncheon," she said sheepishly. The events of the morning had given her an appetite.

"Then let's go have luncheon," Maitland said, taking her

hand. "Perhaps some fuel will help us figure out where the cipher might be."

They were greeted by Serena in the dining room, and Maitland was reminded that he'd never gotten back to Jem with the promised game of soldiers. Making a mental note to see the boy that afternoon, he gave his cousin a questioning glance as she stood behind her chair waiting for the others.

"Greaves told me there was some trouble with Mr. Foster," Serena said with a frown as she took her seat. "I cannot like how many dangerous situations you ladies have found yourselves in since your arrival here. And now a murder in this very house. I cannot think that this was what Aunt Celeste had in mind when she promised you adventures in Beauchamp House."

"Given that Aunt herself requested that Ivy find out who killed her," Kerr said dryly, "I suspect this is exactly what she had in mind, Serena. Though perhaps she did not anticipate a man being stabbed to death in the library. Even so, she was hardly one to wish young ladies to be wrapped in cotton wool. And I think they've handled things admirably."

"Indeed," Maitland agreed, lifting his glass to the table at large. "There's not a heartier group than the one assembled at this table. And I daresay Aunt chose them specifically for their strength."

Serena shook her head in exasperation. "It's all well and good for the two of you to sing their praises. You aren't the one who is supposed to be chaperoning them. And thus far, I've done a poor job of it. First Ivy was compromised into marrying Quill and now you, Maitland, my own brother, have faked a betrothal to Daphne in order to protect her from her father. At this rate, Sophia and Gemma will be embroiled in scandals with the vicar and his curate before the week is out. It's like living in a Sheridan play. With murder."

Maitland wanted to laugh off his sister's worries, mostly because it was amusing when she laid it all out there like that. But he knew that she took her responsibilities seriously. And that her gratitude to Aunt Celeste for offering her this chance to get away from her drab life in the dower house colored her feelings about the current situation.

But before he could speak up to comfort her, Daphne broke in.

"Lady Serena, I can assure you that there is no need for you to worry so about our reputations. Indeed, Ivy needn't concern you at all now that she's married to Lord Kerr. And my reputation was never that much to begin with."

Serena blinked, as if trying to determine if Daphne was serious.

"But really," Daphne continued, patting her chaperone on the hand, "it is sensible for you to be overset about the murder of Sommersby. We have no notion of who might have done it. And they did shoot at Maitland and me the other night. There's no telling when he will strike next."

Maitland was overcome with a coughing fit as he watched his sister's eyes widen at Daphne's words. So much for comforting her, he thought with an inward sigh. At this rate, Serena would have guards stationed at every door.

But his sister was made of sterner stuff.

"Thank you for validating my fears, Daphne," she said, then with a speaking glance at Kerr and Maitland, she continued, "At least someone in this house doesn't think I'm overstating things when I say that we are all in danger."

Wincing, Maitland gave his sister a nod to indicate she'd made her point. "I apologize for minimizing your worries, Serena. It's only because I don't wish to alarm anyone. And I can assure you that we're safe as houses. In point of fact, I myself had Greaves post extra guards at all the entrances the morning after we found poor Sommersby."

At his words, he saw Serena's shoulders slump with relief. He felt a pang of guilt at not having noticed earlier how much this situation had bothered her.

"Thank you, my dear," she said with a genuine smile. "I might have known you would take charge. You were always ordering things to your liking. Even when you were a boy."

"You're just still angry that I ordered *you* around," Maitland said with a grin.

He had been a bit of a handful as a child. Especially since he had for a few years there taken his father as his role model. And the late duke was hardly the sort to take the feelings of others into consideration when he was making decisions. By the time Maitland had come into the dukedom at sixteen, he'd long since realized that it was far more pleasant to go through life with a smile on one's face than with a cold sneer.

It hadn't endeared him to his father, of course, who saw his son and heir's sunny disposition as a sign of weakness. But it had stood him in good stead. And he'd never inspired the kind of fear and loathing he'd seen enter the eyes of his father's circle as soon as the old duke approached.

"Of course, I am," Serena answered pertly, drawing his attention back to the table. "I was the elder, and you tried to lord your title over me like some sort of crown prince."

"You complain," Kerr said with a laugh, "but you were just as bad. And knew exactly the right place to pinch when we didn't bow to your wishes."

"He's right, Rena," the duke said to his sister with a shrug. "And I was manageable enough so long as I was allowed to visit the stables every day."

"You were fond of horses even as a boy, then?" Daphne asked, her eyes bright with curiosity.

"I wanted to live in the stables," Maitland said, a little wistful for those days before he'd realized the enormity of his position in the world. "Mr. Jacoby, the head groom at the Maitland estate, let me sneak in as much as I wanted until my father discovered it. I thought at one point—I was far too young to realize it was an impossibility—that I would become a groom myself when I was older. But Father quashed that flight of fancy soon enough. Fortunately, I was able to convince him not to take out his anger on Jacoby. But it meant less time among the horses for me."

"But you're able to do so now," Daphne said softly, as if she understood how difficult it had been for him to give up the shelter of the stables and the gentle guidance of Jacoby. Their eyes met and he saw recognition there. And sympathy. "That must be counted as an improvement."

"One of the first things I did when I came into the title was to have the stables fully renovated—father didn't have much use for animals or people. Or at least only so far as he could use them." He didn't say that his father had also neglected the buildings just because Dalton had cared so much that they were so shabby. He'd been a cruel man, his father. But he liked to think that he'd got his revenge by living well.

"It's the home for elderly horses that I most love about your renovations, though," Serena said with a warm smile. She had been just as hurt by their father's neglect, but she'd never stopped supporting her brother. He was grateful for her, as he was for Quill and his aunt Celeste, who had shaped him into the man he was today.

"What's this?" Daphne looked from one Maitland sibling to the other.

"My cousin has dedicated a special area of his estates to housing elderly or infirm horses, who through no fault of their own find themselves on the way to the . . . er . . ." Maitland watched in amusement as Quill tried to come up with an alternative to the word "slaughterhouse."

"In straightened circumstances," Maitland finished for

him. "And they are able to live out their days without fear of the lash or any other sort of cruelty."

"That's the most beautiful thing I've ever heard," Gemma said with a sniff. And as he glanced at the other ladies, Maitland felt himself redden under their scrutiny. Daphne was beaming at him, and he got the feeling she would have launched herself into his arms if there wasn't a tableful of people watching them.

"It's nothing," he protested, suddenly very interested in the pigeon pie before him. "Just a good use for that particular piece of land. That's all."

And that was all he had to say about the matter.

Chapter 7

Maitland and the ladies tried to convince Daphne to rest for a little, given the odd circumstances of the last day, but she steadfastly refused.

"There is too much to be done," she insisted, leading the way to the library. "A man was murdered. And if it was over the cipher, then I want to make certain that we haven't missed something in the secret room."

She was made of stern stuff, his Daphne, the duke thought as he and the others followed her down the hall to the book room.

His Daphne. For the time being at any rate. Until he convinced her to turn this betrothal begun in deceit into a real one.

Which would not be an easy task given what she'd said to her father about her feelings on the matter of matrimony in general. He'd known, because of his sister's horror of a union, that in the eyes of the law men held almost all the power in a marriage. But Daphne's wish for autonomy for the sake of her studies was another layer to the issue he'd not considered. With the wrong man, marriage could mean a total loss of freedom for a woman.

He'd just have to make sure Daphne knew he was the right man.

The library was bright with the early afternoon sun, and while the others wandered in, Maitland stood where Daphne had halted just inside the door.

"I know we were in here this morning," she said with a frown, "but I didn't go back in there." She stared at the now closed portal into the secret room."

They hadn't returned to the little room since Squire Northman had come to look at the crime scene. Despite the man's suspicions that Daphne might have had something to do with the murder, his sense of chivalry had prevented him from forcing her to return to the spot where she'd found the body.

She betrayed her apprehension only with her words. Her spine was straight and though she did not take her eyes off the other side of the room, her stance was one of determination. It took every ounce of self-control to stop himself from pulling her to him in a reassuring hug. Only because he knew her better now was he able to see how much she feared revisiting the scene of Sommersby's death.

He contented himself with a touch of his hand to hers. And to his surprise, she turned her hand over and squeezed, taking comfort from him, though she didn't glance his way.

"You needn't go in now," Maitland said, reluctantly letting her go, and following her as she made her way to the secret door. "There are enough of us that the room can be easily searched again without your assistance. I daresay it will only fit a few of us at a time anyway. You needn't be one of them."

She'd stopped just before the shelf with the opening mechanism. The books that had been removed by Sommersby still lay where Daphne had begun organizing them last night. "I must go inside," she said, reaching out to depress the latch. "Lady Celeste left the secret of the Cameron Cipher's presence in the library to me. She wanted me to be the one to find it. And I won't let some beastly murderer keep me from fulfilling her wishes. I owe her too much."

As they watched, the bookshelf swung inward, revealing the darkness of the chamber within. Wordlessly, Maitland lit the wick of the lamp they'd left on the table the night before.

"I'm coming with you," he said, even as she stood in the open door. If she heard him, she gave no indication of it, only waited for him to follow her with the lamp.

Perhaps sensing that this was something Daphne did not need witnesses for, the others remained in the library, searching through the books and shelves for any further clues.

Recalling the hook in the wall just inside the doorway Maitland hung the lamp from it, which illuminated the silk hung walls. He hadn't noticed last night, but the chamber was furnished with every bit as much care as the rest of the house. On the floor, where they'd found Sommersby, was a thick carpet, similar to the one in the library itself, covering the wood floor. A portrait hung in a place of pride on the far wall. He had no memory of seeing it the night before. He'd been so focused on the dead man on the floor, the chamber might as well have been empty.

When he moved to look closer, he saw that the likeness was of Charles Edward Stuart, The Young Pretender, also known as the man for whom the Jacobite cause was fought and lost.

It had been over half a century since the 1745 uprising that had left the movement to put Bonnie Prince Charlie on the English throne in tatters. Prominent members of the cause had been put to death for treason.

Aunt Celeste hadn't even been born when the Jacobites were defeated. But that didn't mean she hadn't found something to admire in the movement. Had Aunt Celeste been a Jacobite sympathizer? Or did this décor simply reinforce the fact that the Cameron Cipher had been secreted here? Given his own knowledge of his late aunt, Maitland was inclined to believe it was the latter.

* * *

Daphne sat on her haunches, examining the small chest that still lay where Sommersby had dropped it. He watched as she gingerly lifted it from the floor and ran her fingers over the velvet lining. Searching for some other items contained there, no doubt.

Leaving her to it, he moved to the painting and carefully lifted it from the wall. It wasn't large. Like every other object d'art in the house, it looked as if it had been made for its particular placement.

He hadn't really been expecting to find anything there. He'd actually chosen to inspect the painting in an effort to distract himself from Daphne's close proximity. When he turned it over to look at the back, he almost missed it. If he had not taken a leaf from Daphne's book and run his hand over the back of the canvas, the frame, and the bits of wood wedged into each of the four corners, he'd not have felt the rolled bit of parchment hidden almost invisibly between the wooden stretcher and the canvas.

He must have made some noise of excitement because Daphne looked up at once. "What is it?" she demanded, her eyes shining in the lamplight. "What did you find?"

"Bring that," he told her, nodding to the box in her hands before carrying the painting back into the main room of the library.

At their quick reemergence, the others came crowding around.

"I hadn't realized there was a painting hidden in there," Sophia said with what sounded like pique. As the artist of the group, she would have a natural interest in such a find.

Daphne rested the box on the nearest table with a thump, while Maitland gently lay the painting face down next to it.

"Which of these are we meant to examine first?" Ivy asked, glancing from the chest to the back of the canvas.

"There is nothing more to the box than what you see," Daphne said with a frown. "I thought perhaps there would be something hidden in the lining, or maybe a secret compartment. But there's nothing here that I can find."

In the bright natural light of the library, Maitland was able to see the parchment wedged into the corner of the picture frame more clearly. "I may have discovered something useful," he said, pointing to the section in question. "Since you are the one my aunt chose to tell about the cipher, I thought I'd let you be the one to have the first look at it. We may have lost whatever was hidden in the trunk, but perhaps this can shed some light on who took—" He broke off as she reached out a hand to remove the rolled document and without ceremony, unraveled it.

When she did not speak, Ivy expressed the impatience they were all feeling. "For heaven's sake, tell us what it says!"

"Is it a clue?" Gemma demanded.

Sophia put her hands on her hips. "Does it tell anything about the cipher?"

Maitland's heart sank as she shook her head.

"It's blank," Daphne said turning the page to show them that there was indeed no visible writing on it. Her mouth was twisted with disappointment. "It was probably used as a wedge to hold the canvas in place. It's not a clue at all."

"I wouldn't be so sure," Sophia said, moving to examine the open structure of the frame, which exposed the back of the canvas it showcased. "It's far more common to use a bit of wood to secure a loose canvas. There is no reason I can think of for placing this page here."

She reached out to turn the frame so that the subject of the painting could be seen in the light, and gasped. "It's a Catherine Read," she said, awe in her voice. "I'm almost sure of it. Perhaps the best I've seen."

"And who is this Catherine Read, pray?" Gemma asked

her sister with a touch of exasperation. "You forget, Sophia, that we do not all have your knowledge of obscure art."

"If you spent more time away from your fossils and bones, sister," retorted Sophia, "you might recognize the name. And she's most certainly not obscure. She's one of the best-known pastel artists of her generation, as well as the member of a prominent Jacobite family. It's no wonder Lady Celeste chose a Read for the room where she'd hidden the cipher. It fits perfectly, in fact."

"There's no signature," Daphne noted from where she peered down at the painting. "How do you know it's by this Catherine Read person? There's nothing at all that indicated who painted it."

"Notice the way the Prince leans his chin on his fist?" Sophia asked, pointing out the specific area on the painting. "Well, that is a characteristic in many of Miss Read's works. Not to mention that I recognize other elements of her style. It's not one particular brush stroke or element that makes me think it's hers. It's the thing as a whole."

Maitland frowned down at the portrait. "The chin thing," he said with a nod toward the work, "I've seen that at the National Gallery. Sir Joshua Reynolds, I believe."

At the mention of Reynolds, the diminutive artist drew herself up to her full height. "You are not alone," she scowled. "Miss Read's work has often been mis-attributed to Reynolds. Mostly by men who cannot possibly believe a woman capable of such skill. Which is absurd, of course. But when has misogyny ever been a surprise?"

All four ladies scowled in Maitland's direction, and he threw up his hands. "I meant nothing by it, Miss Hastings. It was merely an observation. I'm as familiar with art as any man in my position. But I'm hardly an expert. And knowing Aunt Celeste, she was probably making a point by choosing a Read painting to adorn the hiding place of the cipher.

"What's really of interest, here," Sophia said looking somewhat mollified, "is the fact that I've never seen mention of this painting in any collection. I've read through the catalogs of most of the better-known art collections in England and the continent, and I've made a particular study of Miss Read's work. And I cannot recall ever seeing it mentioned."

"What if it has never been made public?" Daphne asked. "If this Miss Read was a Jacobite herself, perhaps the painting accompanied the cipher. As a sort of talisman?"

"I'm not sure how practical it would have been for Cameron to travel across England carrying a portrait that all but shouted that he was a Jacobite sympathizer," Maitland argued. It was a romantic notion, he supposed, but a man hiding from the authorities would wish to keep from drawing attention to himself.

"It's quite impossible anyway," Sophia said. "Miss Read didn't travel to Europe, where she likely met the Prince, until after 'forty-five. And if Cameron brought the cipher through this area before 'forty-five, there's no way he could have even seen the portrait, much less carried it with him along with the cipher."

"So, Lady Celeste was the one who set up this secret room?" Daphne asked, puzzled. "But to what end? Why not simply tell me the location of the cipher in the letter she wrote me and be done with it?" She rubbed her forehead as if she were fighting a headache.

Unable to stop himself, Maitland placed a comforting hand on her back, which was turned away from him. "I know it's frustrating," he said in a soothing tone, "but there is a method to the madness."

"I'm sure I can't begin to guess what that might be," she said in a petulant tone.

"I hate to add to the growing list of questions without answers," Gemma added with an apologetic look, "but has anyone asked yet how Sommersby, who had, to our knowledge, never visited this part of England, knew precisely where to find this secret room? Can Lady Celeste have told someone who passed on the location of the cipher?"

They all stared at the painting, as if its subject would leap off the canvas and give them the answers they sought.

Finally, Daphne sighed. "I cannot imagine that Sommersby, who was not the most intelligent of men, could have discovered the room's location on his own. I spent most of my time since my arrival here searching the library and I never came across it. I think you're likely correct, Gemma, that someone else told him, but who?"

"Let us not get distracted from our current conundrum," Maitland said mildly. "If we begin pulling at every loose thread we'll have nothing but a tangle."

Daphne nodded. "You're right. First things first." She picked up the scroll and stared at it again.

"Aunt Celeste was quite fond of Gothic novels," Lord Kerr said into the glum silence. "I suspect she saw all of this . . . theatre, for want of a better word, as part of the puzzle."

"Perhaps it's just a painting," Sophia said with a shrug. "A significant one, by a female artist of some note, with Jacobite connections. But we may be attributing too much significance to it. And letting ourselves fall prey to the excitement of mysteries and secret codes and hidden messages."

Something about what Sophia said sparked a memory, and with a renewed sense of hope, Maitland turned to his cousin. "Kerr, do you recall how we used to send secret messages to one another when we were boys?"

The marquess met his gaze and frowned. Then realization dawned and he whistled. "I haven't thought about those things in ages," he said. "But she was the one who taught us how to do it, so of course Aunt Celeste would choose it as a way to include another clue here."

"What?" Daphne asked, turning to Maitland in puzzlement. "What are you two talking about?"

"Someone get me a candle," the duke said with a grin. "If I'm right, we're going to unravel at least one mystery today."

"Invisible ink," Daphne said as she watched the duke hold the scrap of seemingly blank parchment over the candle flame. "I should have guessed."

She had read about the use of lemon juice instead of ink years ago in a book about spies in the Colonial Wars in America. Why hadn't she thought of it as soon as they'd found the parchment? She was usually much quicker than that.

Clearly the excitement of the past few days was taking a toll on her intellect.

Leaning against Maitland's side so that she could see more clearly, she watched as writing in Lady Celeste's hand—which she knew well by now—appeared on the parchment in a brownish hue. A shiver of excitement ran through her.

"I knew our boyhood schemes would come in handy one day," Kerr said with satisfaction. Rolling her eyes, Ivy mock cuffed him on the ear.

"This is serious business, Quill," she chided, though her eyes were light with amusement.

Diverted from the matter at hand, Daphne's heart constricted at the interaction between the married couple. Would she and Maitland be that happy if they continued this hasty betrothal? She tried to imagine herself behaving with the easy affection that Ivy showed her husband. And failed.

Breaking into her reverie, Maitland handed her the message, which was still warm from the heat of the flame. "You should be the first one to read this."

She swallowed, suddenly nervous at the prospect. What if it was something mundane, like a shopping list?

Self-doubt wasn't something that Daphne was accustomed to. She was, most of the time, quite sure that she knew at the very least what the most logical course of action should be. But now she hardly knew up from down.

Taking the note from Maitland's hand, she read it aloud:

> If someone steals the prize hid here
> You may find it still, my dear.
> Another version I have hid,
> To find it just do as I bid.
> Three clues I've stashed with trusted friends.
> Each missive toward the map extends.
> For your first clue you now must chase
> The man whose help enhanced this place.

"That's it?" asked Gemma, scowling. "I've seen hiero-glyphs that were more specific."

"It's really only the last bit that's the puzzle," Daphne said with a shrug. "The rest is clear enough. She left more clues to the location of the cipher in case someone else got to it first."

"How on earth could she have known it would go missing?" Kerr asked, clearly aggrieved by the notion. "Aunt was canny, but she hardly had the ability to predict the future."

"She's been clever enough so far," Maitland reminded him. "She somehow managed to matchmake between you and Ivy from beyond the grave. And the Cameron Cipher is one of the most sought after treasures in all of England. It's only logical to think that someone would figure out where she'd hidden it. Aunt was nothing if not thorough."

"The note itself is straightforward enough," Daphne said, drawing their attention back to the matter at hand.

"But who does she mean by 'the man who helped enhance this place'?" Ivy asked. "A gardener? Or the decorator? Is this something perhaps Mr. Greaves would know?"

Maitland cleared his throat, and Daphne turned to look at him. "Are you ill?" she asked, frowning.

"I am not," he said with a grin. "It's just that I might be able to answer this riddle."

When he did not continue, Daphne tilted her head, as if to say, "Well?"

"I think she might be referring to Mr. Renfrew," he said, looking in Kerr's direction. "You recall him, don't you? The steward who was here when we were children?"

Lord Kerr stroked his chin. "I haven't thought about Old Renfrew in years," he said frowning. "Though he does fit the description, since he oversaw the design and work on the gardens. I wonder what happened to him? I must confess I didn't really pay much attention to his comings and goings."

He turned to the ladies. "Aunt went through several stewards after Renfrew left, as I recall, since many of them had a difficult time taking their orders from a lady who knew precisely what she wanted."

"Nor do I," Maitland agreed. "But I suspect Ivy is correct that Greaves will know. He's been here for decades."

Without waiting for the others, Daphne began walking toward the door.

"Where are you going?" Sophia called after her from where she stood with her hand on the bell pull.

"To speak to Greaves," Daphne said without turning back. She could wait for the butler to respond to the bell, but she was tired of inaction. She needed to do something proactive, instead of relying on others to solve the mystery Lady Celeste had left for her.

"If you'll just excuse us," she heard Maitland mutter from behind her.

He caught up to her in the hallway and followed as she strode toward the landing. "I take it this means you've decided which of our many mysteries you'd like to pursue?"

"It's the one that holds the key to all the others," Daphne responded as she hurried down the stairs toward the ground floor. "If we find the cipher, we are likely to find who killed Sommersby."

"I agree," he said trailing after her. "But the murderer might have already got to the cipher by now."

"I doubt that," Daphne said with a shake of her blond head. "Your aunt must have known someone else would try to steal the cipher. Otherwise she would not have left the second set of clues. I think now that whatever was in the box, it was not, in fact, the Cameron Cipher."

They reached the shining black-and-white marble-tiled floor of the entry hall, and Daphne turned toward the door leading into the servants' hall.

Before she could push through it, Maitland laid a staying hand on her arm. "How can you know that?" he asked, looking flummoxed. "You didn't see whatever it was that the killer removed from the box."

"No," she said with strained patience. Did he think she was a simpleton? There was a rational reason for every conclusion she'd drawn so far about the cipher and the trail Lady Celeste had left for her. "Of course I didn't see what was hidden in the box. How could I when I only saw it for the first time with you when we found Sommersby's body?"

"Then how do you know the cipher wasn't in it?" he persisted, looking as frustrated as she felt.

"Because she told me," Daphne said. "I just didn't realize it until a few moments ago."

When he only frowned at her, she sighed. "In the letter Lady Celeste left for me, she said 'I hope you'll find sanctuary here at Beauchamp House—where even Hypocrites could ne'er Soil Eden.' "

"What does that even mean?" Maitland asked with a frown. "It's . . . it makes no sense."

"When I first read the letter," Daphne said with a shrug, "I saw the first anagram referring to the Cameron Cipher, and thought that was the only message hidden there."

"All right," the duke said. "So I take it that means this other sentence contains a hidden meaning?"

"I assumed the bit about Hypocrites was some classical quotation I was unfamiliar with," Daphne said with a slight blush. "My classical education is not what it should be, since I insisted Mr. Sommersby, Senior, devote most of our studies to mathematics. And I did not wish to reveal my weakness, so I did not take it to Ivy, who would likely have told me at once that there was no such quote. And that the reference is religious and not classical."

Maitland sighed. "You are not supposed to know everything there is to know in the world, Daphne. You're allowed to ask for help sometimes."

His words made her stomach flip. It simply didn't feel right to rely on others when she was perfectly capable of finding out something for herself. But if Lady Celeste's quest had forced her to learn anything, it was that Maitland was correct. Sometimes one had to ask for help from others. And it wasn't shameful. It simply was.

And, coming from Maitland, the reminder held more importance than it would have otherwise. She was willing to admit that at least. But not aloud. Not yet.

"Just as with the message about the cipher," she continued, "this second message is a simple anagram of the three capitalized words. *Hypocrites*, *Soil*, and *Eden* can be rearranged to read. *Decoy in Priest's Hole*."

"I'll be da—er, dashed," the duke said, shaking his head

in wonderment. "You are never allowed to doubt your powers of deduction again," he said with a grin. "I would never have figured that out in a million years of trying."

A line appeared between her brows. "You could not possibly try for a million years. You'd very likely die after the first eighty or so. Or sixty, I suppose given your current age."

Maitland stared at her for a second before shaking his head. "You are a true original, Lady Daphne Forsyth," he said, his blue eyes crinkling at the corners, in that way she'd learned meant he was happy.

Which, in turn, made her feel happy. "Thank you, your grace," she said with a shy smile.

"Perhaps you could call me Dalton now?" he asked, dipping his head so that he could see her eyes. "We are, for better or worse, partners in this adventure. And even if it's only temporary, we're betrothed."

At the mention of the betrothal, Daphne's heart began to beat faster. "I suppose so, your . . . Dalton."

With an approving nod, he held out his arm for her. "Let's go see if Mr. Greaves can point us in the direction of Renfrew, now. Because unless I miss my guess, whoever took the decoy cipher is likely growing very frustrated just about now."

"Will he come back here, do you think?" she asked, alarmed at the prospect. After all, this man had been willing to kill Sommersby to get what he thought was the real cipher. What would he do if he came back?

"I don't know," Dalton said with a frown. "But if he does, we'll be ready for him."

Together they went down the servants' stairs in search of the major domo of Beauchamp House.

Chapter 8

"Yes, of course, your grace," said Greaves, whom they found in his office, going over the household ledgers. "I am in correspondence with Mr. Renfrew and know his direction well. He's gone to live with his daughter in Bexhill, no more than a day's drive from here."

"And he is in good health?" Maitland asked. It would be just their luck if they drove all the way to Bexhill only to find him at death's door.

"As far as I know, your grace," said the butler with a frown, as if the notion that an elderly man could be in ill health was troubling to him. Greaves was no spring chicken, after all. "Though now that you mention it, I haven't had a reply from my last letter, sent at Christmastime."

That had been over six months ago, Maitland thought with alarm. He hoped that wasn't an omen.

Seeing that he had upset the older man, he hastened to reassure him. "I'm sure he's quite well, but busy with his grandchildren," he said.

"How far is Bexhill from here?" Daphne asked, cutting to the heart of the matter, as usual.

"Only six miles or so, I should think," Greaves said to

her coolly. The very proper upper servant clearly found Daphne's abrupt manner difficult, though he would never say so aloud. It was indicated only in a slight lessening of the warmth he'd shown Maitland. Still it was noticeable.

Raising his brows at the man he'd known since he was a boy, the duke was not displeased to see him color a little at the rebuke. Daphne might not be to everyone's taste, but she was one of the four owners of the house and an earl's daughter to boot, and as such deserved the man's cordiality as well as his respect.

"Perhaps I can ask cook to pack a picnic luncheon for your drive," the butler said, trying to make amends.

"Oh, but I don't think . . ." Daphne began.

"That would be perfect, thank you, Greaves," said Maitland at the same time.

Looking from one of them to the other, the butler seemed to decide that the duke outranked his new mistress. "Very good, your grace. I will inform her at once."

When he and Daphne had reached the ground floor again, Maitland said, "A kind word goes a long way with the servants, you know. Even if it's just to thank him for his time."

"But it is his job to give me his time," Daphne said, looking puzzled. As if he'd suggested she thank the banister for aiding her ascent of the stairs.

"Of course it is," he said patiently. "But everyone likes to be appreciated. Don't you like to be told you're clever?"

"I suppose," she said, giving the matter some thought. "But I already know I'm clever. So it does me no good to have someone else tell me. I'd be more pleased if they told me I'd done something well that I am not generally good at. Like needlepoint."

He hid a smile. "You're not fond of sewing, eh?" He had a difficult time imaging her dutifully seated before a needlepoint frame, plying her needle.

"I like it well enough," Daphne said with a sigh. "But I am horrid at it. Which is why words of encouragement make me feel a bit better about my less-than-elegant work. It goes against my logical side, of course. Truth is important, but I am beginning to learn that there are times when it hurts."

"Precisely. So you must simply think of thanking the servants as a sort of encouragement for their version of needle-point."

"Your gr—Dalton," she corrected herself, much to his pleasure. "That makes very little sense. They are presumably excellent at their occupations, so, it doesn't follow at all. Though I suppose I will try to do as you say and simply thank the servants when the occasion arises if, as you say, it makes them feel better."

"That's all I ask," he said with a nod.

Eager to be on to the next part of their quest, he took her hand and pulled her toward the main staircase.

"Where are we going now?" she asked, stifling a yawn. "Should we go back to the library and see if we can find anything else?"

"Most assuredly not," he said pulling her hand up to kiss the back of it, making her color up quite prettily. "You, madam, are going to take a nap."

"A nap?" she protested, though her exhaustion was evident in the shadows beneath her eyes. "I am not a child, Dalton."

"No, you are not," he said with a sigh. He was well aware of that fact every time he felt her brush against him. "But, you have had an eventful few days. And if we're to journey to Bexhill tomorrow, you need to get some rest."

When they reached the door to her bedchamber, he pulled her against his body and leaned his forehead against hers. Slowly and deliberately, he kissed her, infusing the caress with some of the passion he'd been holding in check all day.

She was breathless and looking a little dazed when he

pulled away. She said nothing, only held a hand up to her lips as she blinked at him.

Sorely tempted to drag her into the bedroom beyond and continue what he'd started, Maitland got himself under control. When he had her for the first time, it would not be in the middle of the afternoon when anyone might disturb them.

"Sleep well, dear Daphne," he said as she continued to watch him.

She didn't speak until he'd already turned to go.

"I never feel it with you," she said softly.

Arrested by both her cryptic words and the touch of vulnerability in her tone, he turned back.

"The fear," she continued quietly. "Whenever I meet eyes with someone, I get this . . . this knot of fear in my stomach. Anxiety."

She looked down at the floor, then quite deliberately looked up and met his gaze. "But not with you. I can look at you, see you, without that feeling."

It was perhaps the saddest thing he'd ever heard. But also the most exhilarating.

He knew instinctively that he'd just been given a gift beyond price.

"Thank you," he said softly. Not daring to step closer to her lest he break his vow not to follow her in.

"Thank *you*, Dalton," she said with a sweet smile. "I didn't think I'd ever have that with anyone."

Then she stepped into her bedchamber and shut the door behind her.

Alone in the hall, Maitland slumped against the wall, staring at the now closed door.

Unless he very much mistook the matter, he was in serious danger of falling in love with her.

And maybe. Just maybe. She was falling for him, too.

Standing up straight, he strolled down the hallway, tempted to whistle a jaunty tune like a jubilant schoolboy.

The next morning, a picnic basket—put together by the cook at Greaves's request—tucked away beneath the seat, Daphne and Dalton set off in his blue-and-yellow trimmed curricle for Bexhill.

She'd informed the other ladies of their plan last evening when they met in their shared parlor before bed.

"I suppose it would look odd if we were all to go *en masse* to Bexhill to question him," Sophie said, though there was something in her tone that told Daphne she rather wished they could do so anyway.

Then she'd given a squeak, and rubbed her arm. As if someone had pinched her.

The Hastings sisters were quite odd sometimes, Daphne had reflected.

"It certainly would look odd," Ivy said firmly. "Besides, we have plenty to keep us occupied here. What with the number of calls we're sure to receive now that word of Mr. Sommersby's death has got out. I knew we could rely on Squire Northman's wife to tattle all over the village."

That lady had been quite rude to Ivy not long after she'd announced her betrothal to Lord Kerr, and Ivy had yet to forgive her.

"It would have gotten out sooner or later," Gemma said with a shrug. "And we can use the opportunity to question the neighbors about Sommersby's coming and goings. Whoever killed him could still be in the village, you know."

Daphne would like to be there to question the village ladies, but she knew that her talents lay elsewhere. She could never quite figure out what to say to that sort of woman, and always managed to insult them in some way or other. Even when that wasn't her intention. Truth be told she'd be far more comfortable with Maitland.

"Speaking of those who are 'still in the village,' Daphne," said Ivy with an apologetic look, "Quill told me earlier that your father is still in the neighborhood. Staying with the Northmans, in fact. So perhaps it's a good thing that you and Maitland are leaving."

"I thought Maitland's ruse about the betrothal would have reassured him enough to make him go back to London," Daphne said, shocked despite knowing her father was nothing if not unpredictable.

"You don't think he has doubts about the validity of the betrothal, do you?" asked Sophia with a slight frown. "Perhaps he's remained here to make sure you weren't trying to fob him off."

That was something Daphne hadn't considered. She'd been so relieved—after the initial shock of Maitland's outlandish announcement—at the prospect of being freed of her father's demands, even if only temporarily, that she hadn't thought beyond his departure. And once they'd found the clue to the cipher, she hadn't thought of Lord Forsyth at all.

"Even if he is," Gemma said, trying to reassure her, "then we will simply need to spread word of your happy news to the gossip-hungry matrons who come to talk about Sommersby. A few congratulations from neighborhood busybodies will allay any doubts your father might have."

"And, your day trip with Maitland will lend credence as well," Ivy said. "A courting couple might go for an afternoon's drive together without incidenct, but an all-day journey must surely mark you as an engaged couple."

Somewhat mollified by their assurances, Daphne nodded.

"I suppose you're right. And perhaps if we're lucky, by the time we return from Bexhill, Papa will have decided to go back to London."

"You don't suppose there's a possibility that you and the duke could decide to make your betrothal real, do you?" asked Sophia, tilting her head as if she were trying to see more clearly into Daphne's thoughts. "I couldn't help but notice how cozy the two of you were in the hallway."

At the mention of the hallway, Daphne's face flushed. Had their kiss been observed? In truth, she'd been too caught up in the moment to consider it.

"Don't tease, Sophie," chided her sister. "Besides, it's impolite to spy on betrothed couples. Everyone knows that."

"I'm just pointing out that it may not be so easy to dissolve this pretend betrothal as they think," Sophia said, ignoring Gemma's censure. "And it's not as if Daphne is immune to his charms. We all know about her indecent proposal to him the night of Ivy's shooting."

"I'm not sure you're aware of it," Daphne said in seriousness, "but I am still in the room. And I fear that I was carried away yesterday. But there's been no actual declaration from the duke. And aside from that I cannot consider any of this until we've found the cipher and learned who killed Sommersby. Some things are just far more important than . . ."

"Than love?" Sophia asked pertly. "Is that the word you were searching for?"

"Than fooling my father," Daphne returned. Whatever this newfound closeness she had with Dalton, it could hardly be called love. Friendship, maybe. But not love.

Looking disappointed, but thankfully seeing that she would get no more revelations from Daphne about her relationship with the duke, Sophia changed the subject.

"Do you think the duke will let you take the reins?" she asked, genuinely wanting to know. The petite brunette was quite fond of driving and had tried and failed to get Dalton to let her drive his curricle on more than one occasion. "His grays look like they're quite spirited."

"I shouldn't think so," Daphne said with a shake of her head. "I am quite content to let him drive, as you well know."

She paused, recalling what Dalton had said about thanking the servants. Perhaps if she complimented the other ladies about the things they were good at, it would make them feel as she did when someone complimented her terrible needlepoint. They likely knew what they were good at, of course, but it was something. "You are quite good at driving, Sophia."

The other three stared at her in astonishment.

"What?" she asked, when they remained silent. "Did I say something offensive?"

"Quite the opposite," Ivy said with a grin. "Do you realize you just paid Sophia a compliment?"

"So?"

"So," Gemma said, gleefully, "you have never paid any of us a compliment before. Never. In the three months of our acquaintance."

"I'm sure that's not true," Daphne said with a blush. Was she so difficult? It wasn't as if she did not respect them. Of course, she did. Lady Celeste would not have chosen them as her heirs if they were not experts in their fields.

"It is true, I'm afraid," Sophia said. "But clearly something has happened to bring about this change in your manner."

"Or some*one*," Ivy said with a raised brow.

Daphne's cheeks grew hot. So much for stopping their interest in romance. "Of course not. I simply wanted to make Sophia feel good about herself, so I told her she is an excellent driver. Though she likely knows that already."

Though they knew she did not like it, she felt all three girls move closer and hug her one by one.

"I did know," Sophia said as she drew away. "But it was nice to hear all the same."

Now, in the light of day, Daphne recalled the conversation with a small smile as she watched Maitland . . . that is, Dalton . . . handle the reins.

"You're quiet," he commented, as if sensing her scrutiny. It really was extraordinary how he seemed to know what she was thinking much of the time. If only she had a reciprocal ability to interpret his thoughts.

"Did you not sleep?" he asked, glancing at her before turning back to the road ahead of them. "'Journey proud' my old nanny used to call it."

"I slept quite well, thank you," she said, answering the question. She liked to do things in order.

The truth of the matter was that for the second night in a row, she'd slept soundly. She hadn't realized it before Sommersby's death, but even when she'd known he was thousands of miles away in Egypt, she never could quite trust that she wouldn't be jarred awake in the middle of the night by his unwanted advances. She'd even slept with a burning lamp in her bedchamber for a time, that is, until her father discovered the practice and scolded her for wasting fuel.

Before he could speak, and possibly question her more about her sleep habits, asked, "What is 'journey proud'?"

She'd had a nanny when she was small, but she'd been a dour woman who had disliked Daphne's impertinent questions and odd ways. When they'd no longer had the funds to pay her and she left, Daphne had not put up a fuss.

Now, seated beside this handsome man who had clearly enjoyed a different upbringing than she had, she was curious about what sort of nanny his had been. It hadn't really occurred to her before that some children held their nannies in great affection.

"It's the feeling one has," he explained, glancing over at her again with those green eyes that missed nothing, "the night before a trip. You have trouble falling asleep because you're anticipating the next day's traveling. You're far too excited at the prospect of an adventure."

Daphne frowned. "I never knew there was a name for it," she said. There was so much, she'd come to realize, that she didn't know. It was easy enough when she was in the world of numbers, and ciphers, and puzzles to think she knew all. But, she'd come to learn in the past months at Beauchamp House just how ignorant she was on some subjects. Even something as simple as this phrase Dalton's nanny had taught him. "I suppose that's one more thing I can add to my list."

That seemed to intrigue him. "What list?"

They were approaching the outskirts of Little Seaford. But this bit of the road was deserted. And she was glad of it. She felt as if they were cocooned in their own private world where she could speak freely without fear of upsetting someone or saying the wrong thing.

Only with Dalton could she be this comfortable in her own skin. Silently, boldly, she slipped her arm through his and leaned into his body, already dangerously close on the narrow curricle seat. Daring even more, she leaned her head against his shoulder, the hard muscle beneath his arm making her feel protected. Safe.

She'd never imagined how addictive physically touching another person could be.

Rather than object to her forwardness, or questioning her unusual behavior, he instead seemed to welcome it. Silently, he took both reins in his left and used his right to stretch out her arm so that he could clasp her hand.

Then, as if nothing had happened, he said, "Tell me about this list of yours."

Relaxing against him, she said, "I keep a list of things I've learned since I arrived at Beauchamp House. It's getting quite long."

He was quiet for a beat, and she wondered for a fleeting moment if he was about to laugh at her foolish list. Her father certainly would. Mostly because he disliked the fact that she was able to calculate sums and gauge how many cards had been played before he could. He had no compunction about using her abilities for his own profit, but even so, the fact of it seemed to irritate him beyond bearing.

"And what have you learned in your months here?" he asked, sounding intrigued. There was no hint of censure from him. Only curiosity. Still . . .

"It's silly. Forget I said anything."

"Of course, I won't forget it," he said lightly. "You've got me primed now. Besides, if we're going to make this false betrothal convincing then we need to know these things about one another."

His words were said in a teasing tone, but the fact that he used the word false told Daphne all she needed to know about the possibility of their turning the engagement into something more permanent. A pang of disappointment rang in her chest, before she tamped it down, reminding herself that she'd never wished for the betrothal in the first place.

Still, he did have a point about their being able to make it seem real. Especially if her father was lingering in the village in hopes of finding them out.

"Fine," she said grudgingly. "But it's not very exciting. Just a catalog of things I should have known but somehow did not."

Dalton tilted his head, but didn't turn to look at her. "Why are you keeping a list? And what sort of things have you put on it? Besides 'journey proud' of course."

"Before I came to Beauchamp House," Daphne admitted, "I thought I knew everything. Or at least, the most important things."

"Like what?"

Despite her nascent trust in him, she felt naked, but pressed on.

"Mostly information about mathematics and such," she said finally. "Monsieur Fourier's theory of infinite sums, for example. Wherein periodic functions can be expressed as the sum of an infinite series of sines and cosines. I was able to meet him when he came to England. Did you know? My tutor, Mr. Sommersby, had a colleague who knew him from somewhere and he arranged an introduction for me. A brilliant man. Truly."

"I shall have to take your word for it," Dalton said wryly. "I don't think I understand most of what you just said. Except for the bit about the introduction and this Fourier chap being brilliant. I'd guess, however, that you could give him a bit of competition."

Daphne laughed. "Hardly. I am gifted, but I'm hardly the equal of one of the best mathematicians of our time."

"I don't know about that," he said skeptically. "But if you will insist upon it, I must stand down since I know almost nothing about the subject."

They drove on in companionable silence for a few minutes more before they reached the road leading through the village of Little Seaford. Daphne wondered why he had chosen this route, since there seemed to be more traffic, which made for more difficult driving.

Not that Dalton seemed to notice as he skillfully steered the grays around the various obstacles along the way—an apple cart here, a wagon there, pausing so that its driver could ensure the security of its load.

As they moved farther into the center of town, the curricle

slowed near the entrance of the Pig & Whistle, finally coming to a stop just behind a waiting carriage.

"Why are we stopping here?" Daphne asked. She'd thought they'd drive through to Bexhill without stopping. "Is there something amiss with the horses?"

She knew from experience in town that horses could cause all sorts of delays in travel. They seemed always to be throwing a shoe, or coming up lame. Really, it was a most inefficient means of travel, though she could think of no better with the exception of walking on one's own. Which carried its own drawbacks.

Handing the reins to a waiting ostler, Dalton leapt down and moved around to offer her his hand. She turned, and before she could speak, his strong hands were around her waist, and he lifted her easily from the seat and set her firmly on the ground. They stood front to front for a moment, and Daphne dared a peek up into his blue eyes. What she saw there made her look away again.

It was really quite illuminating to know how many occasions for improper thoughts there were in seemingly mundane acts.

"I thought we'd pay a call on Mr. Foster," he said, turning away at last, and offering her his arm.

Remembering how overset Foster had been yesterday, Daphne blinked. "Are you sure that's a good idea? He is very unhappy with us, though I suppose in his position, I would also have been angry. It must have been quite distressing to not know where his traveling companion had gone."

"Hopefully the chap is in a better mood today," Dalton said as the door of the inn swung open and they stepped into the darkened interior.

Chapter 9

He should have told her before they departed Beauchamp
House that he wished to visit Sommersby's traveling companion, Maitland thought as he escorted Daphne into the inn.
But it hadn't occurred to him until they were on the outskirts
of the village and she mentioned her list.

Only Daphne would keep a list of the things she didn't
know.

And one thing no one knew was who had killed Sommersby. The man who'd traveled to the coast with him must
certainly know something about the matter.

They didn't have to wait long for the innkeeper, Mr. Allenby, to approach.

When one was a duke, it was always thus.

In his younger days, he would have thought glumly about
his childhood dream of the anonymity of the stables and
cursed his fate. As an adult, however, he saw and appreciated the privileges of his position, knowing that too much
complaint spit in the face of the everyday difficulties people
without his blessings had to endure. "Your grace," Allenby
said with the broad smile of a man who wanted coin, "what
a delight to see you. Please tell me at once how I may serve

you. A private dining room, perhaps? A cup of tea for Lady Daphne?"

The man's speculative glance at Daphne told Dalton he was already wondering who he could tell about their presence here together.

"Though a pint would be appreciated, Allenby," Maitland said somewhat impatiently, "I'm afraid we are not here to partake of your excellent service. We'd like to speak to one of your guests. A Mr. Foster?"

Allenby's enthusiasm dimmed a bit at the demurral, but he didn't say as much. "Of course, of course, your grace. A bad business with his friend Sommersby." He turned to Daphne. "I hope you ladies were not too overset by the discovery, my lady. It must have been most distressing."

"As it was the first time I'd seen a dead body, sir," she said with her usual forthrightness, "it was indeed most disturbing. I do not recommend it."

The innkeeper's mouth dropped open. Maitland didn't know what he'd been expecting from her, but clearly Daphne's plain speaking hadn't been within his imaginings.

"Mr. Foster?" He prodded.

Allenby blinked. Then, regaining his powers of speech, he bounced back. "Yes, of course, your grace. Mr. Foster is in a private dining room just now, enjoying a late breakfast." In a lower voice, he confided, "He did not wish to be pestered with the questions of the curious masses."

Maitland wondered if the man included himself in that description.

"I'll just take you there, shall I?" Allenby asked, ushering them to a door just off the taproom.

As they walked, Maitland could feel the curious eyes of the patrons on them.

Allenby's brisk knock on the dining-room door was followed by an invitation to enter, and Maitland waved Daphne inside then shut the door behind them, shutting out the inn-keeper.

"What is the meaning of this?" asked Ian Foster, rising from the table where he seemed to be partaking of a rabbit stew. "Your grace, I really must object to this intrusion."

"My apologies, Foster," the duke said easily, pulling out a chair for Daphne, who, looking unusually cowed by the man's outburst, sat. "Of course, you remember Lady Daphne Forsyth."

"Of course I remember her," Foster said with contempt, remaining on his feet despite the fact that the lady in the room was now seated. "She's the one who got my friend killed."

Despite her obvious discomfort, Daphne did not let that pass. "I did nothing of the sort. Sommersby had no right to break into Beauchamp House. And he certainly didn't learn of the Cameron Cipher's connection to the library there from me. I told no one of it. For all I know, you followed him there and stabbed him yourself, sir."

Though Foster scowled, he didn't repeat his accusation. Which told Dalton that he likely knew his allegations were without merit and had only lashed out because he was angry over his friend's death. It was, however, interesting that he also didn't refute the charge that he himself might be responsible.

Deciding to see how Foster would react to a second accusation, Maitland asked, "*Did* you kill your friend, Foster? It isn't uncommon for co-conspirators to fall out. Did he go to Beauchamp House without telling you of his plan to break in? Perhaps plan to take the cipher out from under your nose?"

"This is absurd," Foster said, collapsing into his chair, and shoving aside the plate of stew, clearly no longer hungry. "I cannot believe I'm embroiled in this mess."

"I'd have expected you would feel more sympathy for poor Sommersby," Maitland said mildly.

At that, Foster gave a harsh laugh. "Poor Sommersby. Hah. He got what he deserved."

Maitland stared. A glance at Daphne showed she seemed just as astonished.

Had the man just confessed to murdering Nigel Sommersby?

Carefully, so as not to alert the man to what he may have just said, Maitland said easily, "That's an odd thing to say about your friend, sir."

Sighing, Foster sat back in his chair and shook his head. The shadows beneath his eyes were prominent in his pale face. He looked as if he'd aged ten years since they'd first met him.

"He wasn't my friend, your grace," he said bitterly. "I could barely stand the fellow if you wish to know the truth. But I had a job to do, and so I accompanied him here. Much to the detriment of my own career."

Daphne shot a questioning look at Maitland, but he had just as little explanation for Foster's confession as she did.

"What career is that, sir?" he asked Foster when the other man didn't continue.

Foster, who looked as if he would like to be anywhere but in his current position, said in a weary tone, "I am not an old school friend of Nigel Sommersby's. And I have no personal interest in finding the Cameron Cipher. In fact, I wish I'd never heard of the thing."

"Explain yourself, sir," Daphne said, any guilt she'd felt over the loss of his supposed friend now gone. "If you have no interest in the cipher then why did you come here with Nigel Sommersby? And why did he introduce you as his friend if you were not."

Sensing that this would not be the brief encounter he'd hoped it would be, Maitland took the chair on Daphne's other side and watched as Foster sat thinking. Whether to get his story straight or to recall the details, it was impossible to tell.

Finally, Foster leaned back and admitted, "I'm here because my superiors ordered me to be here. I work for a government . . ." he searched for the right word, finally settling on, "entity, that would like to find the Cameron Cipher and the gold it leads to so that it doesn't get into the wrong hands."

The duke's brows rose. "Home Office?" he guessed. "I should think they would dislike the idea of all that gold funding another rebellion. Though the Jacobites seem an unlikely possibility in this day and age."

Foster indicated that Maitland was right about the government connection with a slight inclination of his head. "I'd rather not say whom they wish to keep from acquiring the gold, but let us just agree that it would be a very bad thing if these people had that sort of largesse at their disposal."

"But how did you end up with Sommersby?" Daphne asked, clearly more interested in the man's connection to her former friend than in who might misuse the Cameron gold. "Surely he didn't agree to take you along if he knew you were working to take the treasure as soon as he found it?"

"That was little more than a few words in the ears of the right people," Foster admitted. "Sommersby wasn't particularly discreet about his plans to search for the cipher. And when I showed up on the scene with an introduction from one of his actual old school friends, and told him I'd heard the cipher was hidden in the library of Beauchamp House here on the coast, he invited me along."

Daphne stared. "You're the one who told him the cipher was hidden at Beauchamp House? But how did you know?"

Foster's eyes turned opaque. "That information is off limits, I'm afraid, Lady Daphne." He didn't sound particularly apologetic to Maitland's ear, no matter what he actually said.

"I'm guessing it was either someone who worked in government who was close to Aunt Celeste," the duke said to Daphne, though he didn't take his eyes off Foster, whom he trusted even less now that he knew his occupation. "Or, it was someone who'd already tracked down the cipher to Beauchamp House and offered the information to Foster's superiors. For a price."

Lady Daphne shook her head in amazement. "For a supposedly secret cipher, it seems as if a great many people knew it was hidden in Beauchamp House. I wonder why they didn't simply break in before Sommersby did and take it themselves."

"It's a bit more difficult than you realize, Lady Daphne," Foster said snidely, "to infiltrate a private residence. Much less the private residence of the well-placed daughter of a duke who is more than usually cautious about the security of her home."

That hadn't stopped the person who killed Lady Celeste, Maitland thought bitterly. But then that had been poison, which was admittedly easier to slip into the house without anyone noticing than a large man with a gun would be.

"But Sommersby managed it," Daphne returned, undeterred by Foster's attitude. "I'll bet that didn't sit well with you at all, having a civilian succeed where you had not."

"Of course, it didn't," Foster snapped. "Because it allowed someone else to take the cipher, and it got that fool Sommersby killed to boot."

"Interesting you should place the two in that particular order," Maitland said thoughtfully.

Scowling, Foster said, "I will not lie and say that the disappearance of the cipher isn't the more pressing issue to me. I didn't wish Sommersby dead, but his loss is not nearly as dangerous for the well-being of the nation as that of the cipher. If the person who's taken it manages to find the gold and deliver it into the coffers of England's enemies, then we are in serious trouble. I won't apologize for seeing the big picture."

"I wonder, however," Maitland said, leaning forward a little, "if it's not something less patriotic that makes you take this loss so hard. I can't imagine the upper echelons at the Home Office are very happy with you just now."

At the other man's flinch, he knew he'd hit his mark.

"I'm guessing you spent years of your life fighting the French, old man," he continued in a companionable tone that he could see Foster hated. "Then, once the war was over you came home and began working in a less-overt capacity. All those years of service, effectively erased by the rash actions of a man you didn't give a damn about. That must really infuriate you."

"If you're asking me again if I killed Sommersby," Foster said sourly, "the answer is still no. I might have disliked the man, and his childish wishes to find the gold at the end of some ridiculous mystery trail may have driven me almost mad, but I didn't want him dead. And I certainly would never have allowed the cipher to fall into enemy hands."

"But perhaps you didn't," Daphne said, looking at Foster like he was some curious specimen she'd found in a museum. "Perhaps you have the cipher. That would surely be a way of keeping it out of the hands of these dangerous people you seem to fear so much."

Before Foster could retort, Maitland spoke up. "An admirable theory, Daphne, but if that were the case, then I think Mr. Foster would be long gone. I believe he's here because he suspects the thief is still in the area. Isn't that right, Foster?"

The agent for the crown didn't respond either way. But his silence was an answer in itself.

Seeing that there was little more to be learned from the man, Maitland rose. "Daphne, we should take our leave now. Mr. Foster very likely has a great deal of . . . searching to do."

With a last look at the spy, Daphne turned and took the duke's proffered arm. They were almost to the door when she turned and asked, "Why did you dislike him so much?"

"Because he was a braggart and a bore," Foster said coldly.

When she didn't turn and leave, he sighed. "Because he actually thought he would find that hidden cache of gold. After almost a century of searching by dozens and dozens of treasure hunters, Sommersby thought that he would be the one to finally do it when no one else could. It was ridiculous."

Maitland thought that said more about Foster's cynicism than it did about Sommersby's optimism.

"I mean to find it, Mr. Foster," Daphne said, her chin raised in defiance. "It's not ridiculous to have confidence. What is ridiculous is to despise someone for having it. If your reach extends your grasp at least some of the time, then what harm is there in having hopes all of the time?"

Turning back to Maitland, she said, "I am ready to leave now."

Without turning back to see Foster's reaction to her declaration, Dalton led her away.

They were more than halfway to their destination before Daphne spoke of Foster's admission again. As if by mutual consent, they'd talked of everything from Dalton's childhood home to the weather, each of them avoiding the scene in the Pig & Whistle. But after she'd had time to think the confrontation over, Daphne was ready to discuss it.

"I should have known he wasn't Sommersby's true friend," she said, one hand on her hat to keep it from flying off in the increasingly turbulent wind. "I should have guessed, and then perhaps none of this would have happened."

"I do not know how," he said, glancing at her with a furrow between his brows. "You hadn't seen the man since you were a girl. A fellow can befriend any number of people over the course of several years."

She made a noise of dismissal.

"The fact remains that I let Foster fool me, just as he tricked Sommersby," she said mulishly. "I should at the very least have questioned him further about his interest in the cipher—what his own feelings were about the prospect of finding such a famous treasure. Given how little he seemed to care about the romance of it in our recent discussion, it's very likely I would have sussed out the truth with only a few pointed queries."

"If you are determined to find yourself at fault," Dalton said with a shake of his head, "then you may as well blame yourself for not knowing someone would shoot Sommersby that night. After all, the all-knowing Lady Daphne Forsyth must have been able to predict such an event, otherwise she is merely an ordinary person."

"You may poke fun," she said stiffly, feeling strangely vulnerable, "but I am not ordinary. And if I cannot understand the motives of ordinary people, then what good is my extraordinary talent? It isn't as if an encyclopedic knowledge of mathematics has contributed to the betterment of the world."

"Daphne," he said softly, "there is no reason you should have guessed what would happen. Especially not when your abilities in one area have clearly caused a deficit in another."

She gasped, not sure if she'd heard him right. "Did you

say I am deficient in some way?" It mattered not that she'd just said essentially the same thing.

They'd been sitting pressed against each other as he drove. But at his words, she scooted as far as she could—which wasn't very far—to the other side of the narrow curricle seat. Rather than looking abashed, Dalton pressed on. "I'm not sure I'd use that term," he said mildly, "but do you deny that you sometimes have a hard time discerning what motives lay behind people's words? That you cannot understand whether something is meant to be taken seriously or in jest?"

She'd never really heard it expressed in such a way, but his explanation did come close to describing what she'd come to think of as her blindness.

"What of it?" she asked cautiously.

"I am simply saying that even with your extraordinary intellect, you were at a disadvantage when it came to catching on to Foster's ruse." Dalton took both reins in his left hand and placed his right one over hers where it lay in her lap. Though they were both wearing gloves, she could feel the warmth of him through the soft kid, and was comforted by the contact. "You are not responsible for what happened to Sommersby. No matter how guilty you feel at your relief that he is dead."

His words struck her like a blow, and she felt tears spring in her eyes. She wanted to deny his accusation, but she could not. Her blissful sleep in the nights since they'd discovered Sommersby's body was proof enough.

"I am horrid," she said, her voice thick with emotion. "Only a monster would rejoice in someone's demise."

"Only a monster would do to you what Sommersby did," he replied, reaching out to take her hand. "Only an unfeeling wretch would not feel some relief at knowing the man she feared for years was no longer a danger to her."

Perhaps he was right, she thought, though some part of her still had doubts.

"You are doing what you can to find his killer," Dalton continued in a soothing tone. "That is more than he has a right to. More than most would do for the man who tried to take her virtue."

"I suppose so," she said, wishing she could go back to her usual unflappable self. These past few weeks had turned her into one of those simpering ladies she'd once scorned. "I only wish I had been able to speak to him about . . . . that night. Before he died, I mean. I wish I could have asked him why he did it. Why he broke my trust as he did."

Dalton didn't speak for a few moments, simply kept his eyes on the horses and the road ahead of them. Daphne had begun to wonder if he'd heard her at all when he finally spoke up. "I cannot pretend to know why a man would do such a thing to someone who trusted him. My sister's husband was often a brute to her, and then would come back to her with tears and promises never to do it again. Then a short time would pass and he would beat her, hurt her, again."

Daphne had not known this about Lady Serena's husband, though she'd somehow known that there was some darkness in her past. Were there so many of these men, then? Who hurt those who loved them with little or no compunction? The notion had never occurred to her. And it was chilling.

"I once asked him," Dalton continued, his steady voice and warm presence beside her giving her much needed succor, "why he did what he did to my sister, who once loved him beyond reason. Do you know what he said? What explanation he gave for brutalizing her again and again?"

She hardly dared ask, yet the words left her in almost a whisper. "What?"

"He said that he did not know. When it came to any sort

of self-reflection, or ability to know his own motives, that was all he could say. He did not know."

She thought about Sommersby for a moment. Was he, too, incapable of knowing himself? Of understanding the impulse that led him to force himself upon his oldest friend? It was a supremely unsatisfactory idea.

Leaning against his shoulder again, she wondered at how different Dalton was from Sommersby. Or even her father. He was a different sort altogether.

Still, she was frustrated at knowing so little of the reasons for Sommersby and his ilk to behave as they did.

"I like to know the explanations for why things happen," she said into the silence. "Not knowing why is one of the things about Sommersby's betrayal that haunted me the most. Not knowing if it was something I said or did that led him to think he could do that to me. Or if he'd have behaved as he did regardless."

"I know Serena would have liked an answer, too," he said. "But I can tell you this, Lady Daphne Forsyth. You didn't make him hurt you. He made the choice to do what he did, and there's nothing you could have said or done that would have justified his actions. I have no respect for a man who takes advantage of a woman. And if I'd known about what he did to you before he had the good grace to get himself murdered, I'd have been tempted to do the thing myself."

There was a fierceness in his voice that was alien to his usual manner. A protectiveness that was both comforting and invigorating. She had once liked to think she could take care of herself—after Sommersby's assault, she'd forced herself to do so, lest he come for her again. But after a lifetime of not being able to rely upon any of the men in her life—excepting perhaps Sommersby, Sr. before he left so unexpectedly—it was bewitching to think that she could count on the Duke of Maitland to stand by her side if the need arose.

Not knowing how to express her gratitude, she went with her impulse and simply squeezed his hand where it grasped hers.

"Thank you."

That was all. Words inadequate to express the depth of her appreciation. But words were all she had at the moment.

Chapter 10

Once they reached Bexhill-on-Sea, or Bexhill as it was known familiarly, a brief stop at the local tavern was enough to give them direction to the Miller farm, where Lady Celeste's erstwhile steward Mr. Renfrew lived with his daughter and son-in-law.

It was a pretty-enough area, with the town itself situated on an elevation that allowed for a clear view in every direction. It was said that William the Conqueror had eaten his first meal in England near here, though Dalton had heard all sorts of tales relating to the King since it was so near the site of the Battle of Hastings. As boys, he and Kerr had come to Bexhill on any number of occasions, to watch the German soldiers who'd come here to escape Napoleon's occupation at the invitation of the Hanoverian, George III.

"It is convenient that Mr. Renfrew was able to retire so near to where he lived and worked for so many years," Daphne remarked as they turned onto a country lane not far from the town proper. "He must be able to keep in close contact with his friends, I think."

"I imagine that is correct," Dalton said as they came nearer to a rather impressive farm house with what appeared to be an extensive husbandry operation attached. "His daughter appears to have done well for herself, at any rate."

"Or rather, her husband has done well," Daphne said dryly. "Unless Renfrew's daughter runs this farm all by herself. It is rare, I think that a woman should be able to do so. Even with the assistance of someone as influential as your aunt."

"I suppose that's correct," he said ruefully. He forgot at times how much women were forced to rely upon their fathers and husbands for their subsistence. Daphne was helping to remind him.

As they neared the front door, a stable lad approached Dalton's side of the curricle to take the reins from him, and as soon as Maitland had helped Daphne to the ground, the entrance of the farm house was opened by a curtsying, mob-capped maid.

"Milord, milady," she said as she bowed and scraped, "how may I help ye?"

"The Duke of Maitland and Lady Daphne Forsyth to see Mr. Renfrew," said Maitland in an amused tone. He had become accustomed to the people around Beauchamp House, who, if they did not precisely treat him like just another resident of the neighborhood, at the very least didn't look as if they were somewhere between a faint and a seizure on greeting him, as this maid seemed to be.

At the mention of Renfrew, however she looked nonplussed.

Fortunately, a pretty woman of middle years entered the hallway and on seeing her visitors, gave an elegant curtsy. "That will be all, Molly," she said to the blushing maid, who looked half-relieved, half-disappointed to be supplanted by her mistress.

"Your grace," said the lady, whom Dalton assumed was

Mrs. Miller, "my lady, I'm afraid my father is indisposed at the moment. Is there something I can help you with?"

Dalton's heart sank at the news. Had they driven all this way on a fool's errand?

"But we need to speak to him most urgently," Daphne said in a brusque tone that revealed her nervousness.

Looking surprised, but not particularly conciliatory, Mrs. Miller said, "Perhaps we can step into the parlor for a moment and discuss this. I shall ring for some tea."

Giving the woman his most charming smile, Dalton took Daphne's arm. "That would be most appreciated, Mrs. Miller."

The farmer's wife ushered them into a small but well-furnished parlor, which seemed to serve the dual purposes of comfort and illustration of prosperity.

Once there, he waited for Daphne to take a seat on a low sofa, while Mrs. Miller sat calmly in an armchair. He remained standing, taking up a position before the handsome marble fireplace.

"Now, perhaps you can tell me what it is you wish to speak to my father about?" Mrs. Miller appeared to be wholly unruffled by their appearance in her drawing room.

Before Dalton could answer, Daphne said, "It is a confidential matter. Having to do with his former employer, Lady Celeste Beauchamp."

"Perhaps you could tell us something about the nature of your father's illness, Mrs. Miller?" Dalton asked hurriedly, before the other lady could respond to Daphne's admission. "My aunt was quite fond of him as I recall, and I know she would wish me to inquire after his health. If there is anything we can do . . ."

The tense line between the matron's eyes eased at Dalton's words. "That is kind of you to ask, your grace. My father was fond of Lady Celeste as well. But I'm afraid he would not even remember her existence if I were to tell him you called." Her eyes grew shiny with unshed tears. "His mind has gone, you see. And he is not the man he once was."

At the news Mr. Renfrew was suffering from senility, Daphne emitted a distressed sound.

"We are quite sad to hear it, ma'am," Dalton said, not sure where to proceed from here. "Is he able to receive visitors at all, or does that distress him too much?" He could at the very least find out the degree to which the man suffered from his mental ailment.

"He has good days and bad days," Mrs. Miller said with a sad smile. "Unfortunately, today is not a good day. Though I know if he were well enough he would love to receive a visit from you, your grace. You were always one of his favorites. You and Lord Kerr."

"But we've come all this way," Daphne said in a weak voice. Clearly, she was not taking the news of their man's indisposition well.

Moving to take a seat beside her, Dalton hoped that his nearness would give her comfort as it had done in the curricle.

Aloud, he said, "Mrs. Miller, perhaps you will be able to help us after all."

Looking from Daphne to Dalton and then back again, Mr. Renfrew's daughter said finally, "I will do what I can, your grace. Your aunt was quite good to my father."

He smiled at that concession. Aunt Celeste had also been fond of Renfrew.

"Did Mr. Renfrew ever make mention of a letter or a note that my aunt asked him to hold for her?" he asked, hoping that the old man had done something to safeguard the clue to the location of the cipher before he lapsed fully into madness.

Mrs. Miller frowned, thinking. "I'm not quite sure, your grace. He gave me a great many items to put up in the attics, but I can have no notion of whether or not the missive your aunt entrusted to him is there. I did not go through them myself, you understand. And he keeps very few things in his bedchamber with him. Papa has always been a man with few needs for creature comforts."

"Mrs. Miller," Daphne began, and Dalton was almost afraid of what she would say. He was growing fonder of her by the minute, but he'd be blind not to notice that she had a way of setting up people's backs with her words. "Do you suppose we could search through his things?"

Already he could see that Mrs. Miller was opening her mouth to deny them, but then Daphne continued, "It's just that a man was murdered in Beauchamp House, and we think that something Lady Celeste gave your father could help us find what the killer was looking for."

At the mention of murder, the other lady blanched, bringing a hand up to her throat. "How awful," she said on a gasp. "Who would do such a thing? And why?"

"The man who was murdered was searching for something we think the killer has already found," Daphne said, cleverly dancing around the truth of just what it was that Sommersby's murderer had been looking for. "And Lady Celeste, being as brilliant as she was, left a clue with your father to the location of this artifact. If we find the artifact, we will, hopefully, find the killer."

"I do not pretend to understand all that you just said, Lady Daphne," Mrs. Miller said with a shake of her head. "But if I understand the gist of it, you need this paper in my father's things in order to apprehend a murderer. In which case, I will be happy to let you look through his things. Though in his right mind, poor Papa would have been most put out to know you were doing so. Still, he was fond of Lady Celeste, and I should think he would be willing to help find the man bold enough to commit murder in her home."

Dalton bit back a sigh of relief, thanking Mrs. Miller profusely for her cooperation.

As she led them upstairs to the third floor, where the attics were located, he said under his breath to Daphne, who walked beside him, "Well done, my dear. You knew exactly what to say."

Her pleased smile told him that he, in turn, had known just what to say to her.

"I spoke from the heart," she said, "just as Ivy told me to do when trying to persuade someone. I never guessed that it would actually work." She sounded both surprised and pleased at her discovery.

They reached the door leading into the attic then. Handing a lit lamp to Dalton, then turning a large key in the antiquated lock, Mrs. Miller opened the door into the storage area. "I'll leave you to it, then," she said with a brisk nod. "Papa's things are just to the left, near the chimney. I'll send up a maid in an hour or so to see if you need any other help."

"Thank you, Mrs. Miller," Daphne told her with a smile that lit up her entire face. For a moment, Dalton was stunned by her beauty.

"I am happy to help, my dear," said the other woman, with a smile. "I hope you find what you're looking for."

When she was gone, Dalton turned to see Daphne staring after her.

"What is it?" he asked, concerned.

"It's nothing," she said with a slight shake of her head. "It's just that I usually do not get on with people so well. It felt . . ."

"Nice?" he asked with a grin.

"Yes," she said. "Nice." Which sounded like the most wonderful feeling in the world when she said it just so.

Then her eyes cleared and she turned to indicate that he should lead the way.

No fool, Dalton followed her orders, and lifting the lamp to shed light on their path, he stepped into the musty attic room.

Unfortunately for Daphne and the duke, Mr. Renfrew had been a man who did not like to throw things away. So the number of crates and trunks they were forced to wade through was more than they had at first thought.

Mixed in amongst a few decades worth of *The Farmers Journal*, Daphne found stacks of letters exchanged between the steward and friends who appeared to be fellow stewards with interests in farming. Not to mention all the correspondence between the man and his eleven (Daphne counted) siblings and four children.

"For a man who didn't speak much," Dalton remarked wryly, as he removed another stack of letters from the trunk he was examining, "Renfrew had much to say when he put pen to paper. I don't know how he found time to work Aunt Celeste's farmland given the number of letters he wrote."

Daphne had wondered the same thing.

She also felt a pang of sympathy for the old man, who must have craved interaction with his peers if he was willing to put so much effort into writing them. Since she'd spent her whole life feeling as if she didn't quite fit in, not only because of her intellectual pursuits, but also because of her odd nature, she could relate. She wondered, suddenly, if when she was gone someone would find her own saved letters from her mathematician colleagues equally as pathetic.

Aloud she said, "I should think if your aunt had found fault with his work she would have done something about it."

She glanced over at him and saw that in his concentration on the task at hand, he'd disarranged his slightly overlong hair so that a golden lock of it fell onto his brow. He really was more handsome than a man should be allowed to be. What with his wide shoulders, trim waist, and face that might have been a Greek statue come to life, he was really more than she could have ever conjured from her imagination.

He must have felt her scrutiny then, because he looked up with a question in his eyes. "What is it? Did you find something?"

Blushing at having been caught staring, she shook her head. "No, I was just wondering if you had," she lied.

With a wry smile, he lifted a small painting and handed it to her. "Does this answer your question?"

She gazed down at the artist's rendering of what looked to be an exaggeratedly large ox. She knew it was an ox—for she'd never actually seen such a thing in her whole life— because affixed to the bottom of the simple frame was a brass plate that read "Beauchamp House Ox—Live weight 464 stone."

"Good heavens," Daphne said, aghast. "It must have been enormous!"

"Indeed." Dalton rubbed a hand over the back of his neck. "I cannot seem to have ever spoken to Mr. Renfrew about the cattle raised on the farms at Beauchamp House, but clearly there were some prize winners amongst them. My aunt certainly never spoke of it."

"It must have meant something to Mr. Renfrew," Daphne said handing the painting back to him, feeling a small jolt of electricity as their hands brushed. She couldn't help but be aware of their enforced proximity in the attic. In the curricle, they could talk, but he was forced to keep his attention on the road so they could do little more than hold hands. But here, alone, she couldn't help but imagine the possibilities. "For him to have kept the painting, I mean."

"Oh, as opposed to the rest of his things, which he threw away?" Dalton gave her a sardonic look, and she laughed. Was she mistaking the light in his eyes for something it was not, she wondered as they shared a look? "Well, when you put it that way." She hoped her voice didn't sound as flustered as she felt. She couldn't remember ever feeling so nervous around a man. Leaning back on his haunches, Dalton sighed as he surveyed the piles of detritus around them. "I don't know if we're ever going to find this letter my aunt gave into his care. Not unless we spend the next month or so rooting around through agricultural artifacts and prize cow paintings."

Moving from her kneeling position to sit on the trunk next to where he crouched, Daphne said, "Perhaps we're not being methodical enough about our search. So far, we've gone through most of Mr. Renfrew's correspondence and found nothing. But what if we look for items that are particular to his work for your aunt?"

"I thought that's what this was?" Dalton gestured to the stack of journals and prizes.

"If he discarded so few of his things," Daphne said, "then he must have also held onto his correspondence with your aunt, including records of payment, and so forth. But I've seen nothing like that thus far. Have you?"

"No," he said with a nod of approval. "I have not. Well done, Daphne."

"Don't congratulate me yet," she said, though she felt a burst of pride at his praise. Which was silly given that she'd always been a step ahead of most people she knew. But there was something about being lauded by Dalton that felt different. It mattered. And fed her soul in a way she hadn't even realized she needed. "It's simple logic. But at least we can surmise that it must be preserved somewhere."

"You're just being modest," he said. Getting to his feet, he stretched a little, and Daphne couldn't help but admire the way his muscles moved beneath his clothes.

Tearing her gaze away, she stood, too, and looked round

the room for likely hiding places for documents. Her gaze lit on a crate against the wall and she moved toward it. "I believe you're the first person ever to call me modest," she said over her shoulder as she attempted to remove the crate's lid.

"Oh, please,' Dalton said with a wave of his hand. "You can be quite modest. It's just that you're so busy trying to prove yourself to most people that you don't give anyone the chance to see your prowess for themselves."

That stopped her in the process of lifting out a stack of books.

She'd never thought of it that way, but he was right. She did spend much of her life trying to prove herself to people.

"I suppose I don't feel the need to do that with you," she said, feeling suddenly shy. This extended period of proximity to him was wreaking havoc on her usual sense of aplomb.

When he touched her hand, she jumped a little, startled at the touch. She hadn't heard him approach.

"I'm glad," he said softly. "I want you to be comfortable with me. To be yourself."

And then he moved back to the trunk beside her, which he'd apparently decided needed his attention, and left her to her thoughts.

Taking a deep breath, she looked down and noticed that the books she had before her were finely bound in leather. Far more expensive than even a prosperous steward would be able to afford. Flipping open the first one, she saw an inscription on the fly leaf. "To Mr. Renfrew, Christmas 1818." Beneath it, was the signature she'd come to know so well, that of Lady Celeste Beauchamp.

Turning the book over, she saw that it was a title on cattle breeding.

Not wanting to raise Dalton's hopes, she searched each of the books from the crate, which all seemed to be Christmas gifts from Lady Celeste to her steward. And it wasn't until she reached the one at the bottom of the stack that she found what she was looking for.

Tucked neatly into the middle of a bound volume of *The Sussex Herd Book,* she found a wax-sealed note.

She must have gasped, though she had no awareness of it.

Dalton was by her side in an instant, kneeling beside her before the crate, staring down in the lamplight at the page in her hand.

"I knew you'd find it," he said with a grin. "Clever girl."

"I feel awkward opening it," she admitted, not meeting his gaze. "What if it isn't what we think it is?"

"Mrs. Miller has given us permission to go through his things with the expectation that we would find the note," Dalton said. "And in his present state, I doubt Mr. Renfrew will object."

With a nod, Daphne slid her finger beneath the upper fold of the page and broke the seal.

Chapter 11

Maitland had begun to worry that they'd traveled to Bexhill for nothing when Daphne hit on the idea to look for things associated with his aunt. His praise for her idea had not been empty flattery.

She was clever, and if he'd been forced to perform this hunt on his own, he likely would have given up in frustration long ago.

And there was no denying that it was quite pleasant to spend so much time in the company of a beautiful lady who looked at him when she thought he couldn't see her as if he were some sort of Adonis. He'd been admired by women before, and was under no illusions about the fact that he was handsome, but there was something particularly gratifying to know that Daphne—who was the most intelligent woman he'd ever known, aside from his late aunt—thought him attractive.

Kneeling there beside her, it was difficult to keep his mind on the matter at hand, especially when he could feel the warmth of her while the lemon verbena on her skin seduced his senses. Forcing himself to focus, he watched as she broke the seal and read aloud the message on the folded page.

Huzzah for you
You've found this clue
And deserve your due reward.
So leave these cattle,
It's off to Battle
And Themis' shining sword.
Secreted there
You'll find a pair
Who'll my next note reveal.
Forget thee not
This puzzled knot
Romance's treasure doth conceal.

"I never knew my aunt had such a knack for penning such awful verse," Maitland said when Daphne finished. "I mean, sincerely, this is terrible."

"I should imagine it's difficult to write lines that rhyme as well as convey the message she wished to hide there," Daphne said, with what sounded like a bit of defensiveness for his aunt.

"Aside from congratulating us for finding this clue," he said taking the page from her to read it again, "what is this message she's trying to convey to us?"

Daphne examined the words, her head close to his as she read.

"Well, discounting the congratulatory note," she said, pointing to the words, "the first part is this bit about 'Battle' and 'Themis' shining sword.'"

"'Battle' is capitalized," Dalton said, "so perhaps she's referring not to an actual battle, but the town of Battle, since it's so near to Beauchamp House."

"I agree," Daphne said. "She showed in her note to me that capitalization denotes something she wishes to call attention to, and in this case I cannot think of an anagram of Battle

that would make any sense. And then moving on to Themis'
shining sword, I'm afraid I'll need to ask Ivy. It looks like
a classical reference, but my knowledge in that area is sadly
lacking."

"Huzzah, indeed," Dalton said with a grin. "Finally, an
area in which I know something that you do not!"

Daphne rolled her eyes, but he chose not to notice. "Themis," he explained to her with what he considered to be great
dignity, "was a Hellenic goddess, who was said to represent
the divine rightness of law."

He grinned at her. "I knew those years at Oxford would
be useful to me one day."

"Congratulations," Daphne said, shaking her head at his
foolishness. "You must be so proud."

He made a show of preening for a moment before she
turned the subject back to the matter at hand. "So your aunt
must in these two lines be telling us that we should go to Battle to see someone related to justice. A solicitor? A barris-
ter? Perhaps some other sort of legal person?"

"If I recall correctly," he said, serious once more. "Aunt
employed the services of a solicitor in Battle. I can't remember the man's name, but I feel sure Greaves will know."

"But she says 'a pair,'" Daphne reminded him. "Could
she have used a pair of solicitors? Or perhaps she means we
should see more than one person there?"

"I'm afraid my powers of recall do not extend that far," he
said with a frown. "We'll ask Greaves, and then perhaps if
he has nothing to add, we can simply travel to Battle and see
what we find there."

She nodded, looking down at the page again. As if the
answer would materialize there.

Unable to resist, Maitland moved closer, taking the opportunity to rest his chin on her shoulder to look down at the
note with her. It had been damned difficult to keep his hands

to himself the whole afternoon. Especially given the way Daphne had of looking at him when she thought he wasn't looking.

"And what of 'Romance's treasure'?" he asked, feeling a tremor run through her at his voice in her ear.

"As in the letter she wrote to me on my inheritance," she said, her voice betraying with a slight tremor that she was not as unaffected by his closeness as she seemed, "R-r-romance is an anagram of Cameron."

As she spoke, he turned and took the lobe of her ear between his teeth. Rather than tell him to keep away, as he half-feared she would, Daphne instead let out a little exhale of want, and turned her head so that he could have more access to her neck.

He would have liked to shout with triumph but settled for smiling to himself as he did as she had indicated she would like, and kissed the spot behind her ear and then worked his way down toward the hollow of her collarbone.

Still, trying to keep them somewhat on topic, she continued, "And . . . t-treasure, is self-explanatory, I sh-should think."

"You're a treasure, Lady Daphne Forsyth," he whispered as she gave up any attempt at ignoring him and slid up a hand to run her fingers through his hair.

He'd just moved to fit himself against her arched back, and taken her breast—still covered by the layers of clothing she wore—in his hand, when the sound of loud footsteps coming up the stairs startled them both.

When Mrs. Miller stepped into the room, there were three feet between them as they each made themself busy putting various items from Renfrew's lifetime of hoarding back into the crates and trunks from whence they came.

"I thought I should check in on the both of you," the lady of the house said cheerfully, clearly unaware of the scene of incipient debauchery she'd just interrupted. "It's been quiet, but I supposed if you found something you'd have come down by now."

"In fact, Mrs. Miller," said Maitland, closing the trunk he'd just pretended to work in, "we just moments ago found the letter we were looking for."

Daphne remained silent as she placed the books given as Christmas gifts to the steward back into the crate.

"I had my doubts, your grace," Mrs. Miller said with a shake of her head. "But I might have known that between you, you'd find something. I don't suppose you could let me see it?" Curiosity shone in her eyes, and he wondered if she knew more about their reasons for coming here than she revealed.

"I'm afraid that won't be possible, Mrs. Miller," Daphne said, rising from the floor and shaking out her skirts as she stood. "The letter involves a matter of the highest important to the government."

At the mention of the government, the farmer's wife's eyes widened. "Oh, I had no idea! To think that my father had something like that for all these years."

Not wanting the woman to be fearful, Maitland assured her, "It isn't as dangerous as it sounds, dear lady. Though more than that I cannot say. And I would please ask that you keep this information to yourself. It is not something that we wish to be known abroad at this time." He flashed her his most winning smile, the one he used to inveigle biscuits from the cook at Beauchamp House.

"Oh yes, of course, your grace." Mrs. Miller blushed at his attention. "I will tell no one. Except my husband if that's all right. We don't keep secrets."

"Of course, of course," Maitland said, taking Daphne's arm as she moved to stand next to him. "An admirable habit, ma'am. Your husband is a lucky man."

He heard Daphne give a slight snort next to him, but when he looked over, she seemed serene enough.

"We really cannot thank you enough, Mrs. Miller," she said with what he saw was genuine effort on her part to make their gratitude known.

"Lady Celeste was good to my father, Lady Daphne," said the other woman. "I know he'd want me to show the same kindness to her nephew and her . . ." she seemed to search for a term to describe Daphne's relationship to Lady Celeste, and settled on "friend."

The note tucked into the pocket of the duke's coat, they followed their hostess back downstairs. And with a promise to come back at a later time in hopes that Mr. Renfrew would be well enough to receive them, they made their way back to the waiting curricle and were soon back on the road east.

They were nearly a third of the way back to Little Seaford by Daphne's calculation when she noticed the dark clouds gathering.

Most of that time had been spent attempting to decipher the meaning of that interlude in the Miller attic. And the rest of the time was taken up by self-recrimination at how quickly she'd become distracted from their reasons for traveling to Bexhill in the first place—namely to search for the cipher and Sommersby's killer. Surely someone as intelligent as she could manage to keep on task without turning into a blushing ninny.

If she felt every shift of his body on the curricle seat, and if the pleasant sandalwood and male scent of him distracted her from the task at hand, well, she would simply have to be stronger. And mindful of the purpose for this drive, she determined to keep her hands to herself throughout the rest of it.

A jolt of the carriage as it crossed a depression in the road, however, brought her attention to more immediate concerns. A glance at the sky ahead of them made her inhale sharply and in turn to process.

It was, in fact, growing quite dark with clouds.

"Dalton," she said, trying not to sound managing. He was after all, a very good driver and had seen them quite safely over the journey thus far. "Have you noticed that there appears to be a storm on the horizon?"

Her companion gave a slight snort of laughter. "Yes, Daphne dear, I see it."

She felt her face warm at the endearment.

"But what are we to do about it? I do not mind getting wet, of course. But we are in an open carriage. Even animals know to come in from the rain."

There, those were reasonable-enough questions. She had not lost all her wits because of a kiss. Or two.

"If it looks as if it will overtake us," he said mildly, "then we will stop in the next village. There is a perfectly respectable inn there where we can wait it out. There's no reason we shouldn't be able to get back on the road once it's passed."

As if he could read her thoughts, he added, "I do have a plan. I won't let you come to harm, you know."

Her stomach gave a little flip at that simple reassurance. Was it possible to trust that someone else would see to her comfort? It was both enticing and a bit terrifying to let him make the decisions.

Of course, there were any number of things that were entirely out of her hands. She was a lady, after all, and thus subject to the rule of her father in one way or other from her infancy. But her maneuver in which she forced him to allow her a tutor had proven to Lord Forsyth that she was no longer going to blindly follow him. So had the incident with Sommersby. After that it had become important that she be the one to make the decisions about her day-to-day life.

Could she trust Dalton to ensure her safety now? He had given her no reason to doubt him thus far. But her experience with men told her that they were sometimes inconsistent. Trust was such a leap, and she wasn't sure she could make the leap yet.

At least not with her heart.

With the curricle, and her safety from the storm, however, she was willing to take the risk.

The rain began just as they arrived in the stable yard of The Bo Peep.

An odd name for a coaching house, but at this moment Daphne only cared that they had tea and a warm blanket on hand. The wind had picked up on the road, and combined with the rain and the chill of early summer, she was shivering in her wet clothes.

Tossing the reins to a stable hand, with orders to give the horses extra oats and a good rubdown, Dalton leapt down and was at Daphne's side before she could manage the step. His mouth a solid line of concern, Dalton reached up for her and when he felt her chill, he cursed, then shrugged out of his greatcoat and placed it around her. She would have argued, but there was something about his manner that kept her silent.

Inside the inn, even their bedraggled state was not enough to disguise the fact that a very important personage had arrived. No sooner had they stepped inside, than the proprietor was before them.

"Milord, milady," the little man said with an unctuous manner, "welcome to The Bo Peep. How may we serve you?"

"A private parlor, a pot of tea, and perhaps a room where the lady may repair to dry her clothes," Dalton said without his usual sangfroid.

The innkeeper, however, seemed used to dealing with high-handed aristocrats. "I'm afraid we are filled almost to the rafters, milord. A local family is having a wedding, and we've got quite a few guests here."

Dalton frowned. "What do you have available, then?"

"Only one bedchamber, milord," said the man, "and it is not the sort of room I would normally offer to someone like yourself. But I'm afraid it's all we have."

Just then raucous laughter erupted from the taproom behind him. Clearly the wedding party was spending the storm enjoying whatever spirits the establishment had on hand.

As if to emphasize their situation, a crack of thunder sounded outside.

Without looking to Daphne for assent, Dalton nodded. "Very well, we'll take it. But I do wish for tea and some food to be brought up as soon as possible."

With a nod, the man led them toward the stairs, where they passed several gentlemen coming down.

One in particular seemed to pause as he saw Dalton.

"I say, is that you, Maitland? What on earth are you doing in this hellhole?"

The innkeeper seemed to stiffen at the description, but did not object, clearly having learned to let his guests have their way.

Rather than greet his friend with his customary warmth, however, Dalton paused long enough for Daphne to see him close his eyes in frustration. Then almost as if it hadn't crossed his visage at all, it was gone and replaced with a friendly grin. "Pinky," he said, nodding to the fellow before indicating to his companions that they should proceed.

But Pinky was not to be ignored. "I should have known I'd see you here, though. Your aunt's place is just over near Hastings, isn't it?" He gave a quick but speculative scan of Daphne. "I might have guessed you'd find the best bit of fluff around. Always did have a good eye, eh?"

Daphne's eyes widened at the insult. She had been subjected to those sorts of glances before, of course, but had never been spoken of so blatantly. And certainly never mistaken for a lightskirt. She opened her mouth to give this Pinky a set down, but was forestalled by Dalton.

"And you always did have a way of mistaking matters, Pinky, old thing," he said in a drawl that sounded as foreign on him as a French accent would have done. "May I introduce my bride? Darling this is Lord Pinkerton. We were at school together."

It was difficult to say who was more shocked by this pronouncement, Daphne or the gaping Pinky. The innkeeper looked surprised as well, but kept his mouth shut.

One glance at Dalton showed his eyes boring into hers, heavy with a message she was quite able to read.

"A pleasure," she said, extending her hand toward Pinky, who bowed low over it.

"The pleasure is mine, your grace," the fop said with a grin. He seemed not to be in the least embarrassed by his earlier assumption about her. "Leave it to Maitland to find such a diamond."

"I'm sure you'll understand if we get upstairs now, Pinky," Dalton said before Daphne could speak. "We were caught in the storm, and I do not wish her to catch a chill."

Not waiting for his friend to respond, Dalton indicated to the innkeeper that he should proceed, and they hurried after him.

Once they reached the door to what was, indeed, a most unimpressive chamber, the innkeeper looked abashed. "Your grace," he said, as if seeing just how bare the little room was, "I can ask one of the other guests to exchange rooms with you. I feel sure once they learn who it is that wishes to use the chamber . . ."

"This is adequate, Mr. . . ."

"Woodley, your grace. George Woodley, at your service." He bowed.

"A pleasure, Mr. Woodley." Dalton's easy manner seemed

to have returned with their removal from the crowded tap-room. "I should like some hot water brought up for my wife, as well as the tea and food. And if you have any clothes that she might change into, that would be appreciated. We were caught unawares in the storm and had not planned to stay over."

With a promise that he would find something, Woodley left them then, closing the door behind him.

Daphne, who had moved to stand before the fire as soon as they walked in, turned to see Dalton watching her.

His hair was almost brown thanks to the rain, though wisps of gold stood up in places. And his mouth was tight as he watched her.

"You have a remarkable habit of making pronouncements about our relationship, your grace," she said with some asperity. "I have found myself betrothed, then married to you in the space of a few days. Both times without my recollection of ever having consented to the match."

"Pinky is one of the worst gossips in the *ton*," he said, stepping forward to take her hands in his. Feeling their coldness, he gave a curse and began rubbing them between his own ungloved hands. "I might have attempted to pass you off as my mistress, but the likelihood of him remembering your face if you were to meet later is strong. He never forgets a face, and worse, he never passes up the opportunity to spread tales."

"Surely he is just as likely to realize once some time has passed that there has been no announcement in the papers." Daphne tried to keep her mind on the matter at hand but she was very cold. And his hands were quite warm.

He was silent for a spell, and was saved from reply by the arrival of both a maid and a footman, bringing clothes, a pot of tea, and hot water.

Once they were gone, Dalton turned back to Daphne, his

eyes never once wavering from her face. "There will be an announcement in the papers, Daphne. There's no help for it. We might have broken things off in front of your father without any sort of ramifications. But I'm afraid that this is one action that cannot be undone."

"But surely, we can simply tell Pinky what happened," she said, knowing as she said it that it was futile. She'd recognized Pinky from some card party or other in London. He was one of those men who traded on gossip for his own amusement as well as in exchange for invitations. There was no way he'd agree to keep quiet about finding the Duke of Maitland in such a compromising position.

"That wouldn't stop him from spreading gossip about it." Dalton sighed, and pulled her against him. "Your reputation would be in shreds."

As would his. Even so, marriage was not what she had foreseen for herself.

"I do not care overmuch for my reputation," she said softly. "I could withstand it."

But even as she said the words she doubted them. She thought of the women she'd seen in town. Who were spoken of in hushed tones, and dared not show their faces in public lest they set off a flurry of whispers. It wasn't as if she cared for the social rounds. But she'd always taken pride in the fact that despite her father's insistence she use her skills at the gaming tables, her personal reputation was flawless. She might be the daughter of a scoundrel, but she herself had escaped being marked with the same brand. Was she willing to sacrifice herself just to keep from marrying a man who had thus far proved to be the most trustworthy she'd ever met?

"But I won't let you," he said kissing her forehead. "There's nothing for it, Daphne. We must marry."

Chapter 12

Dalton waited. Watched as her every thought flashed through her eyes.

He had known, of course, that she saw their hasty betrothal for her father's sake as a temporary thing. A quickly erected levee to stop the flood of Lord Forsyth's demands from overwhelming to the point of destruction.

But his offer had been more sincere than he'd let on. Though he would not force her, he had intended to use every persuasive skill at his disposal to convince her that they should make a go of the match. Since she'd first approached him not long after they met with her scandalous proposal, followed by his rejection, Dalton had come to realize that he was unlikely to meet her equal should he live to be a hundred.

She was lovely, intelligent, determined, and, despite her appearance of arrogance, self-effacing when it came to those things she felt she did not excel at. She just so happened to recognize that she possessed some skills that far outshone the average person. It was perhaps not humble of her to declare the fact, but neither was it sensible for her to pretend to be less than she was.

In that, she reminded him of Aunt Celeste, who had also

known her worth and did not pretend to be a simpering ninny for the sake of other (mostly male) sensibilities.

He wondered as he stood there holding her, waiting for her to accept the inevitability of their match, if Celeste had had some hand in this. If she had engineered the lives of her nephews by choosing ladies as her heirs whom she suspected they would find appealing. Though he hadn't considered it before now, the idea held some appeal. It was comforting somehow to think that Celeste had known just what sort of women he and Kerr needed. That she was still here caring for them long after she was gone.

Even so, Daphne was hardly predictable. And whatever he might wish regarding her decision, he knew she was quite capable of digging in her heels when she wished it. The notion of having her reputation thoroughly ruined was not appealing, he could tell, but if the alternative was something she did not want, she would endure it.

Whether he was willing to endure it was another matter altogether. He had always prided himself on maintaining a spotless reputation—especially when compared to that of his father. He might admit to wanting Daphne for himself, but a part of him wished her to marry him because he did not want to be known as yet another ill-reputed Duke of Maitland. It was selfish perhaps, but he was honest enough to admit it should she ask.

He was about to do so when she raised her eyes to him, dark green in the dim light of the modest chamber. "Not long after we met," she said softly, "I asked you to take me to bed."

Dalton blinked. He had not been expecting her to speak of that just now.

Curious about where she was going with this, he said, "I remember." He had done nothing but remember that moment ever since he turned her down. Any other man would have leapt at the chance to hold such a beautiful woman in his arms. And in the wee hours of the night, for weeks afterward, he'd considered going back to her, to tell her he'd changed his mind.

"It wasn't for the reasons you think," she said, lowering her eyes again, as if she could not speak the words while meeting his gaze.

"It doesn't matter, now." He stroked a hand over her back in a soothing gesture. "We know each other better now. I need no explanations."

"But I wish to explain," she said, pressing on. "You see, I was still unable to get past that . . . incident with Sommersby. I couldn't stand the thought of being touched by any man. Even one I wished to be with."

At the mention of the other blackguard's name, Dalton wished, not for the first time, that he'd known Daphne at the time. He would have made quite sure Sommersby never approached her again.

"But I was drawn to you from the moment we met," she continued. "It was the first time I'd found someone appealing since the incident with Sommersby, you see, and I thought perhaps if I asked you to be with me in that way that it would erase the memory of him, make me whole again."

Dalton was overwhelmed. There were so many things he wanted to say at that moment. He wanted to tell her how flattered, and humbled, he was that she trusted him. To assure her that all men weren't like the bastard who tried to hurt her. To say he wished he'd known all this when she first approached him.

But sensing that she was the one who needed to speak now, he kept silent.

"I know that I shocked you," she said, smiling a little. "You were rather like a scandalized maiden aunt."

"In my defense," he said, feeling his ears turn pink, "it was the first time an unmarried lady had ever approached me with such an offer. You took me by surprise."

That gave her pause. "Does that mean that married ladies have approached you with similar offers?" She looked rather shocked, as if the notion had never occurred to her. For all that she pretended worldliness, she was still innocent about such matters, he surmised.

"We are not speaking about other ladies," Dalton said, deciding that they perhaps needed to make use of the lumpy settee behind them. He for one did not know if his knees would hold out for much more of this sort of talk.

Pulling her with him, he waited until they were seated, his arm holding her close to his side, before he said, "Go on."

In this position, she did not have to look into his eyes, which he thought she would prefer, given how difficult it was at times for her to endure eye contact. But once again, Daphne surprised him. Turning to face him, she lifted a hand to his face, as if she needed to see his eyes as she spoke. "I am asking you again, your grace. We may not have another opportunity like this, when we are away from the prying eyes of your sister and cousin and my friends."

He should have known she was leading up to this. But like before, he found himself caught off guard. If he did marry her, he could envision a lifetime of such surprises. And though he once would have said he longed for a life of calm and content, there was something about the idea of such a life with Daphne that appealed more than he could have imagined.

Taking her hand, he kissed her palm and moved it to rest on his heart, which was beating like mad with anticipation now. "That was not my intention in bringing you here, Daphne. I truly did just mean to wait out the storm for a bit before returning to Beauchamp House."

She smiled. "I know that. You are the most honorable man I have ever known aside from the elder Mr. Sommersby."

Knowing how much she admired her tutor, he felt humbled by the comparison.

"But, I need to know if this is something I can do—endure your touch, any man," she said, looking down again. "I need to know that I will be able to give you what you need if we do marry. Because if not, then I won't force you into a marriage with someone who is broken. Your title requires an heir—and more children to carry on the family name. It is an antiquated system, but I am well aware of how much it means to a man to know that his name will carry on."

Likely she knew this at her father's knee. He was not the sort who would refrain from chastising his daughter for not being born the son he wished for. Yet another reason to despise Forsyth. Especially since his own reputation was the probable reason he had not married again.

"It is true that my title does mean that I would like an heir," he said to her, knowing that he must choose his words carefully if he didn't wish to bungle things, "but I have a cousin, who is not a bad fellow, who will inherit if I should die without issue. He is more than capable of taking the reins of the dukedom. And even if that were not the case, I have given you my word. Honor dictates that even if it were not my choice—and I assure you it is—I would still be required to keep it."

"Such an honorable man," she said, without irony. "That is why I must make sure that I do not trap you."

"And what if I don't see it as a trap?" he asked, the possible consequences of her experiment's failure sending a jolt of fear through him. "What if I promise to marry you regardless of your ability to give me an heir. After all, there are any number of marriages that do not produce sons. Or produce no children at all. Why can we not leave it to fate to decide?"

"Because I need to know," she said firmly. "Either you make love to me here, now, or I must have your word that you will release me from this match."

He pulled away, needing to get away from her for a moment. To think without the nearness of her clouding his judgment.

"You must agree it's the only sensible way," she said, her tone brisk. Just as if she were trying to persuade him of some mathematical principle rather than a decision that could keep them apart forever. "If I am able to be a proper wife to you, then we will wed. If I am not, then we will agree to part ways."

"And what of finding the cipher?" he asked, knowing it was unfair, but grasping at the thing she wanted more than any other in an effort to persuade her. "What of finding Sommersby's killer?"

"Of course we will continue to search for both." She frowned, as if the notion they would no longer search for both was absurd.

At her expression, he couldn't help himself. He laughed. "Daphne, you are the most maddening woman!" He shook his head in amazement. Only she would consider a broken engagement as something to be brushed aside while they worked closely together to search for a murderer.

She didn't reply, only sat patiently watching him. Seeing that he would never be able to persuade her to change her mind, he sighed.

"Very well. We will perform this experiment as you call it. And if for whatever reason you are uncomfortable, we will stop."

Daphne beamed. "I knew you would see things my way. You are a reasonable man, after all."

But he wasn't finished. "However, I demand that you give me another chance to . . . er . . . convince you, if this attempt doesn't work."

He couldn't believe he was speaking about such a delicate matter as if it were some sort of laboratory exercise. Given the amount of pressure he now felt himself under, he was even beginning to doubt his ability to perform. Which had never been an issue for him in the past.

Perhaps sensing his hesitation, she stood and placed her hands on his chest. Leaning forward, she kissed him softly on the lips.

And that decided it. Unable to resist her any longer, he pulled her against him and kissed her back.

Daphne had known from the moment she met him that Maitland had the potential to hurt her. It had been there in his golden good looks and charming manner. In his easy way with everyone—so different from her own often fraught interactions with friends as well as foes.

Even so, she'd wanted him.

And all these months later, with a storm raging around their cozy room, she gave herself over to the need she'd felt deep within her that day.

His mouth was firm, but gentle, as she explored it with her own. He tasted of sin and salvation, and she gave herself over to the heady intoxication of knowing he'd let her take what she needed from him. She was the one who tested, tasted, pressed her tongue into his mouth. Led each step of their dance.

But he was no passive partner. Once she introduced something, he would reply in kind. A taste for a taste. A touch for a touch. A stroke for a stroke.

When she gave her hands license to thread through his hair, he caressed up the curve of her waist to cup her eager breast, straining against the confinement of her stays as he stroked a thumb over the peak. When she bit lightly at his lip, he took that as an invitation to suckle his way down her chin to that place near her collarbone that made her writhe against him.

Somehow he'd managed to lower the bodice of her gown and when his mouth met the sensitive skin of her bosom, she nearly wept at the way he teased the edge of her nipple. The deprivation stirred that place at her core, where she needed him.

She must have made some protest, for Dalton paused, and asked, a little breathless, "Yes?"

"Yes," she exhaled as he loosened the laces of her stays and put his mouth where she most desperately needed it, covering her straining peak with warm heat. "Yes."

And even as she gave herself up to the caresses there, she felt his other hand sliding up her stockinged calf to her knee, and when instinctively she moved to kneel, opening herself to him, he did not disappoint. The soft touch of his caress against that aching place combined with the deep pulls of his mouth almost sent her over the edge.

There was no need for him to ask her consent now, for she was all too eager for his touch. And when he stroked a finger into her, then followed it with two, she could not stop herself from rocking into his touch. She found his mouth so that they could mirror the motion of his hand with their tongues. Higher, higher she seemed to soar with every thrust of his hand, and when finally she went over, it was with a cry of elation as she closed her eyes against the bright burst of her release.

She was gone for no more than a moment and came back to feel his sweet kiss on her forehead as she sprawled against his chest.

"Are you well?" His voice was strained, and an experimental shift against him revealed the cause pressing against her still sensitive body.

"Yes," she said, moving against him.

But he caught her hips and stilled her. "We needn't go any farther," he said, even as he closed his eyes against his desire. "We can wait. I still wish to marry you, but if you aren't ready for the rest . . ." He left the words hanging in the air between them.

She considered the offer. She knew now that she would not flinch at his touch, and they could have a full marriage without the memory of what had happened with Sommersby between them.

But now they were almost there, and in the wake of what he'd just given her, she didn't want to wait. She wanted him to feel the same bliss she had.

And if truth be told, she wanted him, too. All of him.

Pulling away from him, and moving to stand, she saw a flicker of disappointment in his eyes before he quickly masked it with understanding.

He rose, and ran a hand over his mussed hair. "I'll just go check on the horses," he said.

He made to turn and leave, but she stopped him with a hand on his arm. "Stay," she said. And when he'd turned to look at her fully, she removed her gown and finished unlacing her stays, letting the boning fall to the floor until she was standing before him in nothing but her shift and stockings and boots.

The knock on the door forced a very foul word indeed from him.

"The food and clothes," he said closing his eyes in frustration. To his relief, it was mirrored in Daphne's face.

Unable to resist, he crossed the room and kissed her hard. "One minute."

It took only a brief exchange to send the innkeeper away, and when he turned back, he saw that she hadn't moved.

There was something so vulnerable and brave about her standing there, nearly naked, waiting. When he moved toward her, he stopped just far enough away to let her make the choice.

But he needn't have bothered.

"You're sure?" he asked as she stepped close to press herself against him. With a nod, and meeting his gaze with trembling courage, she began unwinding his cravat.

But once he realized she was serious, he pushed her hands away and led her to the bed and threw back the bedclothes. Quickly, he finished removing his cravat, and coats and boots, and when she was seated on the edge of the bed, made haste to remove her boots and stockings. Touching her tenderly every step of the way.

When he stood to pull his shirt over his head, she leaned back against the pillows to admire him.

His body was muscled without being bulky, and she loved the width of his shoulders, the way they tapered down to his waist.

Maitland caught her watching him, and his hands paused at the fall of his breeches. She glanced down to where that hard part of him strained against the placket. And suddenly this moment between them was more real than anything she'd ever known.

Swallowing her apprehension, she gave him a slight nod, and thinking to distract herself from the moment, she rose up and pulled her shift up and over her head.

When she emerged from the lawn fabric, he was kneeling on the bed beside her, and then they were skin to skin.

"I've heard there is some pain for the lady the first time," he said against her ear, even as he caressed over her naked skin. "I will try to be gentle, but I don't know if once I begin I'll be able to . . ."

She stopped his words with a kiss. "I trust you" was all she said. And then she gave herself up to the overwhelming surge of bliss that came from feeling his warmth against her from head to toe.

And when he kissed her now, there was no diffidence, no hesitation, only desire. She opened herself to his touch, and reveled in the primal sensation of his weight against her.

His hands, calloused from driving, were rough against her bare skin as they teased their way over her belly.

When he shifted to kiss his way from her neck to her breasts, then downward, she let him. Only when she felt his arms slide under her knees did she gasp in surprise. "What are you doing?" she asked, both breathless and puzzled.

Maitland looked up at her, every inch the decadent lord sprawled naked in her bed. But also patient. Tender.

"Will you trust me?" he asked, his eyes imploring. She sensed that he wanted this as much as he wanted it for her.

Since he was clearly the more experienced between them, and he hadn't yet broken her trust, she nodded.

Given free rein, he continued his movements, hooking his elbows beneath her knees and opening her wide to his gaze. She closed her eyes in embarrassment at the thought of him seeing her thus. But when she felt his warm breath on her mound, she gasped in a mixture of shock and sensation.

It was thoroughly wanton, but she was unable to stop herself from straining against him where he stroked his tongue against her, reigniting the flames his fingers had lit earlier. And when he sucked the peak, then teased his fingers over her molten core, it had her panting, begging, pleading with him to give her what she needed.

She almost wept when she felt him slide up over her, but just as quickly he placed his thumb where his mouth had been and propping himself over her on one arm, guided himself to that part of her that desperately needed to be filled.

With one strong thrust, he gave it to her.

Chapter 13

He'd tried to hold back. Tried to be gentle. He'd tried his damnedest to make sure she was as prepared as a woman can be for her first time.

But still that first thrust almost send Maitland over the edge.

He clenched his teeth against the need to pound himself into her, to let go of the desire he'd tried desperately to keep banked while tending to her needs. She was worth it, he knew, but dear God, he was desperate to let go.

"Yes?" he asked, echoing his earlier question to her, praying that her response would be affirmative. If he had to stop now, it might kill him.

He'd do it. He had to. But he would weep.

"Yes," she said, and whether consciously or not, her hot, sweet sheath clenched around him, and before she even finished the approving syllable he was lost.

Moving against her, struggling to keep his thrusts decorous—if such a thing were even possible—he felt beads of sweat roll down his back as he pressed into her. Again and again, then needing to be closer, he brought his arms beneath her knees again, this time pressing her wide so that there was not even a breath of space between them.

And all the while, Daphne, moved beneath him. If there

was pain, she gave no indication of it. Instead she writhed and bucked as much as she could in the position, and with each thrust he felt her clench around him.

He tried to hold out as long as he could, but after months of waiting and wanting, the feel of her tight body clasping him was too much for finesse. He sped up his thrusts, and when he stroked his thumb over her sensitive nub, she cried out, trembling beneath him as her crisis took her. Free to let go at last, he pounded into her three more times before he emptied himself within her in a shout of relief.

He came back to himself slowly, but fully aware that the soft body cushioning him was Daphne.

Daphne.

Reluctantly, he withdrew and eased onto his back beside her. "I'm sorry." Keeping her in the circle of his arms, unable to stop himself from touching her, he stroked a thumb across the soft skin of her shoulder. "I must have been heavy."

But she must not have minded, because she curled into his side, and stroked a hand over his chest, toying with the light dusting of hair there.

"Is it always like that?" she asked, her breath soft against his skin as she spoke.

He huffed out a laugh, still a bit breathless. "It most definitely is not." He thought back to his previous lovers, though the very act felt disloyal somehow. But he could never recall being so . . . drunk . . . with passion before. Certainly, he hadn't felt the sort of protectiveness he did for the woman in his arms.

What that said about his chivalry, he didn't like to think.

When he didn't elaborate, she went on, "Ivy seems to think she and Lord Kerr are quite good at it."

Dalton raised his eyelids and found her watching him. He wasn't sure he wished to think about his cousin and his wife together.

No, he was certain he didn't wish to think of it.

Though considering that he and Kerr were cousins, it stood to reason that . . .

"I think we are better," Daphne said, breaking into his thoughts. Then her words sank in.

"You're quite the competitive little thing, aren't you?" He met her mouth for a kiss.

She settled her head back down upon his shoulder. "I'm better than all the other ladies at mathematics of course, but I did think that because Ivy is married she would have surpassed the rest of us at lovemaking. Especially considering that her husband clearly has a great deal of exp—"

He stopped her mouth with a kiss. "Perhaps we shouldn't talk about such things, my dear. It could make things rather awkward for me the next time my cousin and I are left to our port after dinner if I'm thinking about him in bed with his wife."

And that statement reminded him of Beauchamp House and all the changes awaiting them as soon as they left the cocoon of this room and returned to their normal lives. He sighed into her hair.

Before she could continue with her speculation about Lord and Lady Kerr, he said, "When we return home, I'll set out for London to obtain a special license. It shouldn't take above a day or so if the weather holds."

She pulled back a little, eyes wide. "So soon? We still have to visit your aunt's solicitor in Hastings. And there is the matter of informing the magistrate of what we've found."

And just like that, the spell was broken, and they were thrust back into the everyday world.

He sat up against the pillows as she held the sheet to cover her nudity. She'd never been more beautiful.

"There's nothing to be done for it," he said, watching as she examined her hands, not meeting his eyes. "We can't risk

Pinky spreading word of seeing us here. The new vicar has been established at the church, so we can marry in a few days' time I should think."

He could tell that she didn't like the idea, though whether because it was sooner than she wished or because she didn't wish it at all he couldn't guess. Either way she would have to adapt. Because marry they would. On that matter, at least, he would not budge for one reason that was of the utmost importance.

"There might be a child, Daphne," he said. They could both endure ruined reputations if necessary, but he would not place that sort of burden on an innocent.

Her eyes widened, and instinctively she rested a hand on her softly curved belly. "I hadn't considered that," she admitted with troubled eyes.

He didn't like worrying her, but she was an intelligent woman. She deserved to know all of his reasons for wishing to marry her.

"Come," he said kissing her one last time before he began gathering his clothes from the floor, "we should have time to get back before dinner."

He pulled on his breeches and watched shamelessly as she followed suit, though the sheet covered her spectacular bottom as she bent to retrieve her chemise.

Pity, that.

Slipping into her stays, Daphne said thoughtfully, "If we had a child, it would very likely be quite intelligent. And beautiful."

"With my stunning good looks and your brain," he said with a grin, "how could it possibly be otherwise?"

As luck would have it, they were met at the entrance to Beauchamp House by Ivy, who took one look at their disheveled state and called for hot baths and tea for them both. And soon

Daphne found herself in her dressing room, soaking in a lavender-scented tub. Her maid fussed over her tangled hair and damp clothes and made sure that her robe was warmed by the fire before she wrapped herself in it.

Though she would have liked some time alone to consider what had happened with Dalton at the inn, she found her fellow bluestockings waiting for her in the seating area of her bedchamber.

"Here," said Sophia, handing her a cup of tea as she took the overstuffed chair they'd obviously left vacant for her. "Summer might be at hand, but these storms can be quite chilling. We don't wish you to catch your death."

"I am quite warm, thank you," Daphne said, though she took the proffered tea and drank. Dalton had done a thorough job of warding off any chill the rain had left her with. Though she was oddly reluctant to tell her friends that. Their response to her confession that she'd propositioned him before had been swift and scandalized.

"What did you learn?" Ivy asked, settling back with her own tea. For the barest moment, Daphne thought she was talking about that interlude with Dalton, and her eyes widened.

"Did you find the clue with Mr. Renfrew as you'd hoped?" Gemma clarified.

Relieved, Daphne nodded. "Yes, we did. It took a bit of doing because Mr. Renfrew is suffering from the effects of old age, but we did manage after a bit."

She explained how the former steward's daughter had let them search the man's belongings until they found the clue from Lady Celeste. Dalton had the actual note, but she'd memorized it and recited it for the other ladies now.

"So you believe she means the next clue is with her solicitor in Battle?" Ivy asked, after they'd discussed the likely interpretation of "Themis' shining sword." "I can't help but agree. Themis is often used to symbolize justice and the law. Well done, both of you."

Daphne blushed a little at the praise. "It was mostly Dalt . . . um, the duke, who guessed the meaning. As you know my classical knowledge is not what yours is."

"Dalton, is it?" Sophia asked with a sly smile. "Do I take it the two of you grew a bit closer on your journey?"

"Hush, Sophia," her sister chided. "They are betrothed— even if it's only a temporary ruse. It's hardly shocking that she would use his Christian name."

"About that," Ivy said with an inquisitive look. "Was I mistaken or did Maitland not eschew the hot bath I had brought up for him and call for his horse to be saddled and his valet to pack a bag? Surely he isn't going to Battle on his own?"

Daphne didn't bother trying to dissemble. "I believe he is traveling to London for a special license."

Silence fell on the usually chatty group.

"It must have been a very eventful journey, indeed," Sophia said with a speaking look at her sister for chiding her earlier.

"I must say," Gemma said with a little shake of her head, "if my sister and I do not wish to become betrothed, we must of necessity avoid going out in a gentleman's company when a storm is likely."

She referred, Daphne knew, to Ivy's betrothal to Lord Kerr following their being caught out during a rainstorm. Daphne wondered if her friend and her husband had spent their rainstorm in a similar activity. Curious.

Ivy pursed her lips, but ignored them. Instead, she turned to Daphne and touched her lightly on the arm. "Is all well? Are you agreeable to the match? Because if not, I can speak to Kerr and have him put his cousin off for a bit."

But despite her reluctance when Dalton had mention a special license earlier, she was determined to go through with the marriage. Her own reputation might not be of primary importance to her, but she knew that Maitland took his gentlemanly honor quite seriously.

She may not have considered marriage to be something she wanted before, but if she was being honest with herself, she wasn't exactly dreading marriage to the duke. If anything, she was rather looking forward to it. She cared nothing for his title or wealth. But the fact that he was able to rouse fire in her with barely a look was certainly an enticement.

If what they shared in bed was as unusual as all that, she was reluctant to give it up for a life of lonely solitude. That only a few months ago she'd looked forward to such a life was an irony she found amusing.

And she had come, in the past weeks, to value his reliability and even temper. If he'd been a different sort of man, one like her father, for instance, she could have ignored the other benefits. But his passion coupled with his personality made the match that much more appealing.

Then there was the matter of a possible child. Something far too monumental for her to consider as anything more than an abstraction now. Though the very idea made her chest tighten with emotion she dared not name.

So, in answer to Ivy's question, she didn't need to be rescued.

"There is no need for anything like that," she told Lady Kerr with a shake of her head. "We are agreed upon the matter. Indeed, I am sanguine."

"Did you . . . ?" Gemma looked troubled. "That is to say, did you tell him about what Mr. Sommersby did to you?"

At the mention of Sommersby, Daphne was surprised to find that she no longer felt the same sort of dread on hearing his name as before. Had Dalton managed to exorcise the demon of the other man's assault once and for all?

"He knows," she said with a small nod. "And it is likely a

very good thing that Sommersby was dead before he learned of it."

"Speaking of Sommersby's death," Ivy said, "I believe the magistrate wished to speak to you again this afternoon. He called while you were both still gone. He would not tell Quill why he'd called however. Though I suppose that has more to do with their history than anything else."

Quill had had a liaison with the other man's wife in his salad days.

"Perhaps tomorrow we can call upon him," Daphne said, thinking that since Maitland would be away, and it felt somehow disloyal to travel to Battle without him, this would be a way for her to continue their investigation without breaking his trust. "He very likely will not be able to shed any light on the search for the cipher, but he should be aware that the killer likely has another clue."

From downstairs, the dinner gong sounded, and Ivy, Sophia, and Gemma rose.

"I believe I'll have a tray in my room," Daphne said, suddenly feeling exhausted from the events of the day. And if she were honest, dinner without Maitland there to entertain her with amusing stories and silly teases sounded dreadfully dull.

Hanging back from the others, Ivy waited until the Hastings sisters were gone before saying in a low voice, "If you have any questions, Daphne, or would like to know if anything is . . . irregular . . ."

Daphne's brows drew together. It took her a moment to catch the other lady's meaning. And when she did, she felt her whole face turn red.

"Oh, no!" she said with a shake of her head. "There is nothing . . . that is to say I do not have any . . ."

Ivy nodded. "I thought I'd offer my counsel, nonetheless. It can be unsettling at first, but it can be quite enjoyable if you let it."

"I'm not sure I understand you," Daphne said with a frown. Her experience with Dalton had been more than simply enjoyable. "It was . . . magnificent."

At her pronouncement, Ivy grinned. "I am relieved to hear it. I don't mind telling you Kerr was brilliant that first time, too, but my mama refused to hear it. I thought perhaps my experience was singular. And feared yours would prove to be more as she described."

Daphne shrugged. "Perhaps it is a generational difference?"

Ivy nodded. "I confess I don't like to think of it too closely since it means thinking about my parents together like that." She gave a delicate shudder.

Having never met Ivy's parents, Daphne couldn't say one way or the other.

"In any event," Ivy continued, "I am glad to hear you are content with that aspect of the relationship. But I do hope you'll come to me if that should change. I like to think we ladies should stick together in such matters, though there seems to be a societal taboo about talking openly about them."

"I will keep that in mind," Daphne said. "Though I am perhaps not the one who needs to be encouraged to strive for more candor."

"And on that note," Ivy said with a laugh, "I'll be off."

When she was gone, Daphne crawled into her bed, and as soon as she closed her eyes she was back in the little room at The Bo Peep.

She fell asleep remembering just how safe she'd felt in Dalton's arms.

Chapter 14

Maitland made good time to London, and though it meant rousing the sleeping servants, he decided to stay the rest of the night at his London house rather than going to a hotel. His mother slept soundly, so he didn't see her until the next morning when he stepped into the breakfast room and found her eating her customary toast and tea.

"Maitland," she said with surprise as he stepped over to kiss her cheek. "I wasn't expecting you. Though I suppose I should have guessed given the amount of food on the sideboard."

His mother disliked excess, which made her a most unlikely duchess. Especially given his late father's love of it.

He filled a plate for himself and sat down near her. "I arrived quite late," he told his mother. "And didn't wish to wake you."

Her blond brows rose in question. "Was there some reason for you to ride in haste?" He watched as she considered the matter. Before he could speak, she said, "There's nothing amiss with Serena or Jeremy is there?"

"No," he assured her, feeling like a cad for letting her worry. In truth, he'd been trying to come up with a way to explain his actual reason for coming to town, but it hadn't occurred to him that she'd interpret his silence as dire. "Both Serena and Jem were well when I left them, I assure you."

She relaxed at his words. "I don't believe I'll ever stop worrying about her after what that monster Fanning did to her," she said with a scowl. "Horrid man. Your father was a fool to let her marry him."

Not wishing to rehash the circumstances of his sister's marriage, Maitland was silent, and took a bite of eggs.

When he looked up he found the duchess watching him. "Why did you come back in such a hurry?" she asked again, scanning his face for an answer. "Has another of Celeste's bluestockings got herself into trouble? I hope she knows better than to try to trap you into marriage!"

The duchess had been rather jealous of her children's close relationship with her sister, and the news that one of them had actually married Quill, her nephew, in haste had only served to prove that Celeste's choice of heirs had been faulty.

At her choice of words, Dalton winced. He had imagined this conversation in a more comfortable setting than at the breakfast table while she interrogated him like a cardinal of the Spanish Inquisition.

"I would hardly call Kerr's happy marriage a trap, Mama," he said with a frown. "Indeed, Quill and Ivy are quite blissful, which you would know if you had accepted their invitation to come for a visit at Beauchamp House."

"Oh, piffle," the duchess said with a wave of her hand. "I have no wish to travel to the seaside unless it's Brighton. And you may make all the assurances you like about the happiness of your cousin's marriage, but your Aunt Estelle is convinced that that hussy lured him into a trap. A mother knows these things, Maitland."

Estelle was Lord Kerr's mother, the dowager Lady Kerr, and incidentally the sister of Celeste and the Duchess of Maitland.

Pushing aside his plate, Dalton took a fortifying gulp of tea before saying, "I wish you would not speak of Ivy in that manner, Mama. She is a lovely lady and has made Quill very happy, I assure you."

At her grunt of disbelief, he sighed before pressing on. "As it happens, my reason for coming to town is somewhat tangentially related to Quill's recent marriage. I have come to procure a special license, in fact. For myself and Lady Daphne Forsyth, another of Aunt Celeste's heiresses."

The Duchess of Maitland's jaw dropped. "What? I was only engaging in a bit of hyperbole when I asked if you'd been trapped into marriage. Maitland, please tell me this is some jest on your part!"

"I'm delighted to say it is not," he said firmly. "Lady Daphne and I will be married as soon as I return to Beauchamp House." Despite his fervent wish that she would reject the invitation, he added, "I hope you will return with me to celebrate the nuptials."

"I most certainly will not!" she said, her eyes wide and her back ramrod straight. "Because you will not be marrying the daughter of that . . . that rapscallion Lord Forsyth. Do you know who the man is?"

"He is currently in Little Nodding, so yes, I do," Dalton said through clenched teeth, not wanting to admit that her assessment of Daphne's father was not far off his own. "And it makes no difference to me who her father is. I am marrying *her,* not the earl."

"It is a *mésalliance* of gigantic proportions," the duchess said, her voice rising with every syllable. "Even worse than your cousin's marriage to that scholar's daughter. At least her father is respected and conducts himself with dignity. The Earl of Forsyth is a drunkard and a gamester. And he has made a practice of carting the chit all over town to play cards at his behest. Like some sort of gambling pander."

At her slander of Daphne, Maitland stood, glaring down at his mother. "Hear me well, Mama," he said, his voice barely controlled in his anger. "You will speak that way again about Lady Daphne Forsyth at the risk of damaging our relationship forever. She is not her father, and she is not to blame for his bad acts. No more than Serena or I are to blame for our father's."

At the mention of the late duke, his mother flinched.

"Yes," he said with a feral smile, "remembering now, are we, that the previous Duke of Maitland was also a rapscallion?"

"Maitland," she said, looking contrite, but unbowed, "I never meant to say that Lady Daphne was—"

He cut her off with a gesture. "I do not wish to hear you say it again. I am quite serious about the consequences should you defy me on this matter, Mama. I am the head of this household, and I have chosen my bride. If she does not please you, then that is lamentable, but it is my choice to make."

"But her reputation," the duchess said with a shake of her head. "Your father's reputation makes it doubly necessary for you to behave like . . ."

"Like a gentleman?" he asked with a raised brow. "That is precisely what I am doing. I have compromised her, Mama. And my own scruples mean that I must marry her. But aside from that, I wish to marry her. She is quite the most intelligent person I have ever had the pleasure to know. And the loveliest."

At the word "compromise" the duchess raised a hand to her chest in horror. "Oh Maitland, did you not heed my warnings about the schemes young ladies will try on an eligible nobleman? How could you have let this happen?"

Seeing that she found it impossible to believe that he could have been the one to do the compromising, Maitland sighed.

Pinching the bridge of his nose, he said, "Mama, I will not go into the details with you, but rest assured that every step of the way, I was the one at fault. Not Lady Daphne."

His words must have given her pause, because she shut her mouth on whatever it was she was about to say, and nodded.

With a sigh of relief, he continued. "Now, I hope that you will write a cordial letter to Lady Daphne welcoming her to the family if you still refuse to return to Beauchamp House with me for the wedding."

He thought for a moment that she would change her mind—something he very much did not want to happen—but fortunately, she said with a shake of her head, "I truly cannot leave town at the moment, my dear. Though I hope you will bring her to meet me as soon as you think you are able. I will oversee her introduction at court. And doubtless she will need a new wardrobe."

Though he was a grown man capable of making his own decisions, he would not put it past his mother to attempt some sort of intervention to keep the wedding from happening.

"I have little doubt that Daphne will welcome your assistance," he lied. Daphne would very likely chafe under his mother's guidance, but that was a bridge he'd cross when he came to it. "Now, I would like to discuss this further"—another lie—"but I must go find the bishop so that I can get back to the coast."

"I am sorry I reacted so badly, my dear," she said with a sad smile. "I suppose I do not only worry about your sister. It is quite hard to accept that my children are all grown up now and able to take care of themselves."

He looked at her, noticed the threads of silver in her blond hair that was so like his own. Her marriage to his father had not been a happy one. And she considered Serena's disaster of a marriage as something she should have been able to prevent. It was little wonder she greeted with shock and dismay the news that he was to be married by special license to someone she knew only by reputation.

"I know," he told her, bending to kiss her on the head. "But we are quite grown. Though it doesn't mean we don't need your affection and guidance."

She nodded and surreptitiously dabbed at her eyes with a lace-edged handkerchief.

When he left to find the bishop, she was bent over her escritoire, penning a letter to Daphne.

He could only hope it did not include references to Lord Forsyth.

When it came to speaking frankly, his mother and Daphne had that trait in common.

"I'll inquire as to whether the Squire is available to receive visitors," said the Northman's butler with a scowl.

Daphne and Ivy had risen early and set out after breakfast for the magistrate's house. After yesterday's storms, the sky above them was clear and blue, and they decided to walk rather than take the carriage.

"Perhaps I wasn't the best person to accompany you," Ivy said as they watched the dour man leave. "I still don't think I've been forgiven for the scene at their dinner party."

Ivy and Mrs. Northman had argued over something having to do with Lord Kerr, Daphne recalled. And the elder lady had been quite angry about the fact that Lord Kerr had become engaged to Ivy—though from Daphne's point of view, the woman had no right since she was already married herself.

"We are not here to see the lady of the house," Daphne reminded her. "And even if we were she would be obliged to be polite to me since I outrank her rather significantly." Daphne found that reminding unpleasant people of her due as an earl's daughter sometimes led to an improvement in their attitude.

Ivy hissed a laugh. "You should not say that," she said in a low voice, shaking her head. "And yet, I would very much like to see you tell Mrs. Northman that to her face."

"Where else would I tell it to?" Daphne asked, puzzled. Why did people insist upon speaking words that made no sense? It was most frustrating.

Then the butler returned to inform them that the magistrate would see them, and soon Daphne and Ivy found themselves seated before a very large desk in the Squire's study.

"I was quite displeased to find you gone from home yesterday, Lady Daphne," he said once they were settled. "I needed to ask you some questions about Sommersby's death, and you were not there."

"Yes," Daphne said, puzzled. "Because, as you say, I was gone from home."

"There is no need to be flippant, Lady Daphne," he said, his heavy brow furrowed. "This is a serious business. A man was killed in your home, and it seems very likely it was related to an artifact you yourself are searching for."

If he was going to investigate the matter, Daphne thought petulantly, then he should use the proper terms. "As it happens I am searching for a coded message, a cipher, if you will. Not an artifact. Though it is around seventy years old so it is not precisely of current origin. A cipher is a . . ."

Ivy touched Daphne on the arm, startling her into pausing in her explanation. Ivy was quite good at placating men when necessary, Daphne thought with a touch of jealousy,

"I think what my friend is trying to say, Mr. Northman," Ivy said with a sweet smile, "is that she is very sorry for not being available when you wished to speak to her. But she has some news that might help in your investigation."

Daphne scowled. That was not what she had meant to say at all, but her friend's placating tone must have worked, for the Squire sat up straighter.

"What is this news? I've had my men search high and low for this other man whom you and the duke say shot at you," he said with frustration, "but if he is still here, he's hidden himself well."

Ignoring the magistrate's complaint, Daphne quickly outlined how they'd found the note from Lady Celeste behind the painting and how it had led them to visit Mr. Renfrew in Bexhill.

"Why in the blazes would Lady Celeste hide all of these bits of verse across the county?" the Squire asked with a moue of distaste. "If you ask me it's a havey-cavey business. She should have just left the coded message with her will and had her solicitor hand it over when you inherited. Then there would have been no need for Sommersby to search high and low for it, breaking into other people's homes, and what not."

Though it felt disloyal to her benefactress, Daphne tended to agree with the man. Except for one particular point. "At the time, secrecy about the location was quite necessary because the gold was intended for treasonous purposes," she said, trying to be polite. But really, was the man so foolish that he didn't know as much?

"And," Ivy added, with a speaking look her friend, "Lady Celeste enjoyed creating puzzles. She thought she was leaving a game for one of her heirs to solve. I'm sure she had no notion that Mr. Sommersby would come to harm in the course of searching for it."

"Hmph." The Squire didn't argue, but nor did he seem convinced. "So you intend to follow these clues until you locate the cipher?" He folded his arms across his chest, the picture of skepticism.

"I do, indeed, sir." Daphne raised her chin a bit. "And I will solve it, and find the gold."

"And what of the murderer? He has the original version of the cipher. What if he beats you to the treasure?"

Daphne couldn't stop herself. She laughed.

"I don't see anything amusing about this matter, Lady Daphne." The Squire leaned forward. "A man is dead."

"I am well aware of that fact, Mr. Northman," she said before Ivy could intervene. "But I find it very hard to believe that the murderer has my mathematical and ciphering abilities. If he is able to unravel the message, then I shall be very, very surprised."

The magistrate just stared at her for a moment. Daphne was used to this reaction to her pronouncements about her abilities, and did not flinch.

"I'll say this for you, my lady," the man said with a shake of his head. "You've got bottle. I only hope you've got someone looking after you while you're haring about the countryside searching for Lady Celeste's bits of paper."

"I am perfectly capable of—" Daphne began, but was interrupted by Ivy, who rose and locked arms with her.

"Thank you so much for your time, Squire Northman," Ivy said inclining her head. "We will keep you informed of our progress. As we hope you will do with your own progress in finding Mr. Sommersby's killer."

Once they were in the hall, Ivy whispered, "I thought we'd agreed you would not argue with the man overmuch. He already is suspicious about this entire affair. We do not wish him to decide that you are acting strangely or had reason to want Sommersby dead yourself."

"But I did," Daphne said in an answering whisper. "Though not because of the cipher, you realize."

"I'm not a mathematical genius, Daphne," said Ivy with a huff, "but I am not a simpleton. Of course I know you had other reasons. But we haven't told the Squire about that, and if you intend to keep it that way then you had best not speak of it here in his hall where the servants might be listening."

That gave Daphne pause. She truly didn't want to explain what had gone on with her and Sommersby in the past. And Ivy was right. It would give him reason to suspect she had even more reason to kill him.

They were almost to the bottom of the main stairs when Daphne heard a familiar guffaw coming from below.

As she and Ivy reached the ground floor, she was shocked to see her father there, with Mrs. Northman's arm in his, as if they had just returned from a walk.

"Father," she said as the couple handed their hats and coats to the waiting footman, "I didn't expect to see you here."

As if he'd only just seen her, the Earl of Forsyth gave a theatrical start. "My dear daughter," he said. "What a pleasant surprise."

That was a lie, she knew, since he could hardly be surprised to see her in the home of a neighbor.

"I thought you'd returned to London but imagine my surprise when I learned through gossip you were still here," she said, watching as Mrs. Northman's glance flitted from one Forsyth to the other in barely disguised glee. "Why did you not tell me you were staying in the neighborhood?"

"Did I not?" Forsyth asked. "It must have slipped my mind after our disagreement the other day. Though I must admit that I was able to come to quite agreeable terms with your betrothed. How is Maitland?"

At the mention of Maitland, Daphne felt herself color. "Maitland is none of your concern. And he told me that he gave you enough funds that you shouldn't bother us again anytime soon. Which makes me ask again, why are you still here?"

If he felt the sting of her rebuke he did not let it show. "If you must know, I was at school with Northman. And when I met him on the road to Little Seaford, he was kind enough to invite me to stay. And since I would like to be here for your nuptials, I thought I would accept."

His eyes narrowed. "You are going to wed soon, are you not? A little bird told me that you were seen at The Bo Peep looking very cozy indeed. In fact, someone said that Maitland claimed you were already wed, which I know cannot be true. Why it takes a day's hard riding at least to get to London for a special license."

Before Daphne could respond, Mrs. Northman spoke up. "Lady Daphne," she said with a catlike smile. "I was rather shocked to hear of your hasty betrothal. Though I suppose that is becoming quite typical of the way things work at Beauchamp House. If we are to go by the precedent set by Lord and Lady Kerr, that is." She nodded in Ivy's direction.

"Now listen here, Mrs. Northman—" Ivy began with a scowl.

Daphne, knowing that no good could come of a sentence begun that way accepted their pelisses and hats from the butler and led her friend to the door.

"Good-bye, Father," she said over her shoulder as she hurried her friend away from danger.

"But what of your wedding?" he called after her.

"Why didn't you let me speak my mind to her?" Ivy complained as they hurried away from the Northman home and toward the lane leading back to Beauchamp House. "I'm a Marchioness now and outrank her. Didn't you say that reminding people you outrank them helps?"

"Not when Mrs. Northman loathes you as much as she does," Daphne explained. "And besides that, you shouldn't get overexcited. Lord Kerr won't like it."

"Oh piffle," Ivy said with a scowl. "Kerr knows how I feel about her. And I'm not an invalid."

Daphne thought about the possibility that she might soon be saying the same thing. If Lord Kerr was any indication, men became quite overprotective when their wives were breeding. "Very well," she said, stopping as they reached the end of the Northman's drive. "Would you like to go back and rip up at her?"

"No," Ivy replied grumpily. "I'm no longer in the mood. Besides I do not wish you to have to see your father again. What on earth was he thinking to stay in the neighborhood without informing you?"

"I don't know," Daphne replied. "But it can't be good."

Chapter 15

"I'm afraid his lordship and the ladies have walked over to the vicarage to meet the new vicar, your grace," Greaves informed Maitland when he arrived back at Beauchamp House the following day.

He was bone tired, and still troubled over his conversation with his mother the day before. But he needed to see Daphne before he could rest—because, truth be told, he missed her.

Handing his hat, gloves, and greatcoat to the butler, he asked for hot water to be sent to his room. Then, recalling what Lady Celeste's note in Renfrew's belongings had said, he asked the older man if he could recall the name of his aunt's solicitor in Battle.

"Yes, your grace," Greaves said with a nod. "It was a Mr. Hargrave."

A flash of some emotion Maitland couldn't read crossed the butler's face, and something about how quickly the man was able to recall the name told him it wasn't the first time he'd heard the question. "Lady Daphne asked after Hargrave while I was away, didn't she?"

"Indeed, your grace. Though she did not ask for the man's direction." He gave a small smile. "I believe she was waiting for your return, if I may say so."

Well, thank heavens for that, at least. Maitland had been half expecting to learn Daphne had traveled to Battle on her own when the butler told him she was home.

With thanks to the man, he hurried upstairs to wash off the worst of his travel dirt and change clothes, then because he was mindful of getting to the vicarage before the others left, slipped through the secret passageway off the kitchens and took the shortcut along the shore.

"When the vicar's housekeeper showed him into the comfortable drawing room of the tidy manor house, his cousin, sister, and the four bluestockings looked up in surprise at his entrance. Daphne was seated beside a handsome man with curling light brown hair and smiling eyes.

Maitland hated him on sight.

"Your grace," the man, who must be the new vicar, said with a warm smile. "I am glad to meet you. From what your sister and her friends have said, you are a most amusing fellow."

The duke glanced at Lord Kerr, who gave a slight shrug as if to say "What did you expect?"

Then his cousin stood and performed the introductions. "Reverend Lord Benedick Lisle, may I introduce my cousin the Duke of Maitland?"

"That sounds rather imposing, doesn't it?" said Lisle after he and the duke exchanged bows. "Among friends, I am just Ben."

"And are you?" Maitland asked, with a raised brow. Something about the fellow set his back up. Perhaps the fact that he'd seemed so cozy sitting next to Daphne when he arrived. "Among friends, I mean. You've only just met us all today, as I understand."

Before the vicar could respond, Lady Serena spoke from where she was seated beside Daphne on a rather hideous green chintz settee. "We have actually determined that

Benedick shares many acquaintances in common with us, Maitland. And he is the brother of Lord Freddy Lisle. Were you not at school with him?"

On closer inspection, Lisle did bear a striking resemblance to his brother Freddy, whom Maitland had known at university. And in that context, his good looks and charm made absolute sense. The Lisle brothers were known for their way with the ladies.

"Indeed, I was," he said. "Though Freddy was a year ahead of me. We did run in some of the same circles."

"Freddy knows everyone," the vicar said with a laugh. "I have yet to visit any part of England where I haven't met someone who has at the very least heard of him."

"But surely it is your brother Lord Cameron Lisle who is the more famous of the two," Gemma said from where she was examining a shelf of books. "He is quite well known as one of England's foremost natural scientists. I've read all of his treatises. They're quite fascinating."

Benedick hid a smile. "I would promise to tell my brother of your praise in my next letter," he said, "but I'm afraid his sense of his own importance is already quite outsized enough."

"One cannot blame him for being proud of his achievements," Daphne said, coming to the absent man's defense. "There is nothing wrong with being aware of one's own strengths."

Further conversation was stalled by the arrival of the tea tray, which Lady Serena offered to preside over.

"Your cousin and the ladies were telling me a bit about what happened here before my predecessor retired," the vicar said as cups were handed around. "I must confess, it does not sound like the sort of thing I am used to as a general rule. Most parish scandals are rather dull."

He was referring, of course, to Ivy's kidnapping and the former vicar's harm at the hands of Lady Celeste's killer.

"Unfortunately, we seem to be prone to some rather unusual happenings in the area," Lord Kerr said, taking a seat on the divan beside Ivy. "I suppose you've heard by now about the business with Sommersby at Beauchamp House?"

"A bad business," Lord Benedick agreed. "Mrs. Northman was quite happy to fill me in on the particulars." He gave a slight grimace. Clearly, he had not been charmed by the magistrate's wife, Maitland thought wryly. The matron would be quite disappointed.

"She is a very unpleasant woman," Daphne said with her customary certainty.

Maitland was prepared to defend her to the clergyman, but he only said mildly, "I cannot disagree, Lady Daphne. Though it is perhaps un-Christian of me to say so."

"She is hardly in a position to cast judgment." Sophia turned from her examination of a small landscape hanging above the fireplace. "Mrs. Northman, I mean. She who is without sin and all that, after all."

The vicar raised a brow. "I hope no one here will be casting stones any time soon."

"Only into the sea, Lord Benedick," said Sophia with a hint of color in her cheeks. "Much as it would satisfy me to take Mrs. Northman down a peg. She has been quite unpleasant to several of my friends now. And I do not tolerate such for long."

"Most loyal of you," replied the vicar with an approving glance.

The conversation then turned to other, less-inflammatory topics, like the local congregation and how the newcomer was settling in. Before long Lady Serena rose, as did the others, to take their leave.

When Maitland lingered behind the others, Daphne did as well, telling them that they would be along soon.

"I had hoped for a word alone with the vicar," he said in a low voice as she placed her hand on his arm.

"But this involves me as well as you," she said with a frown. "Why should I not be here when you speak to him?"

Lord Benedick, who watched them with some amusement in his eyes from his place before the mantle, bit back a grin. "I take it you wish to speak to me about performing a marriage?"

Startled, Maitland turned to him. "What makes you guess that?" Perhaps he and Daphne wished to speak to the fellow on some arcane matter of theological importance. Or they wished to invite him to supper at Beauchamp House. They could be here for any number of reasons.

"For one thing," the vicar said, looking from one to the other, "as soon as you entered the room, your grace, Lady Daphne's entire demeanor lightened."

Daphne frowned, and placed a hand to her cheek as if to verify the statement.

"And you, Maitland," he said to the duke, "scanned the room until you found her, then relaxed, as if knowing her location allowed you to be calm again."

Maitland wasn't sure if he was pleased or annoyed at the other man's assessment.

"The duke has just returned from London where he acquired a special license," Daphne said. "That is, I presume you were successful?"

"Of course." Maitland was not a mathematics genius, but he was quite able to exert his ducal influence when necessary. "And, as you guessed, we should like you to perform the ceremony. Here in your church preferably."

He hadn't discussed the matter with Daphne, but Maitland had fond memories of sitting beside his aunt in the family pew here as a boy.

But the idea seemed to appeal to Daphne, and she nodded her agreement.

"I would be delighted," said the vicar with a warm smile.

They made plans for ceremony in three days' time with just their friends in attendance.

As he walked them to the door, however, Lord Benedick stopped. "I just remembered. There was something I found while going through some papers my predecessor left behind. If you'll wait for just a moment?"

And before they could protest, he hurried from the room, returning a moment later carrying a sealed letter.

"I didn't make the connection until you arrived this afternoon, Lady Daphne," the vicar said as he handed it to her. "And then there was no convenient moment to bring it into the conversation. I suppose you met the old vicar before he departed and he wished you to have it?"

But when Daphne held out the missive, her scrawled name was in Celeste's handwriting.

"Thank you very much," she said, staring down at the page. She made no mention of what the note could pertain to. Noting the seriousness of her expression, the vicar didn't ask.

Ready to get her alone so that they could open it, Maitland bowed to the clergyman and they made their farewells.

They made their way to the path leading from the vicarage to the sea stairs in silence.

As if by mutual agreement, they didn't stop to read the note until they were at the bottom of the stairs, out of sight of both the vicarage and Beauchamp House, which loomed over the cliffside cave entrance that served as the portal to the secret passageway.

There, Maitland handed Daphne down to sit on one of the lower steps, and he sat down beside her.

She slid a finger beneath the seal and opened the folded page.

Daphne had felt such a cavalcade of emotions since arriving at the vicarage that morning, she almost suspected she was sickening with something.

If the Reverend Lord Benedick Lisle was to be believed, she was love sick, though she knew very well that whatever it was she felt for Maitland was something far less hysterical. She wasn't even sure she was capable of such a thing as love. Affection? Absolutely. Attraction? Certainly. But love implied flights of fancy and public declarations. And she was as prosaic as ever.

Even so, when he'd arrived in the parlor of the vicarage, she had felt a spark of elation to see him after his absence. Had it only been a day or so? If one measured by how much she'd missed him, it would have been a month at least.

She hadn't realized just how transparent her affection for him had become—for that was what it was—until the vicar mentioned how she'd looked on seeing Maitland's arrival. She wasn't normally one to wear her emotions on her sleeve. But then the past few days had been far from normal.

She'd been so pleased to see him, in fact, she hadn't even argued with him over his decision for their wedding to take place in the church. It wasn't that she was against having it there, but she had thought perhaps the gardens of Beauchamp House would be pleasant. The wedding was just a legal formality, however, so it hardly mattered where it took place. And Maitland seemed to be sentimental about the area, so he likely had his reasons for wanting it in the tiny church.

Their silence on their walk back toward Beauchamp House was comfortable, rather than awkward, as silences could sometimes be. And she was pleased to have him beside her, feeling the pleasant zing of attraction between them even as they did something as ordinary as walk home.

Now, seated beside him on the sea stairs, Daphne read aloud from Celeste's letter.

> *My dear Lady Daphne,*
>
> *I gave this letter to the vicar to, in turn, give to you should you come to him for assistance in the quest I left for you.*
>
> *It is my hope that if someone should get the cipher before you, you will find the second set of clues I've left for you. I have always believed it is better to prepare for the worst while hoping for the best, and unfortunately, there are those who would like very much to know the location of the prize I left for you. One of the paths to it is more straightforward than the other, but I have faith that no matter which you take you will emerge the victor in my little game. Certainly no other is as quick with numbers and ciphers as you are.*
>
> *It is also my hope, though he will not thank me for meddling, that my nephew Maitland will be of some use to you in this matter. He has never considered himself to be a good student, but I know him to be quite clever when it comes to handling people. And you, my dear, for all that you are an intelligent woman, are not. I have left instructions for him to take charge of your comfort at Beauchamp House and to assist you in any way he sees fit in your quest. Please allow him to help you should you need it.*
>
> *You are a bright and lovely lady, Daphne. And I trust you to do whatever is best when you reach the prize. It's why I chose this particular puzzle with you in mind.*
>
> *Yours affectionately,*
Lady Celeste Beauchamp

"What does she mean she 'left instructions' for you?" Daphne asked a sheepish Maitland. "You never mentioned anything about that?"

As she watched, he rubbed a hand over the back of his neck. "It never came up," he said in a defensive tone. "And I did not think you would be particularly pleased to learn my aunt was concerned about your lack of . . . that is to say your problems with . . ."

"My brusque manner?" Daphne asked sweetly. She was rather enjoying seeing the normally self-assured duke off his pedestal.

"That isn't what I said," Maitland returned with a frown. "Though you must admit that I do have a charming way about me. And I'm not nearly as good as you are at maths."

"The fact that I am your superior when it comes to calculations is beside the point," Daphne said with a huff. "I am more concerned about the fact that you kept your aunt's message to you from me, when I have been thoroughly honest with you."

"I thought she was meddling, as she said," the duke replied, staring out at the rolling waves. "And I didn't wish you to think I was helping you only because of what my aunt said."

"But weren't you?" Daphne asked. She suddenly wasn't quite so sure that the connection she'd felt between them was as strong as she'd at first thought. Had he sought her out only because his aunt had suggested it?

She felt her heart constrict at the thought.

Folding the letter, she stood and hurried toward the cave entrance, suddenly needing to be alone to think the matter over.

"Daphne, wait!"

She heard him behind her as she stepped into the coolness of the cave. After the brightness of the seaside, her eyes took a minute to adjust to the dark, though the others had left a pair of lamps burning where they hung from hooks on the wall.

To her surprise, she felt tears well in her eyes. She hadn't realized how much she had trusted Maitland's attraction to her before it was in doubt.

"It isn't what you think," he said softly, stopping her with a hand on her arm. "My aunt's letter had nothing to do with my interest in you."

"I don't see how that can be true," she said, turning to face him, though she once again found herself unable to meet his gaze. "Indeed, your initial rejection of my advances seems to indicate that you could not see me as a potential lover because your aunt had already got you thinking of me as someone for you to look after."

"That had nothing to do with it," he said, grasping her by the shoulders. "Daphne, look at me."

She swallowed, terrified at what she would see if she let her eyes meet his. But when he asked again, she looked up.

"I rejected you for the reasons I gave you at the time," he said, his eyes intense with some emotion she couldn't read. "Because I do not debauch innocents. And because you were my aunt's heir, and as such off limits to such things. That is not to say that I wasn't attracted. You know I was, from that first moment we met."

"But I don't know what to believe, now," she said with a shake of her head. She looked down at the front of his coat, unable to meet his gaze any longer. "And this calls all of your actions into question. Your announcement of our betrothal to my father. Your ruse with Pinky at The Bo Peep. How do I know this wasn't all part of some plan you concocted at your aunt's behest?"

"All of that was genuine," he said, tipping up her chin with his finger. "All of it. Daphne, I've never been more drawn to a woman than I am to you. I think of you every moment of the day. I rode for almost twenty-four hours straight just so that I could get back to you."

She wanted to believe him. She truly did. Before Maitland she'd come to believe that she would never find a man she could truly trust—not outside of her tutor Mr. Sommersby. And there were so many things about him she had come to appreciate. His warm smile. His—yes—his charm. Even the crooked grin he seemed to save only for her.

"But what if I trust you and you let me down?" she asked in a voice so low he had to lean down to hear her.

"Oh, sweetheart." He wrapped her in his arms, and unable to resist his nearness, she went willingly, slipping her arms around his neck and lifting her face to his. "I will let you down. Because that's what it means to be human. But I promise you, I will try not to."

He bent his forehead to touch hers.

"I don't know if that's enough," she whispered.

"Then perhaps what's between us can be," he said, just before he took her mouth.

Chapter 16

Daphne felt the cave wall at her back as he worshiped her mouth, every touch more devastating than the last.

She'd missed him while he was gone. Far more than she could ever have imagined.

It wasn't just that she enjoyed his company, but she admitted to herself, as she reveled in the feel of his hard body beneath her hands, that she craved him physically. Like the perfect equation, there was something about his particular combination of body and soul that, when combined with hers, rendered the most elegant solution.

"I missed you," he said against her throat as she slid her hands beneath his coats, to feel the warmth of his skin through the fine lawn of his shirt. "Missed this."

She replied with a sigh as he tugged down the top of her gown and put his mouth where she most needed it, on her exposed breast. Bold in the circle of his arms, she grasped his buttocks and pulled him closer, the jut of his erection pressing into her belly, reminding her of how much he wanted her.

As if he could sense her need for contact there, Maitland shifted, lifting her skirts with one arm as he kept suckling her peak. When she felt his fingers at her aching center, she gave a whimper of relief. Desperate now, she moved restlessly against his hand and almost cried out her disappointment when he drew away. She bit her lip as she followed him with her hand, stroking where he pressed against the falls of his breeches.

"I'm coming back," he said in a strained voice, making quick work of the buttons there, before raising her gown to her waist. "Hold on," he said, lifting her in his arms.

Instinctively, she wrapped her legs around his waist, fitting him against the aching heart of her. With one thrust he plunged into her, and Daphne cried out with the rightness of it.

They clung together for what felt like hours like that, Maitland's breath warm against her neck as she felt a tremble run through him, like a racehorse eager to sprint away. Then when the stillness was almost unbearable, he began to move. Slowly at first, so that she felt every inch of him as he withdrew from her clasping body. But soon they were both writhing together in an erotic dance, Daphne welcoming his every surge forward with a rising sense of urgency.

At last, before she even knew it was upon her, she felt herself hurtling over the edge as she seemed to splinter into a thousand pieces of profound joy. Aware only in some distant part of her consciousness of the pulsing waves of her body where he claimed her with his own. Still clinging to him, she felt his rush toward his own release, until with a strangled cry he thrust one last time before relaxing against her.

They clung there to one another for several minutes, both trying to catch their breaths. When she let her feet drop to the ground, she found that her knees were a bit wobbly and was grateful for his steadying arms around her.

"Easy," he said with a smile in his voice. "I wouldn't want to follow up the most incredible experience of my life with a visit from the doctor. It tends to reflect poorly on a man's sense of his own lovemaking skills when his partner ends up with broken bones."

He was absurd, she knew. But it was one of the things she most loved about . . .

She stiffened as she realized what she'd just thought.

Loved? Why had her mind gone to that word?

Which Maitland misinterpreted as offense at his joke. "Not that that's ever happened before, of course. I wouldn't wish you think that I . . ."

Shaking off her momentary lapse, Daphne forced herself to smile. "Of course I don't think that."

He seemed to be skeptical of her reassurance for a moment before he smiled back and stepped away. "Good."

While they both began setting their clothing to rights, Daphne reflected on her lapse in thought.

Perhaps it was perfectly natural for a lady to fancy herself in love with the man who'd just brought her such carnal bliss. That was what it was, she decided. Gratitude. She'd mistaken her natural response to his very considerable skills at bringing her pleasure for love.

Relief at having found a likely explanation for her momentary slip, she pulled up the sleeve of her gown and straightened her bodice.

Just because she was going to marry Maitland, she reasoned as she watched him turn his back so that he could discreetly refasten his breeches, did not mean that she had to give him her heart. Before this week, she'd been content to think of spending her life as a spinster bluestocking. While other women were toiling as wives and mothers, she would use her superior intelligence to blaze trails where no lady had gone before.

Circumstance and necessity had changed those plans, and she had agreed that marriage to the duke was now necessary both to protect their reputations and that of their as-yet hypothetical child. But that didn't mean she had to give all of herself to him. Surely it was allowed for her to hold some part of herself back from him. No matter how much she trusted and admired him, there was some resistant corner of her mind that did not, might not, ever fully believe he could remain such a paragon as he seemed now.

And, she couldn't help reminding herself, he had kept his aunt's letter to him from her. As betrayals went, it was small, but it could be the first in a series. Or worse, might lead to larger and larger ones.

"You're quiet," Maitland said as they walked in single file through the hidden passageway leading from the cave up into the kitchens of the main house. "I wasn't too rough, was I?"

She heard the concern in his voice and felt a pang of affection—that's what she'd call it—for this man who seemed so careful not to do her harm.

"Not at all," she said, glancing back to give him a reassuring smile. She'd never been overly concerned about the feelings of others—mostly because she managed to hurt them without meaning to again and again. If she allowed herself to care too much, she'd be always in tears—but perhaps because of his gentleness with her, she wanted desperately not to hurt him. Hopefully, there would be no reason to do so.

She couldn't help but recall his words to her earlier about letting people down being part of the human condition.

Not really giving a damn if the whole household guessed what they'd got up to in the cave, Maitland left Daphne at her bedchamber door with a kiss before going in search of Kerr.

Unfortunately, he was forestalled by the appearance of his sister, Lady Serena, bearing down upon him in the hallway leading to the study.

"I'd like a word please, Maitland," she said with a speaking look that reminded him of their mother in one of her moods.

Without waiting for him to agree or disagree, she stalked down the hall past the study, where he'd hoped to find Kerr, and toward her own little parlor.

By the time he stepped into his sister's *demesne,* she had already taken up a position behind her writing desk, reminding him of a father about to reprimand his heir. Their father had been particularly fond of the pose, though he'd often employed a birch as well. Fortunately, he needn't worry about any sort of corporal punishment from Serena.

Closing the door behind him, he couldn't help straightening his coats before he perched on one of the painfully small chairs before her desk. Really, had it been too much to ask that his aunt, who had furnished the entire house, would ensure at least one man-sized chair per room?

"I trust your trip to London was a success?" Serena asked. "I know you at least were able to speak to Mama, because she sent a letter informing me of her intention to come down for the wedding. Which, by the by, she has instructed me to tell you, should really be at St. George's Hanover Square."

Maitland gaped. "How the devil did she get a letter here so quickly? I only made it there and back in such haste because I rode as if the hounds of hell were on my heels."

"I daresay she told her messenger to do the same," Serena said with a shake of her head. "You know when Mama is determined, she can make whatever she wants happen."

"She told me she would not attend the wedding," he continued, wanting to tug his hair from its roots. "That she was far too busy. I should have known it was a feint. Just once I'd like her to do what she says she'll do."

"You had just as well wish for the moon to fall to the earth to be bowled like a ball," his sister said. "She will always do as she pleases, as you well know."

"Then so shall I," he said with a scowl. "Daphne and I have arranged to be married in the village church in three days' time. If Mama is not here by then, she'll simply have to settle for meeting my duchess after the fact."

Serena, who had come to respect their mother's whims like the unpredictable imps they were, made a tsking noise. "Are you sure you want to do that? She can be most disagreeable when she's been thwarted."

"So can I," he said simply. "And I am more concerned with disappointing Daphne, who must be my main concern now. Mama will just have to adjust."

"Speaking of Daphne," Serena said with a chiding tone, "I would prefer it if you could manage to behave yourself until you are wed. It's bad enough that Ivy and Quill compromised themselves into marriage on my watch, but now my own brother has got himself a bride in the same way. Beauchamp House is beginning to get a reputation in the neighborhood for mayhem."

He felt his ears turning red. He had thought Kerr might tease him about the extra time they'd taken on the return from the vicarage, but not Serena.

Still, he felt a need to defend himself, if only to preserve the upper hand as a sibling. "I would think that finding a dead man's body in the library would do more damage to Beauchamp House's reputation than the hasty marriages of two of Aunt Celeste's protégés."

His sister scoffed. "You know full well that sex is far more scandalous than murder, Dalton." She only used his Christian name when she was truly annoyed. "And if you had the decency to keep your . . . um . . . escapades confined to other places besides the house, I would perhaps be less incensed."

"But we did," he protested, because technically the cave

was not inside the house. At least not the part of it where he and Daphne had . . . escapaded.

But his words fell on deaf ears. "I don't wish to hear it. I know what I heard when I was in the wine cellar looking for something for dinner tonight, and it was not the soothing sound of the sea, let me tell you." She gave him a pointed look.

If possible, his ears got redder. He had never enjoyed the sort of relationship with his sister—or any family member aside from Quill—where he felt comfortable discussing his sexual exploits. And certainly he didn't relish the thought of his sister overhearing him with Daphne.

He shuddered. He couldn't help it.

"Oh, I heartily agree," Serena said with a pained expression. "So, perhaps now you'll agree with me that at the very least you should confine your amours to the bedchamber?"

"But you just said you didn't want us doing it in the house!" He couldn't help pointing out her inconsistency.

"I don't want to know about 'it' at all," she said, her voice rising with exasperation. "But at least in either of your bedchambers, I won't be in danger of overhearing you."

She had a point there. Being overheard by his sister was about as strong a cockstand killer as he could imagine. In fact, some of the afterglow from the cave had been destroyed knowing she'd heard them.

"Very well," he said with some remorse. "You've made your point. I apologize for scandalizing you. It's just that Daphne and I are . . ."

There was no way he could describe just how impossible it was to keep his hands off his betrothed without embarrassing them both. So he settled for saying, "very compatible."

Serena smirked at the euphemism. "I could have told you that from the first day you met," she said with a shake of her head. "I am happy for you, Dalton. More than I can say."

Her smile was genuine, and he felt the warmth of her

affection in a way that had been missing from his interview with their mother. It was Serena whose support he wanted most.

"I will admit," she went on, "that at first I was not overly fond of Daphne. She can be quite abrasive at times. And her insistence upon her own intelligence was grating before I realized that it is her insecurity about all her other abilities that makes her flout it so."

"And she is correct that she knows more about maths than the rest of us will ever forget," he said wryly. It should perhaps be a bit intimidating for him to contemplate marrying a woman who could think circles around him, but he sensed that there was something about *him* that she was drawn to. Something only he could give her. Something she needed—and not just carnally, though that was one connection between them certainly.

"But I think she's beginning to realize there is more to life than just intellectual pursuits," Serena said. "And you are not a simpleton, brother. Just because you haven't devoted your life to scholarship doesn't mean you know nothing."

It was true he'd been rather good at school, but Dalton knew that his true skill lay in his ability to read people. And to navigate the sometimes troubled waters of personal relationships, be they business or social. He was good at people.

He said as much to Serena.

"I think that's why you complement one another," his sister said with a smile. "Though I do worry about how she'll manage the political intricacies of being a duchess."

At that, he laughed. "Are you mad? She already behaves like a duchess. All she lacks is the title and power to follow it through. She'll be far more successful than Mama has ever been. With the difference being that she won't be manipulating people for the sake of her own ends. And if she offends anyone it will be accidental rather than purposely."

"You truly are in love," his sister said with a laugh.

At the mention of love, he shook his head. What he and Daphne had together was powerful, and he felt great affection for her, but he wasn't ready to call it love. Not yet when they'd only given in to their desires three days ago. "I wouldn't go that far," he said, "but perhaps it will grow into love. At least that is my hope. At the very least I want our marriage to be more affectionate than that of our parents."

"Or mine," Serena said with a sad smile. "Do not apologize for thinking it. I was, too. In fact, I sometimes look at Ivy and Quill, and you and Daphne and wonder if I will ever find that sort of happiness for myself."

Dalton's chest hurt for his sister. Her marriage had been, with the exception of Jeremy, a nightmare. But the very fact that she was even considering the possibility of finding love meant that she'd healed in some way. And he counted that as a blessing.

"I know you will, my dear," he said, grasping her hand where it lay on the desk. "I have every faith that there is some man out there who will appreciate and love you as much as Jeremy and I do. Indeed, as the whole of Beauchamp House does."

"Even Daphne?" Serena asked skeptically.

"Especially Daphne," he replied with a grin. "How can she not love the lax chaperone who allowed her to go cross-country with me?"

Her shout of offended laughter rang in his ears for a long time afterward.

Chapter 17

The next morning found Daphne and Maitland riding in Lady Celeste's ancient barouche with Ivy and Kerr, on their way to the town of Battle only a few miles from Beauchamp House.

That they bring along the marquess and marchioness had been Lady Serena's suggestion that morning at breakfast, and Daphne had seen some silent communication pass between Maitland and his sister before he declared it to be a fine idea.

She'd not seen him again after their encounter in the cave. Maitland having declared himself exhausted after nearly twenty-four hours in the saddle, retired early. Daphne had missed him at dinner, but had taken the opportunity to continue her organization of the library. And somehow, she'd been calmer knowing he was in the house, even if they weren't in one another's pockets.

"It was rather clever of Lady Celeste to engineer another way for you to obtain the cipher," Ivy said as the carriage rumbled along the road overlooking the sea. "It's almost as if she knew someone else would get to it before you did."

Daphne considered the notion. She didn't believe in premonitions, or anything of the sort, but she thought it very likely that Lady Celeste had used her reasoning powers to make the deduction. "It's not as if the existence of the cipher was a complete secret," she said aloud. "Though it was considered by many to be a romantic legend, I think there were an equal number of those who thought the legend was rooted in some truth. I first learned of it from my tutor, who said he heard of it while he was at school. So, it was known in mathematics circles."

"Aunt Celeste was at the very least concerned about ensuring you would be the one to eventually solve it, however," Maitland argued. "She must have chosen you as one of her heirs because she thought you could figure it out."

"I wonder that she didn't attempt to solve it herself," Lord Kerr said from where he sat beside his cousin in the rear-facing seat. "She was quite formidable at solving puzzles and the like."

"She did," Daphne responded, putting a hand on her hat to keep it from flying off in the wind. "She told me as much in her initial letter to me. I do believe that's why she sought me out. She wished her heirs to be good at different areas of expertise, but she wanted a mathematician in particular because she thought it would make the cipher easier to solve."

"If only we could find the blasted thing," Ivy said, holding on to her own hat. "I do appreciate Lady Celeste's attention to detail, but I do hope this other trail she left is shorter. If we reach the solicitor's office only to find another clue that leads to more clues, I will be most put out."

"I am more concerned that whoever killed Sommersby and found the other cipher has already unraveled it and found the gold," Daphne said. It was something she worried about more than she let on. Because if he'd found the gold, they might never know who had killed Sommersby. And though Squire Northman seemed to accept the notion that someone outside the household had killed the man, Daphne couldn't help but fear that their lack of success in finding the murderer would lead the magistrate to turn his suspicions back to her. Especially if he ever learned of Sommersby's assault on her.

"If it was too difficult for my aunt to solve," Maitland said in a reassuring tone, "then I doubt the killer has managed it either. It's said that Cameron was fond of maths and codes himself. So it's likely that he created something that was difficult for anyone but a truly gifted scholar to solve."

"I hope you're right," Daphne said with a sigh. "Otherwise we're wasting our time haring about the countryside."

"I wouldn't say that," Ivy said, grinning. "It's rather exciting to be on the hunt. Especially if we manage to catch a murderer at the end of it as well as find the lost gold."

"I fear your success in unmasking my aunt's murderer has made you bloodthirsty, Ivy," said Lord Kerr in mock exasperation.

Daphne watched as they shared one of those looks that seemed to convey hours of conversation in a single glance. What must it be like to be so in tune with another person that you could read their feelings as easily as she could read the pattern in a series of numbers? She'd only just learned to meet Maitland's eyes without looking hurriedly away. She certainly couldn't tell what he was thinking.

But the same could not necessarily be said for Maitland when it came to him fathoming her thoughts. When she chanced a look at him, he raised a brow in question. He knew something was bothering her. She was able to read that at least, she thought, as she gave a small shake of her head in reply.

When they reached the village of Battle, so named because it was the site of the Battle of Hastings that put William, Duke of Normandy on the throne, it took only a few moments to find the office of Mr. J. Hargrave, Esq.

At the news that not one, but four noble visitors wished to see his master, the pale-faced clerk, a Mr. Fleet, in the outer office turned even whiter. "One moment please, your grace, Lady Daphne, Lord and Lady Kerr."

Alone with the clerk's underling, a thin young man who stood gaping at them like a circus exhibition, they waited.

"I take it Mr. Hargrave's clientele does not generally hail from the aristocracy," Kerr said in a low, amused voice. "I wonder what possessed Aunt Celeste to give him her business."

It was a well-appointed office, Daphne noticed, but hardly the sort of place one would expect of someone who enjoyed a thriving trade. At least, not that she imagined. She'd never had occasion to visit a solicitor's office before.

Before any of them could respond to Kerr's remarks, they heard a shout from the back room where the clerk had gone. Daphne looked at Maitland, who said, "Wait here." And though she chafed at the order, she and Ivy stood where they were as they watched the gentlemen, followed by the assistant clerk, disappear into the back office.

"I hope all is well," Ivy said nervously. "I wish I hadn't said that about this exciting me. I don't wish people to be harmed. Goodness knows."

Wanting to comfort her friend, and perhaps needing a bit of comfort herself, Daphne placed a hand on Ivy's shoulder. "I know you don't. And perhaps it was nothing. A book falling on someone's foot. The clerk tripping over his own feet."

But the longer they waited for the gentlemen to return, the more she knew it couldn't be anything as benign as she'd described.

When Lord Kerr came back alone, her heart caught in her throat. Where was Maitland?

"I'm afraid Mr. Hargrave has met with an accident," said Kerr without preamble. "I'm going to find the local physician, though I fear the man is no longer able to benefit from his services."

Daphne clasped a hand to her chest. "He's dead?" she asked, horrified.

"What happened?" Ivy asked.

"We're not sure," Kerr said. "I'd better go find the doctor. Maitland will be out in a moment to tell you more."

And with a quick kiss for his wife, Lord Kerr was out the door.

Not content to stay where he'd left them, Daphne and Ivy moved as one to the door and stepped into the office.

Maitland, who knelt beside an unconscious man behind the desk, looked up at their arrival. "I told Kerr to keep you out of here," he said with a frown. "Go back outside."

"We aren't children, Maitland," Daphne said with a firmness she did not feel. "Perhaps we can help."

Brushing past Ivy and Fleet, the clerk, who stood wringing his hands, she moved to kneel beside the duke and saw that Mr. Hargrave was bleeding from a rather large gash in his forehead. Beside him lay an open box, the twin of the one they'd found in the secret room in the library at Beauchamp House—and it was glaringly empty.

Ignoring the clue for a moment, she concentrated on the bleeding man. "Give me your cravat," she said to Maitland, who unwrapped the cloth from his neck and handed it to her.

Taking the starched linen, she folded it into a pad and placed it against Hargrave's bleeding wound. He had lost a great deal of blood, which ran down the side of his head to pool on the carpet beside him. "What can have happened, Mr. Fleet?"

When the clerk didn't respond to her question, Maitland turned to the man. "You there, Lady Daphne asked you a question. I know you're overset by finding your master in this state, but we must find out who did this."

Blinking, the clerk turned to look away from the pool of

blood at Daphne. "I don't know. I left to visit the stationers and I sent Henry here to collect the post. We were only gone for a half hour or so. Someone must have come in while we were gone.

The man left off with a broken sound. "If only I'd thought to check on him sooner."

"You can have had no notion of what happened," Ivy said in a soothing voice. "It's not your fault. It's the fault of whoever did this."

"Has your master had any visitors in the past couple of days?" Maitland asked, rising to begin looking through the papers on the unconscious man's desk. "Anyone you might have found suspicious?"

"There are always strange characters in and out of the office," Fleet said with a shake of his head. "It's part and parcel of the work. Mr. Hargrave isn't snobbish like some. He will take on work so long as the client's coin is real."

"So, you cannot think of anyone who might have done this?" Daphne asked, looking up from where she held the cravat to Hargrave's bleeding head. "Has anyone else been here asking about Mr. Hargrave's work for Lady Celeste Beauchamp?"

The clerk blinked. "Yes, there was a man here this morning before we left. But Mr. Hargrave sent him away."

Daphne and Maitland exchanged a look.

"What did he look like?" Maitland asked, turning from his search of the desk to look more closely at the clerk. "Describe him."

Sagging a little on his feet, the clerk said, "He was of middle years. Respectable-like, but his clothes weren't so fine as yours. I knew he wasn't from around here, though. I didn't recognize his name."

"He gave you his name?" Daphne asked, surprised.

"Yes," the clerk said shakily. "Sommersby. Mr. Richard Sommersby."

Maitland watched, arrested, as Daphne gasped at the clerk's pronouncement.

"Are you sure that's the name the man gave?" she asked, her face losing all color. "Richard Sommersby?"

Moving to her side, and indicating with a nod that the underclerk, Henry, come tend to his master's wound, Maitland pulled Daphne to her feet and saw her to a chair. "What did this person look like?" he asked once she was settled.

Fleet took a deep breath and closed his eyes for moment, as if trying to recall. Finally he said, "Not quite as tall as you, your grace. Dark hair with some gray mixed in. And spectacles."

"That's him," Daphne said with a helpless shake of her head. "My former tutor. Perhaps it's only a coincidence that he was here this morning."

Hearing the hope in her voice, Maitland's heart ached for her. It was possible that two men had called upon Hargrave that morning, but unlikely. The man who had assaulted the solicitor was almost certainly the elder Mr. Sommersby.

Ivy, who had been watching aghast from the other side of the desk, came forward and lay a hand on Daphne's shoulder. "I see some brandy, there," she said in a soothing voice. "Perhaps Maitland will pour you some?"

Grateful to have something to do, Maitland moved to the sideboard against the wall, and set about unstoppering the decanter and pouring a glass.

"I'm perfectly fine," Daphne protested, even as she took the glass from him. Their eyes met, and he saw how upset she was at the idea her mentor was tied up in all of this business. Even so, she squared her shoulders and took a sip, closing her eyes against the fiery taste. "I haven't seen Mr. Sommersby in a long time," she continued. "We're practically strangers now."

But Maitland couldn't help but remember what she'd said about her tutor being the one man she'd been able to trust in her life. Of course, that had been before he left their home unexpectedly, but she'd seemed to explain that away, blaming it on her father. What would she do if she discovered that he'd turned out to be just as unreliable as everyone else?

He didn't like to imagine the effect that would have on her. On them.

Just then, the door leading into the office opened and Lord Kerr entered, followed by a man of middle years carrying the black bag that denoted his profession.

"Dr. Eustace," Kerr said to them as the physician hurried to the prone man's side and began examining him. "We've arranged for a couple of men to come with a litter to carry him to the surgery if necessary."

"Perhaps we should get out of their way," Maitland said, moving to offer Daphne his arm. She looked over to where the doctor was examining Hargrave's wounds, then with a sigh, she rose and allowed him to lead her out.

Fleet, who had regained some of his composure, remained behind to assist the doctor, sending his assistant, Henry, back to watch over the outer office.

Once they were back out in the outer room, Maitland explained in a low voice what they'd learned about the solicitor's visitor that morning

"Sommersby's father?" Kerr asked in surprise. "What is he doing in Battle? Wouldn't he have come to Beauchamp House or Little Seaford to collect his son's things?"

"I'm afraid it appears as if Mr. Sommersby is searching for the cipher," Daphne said, her disappointment evident.

"We still don't know that he is the one who hurt Hargrave," Maitland said, trying to reassure her.

"But logically, it's the only explanation that makes sense," Daphne said. She ticked off her points one by one using her fingers. "First, he is the one who initially told his son and me about the Cameron Cipher. Second, he may very well have been the one to encourage Nigel to go in search of the cipher. Third, he was not a wealthy man, and certainly would benefit from the hidden cache of gold.

"Most damning of all, however," she continued, "is that he could have had no reason to visit Mr. Hargrave other than to see if Lady Celeste left any other clues about the cipher with him. He was her solicitor—and people often leave important papers in the care of their solicitor."

"But why attack the man?" Maitland asked, not sure he understood the connections Daphne made between the tutor and the attorney. "It certainly doesn't help him find a solution for the cipher."

"We can have no idea what actually happened until we talk to one of them," Daphne said, "but the fact that the box was lying empty beside Mr. Hargrave seems to indicate that Sommersby took what was inside."

"I saw some blood on it," Maitland said. He'd wanted to keep the information from Daphne for as long as possible, but she was already leaping to the same conclusions he was. "Before you came into the room, I examined it. I'm quite sure it's what was used to bludgeon him."

"Dear God," Ivy said, raising a hand to her chest.

They'd all seen how strong the blow had been that cracked Hargrave's skull. It had taken a great deal of strength, and perhaps anger, to do that sort of damage.

"He would be quite frustrated," Daphne said softly from where she stared out the window. "He's likely already tried and failed to solve the decoy he stole from the hidden room.

And I suspect he hoped that whatever was in the second box would make his task easier. If it was the real cipher, then he was met with just another puzzle impossible for him to solve."

"Why impossible?" Ivy asked, from where she perched on Kerr's chair. "I thought he taught you everything you know about mathematics and ciphers and the like?"

Daphne, turned, and gave a bitter laugh. "Actually, that's not correct. I did learn a great deal from Mr. Sommersby, it's true. But he was only my tutor for a year or so before I surpassed his ability to instruct me. He guided my studies, of course, but he didn't fully understand everything I worked on."

"But if you believe he's been after the cipher all along . . ." Maitland began. He stopped because to finish would mean putting into words what was for Daphne a horrific discovery.

She pressed on. "If he is the one who's now in possession of the cipher," she said in a sad voice, "then it is almost certainly the case that he murdered his own son."

Chapter 18

After ensuring that Mr. Hargrave, who was still clinging to life, was safely settled into Dr. Eustace's surgery, the party from Beauchamp House made the journey back home in a much more somber mood.

Without discussing the matter, Maitland and Ivy had switched seats, so that he could ride the entire way back with his arm holding Daphne close. She felt as if she should protest, but she had to admit that she needed the comfort of his nearness. Perhaps she had learned that the one person she thought she could trust above all was a murderer, but she still had Maitland.

When they reached Beauchamp House, they were met at the door by Serena, who informed them that Mr. Ian Foster was waiting to see Daphne in the drawing room. Wondering what the crown agent could want, Daphne hurried upstairs with Maitland hard on her heels. When she stepped into the blue-and-white room, it was to find Foster impatiently tapping his fingers on the mantle.

"Finally," he said without greeting as they stepped into the room, Maitland closing the door behind them. "I thought you'd eloped to Gretna."

Ignoring the man's complaint, Daphne stalked over to

where he was standing with his back to the fire. "We're here now, Mr. Foster. And it's been a trying morning, so I hope you will get on with whatever it is you wish to say."

She knew she was being unforgivably rude, but what she'd said was true. It *had* been a trying morning. And she wanted nothing more than to hide away in her bedchamber and think about what she'd discovered about her tutor.

Foster frowned and turned to Maitland for support, but he didn't get it, because he said, "Well, I suppose I should have known you'd not exactly welcome me with open arms."

"How clever of you, Foster," said the duke with a pointed look. "But then, I daresay you Home Office spies are used to being given the cold shoulder. That happens when you lie to everyone around you and get a man killed in the process."

"For the last time," Foster said with a grimace, "I didn't tell Sommersby he should break into Beauchamp House. If I'd known what he was planning, I'd have warned him against it. And I certainly didn't stab the fellow to death."

"But it was your information that made him think the cipher was hidden there," Daphne retorted, feeling all the anger and frustration of what they'd found that morning bubbling up within her. "You are just as responsible for Sommersby's murder as the man who actually killed him. If not more so, because as a representative of His Majesty's government you're supposed to protect the lives of his citizens."

"I can't be responsible for every damned fool who decides to go in search of hidden treasure," Foster protested, looking aggrieved. "I wasn't even sure the tip about the cipher being hidden in Lady Celeste's library was even true."

"Where did you get that tip, by the by?" Maitland asked from where he'd stopped beside Daphne. "As far as we know, Lady Celeste told no one but Daphne, and that was in a letter she didn't receive until after my aunt's death."

Foster looked defiant for a moment, then as if coming to some decision, he gave a short nod. "Fine, but if I tell you, you must promise not to hold it against the man. He's been useful to us in the past. And he is actually quite good at his profession."

Daphne, who hadn't expected Foster to tell them anything caught her breath.

"I learned of it from Lady Celeste's solicitor. A man who keeps offices in Battle, by the name of Hargrave."

"What?" Daphne and Maitland asked in unison.

Thinking they were shocked because of the breach of ethics on Hargrave's part, Foster raised a hand. "I know it sounds as if the man broke his client's trust, but in matters of national security such as this, it's not unusual for a solicitor to give us information about his clients. In this case, Hargrave was privy to Lady Celeste's possession of the cipher because he was also her man of business. So he knew about all of her assets. And it was his idea that she create the secret room—a playful replica of a Priest's Hole as the Catholics used during the Reformation, and later the secret rooms Jacobites used during the rebellion."

"Who else knew about this?" demanded Maitland, while Daphne looked on in horror. Was it possible that Foster was indirectly responsible for both Sommersby's murder and Mr. Hargrave's attack?

Foster frowned. "I told only Sommersby," he said, some of his defiance seeping away. "Though I have no idea whom he might have told. I didn't say so before, but I suspected he had an accomplice. I mean, it's obvious, I suppose, considering his murder."

"Hargraves was assaulted this morning in his offices in Battle," Daphne said coldly. "That is where we've been this morning. Picking up the pieces of another man who was harmed as a result of your callous disregard of the safety of others."

Ian Foster paled. "What?" he asked, his voice strained. "That's not possible. I only spoke to Hargrave the day before Sommersby's murder. He was fine."

"I hope I don't have to tell you that there is a difference between then and now," Maitland said severely. "I daresay whoever it was that killed Sommersby sought out Hargrave thinking he might have more information about the cipher."

"But I don't understand," Foster said, oddly deflated. "If he has the cipher, what more does he need? He only needs to solve it and find the gold. There's no need to search for more information."

"We believe that the man who stole the cipher from Sommersby is unable to decode it," Daphne said wearily. Was it really only a week ago that she'd been excited at the prospect of finding the cipher and discovering the treasure? It seemed like a lifetime ago.

"Then why did he seek it out in the first place?" Foster asked, clearly baffled by the idea. "I was planning to take it to an expert the government consults with sometimes at Oxford. I certainly know my limitations and that there's little to no possibility that I'd be able to crack it. Though I'd likely give it a try for a bit at first.

"This man may have an elevated sense of his own abilities," Maitland said, exchanging a look with Daphne. He seemed to be asking how much she wished to tell Foster about her tutor's involvement.

"Who is it, for God's sake?" the agent demanded. "I can have the man taken into custody in a day's time. Or less, if the weather holds."

"We don't know where he is," Daphne said tightly. "If we did, we would have turned him over to the authorities ourselves when we found Mr. Hargrave."

"But who is it?" Foster pressed. "Is there some reason you're not telling me? Is it someone you're close to?"

Daphne sighed. She wasn't sure why she still felt any loyalty to Mr. Sommersby, considering all he'd done, but somehow she did.

Then, before she could even decide whether or what to tell, Foster's eyes grew wide. "It's Richard Sommersby, isn't it?"

She must have revealed he'd guessed correctly through her expression, for Foster's mouth gaped. "I knew it was no coincidence that Sommersby's father was visiting the seaside when we arrived in Little Seaford."

"Why didn't you tell us the elder Sommersby was here before?" Maitland demanded, looking as if he wanted to lift Foster by the cravat and shake him. "He's the one who told Daphne about the cipher in the first place, years ago. He's likely been on the hunt for it for decades."

"He went on his way—or seemed to—after we met him in the village that day," Foster said, looking ill. "But it's quite possible he came back while I was traveling to Battle to visit his son. And I did tell Sommersby where I was going and whom I was planning to see."

Daphne said the foulest curse word she could think of, and far from looking shocked, Maitland nodded.

"Agreed."

"I've made a mess of this from the beginning," Foster said with a groan. "The Home Office will never trust me with anything again."

The duke scowled. "We aren't concerned about your career with the government, just now, Foster. A man is dead. And another is fighting for his life. In part because you conducted yourself with all the circumspection of a circus performer."

To his credit, Foster looked abashed. "What can I do to make it right?"

But the thing was, Daphne, who had always prided herself on her intellectual abilities, simply had no idea.

Once Foster had gone, Maitland watched helplessly as Daphne, all but vibrating with nervous energy, paced the area between the window overlooking the gardens and the fireplace.

And unfortunately, what he had to say would not make her any less agitated.

"Daphne," he said, stopping her motion with a hand on her arm, "I want you to go to London."

She stopped, her body stiff with shock. "Why on earth would I do that? I'm the only one here who really knows Sommersby. How he thinks. I cannot possibly leave now."

"You are also the only one who can solve the cipher," he said carefully. He'd known she would object to his plan, but knowing Sommersby had been brazen enough to kill his own son, he couldn't risk allowing him to get to Daphne. What if, somehow, she was unable to solve the cipher? He had every faith in her quick mind, but in times of stress, surely even she would falter. And the consequences would be fatal. "I don't want you here, at risk of being kidnapped by Sommersby so that he can use your mental acumen to solve the damned cipher."

It was a testament to his degree of concern that he swore in front of her. Like most gentlemen, he'd been raised to refrain from coarse language around ladies. But these were trying times.

"Who's to say he won't follow me to London?" Daphne was clearly not going to meekly do as he asked, it would seem. "Much better that I stay here in case he does decide to seek me out. At least here, I know I'm among friends."

"You're being ridiculous," Maitland said, knowing it was

the wrong thing to say, but past the point of finesse. "He has killed his own son. He won't stop at killing you, should you fail to give him what he wants. Sommersby is a dangerous man and he knows how capable you are of unraveling the cipher. He knows first-hand how brilliant you are. It's only a matter of time before he comes to you with the cipher. I am only shocked that he hasn't done so sooner."

He moved closer to her, but when he tried to pull her to him, she resisted.

"You seem to think that I am unable to work that out for myself," Daphne said, mouth tight with anger. "I am well aware that I am in danger. In fact, the only reason I would go to London is because leaving here would remove the rest of you from danger. But the fact remains that Mr. Sommersby needs me. His own skills are not up to the challenge, and he needs help. And if he can't get that help from me, he will go to some other great mind for it. I cannot in good conscience allow that to happen. Besides," she continued, her eyes meeting his, pleading for understanding, "there's no guarantee that he won't figure it out on his own. It is a small chance, but if he found some clues at Hargrave's office, then he may even now have found the gold.

He heaved a sigh. "You're never going to agree to leaving, are you?" he asked, torn between admiration for her bravery and exasperation at her refusal to see sense.

"I can't, Dalton," she said stepping closer so that he could pull her into the circle of his arms. "And I wouldn't want to be separated from you, anyway. We are at our best when we're working together. Haven't you realized that yet?"

It was hard to maintain his anger when she said things like that. Dash it all. He needed his anger to keep her safe.

"I don't want to be away from you either," he said, resting his forehead against hers. "But just for clarity's sake, if you'd agreed to go to London I would have gone with you. There's no way I'm letting you out of my sight while there's a murderer on your trail."

She was silent but did not argue. Instead she lifted her face to touch her mouth to his, and Maitland lost himself in the maelstrom of passion that swept over them whenever they touched. But they had work to do, so after a few moments, he pulled back. "We should go tell the others what Foster said."

Nodding, Daphne walked over toward the door, but Maitland almost ran into her when she stopped just short of the threshold. "What's wrong?"

"Look at this painting," Daphne said, pointing to a still life he'd always thought rather ugly. It depicted an ancient Greek man, complete with toga and a wreath of leaves in his hair, holding a scroll.

"What about it?" he asked, puzzled.

"There's a message written on the scroll," Daphne said as if that would explain everything. Then, to his further surprise, she flung open the door and all but ran down the carpeted hallway toward the library doors.

When he followed her at a jog, his cousin Ivy, Sophia, and Gemma all looked up from where they were each poring over separate tomes. They'd been searching for clues to where Lady Celeste might have hidden the second cipher while he and Daphne met with Foster.

"What's amiss?" Ivy asked, frowning as Daphne hurried to the shelf that served as the door to the secret room. She didn't respond to Ivy's question, so Maitland answered for her. "She's found a clue, I think. Or something." He wished he knew more, but he was as puzzled as they were.

He made his way toward the secret room, and met Daphne coming back out, the painting of Bonnie Prince Charlie in her hands.

"Bring the lamp," Daphne said, laying the painting flat on one of the wide library tables.

Kerr, who had hung back from the rest, picked up the lamp he'd been using to read by and brought it over. When it was close enough to illuminate the painting, Daphne pointed to a plaque in the background of the scene. "Look there. At the inscription on the wall."

Squinting, Maitland leaned down to examine the section she'd pointed out. But there didn't appear to be any meaning to the jumble of letters there.

"It's nonsense words," he said, standing up to look at Daphne quizzically.

"It's the cipher," Daphne said, barely able to contain her excitement. "It was hidden here in plain sight the whole time."

He looked down at the painting again, then back at Daphne. "You're serious? But if the cipher is there, why leave clues leading us around the coast on a wild goose chase in search of it?"

But Daphne was already sitting down at the table holding her notebooks and pencils.

"I daresay she was doing a bit of matchmaking," his cousin said from behind him. "From what you said about the note Aunt Celeste left for you, Daphne, she wanted you both to spend a great deal of time together. Not unlike her scheme with Ivy and me. What better way to bring you together than on the hunt for a cipher that was here all along?"

"It's mad," Maitland said, though he had to admit the theory made some sense. "Why couldn't she introduce us while she was alive and let nature take its course?"

"I daresay because planning all this was a great deal more amusing for her," Kerr said with a grin. "Aunt always did enjoy plotting."

With a sigh, Maitland walked over to where Daphne had

begun scribbling in the margins of the page where she'd written the code. She didn't look up, and appeared to be lost in thought as she attempted to work out a solution for the cipher.

"Perhaps we'd best leave her to it, then?" Sophia asked from where she stood beside her sister. They all were watching Daphne as she worked, as if they would miss something if they looked away.

"You all may go," Maitland said with a nod in the direction of the door. "I'll stay here and keep watch."

But, clearly not as wrapped up in her thoughts as she seemed, Daphne looked up then. "You must have something to keep you occupied," she said to him with a sheepish smile. "I'm afraid I'll be at this for a while. It's as difficult as I could have hoped." Then she looked a little stricken. "I suppose that's awful of me when it's caused so much heartache."

Maitland, however, could understand her excitement. It gave her the opportunity to use her gift, and perhaps that was why his aunt had left the cipher to Daphne in the first place. "Not awful," he said aloud. "Just competitive. Which isn't a bad thing."

She gave him a thankful smile, and said, "You really may go. I will be perfectly safe here. And my table is far from the French doors, so there's no danger of flying bullets."

If she thought the jest would make him feel better, she was mistaken. "He was able to break into this room before," he reminded her. "There's nothing to say he won't do it again."

"Fine," Daphne said, throwing up her hands. "Stay. But you must be quiet and still. Otherwise I won't be able to concentrate."

Hiding his satisfaction at convincing her, Maitland watched as the others left, and mindful of her admonition about bothering her, he picked up a volume of Byron's poetry and settled into the only comfortable chair, which happened to be on the other side of the room.

And waited.

He'd only got a short way into the first canto when the door opened to reveal a nervous-looking Greaves.

"Your grace," the older man said with a glance in Daphne's direction, "I'm afraid Lord Forsyth is below asking for you."

Maitland's eyes also went to Daphne, who was in deep concentration. "He didn't ask for Lady Daphne?" he asked the butler in a low voice.

"No, your grace. You specifically." The butler looked as if he would like to say more, but clearly having been warned that Daphne needed quiet, he said in a low whisper, "Please, your grace. He says if you do not come he will come up. And Lord Kerr told me how important it is that Lady Daphne is not disturbed."

With a sigh, Maitland called to Daphne, "I'm just going downstairs for a moment. I'll be right back. Don't move."

But if she heard him, she gave no sign of it. Clearly, when she was immersed in her work, Daphne was deaf to anything else.

Following Greaves from the room, he prepared himself for a difficult conversation.

Chapter 19

Daphne stared at the series of letters she'd jotted down from memory from the painting of The Young Pretender.

As had happened since she was a small child and first began to notice patterns, she let herself go to the place she thought of as the aether. Where everything else ceased to exist. It was just her and the numbers.

She found it impossible to explain how it happened. Her tutor and her father had both tried to have her explain it to them—perhaps so that they could do it themselves? But she honestly had no notion of how it happened. It just did.

And it worked with other patterns as well. Cards for example.

When she was dealt a hand at whist, a glance at the cards in her hand was enough to set her mind calculating odds and possibilities. And every play set her to recalculation, reassessing, mentally building a list of which cards had yet to be dealt.

With codes, it was a bit more complicated. Instead of letters on the page, she saw numbers that were the sum of two other numbers. The first corresponded to a letter of the alphabet. "A" was equal to "0," "B" was equal to "1," and so on. The second was added to each of the letters in the solution. So, if she were to add 3 to every letter of the alphabet, "A" would be represented by $0+3$, "B" would be $1+3$, and so on.

It fell to Daphne to figure out what the second number or, perish the thought, numbers were that had been added to the original message's letters.

Of course, this was if Cameron had used a substitution code. It was entirely possible he'd done something else entirely. But Daphne thought not. Substitution codes had been used for centuries, and the fact that the message in the painting had been composed of letters only told her it was not a symbolic code or anything more complex. The true challenge would be to determine if more than two numbers had been added together to come up with the coded message. It was a typical form of substitution code—the type of code she hoped Cameron had used to write the location of his treasure.

The cipher in the painting had read:

Gdbpc Opiw Hjbbtgatp Thipit

She set to work, trying out various combinations and subtracting important numbers in Jacobite history from the letters in the message.

So engrossed in her work was she, that she was completely unaware of the silent figure creeping up behind her.

One minute, she was scribbling a notation in pencil.

The next, she was unconscious.

Maitland found Lord Forsyth pacing the same path between the window and the drawing room fireplace that Daphne had so recently walked.

As soon as he stepped into the room, the earl looked up with ill-disguised impatience. "You took your time," he said with a scowl. "Am I not to be afforded the courtesy of prompt attention? I am to be your father-in-law, Duke."

Biting back a sharp retort, Maitland said, "What is it you want from me, Forsyth? I gather you wished to speak to me, and only me about this matter? What is it you cannot share with your daughter, pray?"

The earl pokered up. "It is a matter of my daughter's safety," he said with a touch of asperity, "which I thought would better be handled by her betrothed than her father. I am not, after all, in her good graces at the moment, and I doubt she'd listen to me."

That was an understatement, Maitland thought wryly. He doubted Lord Forsyth had been in Daphne's good books since she was a babe and had no way of knowing how corrupt the man was. "By all means, tell me. I will do what I can to see that she is kept safe. Though by demanding to see me in person you took me from that very task."

"You will know much better how to protect her when you learn the man's identity," Forsyth assured him with a flourish. Clearly the man had a flair for the dramatic.

"Who?" Maitland asked, prepared to hear the name that had been racing through his own mind ever since they'd learned of Sommersby's visit to Hargrave's office.

"He has been passing himself off as an agent of the Home Office," Lord Forsyth said, his nostrils flaring in annoyance. "A Mr. Ian Foster."

Maitland felt a frisson of alarm. "But surely Foster is who he says he is. Squire Northman assured me he knew the man as such from his own dealings with the Home Office."

"Perhaps it once was true," Lord Forsyth said, his vehemence convincing Maitland of his sincerity, "but no longer. I had dealings with the man on a separate matter some years ago, and the fellow assured me he was no longer in their employ."

"What 'separate matter'?" Maitland asked, suspicious. He doubted it was anything aboveboard or Daphne's father would have told him as part of the explanation of how he knew Foster.

"That is neither here nor there," Lord Forsyth said pettishly. "What I am telling you is that Foster is likely the man responsible for the murder of Nigel Sommersby. If you had been more forthcoming with me about the matter, I might have made the connection earlier. As it is, I only learned from Northman this morning that Ian Foster was traveling with Sommersby, at which point I knew he was responsible."

"Is it not possible that he only told you he was no longer working for the Home Office in order to gain your trust?" Maitland asked, not quite sure he was ready to follow Forsyth down this particular avenue of speculation. He accounted himself a rather good judge of character, and he'd seen no hint that the man was lying.

Of course, he was not infallible.

"It's possible," Forsyth said. "If you must know the truth, I bought some claret and brandy from free traders through him. I do like a good brandy, you know. And his name was given to me by a friend, who said he'd once worked for the government, but now wished to get a bit of his own against them. He had the connections on the coast, and saw that I received the items I asked for.

"But surely," he continued, "I would have been taken into custody, or at the very least fined, if he was attempting some sort of trap. And there was none. I got my claret and brandy, and never thought of the man again until Northman mentioned him today."

Maitland didn't bother asking why Northman had been speaking to Forsyth about the murder at Beauchamp House. Northman didn't strike him as the most discreet of fellows, and he likely wanted to tell his old school chum the details of the murder that had taken place in his daughter's new home.

"What makes you think he poses a threat to Daphne?" Maitland asked. "We already believe that Nigel Sommersby's father is the one who killed him. And attacked a solicitor in Battle."

"Richard Sommersby?" Lord Forsyth asked, looking pale. "Of course—it makes perfect sense."

"What does?"

"It was from Richard Sommersby that I got Foster's name." Lord Forsyth looked grim.

"Are you sure you don't mean Nigel Sommersby?" Maitland asked.

"No, I'm quite positive," the earl said with a quick shake of his head. "I had little to do with the son. He showed a bit too much interest in my daughter, if you must know. It was impossible to convince the lad that he was beneath her, however. I tried to drive the message home by treating him in the manner his station deserved."

And perhaps stirred resentment against the girl who was so far above him, Maitland thought with a pang of contempt for Daphne's father.

"Why not forbid him from taking his lessons with her?" he asked.

"I had an agreement with Daphne that I wouldn't interfere in her lessons," Forsyth said curtly. "That included who was present for them."

He wanted to know more about this arrangement, but Maitland had a fair idea that it involved the blackmail she'd used to get a tutor in the first place.

"How did you find Sommersby?" he asked, realizing it had never occurred to him to wonder just how the man had ended up in Forsyth's employ.

"Daphne met him at some sort of meeting for scholars."

Forsyth furrowed his brow. "I don't think it was the Royal Society or anything official. To be honest, I didn't ask many questions given the circumstances."

Which the duke took to mean that Lord Forsyth had done exactly what Daphne told him for fear she'd reveal that she was his secret weapon in the card room. If he hadn't already despised the man, he would have begun now.

"I don't suppose you've had any luck finding this missing cipher that Northman told me about," Lord Forsyth said with a hopeful note in his voice. "It's been the cause of a great deal of trouble, but I must admit that the idea of finding a cache of lost gold is tempting. I can see why Sommersby and Foster would be so desperate to get their hands on it."

Maitland stared at the man in disgust. "Did you even come here to warn Daphne?" he asked. "Or did you come to pump me for information about the hidden gold? Because if that was your reason, then you can take yourself off now."

Turning, he began to leave the room, but was stopped by Forsyth's plea. "Maitland, I do want to find the gold. I won't lie. But I also wished to warn you about Foster. There was a vicious streak that the fellow only showed me once. But it was enough to confirm that I never wanted to see him again."

At the door, the duke looked back and saw that Lord Forsyth did indeed appear to be sincere. His face, which showed signs of the dissipated life he'd led, was no longer wearing his usual mask of ennui. "Protect my daughter, Duke," he said. "Don't let that villain kill her like he killed Sommersby."

Something was wrong, she was sure of it.

Consciousness came back to Daphne slowly, like the sun creeping up over the horizon. First one thought, then another, then another, until she was fully awake and aware of the fact that she was no longer in the library at Beauchamp House.

Her head ached terribly, and she had some vague recollection of being transported across rough ground in some sort of cart.

"So," a familiar voice said from nearby, "you're rousing at last. I am afraid I was a bit rough when I hit you. But I couldn't take the chance that you would run. Fortunately I was able to let a strong fellow I hired in the side door and he carried you out to the cart. It's amazing what a man will do for a few pounds. And he earned his money. As I'm sure you know, you're no featherweight, my dear."

Her eyes were still closed, and she didn't need to open them to know the speaker's identity, but she slowly raised her lids anyway. She preferred to confront her captor face to face, rather than cower before him with her eyes closed against her inner terror.

Mr. Ian Foster, looking somewhat the worse for wear since her meeting with him that morning—had it truly only been a few hours ago?—stood before her, a glass of water in his hand. Stepping closer, he lifted the glass to her lips, and made her drink. Daphne wanted to take it from him and toss the liquid in his face, but her limbs weren't cooperating. Frowning, she realized that was because her hands were tied behind her back.

"Drink it," he ordered when she pulled away a little. "You need to be in some semblance of comfort so that you can use that lovely quick brain of yours."

Despite the nausea roiling in her gut, she took a small sip. Then realizing how dry her mouth was, she drank more.

Satisfied that she'd complied, Foster took the cup away and placed it on a nearby table.

Blinking, Daphne scanned her surroundings, careful not to turn her head too quickly. They were in a small chamber in what looked to be a cottage. The furnishings were neither very elegant nor too mean. The walls were painted in a pleasant light green shade that reminded her of the sea. And from where she was sitting she saw a seascape hanging over the fireplace. On the other side of the room, however, there was a tester bed. At the sight of it, she gave an involuntary gasp and couldn't help turning her eyes to her captor.

"As lovely as your person is," Foster said with a slight shake of his head, "I have no interest in harming you that way. That was more Nigel Sommersby's line than mine."

Despite the overall awfulness of the situation, Daphne heaved a sigh of relief. She could withstand anything, she knew that now. But she couldn't deny that his assurance gave her some little comfort.

"I want you instead for your mental acumen, Lady Daphne," he said, turning to leaf through some pages on a low desk in the corner. Over his shoulder, he said, "I knew when Nigel first told me about your skills at ciphering and calculating odds and numbers with such speed and accuracy that it would come in handy someday. I just wasn't sure how."

She wasn't sure what to say to that.

"When he told me what your father was doing with you— sending you into the card rooms of the *ton* for fun and profit—I was awed, I must admit. Lord Forsyth has always struck me as a bit of a rapscallion, but I must say that he was able to harness your abilities in that way, well, it was quite admirable. He even bragged about it to me."

That gave her pause. "When did you have dealings with my father?" she asked, her mind racing at the thought. "And won't this scheme of yours put you in the bad books of your superiors at the Home Office? I should think they frown on kidnapping."

Turning, a single page in his hand, he gave her a rueful smile. "I'm afraid I misled you about my connection with the Home Office. We parted ways some years ago when they took issue with my too-friendly relations with some free traders here on the coast."

So much for using his government connections as a deterrent, Daphne thought with an inner grimace. "But that doesn't explain how you know my father," she pressed him. Perhaps if she could keep him talking to her, someone would realize she was missing from Beauchamp House.

Foster moved to stand before her. "He bought some claret and brandy from me," he said with a shrug, as if that should explain everything. "I had no use for him at the time. He really is a rather stupid fellow. But, I'd known about you for some time, and I was eager to learn if he too possessed your skills. So much easier to deal with men than ladies, I find. Even intelligent ladies like yourself can be ninnies at times, you must admit. Alas, however, Lord Forsyth was a sad disappointment."

She ignored his complaint about women. Much as she abhorred his words, there were more important things to think of just now.

"Fortunately, I found another gentleman who seemed to possess your abilities with numbers," Forsyth continued conversationally as he got behind her chair and began to push it across the floor so that it faced the writing desk where he'd placed the page. When he was satisfied with the position, he went on. "Mr. Sommersby, the elder, was much more reliable than Nigel ever was. And he claimed to be far better at figures than even you were. It's too bad that turned out to be a gross falsehood."

Daphne's eyes widened as she stared up at him, just over her left shoulder. It made sense that he knew Nigel Sommersby's father, but the idea of her tutor discussing her maths skills with this man she hadn't even known at the time made her skin crawl. And the way he spoke of Richard

Sommersby made her worry for her former tutor, Hargrave's attacker or not.

"Why would Mr. Sommersby say that?" she asked, trying to draw him further into the conversation.

"I thought at first," Foster said, annoyed, "that it was an overdeveloped sense of his own importance. But later I came to realize that he was only being gallant. Trying to divert my attention away from you. I needed the Cameron Cipher, you see, and I needed it to be translated."

"How did you learn the cipher was located at Beauchamp House in the first place?" Daphne asked, truly puzzled. Surely Lady Celeste hadn't told the sort of person who would gossip about it.

At that, he smiled. "I truly did learn of it when I was at the Home Office," he said. "Lady Celeste told a friend, who told a friend, who told one of my superiors. At the time I was far too busy working on . . . other things . . . to pay attention. But recently, I found I was in need of funds. And by happy coincidence, I learned that you'd inherited your very unusual portion of the Beauchamp House estate. So, I sought out both of the Sommersbys and we concocted a plan."

He looked almost apologetic as he continued. "I truly had no notion of involving you in this, my lady. Well, not for decoding the cipher in any event. Nigel was supposed to use his former friendship with you to garner an invitation into the house. Then he would search for the cipher, and when we found it, his father would decode it. We'd go retrieve the gold, and no one would be any the wiser."

"But that's not how it went at all," Daphne said, appalled at the whole notion of two men who'd been so close to her once using their connection to her as a means to get rich. They were no better than her father. Indeed, the Sommersbys were worse because at least Lord Forsyth made no secret of his intentions.

"Sadly, no," Foster said, moving to lean his shoulders against the wall, warming to his story. "Nigel, ever the hothead, decided to go to Beauchamp House the very evening after we met you by 'chance' on the road to town. He didn't tell me—likely because he knew I'd object—and using the knowledge I'd worked so hard to obtain from a former footman about the secret room, he slipped out and broke in. Fortunately, I suspected he'd try something rash like that, and I followed him."

"And killed him," she said, remembering with a shudder the sight of Nigel Sommersby dead of a stab wound on the floor of the secret room.

"The damned fool was planning to take the cipher without telling me," Foster said with a grimace. "Is there no loyalty anymore? He'd never have known that the cipher was even at Beauchamp House if I hadn't told him. He thought he was so clever, but in the end, that got him nothing but grief."

"But why didn't you simply take the cipher and disappear then?" Daphne asked, truly curious. It seemed foolish of him to remain behind, where he might be caught. "And why did you shoot at us?"

"Because running would make me look guilty," Foster said to her as if she were a simpleton. "And I shot at you because I could have no notion of whether you'd seen me leave through the window. I could hear your voices even as I shimmied down the tree outside. I haven't come this far only to be caught fleeing a murder scene. I was not made for such an ignominious end."

"If you think I'm the only one who can solve the cipher, then that wasn't the cleverest move on your part," Daphne couldn't help but point out.

At the criticism, Foster snarled. Clearly, he did not like being called foolish. "I thought I didn't need you," he said scowling. "Remember Sommersby had assured me that he was your better or equal when it came to codes and ciphers and the like. But, just as his son had done, he, too, betrayed me."

"What have you done to Richard Sommersby?" Daphne asked, fearful despite her disappointment in her mentor for allying himself with a man like Foster.

"After his little mishap with Lady Celeste's solicitor— really, it was too much of him to think the man would freely hand over all of his notes on the cipher—I saw to it that he was no longer able to impede my progress."

Daphne closed her eyes. "He's dead then?" Somehow she'd hoped that Mr. Sommersby, for all his faults, would at least escape this imbroglio with his life.

But to her surprise, Foster shook his head. "Don't get me wrong, the fellow deserves to die for the mistakes he's made on this operation. It's been one blunder after another for the man. And I can hang for one murder as well as two."

She suppressed a shudder.

"However," Foster said with a shrug, "there is the possibility that alone, you will be unable to unravel the cipher. So, I have kept Richard Sommersby on hand just in case you need his assistance in breaking the code."

Something relaxed within her chest. At least Mr. Sommersby was still alive, she thought. And really, he may very well have saved her from being taken earlier by Foster. She wondered if that had been at least part of his reason for touting his own skills at coding.

"Enough of this chatter," Foster said, stepping away from the wall, and lighting the lamp on the table. "It's time for you to begin."

Daphne looked down at the page, which contained the same set of jumbled letters as her own paper back in the library at Beauchamp House.

"I'll need a pencil," she said, looking up to find him giving her an assessing gaze. "Or barring that, a slate and a bit of chalk."

"I'm not comfortable untying your hands," he said with a shake of his head. "You'll simply have to work it out in that beautiful head of yours."

"But I need to see the calculations on the page," she protested. He was right to resist untying her hands. Her first order of business if he had was to toss the lit lamp at him. "And I need to write out a key once I'm able to get one or two of the letters figured out. It's standard for such work."

He would not budge on the matter, however. "You're a resourceful lady. Figure it out."

And without a backward glance, he left her alone in the tiny room, with only the Cameron Cipher for company.

Chapter 20

When he returned to the library, Maitland was startled to find Daphne was gone. Thinking she'd gone to lie down, or to speak to one of the other ladies, he went first to her bedchamber—which was empty—then to the shared sitting room where the heiresses sometimes congregated.

"No," Ivy said, her eyes worried, "I thought you were with her."

With a curse, Maitland noticed that her page, with the coded message from the painting, and her calculations, had fallen to the floor. Picking it up, he scanned it for some clue, but there was no "help me" written in the margins.

Quickly, he stepped over to the shelf with the lever for the secret passage on it. But a check of the hidden room showed it to be unchanged from their visit earlier.

"Where is she?" Sophia asked as the three heiresses, followed by Serena and Quill, entered the room. "Who's taken her?"

It was a measure of just how odd the past few months had been, Maitland thought, that their first conclusion was that Daphne had been kidnapped.

Quickly he explained to them what Lord Forsyth had told him about Ian Foster.

"But I don't understand," Gemma said, her brows drawn. "I thought it was Mr. Richard Sommersby who was seen at the solicitor's office. And that he was the one who killed Nigel Sommersby."

"I don't know the whole of it," Maitland admitted, "but at the moment, that doesn't matter. We need to find Daphne. It's clear enough that the man is looking for someone to solve the cipher for him. And if he was willing to take her by force, then he's growing desperate."

"But we know nothing about the man," Kerr said, looking troubled. "We don't even know if he has ties to the area."

"I think that's not entirely true," Maitland said, moving to the French doors to look for signs that the former government agent had used this way to escape. "Remember, he worked with free traders. Perhaps he still has connections to them."

The small balcony overlooking the gardens looked no different than it had the last time he'd been out there. How the devil had the man gotten Daphne out of the house?

"I can ask Mr. Greaves if he knows of any particular places where the smugglers gather," Ivy said, moving to the door. "He knows everything that goes on in the neighborhood, good and bad. And perhaps he knows of some hideaway where they meet."

She left, and the others looked to Maitland for guidance. He wished he knew better what they should do to find Daphne. At the moment, he was just as much at a loss as they were. Still, there was one thing they could try.

"Since it's pretty clear that Foster didn't get Daphne out of here by lowering her out the window, I want to know how he got her out of Beauchamp House without being seen. I cannot imagine Daphne going quietly."

"Unless she was unconscious," Kerr said carefully, not

wanting the notion to wound his cousin. "It might make it easier to get her out, I should imagine."

But Maitland had already considered the possibility and was well and truly terrified at the notion. But his terror wouldn't help find Daphne. "Let's go question the footmen. Perhaps they saw someone posing as a delivery man. Or someone who didn't belong."

"We'll speak to the maids," Sophia offered, already heading for the door leading into the hallway. "Let's meet back here in fifteen minutes to compare notes."

Nodding, Maitland followed them and felt his cousin step up to walk beside him as he headed toward the servants' hall. The ladies, meanwhile, went to the hall where the bedrooms were located, where the maids would be working at this time of day.

"We'll find her, Dalton," said Lord Kerr, using the duke's Christian name as he had done when they were boys. "If he needs her to solve the cipher, then at least we know he won't harm her."

But what would happen once she'd done what he wanted? Maitland wondered.

They found the footmen polishing silver in the dining room while the housekeeper looked on.

"If you're looking for Mr. Greaves," she said to them, "he's with Miss Ivy . . . I mean Lady Kerr in his parlor."

"In fact, Mrs. Bacon," said Maitland, "it's John and Andrew we'd like to talk to if that's all right. And you, if you have anything to add."

Looking surprised, the housekeeper nodded. Quickly, Maitland explained to them that Daphne was missing and had likely been taken against her will from the house.

"Oh, goodness," Mrs. Bacon said, aghast. "What is the world coming to? First Lady Celeste, and then that poor gentleman in the library." Daphne had never been a particular favorite with the servants—she was much too blunt for their liking—but the housekeeper's agitation seemed genuine enough.

"You must tell his grace at once if you know anything, lads," she said to the footmen. "Any little detail might help."

The two men were of similar height and build, and quite handsome—footmen were often chosen for their looks and similarity, and his aunt had been no different about that being a standard for hiring than any other society hostess.

"Did you see anything unusual?" Maitland asked them. "Someone who was somewhere they didn't belong. Or maybe a visitor you didn't know showed up?"

Andrew looked thoughtful. "That Mr. Foster was here this morning, your grace. But you saw him in the drawing room with Lady Daphne."

But John shook his head. "That was this afternoon," he corrected the other man. "I showed him up to the library myself. He asked to see Lady Daphne, and since he'd been here before I didn't see that it would be a problem. You were with Lord Forsyth at the time, your grace."

Maitland closed his eyes in frustration. He should have warned the servants to alert him to anything odd, or to any visitors asking for Daphne. "You saw him go up? What about when he left?"

The footman shook his head, "I'm sorry, your grace, but I didn't see him leave. Which was odd now I think of it. But I just assumed he was having a proper discussion with her ladyship."

"And you were in your place in the hall for how long?" Kerr asked.

"For an hour at least," John said, looking to Andrew and Mrs. Bacon to confirm it. "I stayed there until Mr. Greaves asked me to come polish silver with Andrew. And we've only been here for about a quarter hour now."

"What other way might Foster have used to get Daphne out of the house?" Maitland asked his cousin.

"If you please, your grace," said Mrs. Bacon, "but there's no way he could have gone out using the cellar door or the kitchen door without being seen by me or cook. Or any number of servants coming in and out of this area. Which means he must have used the doors off the gallery that lead out into the garden."

"If Daphne was unconscious," Kerr said thoughtfully, "how the devil did Foster manage to carry her all that way? He doesn't strike me as a particularly strong fellow. And no offense to her, but Daphne is rather tall."

Before he could respond, Ivy and Mr. Greaves stepped into the room.

"I believe we know where he may have taken her," Ivy said without preamble. With a nod to Greaves, she let him talk.

"There is a cottage off to itself, not terribly far from here," the butler said, his expression revealing how important he knew this information was. "It is known to the local authorities as being used from time to time by the local free traders. Lady Celeste never held with such goings on, so they never used the caves below Beauchamp House for their activities, but the owner of the Summerlea Estate a few miles away, is often away. And often turns a blind eye."

"Summerlea?" Maitland asked. "Isn't that Sir Thomas Devaney's place?"

"Yes, your grace," the butler said with a nod. "Sir Thomas's family has owned it for some years, but he has another home in Kent, I believe courtesy of his mother's family."

It was not uncommon for landowners all over England to only visit their estates once a year, or sometimes even less frequently. Maitland himself owned seven as part of the entitled properties of the dukedom. And it was simply not possible for him to spend a great deal of time at each of them. Considering what had been going on at the Summerlea, he made a vow to ensure that his own properties were not harboring criminals as soon as this business was finished and Daphne was safe.

"Let's go," he said to no one in particular as he turned to leave the dining room. But his cousin laid a hand on his arm.

"We cannot just go break down the door," he explained, though he did seem sympathetic. "We should inform Northman, and perhaps the local watch."

But Maitland was not willing to wait that long. "You can do both of those things. Indeed, I would appreciate if you would, but I won't wait another minute while Daphne is being held captive by a man who has killed one man and severely injured another."

"At least take one of the footmen with you," Kerr said, as Maitland strode away.

"They can both come," the duke called over his shoulder. "But only if they're prepared to fight."

And not waiting to see if they followed, he made his way to the stables to have his horse saddled. The footmen would just have to follow . . . on foot.

Her head aching, Daphne stared down at the coded message. She was grateful that Foster had left her alone to work on the code. Her head injury was making it difficult for her to concentrate with the same degree of rigor as she'd done in the library.

Still, she was able to recall some of the letters she'd already worked out when he took her.

So far, the message read: *o*a*—Ba**—S*mm**l*a—*s*a**

These she arrived at by adding 15 to the number designation for each letter of the alphabet, so if $a = 0$, then in the message, each letter would $a = 0 + 15$, which meant that the a in the puzzle translated to p. She'd tried a few other key numbers from Jacobite history before deciding on 15. She'd discarded 45 because she reasoned that Cameron hadn't wanted to make the solution that complicated. But 15, which was the year that the first rebellion happened, seemed less cumbersome. And, though she'd never admit to it, she had a gut instinct about 15.

She was working out the rest of the letters in the message when she heard the door to the chamber open.

Though she was tied to a chair facing the opposite direction from the door, she managed to turn just enough to see Mr. Richard Sommersby standing there.

"It's true then," she said, watching the man she'd once loved like a father. The man who'd taught her to harness the natural abilities her actual father had exploited for his own gain. "You did betray me. And your son."

Sommersby flinched a little at the accusation.

He looked exhausted. Dark circles shone beneath his once lively eyes. And in the years since she'd seen him last, his hair had turned completely white. When she'd known him, he'd been a handsome man of middle years. Now he looked as if he'd aged thirty years in the space of seven.

"It's not what you think, Lady Daphne," said Sommersby, moving farther into the room, crossing to stand on the other side of the table from her. "At least, I didn't start out with the intention of betraying you."

"Then how did it start out?" she asked. "Tell me why you got involved with the man who murdered your only son."

Sagging a little, Sommersby said, "I knew Foster through my son. I knew he was involved in some questionable activity, but when your father approached me about where he might find some smuggled brandy, I passed Foster's name along to him. In exchange, your father promised to let you finish your studies in peace. Without his constant interruptions and attempts to have you win more money for him at cards."

Daphne hadn't known, though she did recall a sudden cessation of her father's attempts to persuade her away from her studies.

"I thought that was the end of our association," Sommersby continued. "Indeed it was for a while. But then Nigel told him about the Cameron Cipher. And Foster began to press me about it. By that point, Nigel had already left your father's house and Foster was becoming more and more insistent. He'd heard from one of his connections here on the coast that Lady Celeste Beauchamp had the cipher in her home. I didn't want to leave you, but he left me no alternative. If I hadn't, he'd have forced me to do things that went against my conscience. He was like a man possessed."

"Why didn't he simply steal the cipher himself?" Daphne asked, puzzled. "It's not as if he was bothered by breaking the law."

"I was a little acquainted with Lady Celeste from the Royal Society," Sommersby explained. "Indeed, I am the one who told her about you and your gifts. Foster wanted me to trade upon that acquaintance to ask her to show me the cipher. So that he wouldn't have to do it himself. It was like a game to him—he preferred pulling at my strings, as if I were some sort of puppet, to doing his own dirty work."

"What hold did he have over you?" Daphne asked, almost afraid to hear the answer.

Sommersby looked away, unable to meet her eyes. "Nigel had got himself into a bit of trouble. You were not the first young lady he'd . . ."

"Attempted to take by force?" Daphne asked bitterly. "You

brought him into my home? Left me alone with him when you knew his proclivities?" If Sommersby's other betrayals had stung, this one pierced her heart.

He swallowed, looking down, dejected. "He was my only child. I'd already lost his mother, and I couldn't risk losing him, too. I did my best to keep him away from you. Indeed, I told him that if he touched you, I'd never speak to him again. And I meant it."

"But he couldn't help himself?" Daphne asked.

"He didn't care," Sommersby corrected softly. "He lied to me and said he'd never harm you. But then when my back was turned, he . . . did what he did. I sent him away the very next day. He went to Foster, who either guessed what had happened or to whom he told all. Either way, Foster conceived of a way to force me to do his bidding."

"So you agreed to help him find the cipher." Daphne's voice was flat. She'd never have guessed how weak her mentor had been. There was a time when she'd thought he was the most intelligent man in the world. And that he loved her as if she were his own daughter. She'd been wrong on both counts.

"I did," he agreed. "But I convinced him for a time that Lady Celeste didn't have it. We went instead to Paris, where Cameron had been trying to escape to. When we'd searched for a couple of years without success, however, Foster guessed at my subterfuge. And that's when he decided it was time to return to England and pay a visit to Little Seaford."

"How did he come to be working with Nigel?" Daphne asked.

"He'd been in Egypt, exploring treasure hunting opportunities there, but when Foster invited him back home to search for the Cameron gold, Nigel returned at once. We agreed to come to Little Seaford. And over my protests, Foster decided that Nigel approach you, since you and the other ladies had inherited Beauchamp House in the interim. You, he'd reasoned, were a much closer connection than Lady Celeste had been."

"But Nigel decided to search for it on his own," Daphne guessed. Nigel Sommersby had never been very patient. It didn't surprise her that he'd double-cross his own father.

Sommersby nodded. "And Foster followed him. Killed him. My only son."

His only son who had been a liar, a thief, and a rapist, Daphne thought bitterly.

Sommersby must have sensed some of what she was thinking because he looked up at her with remorse in his eyes. "I know I betrayed you, my dear. But I did try to keep Foster away from you. I told him I would be able to decode the message easily. Though I was aching at my own loss, I made every effort to solve the riddle for him. But it hadn't taken long for your skills with numbers and ciphers to fully eclipse mine. I stalled him for as long as I could. I even convinced him that Lady Celeste's solicitor might have some clue in his office."

"So you *did* attack Mr. Hargrave," Daphne said, shaking her head at the knowledge. Had she ever really known Mr. Sommersby? she wondered.

"No," Sommersby said vehemently. "It was Foster who did that. He took my spectacles and introduced himself as me—another bit of blackmail he could hold over me."

"But why try to hurt Hargrave? Surely if Foster threatened enough, he'd have given over whatever he had from Lady Celeste willingly."

"I don't know," Sommersby said, looking genuinely puzzled. "Perhaps Hargrave guessed that he wasn't who he said he was. Perhaps he sensed something was wrong. All I know is that Foster returned yesterday morning with a page of information on local springs and wells that he'd found in

Hargraves's file on Lady Celeste. But without a solution for the cipher, it was useless."

"And so he decided to kidnap me," Daphne said. "Because you couldn't solve the cipher for him."

"I did try, Daphne," said Sommersby, a beseeching note in his voice. "But you know I was never as naturally gifted as you are with this kind of thing. And I thought perhaps if he brought you here, you could find a solution, and then he'd let you go."

"He will not let me go," Daphne said coldly. "Once he has the gold, he'll rid himself of us both. Because we have enough evidence to testify against him."

The sound of someone clucking their tongue came from the doorway. "My dear Lady Daphne, what a cynic you are. I can assure you I am wholly committed to your health and safety."

Foster walked leisurely over to the table where Daphne was still seated, tied up. He looked over her shoulder at the coded message. But since he hadn't untied her hands or let her use a pencil, the solution she had thus far was inside her head.

"Have you arrived at a solution in that brain of yours, Lady Daphne?" Foster asked in a darkly cheerful tone.

"If I have, I'll never tell you," she spat out. "You're a murderer and a manipulator. There's no way I'll ever tell you the solution."

Foster's expression grew cold. "If you don't tell me then I'll simply have to force your hand. Perhaps by harming the handsome Duke of Maitland. Perhaps I'll do something to harm all of your friends at Beauchamp House. Who is to say a fire won't break out there tonight while they're all snug in their beds. It will be dreadful if they cannot escape because the doors are nailed shut."

His words struck a bolt of fear through her. She didn't need to ask if he was serious. That was evident in the steady gaze of his eyes on her.

"Do not test me, Lady Daphne," he said softly. "Because I will win."

Blinking back the tears that had threatened at his words, Daphne took a deep breath. Perhaps if she told him what the cipher said, he'd go to find the gold and leave her here alone. She could perhaps convince Mr. Sommersby to untie her.

"Tick tock, Lady Daphne."

With a silent prayer that this would be all he asked of her, Daphne said, "All right. I will tell you. If you'll only promise not to harm my friends."

"I am a man of my word, Lady Daphne." He actually looked offended that she would think otherwise.

Deciding she'd find a way to escape somehow, she told him what she'd translated the cipher to mean.

Roman Bath Summerlea Estate

Chapter 21

It was already nearing dusk when Maitland tied his horse in the little wood not far from the smuggler's cottage. He didn't bother waiting for the footmen, who would only get in his way as he tried to effect Daphne's escape. Much easier to slip in alone, retrieve her, and slip back out.

On foot, he approached the cottage, which was sitting on a hill overlooking the sea. It would be quite close to some of the caves used by the smugglers to store contraband goods, he thought.

He had thought there would be some activity at the house, but he could detect no lights burning through the windows, and there was no sound coming from it either. Pray God they'd not harmed Daphne, he thought.

His heart in his throat, he walked softly to the kitchen door, and on trying it, realized it was not locked. Wishing he'd brought some kind of weapon, he opened the door but saw immediately that the room was empty. There was evidence that someone had been here earlier, however. Dirty dishes were on the table with the remains of a meal of bread and cheese. And he could smell the lingering odor of a fire in the hearth.

He listened for a moment, trying to detect any sort of

hint that there was someone in the cottage, but it was silent. Perhaps a little too quiet for his peace of mind. Slowly he walked from room to room, every one empty of people. When he came to the bedchamber, the last room he'd had to search, he was both relieved to find it empty and concerned that he'd not yet found Daphne.

Crossing to the table in the corner, he saw his first clue that she'd been here. On the floor beside the chair that sat next to it, he saw a couple of discarded bits of rope. As if someone had been tied to the chair, then freed.

Daphne had been here. He knew it.

Then, as if she were sending him a message, he noticed something on the floor beside the chair. Kneeling, he saw it was the ruby ring she'd said belonged to her mother.

The ring she said she'd never taken off since the day her father gave it to her after her mother's death.

Plucking the ring off the floor, he stared at it for a moment as it lay in his palm. Then he closed his fist over it before shoving it into his pocket.

Voices below alerted him to the fact that the footmen had arrived.

As he hurried down the stairs, he saw Andrew clutching a piece of paper. "Your grace," the footman said, his excitement barely disguised as he brandished the page, "I believe I know where they've gone."

Curious despite his annoyance at their ham-handedness, Maitland strode over and took the page from him.

"Where did you find this?" he asked, his heart beating faster as he read the note, which was in an unfamiliar hand.

Roman Bath Summerlea Estate

"It was stuck out here beneath a stone on the path," Andrew said. "What does it mean?"

Not bothering to answer him, Maitland said, "I want you both to go back to Beauchamp House and get Lord Kerr. And bring any weapons that are available in the house. A shovel if there is no pistol or sword."

"Where are we to bring him, your grace?" asked John, the other footman.

"We're on the Summerlea Estate here," Maitland explained. "But the Roman Bath is only a mile or so from here. Kerr will remember it from when we were boys. And I know I do not need to remind you that time is of the essence."

He'd been foolish to strike out here on his own, he realized now. Because contrary to what he'd thought, Foster wasn't alone.

Sommersby had left the translation of the cipher for him, he was almost sure of it. But he didn't know whether he could count on Daphne's mentor to do more than that to help her. He'd already betrayed her more than once. If he was suffering a pang of conscience now, there was no guarantee it would last.

Praying that Kerr still recalled the location of the Roman Bath, he hurried around the cottage, climbed onto his waiting horse, and galloped away.

"My apologies for making you walk all this way," Foster said from behind her, his knife prodding her back. "But we really cannot risk the noise and attention a cart would cause."

Daphne hadn't seen a single person on their trek across the Summerlea lands. But she guessed that their reasons for walking were less about noise and more about the fact that there was no road leading to the Roman Bath. Their way so far had been through woods and across fields.

She'd had no notion of what the cipher was talking about, but clearly Foster knew where he was taking her.

Them.

Sommersby still trudged along at her side, though she thought he was looking worse than he had when he'd spoken to her earlier. He was not a young man, and the stress of the past week was catching up to him, it would seem.

They walked in silence for a while through the dimness. Despite his claim of not wanting to draw attention, Foster held a lantern to light their way. It wasn't strictly necessary, but Daphne supposed she should be grateful for it. A sprained ankle was the last thing she needed when she was looking for every chance she had to run.

Finally, after it felt as if they'd been walking for hours, they approached a clearing. In the light of the lantern, she saw to the left were stairs leading into the smallest of the three arches. It was impossible to tell from this far away, but there seemed to be a small room beyond the arch. In the center, the largest of the three arches led into a moss-and-vine-covered grotto. There was nothing in the recessed areas, but it might have once contained some sort of display or statue. The third arch was in the side of a small stone tower built into the side of the hill.

But it was the rectangular pool leading out from the second arch that they were looking for, she realized. The light from the lantern reflected off the gently moving water of the bath, which she guessed was supplied from a natural spring.

"Here we are," said Foster with barely suppressed excitement. "The Roman Bath on the Summerlea Estate."

When Daphne held back, he shoved her forward until she stood at the edge of the pool.

"Watch your step," he said in mock concern. "I wouldn't want you to hurt yourself."

"Just get on with it," Sommersby said in a heated voice.

But if Foster was upset, he didn't show it. "I intend to, sir," he said easily. "Or rather, I intend to let Lady Daphne."

Her heart stuttered. "What do you mean?" But she'd already guessed.

"I intend for you to climb into the pool and get my gold, Lady Daphne," Foster said. "Let me help you off with your gown."

Because she was at the edge already, she couldn't run. And if he pushed her in, the weight of her skirts would undoubtedly pull her under if the pool was deeper than it looked.

"See here, Foster," Sommersby all but shouted, "there's no need to demean the lady like this."

Showing the first sign of temper, Foster said, "Shut up, old man. I don't even know why I brought you with us. You've already proved your usefulness. Now you are a liability."

"I have done everything you asked," Sommersby said, strain in his voice. "Let the girl go, and I will get your gold."

But Foster hadn't stopped unbuttoning the back of Daphne's gown. "We are both too large to search the bath thoroughly," he said as if he were speaking to a child. "Lady Daphne is the perfect size. And without her skirts to weigh her down, she'll easily be able to move within it."

The evening air was cool, and Daphne began to shiver as her back was exposed to it. She felt a wave of humiliation wash over her at the thought of standing before these men in only her shift. But the alternative was drowning. And she fully intended to survive this ordeal and go back to Maitland.

If he would have her after this fiasco.

Like an abigail helping her mistress undress for bed, Foster eased Daphne's gown down over her shoulders and helped her step out of it. Fortunately her stays tied in the front, so she was able to undo them herself and blocking her mind to the reality of her situation, she stood waiting for Foster to move away so that she could remove her slippers.

But he didn't move, only stood there behind her, no doubt memorizing every detail of her exposed body.

Finally, when she could endure no more, Daphne decided to take matters into her own hands. Though she still wore her shoes and stockings, she stepped off the edge and into the rectangular pool.

He was still a quarter mile or so from the Roman bath when Maitland dismounted and tied his horse to a tree.

There was a need for stealth if he was going to catch Foster off guard.

It hadn't taken long for his eyes to adjust to the dark, and he managed to make it to the clearing without calling undue attention to himself. The closer he got, the lighter it became because Foster had a lantern that he held over the water.

Maitland didn't see Daphne, though, and her absence terrified him for a moment before he heard her voice calling out from the water. "There's a great deal of debris down there. It would take less time for me to search if you held the lamp closer to the water."

A splash told him that she was indeed in the water. He recalled from his visits there as a boy that the spring was warm, and with Daphne's height, it shouldn't be much higher than her waist.

"I can't get any closer without climbing in myself," Foster said in an aggrieved tone. "And I don't think you would like that, Lady Daphne."

There was a thread of menace in the man's tone that made the duke's blood curdle.

"No," Daphne responded hastily, as if she truly did fear what would happen if he joined her. "I will simply have to try harder. It's just that not knowing whether the gold is in some sort of box or purse makes it difficult to tell. But I will just be systematic about my search."

"Perhaps I should trade places with Lady Daphne," said Mr. Sommersby, who was seated against the stone wall of the grotto. It was difficult to tell from his position, but Maitland thought his hands were bound.

"Stay right where you are, old man," said Foster grimly. "You've already shown how useless you are. I don't wish you mucking this up as well."

"It would be easier if my hands were free," Daphne said. Maitland froze. He had to get her out of there sooner rather than later, dammit. It would be so easy for the rope around her wrists to get caught on something below the surface.

He was about to make his presence known when he heard Foster say, "Fine," in a petulant tone. "Give me your wrists."

Crouching beside the bath, he took out a knife, and as Maitland watched, cut the ties holding her hands together. "Now, no more excuses. Find my gold, or I won't be answerable for the consequences."

Daphne rubbed the skin at her wrists but then turned away from Foster and went below the surface.

The silence as they waited for her to come back up was one of the worst Maitland had ever experienced. Every part of him longed to burst out of the woods and attack Foster. But he couldn't do so while Daphne was under the water.

Finally, after what seemed like an eternity, she broke the surface, and the sound of her gulping for air made his gut twist.

"I . . . I . . . found something," she gasped out. Then extending her closed fist, she uncurled her fingers for Foster, who knelt so that he could see what she held.

Then, in a quick motion, Daphne struck while Foster was leaning over the bath, grasped him by the arm and pulled him over the edge and into the pool with a loud splash.

Maitland burst out of the woods and jumped into the pool beside them, boots and all, and pulled Foster off Daphne, whom the villain had been attempting to keep under the water.

He was much larger than Foster, but the other man was well muscled, and the water made it difficult to maintain a grip on him. Still, his anger lent him enough strength to swing his fist against Foster's jaw, and while he was still stunned, Maitland got him by the throat and pinned him against the carved-stone side of the pool.

A rage unlike anything he'd ever felt before filled him as he thought of the danger this man had put Daphne in. What if she'd drowned? What if he'd come to find her dead beside the Roman bath? Foster had already killed one man and wounded another, and he'd almost done the same to Daphne. He deserved to . . .

"Maitland! Duke!"

Somewhere in the periphery of his mind, he heard his name being called, and when he registered Daphne's grip on his back, he came back to himself and realized what he'd almost done.

"Dalton, stop!" she cried, and he loosened his grip on Foster's throat. The other man sputtered and choked.

Suddenly Kerr was there, pulling Foster from the water. "I've got him, Dalton," his cousin said. "Let go."

Nodding, Maitland let go and turned to see Daphne behind him.

"Come here." He pulled her to him and she flung her arms around his neck. "I thought I'd lost you."

"I knew you'd come for me," she whispered against his shoulder. "I knew it. But I had to try to escape him."

"Brave girl," he said, though he shuddered to think what would have happened if he hadn't arrived when he did. He'd had a hard time subduing the man—what chance would Daphne have had against him when he did. "Don't ever frighten me like that again. I love you too much to live without you."

She gasped at his admission, then, almost shyly, said, "I love you, too."

"Thank God," he whispered against her mouth as he took it in a firm kiss. "I was determined to plead my case, but you can be quite stubborn. And I had no certainty that I'd win the argument."

"I can be quite reasonable when the occasion calls for it," Daphne said with a small frown that was belied by the smile in her eyes. "In this case, I would be unreasonable to resist you."

He kissed her again. Until the sound of a throat being cleared interrupted them.

"I don't suppose you two would like to climb out of the pool now?" asked Lord Kerr from where he stood beside the footmen, who held a bound Foster between them.

Daphne stiffened in Dalton's arms. "I'm only wearing my shift," she said in a whisper. "And my slippers are on the bottom of the pool."

"Can you give us a moment?" Maitland asked his cousin, who wordlessly removed his greatcoat and placed it on a bit of dry ground.

Then, Kerr, the footmen, their prisoner, and a much-subdued Sommersby stepped away to give them some privacy.

"What about the gold?" Daphne asked, her brow furrowed as Maitland moved to hoist himself out of the water.

"The gold will just have to wait," he said from where he had twisted himself up to sit with his feet dangling into the pool. "Come here and I'll help you out."

But a mulish look came over Daphne's lovely countenance. "Dalton, I was almost killed because of this gold. If it is in this pool, I want to find it now. Before anyone else is hurt because of it."

Then, before he could argue, she disappeared beneath
the surface and with a sigh, he slipped back in, wishing
he'd removed his boots so that he could feel the bottom with
his feet.

But he didn't have to wait long for her to surface with a
shout of triumph. "It's there!" she cried. "A chest, in this
corner. It's too heavy for me to lift, though."

Maitland nodded, and moving over to where she'd indicated, he dove under the water and felt around on the bottom
for the chest. Just when he thought he'd run out of breath,
he found it, and grasping it with both hands, he pulled, dis-
lodging half a century's worth of dirt and leaves and other
debris.

Surfacing, he lifted the chest onto the stones beside the
pool. "There. Now will you let me take you home?"

Nodding, Daphne let him lift her to the edge and immediately began to shiver in the cool evening air.

Dalton wrapped her in Kerr's coat, then picked up the
chest and led her to his horse.

Chapter 22

The morning of Daphne's wedding had dawned sunny and with no hint of the rain that had plagued them ever since they'd found the Cameron gold.

They'd had to postpone the nuptials for a few days because, despite the warm temperature of the Roman bath's water and Daphne's insistence that she was fit as a flea, Maitland insisted that she have time to recover from her ordeal. Also, Squire Northman took his sweet time interviewing them all about the events leading up to the capture of Foster. So even if Maitland had been more reasonable, the wedding would have had to be squeezed in between meetings with the magistrate.

"Are you nervous?" Sophia asked as the four Beauchamp heiresses stood waiting for the carriage to convey them to the church. "I would be quite nervous."

Daphne, who had chosen one of her favorite gowns—a white muslin shot through with jonquil—her favorite India shawl, and a rose-trimmed chip straw bonnet tied with matching jonquil ribbon, was pulling a pair of kid gloves over her trembling hands. "A little," she admitted. "But only because I do not wish to do or say the wrong thing. If it was a mathematics drill, however . . ."

"You would trounce the competition," Ivy said with a grin. "But you needn't worry. Maitland is head over ears for you. And no one else there matters."

"I suspect Maitland's mama would disagree," Gemma said as she tied her own bonnet beneath her chin. "She seems to have some very strong ideas about her own importance."

"No more than my father," Daphne said as they stepped outside onto the portico. "I was rather surprised that they seemed to get along with one another."

They walked down the few stairs and allowed one of the grooms to hand them into the open brougham.

Soon they were rolling down the lane toward the church where Maitland, Lord Kerr, and the few invited guests were waiting for them.

They were turning onto the road leading to the church, when Daphne spoke up. "I know I can be somewhat cold at times, but I wished to let you know, on today when my life will change irrevocably, I am grateful for all of you. And that Lady Celeste somehow knew that we would become friends."

"You're making me cry and the wedding hasn't even begun yet," Ivy protested from beside her. Though she took Daphne's hand in hers and squeezed it.

"I must admit that I wasn't sure of you at first, Daphne dear," said Sophia, dabbing at her own eyes, "but I cannot imagine Beauchamp House without you now."

"Has Maitland agreed to live there for the rest of the year?" Gemma asked, looking worried about the possibility that he would not.

It was difficult to imagine that any of them would have missed her if she'd left earlier in their tenure at Beauchamp House, Daphne thought wryly. Had the situation been reversed, she would not have missed any of them. But somehow over the course of their first four months together they'd forged a bond. And now she couldn't understand how she would ever get on without them.

Aloud she said, "Yes, thank heavens. I was prepared to use every wile at my disposal to convince him, but fortunately it seems that he doesn't need convincing."

"Because, as I said before, he's smitten," Ivy said wryly. "Just as you are with him."

She didn't protest the assessment because it was quite true. Once upon a time, she'd never have imagined a man existed whom she would willingly give her hand to in marriage. From her perspective, the institution itself was like a pair of loaded dice with all the advantage going to the husband.

But, then, she'd never imagined there could be a man she trusted as she did Maitland. But he did exist, and she was lucky enough to be about to marry him.

The carriage pulled to a stop, and they saw Lord Forsyth and Squire Northman waiting outside the door, which had been festooned with roses from the gardens at Beauchamp House.

Ivy, Sophia, and Gemma all kissed Daphne's cheek, and, with a flutter in her stomach, she followed them into the dim outer chamber of the church. Then she watched as they stepped down the aisle, one by one.

"Are you ready, daughter?" asked Lord Forsyth, with a suspicious dampness around his eyes. Daphne had never seen her father in the throes of any emotion but anger, but it seemed that he did feel something for her after all. And since it was her wedding day, and the last one she'd ever spend under his control, she kissed him on the cheek.

"Yes, Papa," she said slipping her arm through his as they stepped to the double doors leading into the nave.

And the rest was like a dream. She walked beside her

father down the aisle to the sanctuary where Maitland stood waiting for her with that light in his eyes that he seemed to reserve only for her.

And then the vicar began the ceremony. Daphne repeated her vows in a clear voice, with only the slightest hint of a tremor, and Maitland's eyes were intense as he slid the ruby that had been in his family for generations over the fourth finger of her left hand.

It was over with far more speed than she could have imagined, and it wasn't until they were back at Beauchamp House celebrating the wedding breakfast in the ballroom that she had a moment to breathe.

She was sipping a cup of punch behind a pillar, when she felt someone watching her. Turning, she saw that Mr. Sommersby was behind her.

"I didn't mean to startle you, my dear," her former tutor said with genuine remorse. "I only wanted to wish you happiness. And to apologize for my role in the business with Foster."

It was painful to think about how much she'd been let down by his role in Foster's schemes. She had once thought Richard Sommersby the most honorable and intelligent man she could ever know. But that, like so many of her beliefs then, had been no more than an illusion concocted by a lonely girl who desperately needed someone to believe in.

The toll his time under Foster's thumb had taken on him showed plainly on Sommersby's face, which bore the signs of worry and fatigue even now, days after Foster had been apprehended. She didn't wish her mentor to suffer any more on her behalf. It was as much her fault for putting him on a pedestal as it was his for not living up to her elevated expectations.

"There is nothing to forgive, Mr. Sommersby," she said, taking his hand in hers. "Truly. Foster was an evil man who used us both for his own purposes. And you lost your son because of him. I cannot hold you responsible for his actions."

At the mention of Nigel Sommersby, the tutor looked even more dejected.

"I am sorry," she said hastily. "I should not have brought him up. It's too soon."

"No," he protested. "It's not that, not grief over his death at any rate."

She frowned. "Then what?"

"I wish I had done more to keep him from hurting you, my dear. I should have done more."

But this was not the time for talking about Nigel Sommersby and his sins.

"I will say this once more, Mr. Sommersby," she said firmly, needing to make sure that he understood her well. "I do not hold you responsible for anyone else's crimes. Not Foster's and not Nigel's. Now, please, I want you to enjoy yourself. This is a day for celebration."

She might have imagined it, but it seemed to Daphne as if some burden lifted from the old man, and he seemed to brighten.

With one last wish for her happiness, he left, and Daphne stood for a moment looking after him.

"Here you are," said Maitland, who slipped up beside her and slid a hand around her waist. "I thought you'd run away from me already."

"Of course I haven't," she said, turning to step into the circle of his arms. They were shielded here from curious onlookers, and she took advantage by lifting her face for his kiss. "I would be a fool to run away from a man like you."

"And one thing you are not," he said, leaning his forehead against hers, "is a fool."

"I might be particularly gifted at mathematics," she said playfully. "Perhaps you've heard?"

Maitland's brows rose in mock surprise. "No. Tell me more about this mathematics you speak of."

"I would," Daphne said with a wave of love for this silly, brave, adorable man, "but we have the rest of our lives for that."

"Do we indeed?" he asked, grinning at her.

"Besides," she said, slipping her arms around his neck, "I've found something I'm better at than ciphering."

"What's that?" His eyes met hers, and the devotion in them made her breath catch.

"Loving you," she whispered as she took his mouth.

Maitland didn't speak, but she strongly suspected he agreed with her.

THE END

Acknowledgments

As with every one of my books with St. Martin's Press, I'm so grateful for the guidance and support of my team there: Holly Ingraham, Jennie Conway, Marissa Sangiacomo, Meghan Harrington, Jordan Hanley, and I'm sure dozens of other people who work tirelessly behind the scenes.

Thanks also to my lovely and talented agent, Holly Root, who is top 'o the trees as my Regency heroes would say, and is cheerleader, guide, friend and bulldog all rolled into one tiny charming package.

My fur companions—Charlie, Toast, Stephen Catbert, and Tiny—have kept me company through the writing and editing of this book and are wonderful at reminding me that though I'm a published author now, I'm still required to man the feed bag on a regular basis. Thanks for keeping me humble, you guys.

And finally, to my friend, the inestimable Lindsey Faber, who has saved my bacon more times than I can say. And without whom this book would not have emerged from the creative fires intact. You, madam, are awesome.